About the Au

Nash Ramji was born in Soroti, Uganda. He arrived in the UK as a refugee at the age of twelve and settled with his parents in Birmingham in the early 1970s. His secondary education was at a comprehensive school there. Following obtaining a law degree from Wolverhampton Polytechnic in the 1980s, he attended The College of Law in Chester. In 1991, he was admitted on the roll of solicitors and has since worked in the legal profession as a solicitor. He settled in Loughborough in 1995. Currently he is a director in a law firm in Leicester.

During his long career, one of his proudest moments, apart from the birth of his two children, was that he served the community as a JP. Being appointed and to serve as a magistrate in 2005 was an absolute honour for him. He sat on many cases in the magistrate's court, dealing with adult criminal cases. One particular case concerned honour killing. This is where the idea about writing this book came from.

Dedication

To my children, Ali and Mariam-Sara
And my mom and dad.

Nash Ramji

THE PRICE OF HONOUR

SEEKING JUSTICE

AUSTIN MACAULEY PUBLISHERS™

LONDON • CAMBRIDGE • NEW YORK • SHARJAH

A CIP catalogue record for this title is available from the British Library.

ISBN 9781398434301 (Paperback)
ISBN 9781398434318 (ePub e-book)

www.austinmacauley.com

First Published (2021)
Austin Macauley Publishers Ltd
25 Canada Square
Canary Wharf
London
E14 5LQ

Acknowledgements

Thanks go to:

Zul Khimji (Toronto)
Zahra Rumani (Birmingham).
Moazzam Shamsi

Author's Note

I was happy when my first book *The Price of Honour* finally reached its ultimate journey to publication. It was a feeling I cannot describe, but I can say I was completely thrilled. I was honoured to receive good positive feedback which was very encouraging. My son Ali helped me with a great deal of research, despite his busy work schedule as he works and lives in Dubai, often speaking on video call. Similar to Ali, Mariam was at hand too whenever I got stuck despite being busy at university. She came to the rescue every time. I am truly honoured to have such wonderful, loving children.

Preface

This is my second novel which is a sequel to *The Price of Honour*.

Faizali's inability to drag himself into the twentieth century or even to realise or understand the importance of it and bring about change, which was something he still had the power within his grasp to do, yet he seems blind to even realise or consider his failure may unleash more catastrophic consequences, brought about by his actions hitherto upon his family in slavishly adhering to his tradition and values which could have dire consequences. His family is broken by the brutal killing of Saleena, especially Raazia, who is tormented by her dilemma, desperately seeking to have justice for her sister and closure to be able to move on with life. Abdel waits to see what his father will do. The family is fragmented and things could reach breaking point. What will the protagonists do now? But more importantly what, will Raazia do?

I dedicate this book to my late parents – Dad: Pyarali Juma Ramji and Mum: Nurbanu Ramji.

Chapter 1

"You are not in Karachi, you dozy bitch. Watch where you are going," a taxi driver shouted from the window of his car as he swerved sharply to avoid colliding with Raazia on Green Lane as she crossed the road. Raazia began to gain pace walking faster, ignoring the driver whose window was wound down fully by now and who continued to shout some obscene words in Urdu which were inaudible to her. Raazia, however, was oblivious to her surroundings. She did not stop to listen to the rantings of the driver as she carried on walking in a daze with her mind in complete turmoil. As she reached home, she opened the porch door with her key, closing it behind her, and then opened the second door to the house, but as she entered, she forgot to take the key out of the Yale lock, closing the door behind her as she went in.

Gripped by a strange feeling never before had she experienced, Raazia began to shiver as a cold chill ran down her spine. She went straight through to the lounge, took her shoes off, sat down on the settee and tucked her legs in towards her body as she began to shake uncontrollably. Raazia had gone through some challenging, often trying, situations, but this one, unlike any previous ones, was different.

Raazia's house was a 1960s-built semi-detached property with a modern look to it. A tarmac drive at the front juxtaposed her garden, a single garage with an up-and-over door which had been painted gloss white. The front of the house had a small porch with a glass door, glass panel on the front and one side. An abandoned shoe rack occupied one corner. By it, there was a disarray of shoes, *chappals*, school shoes and adult shoes strewn on the floor by the empty shoe rack. At the other end was a large house plant.

As you entered through the second door, it led into a small hallway. On the left was a staircase leading to the first floor of the house. Towards the far end, it had two French Louvre doors painted magnolia. The one on the left led to the kitchen; the one on the right into to the lounge. The house enjoyed a homely feel with maroon-coloured plain carpets throughout the house and house plants in every corner. It was a neat little place.

They had moved to this house in the New Year shortly following Saleena's death. Akeel had kept himself busy looking after the grocery shop with his elderly father, Malik, who came to the shop now and then to help him run the busy store. Akeel seemed to have endless amount of energy. He was industrious in whatever occupied his time. The summer of 1998, not only did he look after the family business, but he decorated the house inside as well as outside and helped Raazia with the twins who had endless activities after school. The twins had both joined dance classes which they attended religiously four nights a week. Akeel always wanted them to feel safe so he would pick them up by car from their dance classes.

"What am I going to do?" she kept repeating to herself over and over. A sudden cold chill ran down her spine, and the house suddenly felt cold to her. Her brain eventually switched off from sheer exhaustion from overthinking as she fell asleep for a few minutes only to be woken up some half-hour later when Akeel walked into the house with the twins.

"Mum never leaves the keys in the door, Dad. I wonder what's up with her? I hope she is fine," Meesha commented as the trio walked into the house. "Mummy…Mummy, where are you? Your favourite daughters are home with Abbaaji."

The twins were eleven years of age. Meesha walked into the lounge as Raazia began rubbing her eyes vigorously still half-asleep feeling dazed.

"Mum, how come the keys were left in the front door Yale lock outside? Anyone could have come in whilst you were alone," Meesha asked.

"Oh, did I? I don't remember coming into the house, sweetie, as I was so tired after your aunt Saleena's *barsi* (first anniversary remembrance service) at *Nanaji's* house. I must have forgotten," Raazia responded, trying to force herself to get up off the lounge settee.

"Mum, sit down, you look terrible. I have never seen you look like this before. You have gone really pale and off-colour. Is anything the matter? Tell me."

"No, nothing is the matter. I am just tired," Raazia responded.

Shakeela and Akeel trailed behind Meesha. As they entered the room, they heard the conversation between Raazia and Meesha. They all sat down on the long lounge settee. Shakeela sat on Raazia's right-hand side partially on the armrest leaning onto her, at the same time hugging her with her arm, almost to the point of smothering her mother which Raazia did not seem to mind.

"I can't believe a whole year has gone by, Raaz; Sal gone just like that," Akeel said.

Raazia burst into tears. The loss of her sister and the feelings of bereavement for her were still pretty much raw. Nothing could have contained her from crying so intensely hearing those words; it worried the twins. The passage of time had not healed the deep wounds felt at the loss of her sister in such a tragic way. The loss had been intense. For her, it was like someone had driven an arrow through her heart. The revelation that evening made things much worse for her. Akeel's comments were untimely though quite innocent. He did not mean it in a hurtful way. The observation exacerbated the hurt his wife felt very deeply. It was as profound as at the time of Saleena's death. The intensity was like a fire erupting in her heart. Akeel thought Raazia had got over the worst of it, but clearly not from Raazia's reaction.

She stood up off the sofa, groaned, and was about to dash off, but no sooner she did, she collapsed on to the floor, losing consciousness. Shakeela and Meesha leapt from the sofa almost tumbling over each other to get to her.

"Mum, Mum, Mum…c'mon wake up, please. What is wrong with you?" Shakeela said frantically with a crackly stumble in her voice, repeatedly calling her 'mum' as she held her mother's hand and continued to pat her on the cheeks to get a reaction from Raazia.

There was no sign of movement or life as Raazia lay there completely still for a moment. Meesha dashed to the kitchen to fetch a glass of water and smelling salts. Akeel and Shakeela knelt by each side of Raazia trying to bring her round. Two minutes later, Raazia came to but seemed agitated at all the fussing. She snapped at Akeel, shrugging off the episode.

"I am fine. I have just had a tough day; remembering Sal today brought back the bad memories of how she died so horribly."

Akeel knew his wife too well to accept everything was good, but he knew also not to persist in labouring the point as this would upset his wife even more than she already was. Raazia carried on in a strange but unpredictable mood, so he let it be for now. He knew his wife well enough confidently to know it would not be too long before Raazia would speak about what was troubling her mind.

It was late that evening; Abdel was getting ready to hit the road. He hung around the house for a bit longer hoping Papaji would finally break his long silence and at least speak a few words with him which he longed to hear. Fauzia convinced him to stay the night at the house and said things may be different in the morning. Fauzia said she would try and prick at his conscience to see if she could persuade him just as Malik and Sheikh Ahmad had done some years back that day when they persuaded Faizali to attend *Juma* prayers after his long absence following Abdel's huge lottery win reports in the press. Abdel had longed for Papaji to at least acknowledge him by saying something directly to him. It did not matter what he said, as long as he said something to him. Amii's words were reassuring creating a tiny ray of hope for Abdel, though he avoided raising his expectation for he knew Papaji was stubborn.

It was a virtually sleepless night for him. No matter how hard he tried, Abdel could not get to sleep. He stared at his little square white bedside clock every few minutes, then the frequency at which he glanced at the clock gradually increased as time ticked on that night.

It was virtually a sleepless night for Raazia too. "Akeel are you asleep?" Raazia asked.

"Hmmm…Yes, I am, my dear, in fact, I am fast asleep," Akeel responded.

"I cannot seem to get off to sleep."

"I know."

"Have you been awake the whole time?"

"Virtually, apart from, I dunno, maybe ten, fifteen minutes or so!"

"Akeel, I am so sorry for being so restless in bed. I should have just got up out of bed. I feel so guilty, selfish, not letting you sleep."

"Why, is there summut bugging you then? I couldn't tell."

"You are as funny as the day I met you, Akeel, so calm as well. I don't know how you do it!"

13

"What did Allia say long time ago?" Akeel paused for a few seconds as he scratched his head. "Ah yes, I was 'a knight in shining armour'. I loved that expression; I still do. Your sister had a way with words which is what I loved about her. She still funny, your sister? I don't see much of her these days."

"She has two beautiful children. She cares for them so much. I remember her childhood. It was terrible. *Amii* did not let up with the abuse. I often felt very sorry for her, and Allia could not wait to escape. She would have married anybody just to get away from that witch. She told me she went on her bended knees and thanked Allah when Sajj proposed. Oh, she was so excited. She is a good mother to her children."

"You, Raazia, are not bad yourself, you know. By the way, I want you to know that I am still your knight in shining armour. I am here."

"I know, Akeel. I am so happy you are, truly. I don't know where to start, to be honest, but Papaji had something to do with Saleena's murder. I know he did. I overheard a conversation between Papaji and *Amii* when I was in the kitchen tidying up."

"Are you serious, Raazia?"

She talked to Akeel about what she had heard in the kitchen at Papaji's house.

"Raazia, are you sure you heard it right?" he asked.

"Akeel, I am one hundred and ten percent sure of it."

"Wow, I never thought he would do such a horrible thing. I cannot believe it as I always respected him to be an honourable man. He is your father! My God, Raazia, what a dilemma you got there. What will you do now?"

"I don't know, Akeel. This will tear the family apart whatever I decide to do."

It was 9:00 a.m. Sir Rupert Whitwick's phone rang at the British Embassy in Kampala. His PA picked up the phone.

"Sir Rupert's Office, Elizabeth speaking."

"President Otambu is speaking here. Where is Sir Rupert? I wish to speak to him on an urgent matter," he said in his African accent.

"Mr President Sir, I believe his wife Lady Whitwick is unwell, and she is travelling to England today. He is seeing her off at Entebbe Airport, Sir. May I take a message?"

"Well, I am sorry to hear about Lady Whitwick. I hope it is nothing serious, and I wish her a speedy recovery, but can you have Sir Rupert call me as soon as possible, please? It is urgent."

"I will pass the messages on, Sir, as I will your good wishes to Lady Whitwick immediately, Mr President Sir."

"Thank you, Madam, and I wish you a pleasant day."

"You too, Sir."

Elizabeth sent a text message to Sir Rupert advising him the President had called and that he said it was urgent.

"Oh dear, what could be the matter now?" Sir Rupert asked by return message.

"Sir, I don't know; he did not say," she responded.

Breakfast at the table was unusually a quiet affair. The girls assumed their parents may have had an argument. They looked at each other; Shakeela lifted one eyebrow and squinted her other eye slightly. Meesha made a hard facial expression making a sign intimating to her sister to say nothing. They quietly finished their breakfast cereal after signalling to each other. Akeel did not say anything at breakfast either. He sat quietly, ate his breakfast which was uncanny for him. Raazia looked terrible with huge bags under her eyes.

"C'mon, young ladies, I will drop you off to school then get to the shop after. I think your mum will be calling in sick today. That right, Raaz?" Akeel said.

"Akeel, you know I think I will. I feel awful; my head is thumping."

"Mum, are you okay as you don't look it?" Meesha enquired looking worried.

"C'mon, Meesh, we have to go otherwise we'll be late for school," Shakeela said sharply as she pulled her sister's arm towards her.

"I am all right, babies, really, I am. I did not sleep very well last night. I have a thumping headache, like I said, and that's all, girls. It came on after your aunt Saleena's *barsi*." Raazia reassured her daughters.

The three hugged and said bye to their mother. Raazia sat down to think on what she would do next.

It was about 3:30 p.m. when the British High Commissioner Sir Rupert rushed into his office.

"Elizabeth get me the President on the line straightaway please, quickly my dear. I could do with a cup of strong black coffee too."

Sir Rupert was in his mid-fifties, had short, wavy blond hair neatly brushed to one side, some slight greys showing on his sideburns above the ears, green eyes, podgy belly showing above his waist belt in his Armani pink shirt. He was wearing a white coloured suit. He spoke softly but with a stiff upper lip. Elizabeth was thirty-two, smartly dressed with tons of makeup despite the sweltering heat, her hair tied in a neat French braid. She stood under the fan above her which hung from the ceiling rotating at full speed.

His phone sat in a corner of a Victorian Chinoiserie black-lacquered pedestal desk. On the opposite side of the table was a heap of paperwork in the wire tray which had an 'in-tray' label stuck to it on the front. Next to the wire tray, there was a beige-coloured folder with 'CLASSIFIED' stamped in red ink all over on the front cover.

Elizabeth picked up the black telephone and pressed one of the transparent square buttons from a row of four at the top next to the receiver. It lit up red as she pressed it in.

"Mr President, I have the British Ambassador for you on the line," Elizabeth said as she passed the receiver to Sir Rupert.

"Mr President, sorry, I had gone to Entebbe Airport to drop my wife this morning when you rang," Sir Rupert said slightly out of breath.

"Elizabeth told me you had. I hope nothing too serious, and of course, I wish Lady Whitwick a speedy recovery."

"Thank you, Sir, for your very kind wishes. Now, I understand there was an urgent matter you wished to discuss with me?"

"Yes, I do. It has been over a year since the murder of our dear Saleena Khan and her friend Calvin. Have the culprits been caught yet?" the President asked directly.

"Sir, I do not believe the police thought it to be murder. Do you have any evidence to prove that?"

"Sir, I do not mix my words. Now listen to me very carefully. The circumstances in which they were killed were highly suspicious. I tell you it was murder. That is *my* strong belief. My citizens were killed in your country, Sir, and I expect justice for them."

Sir Rupert bit his lip, stayed silent as he had not been briefed. It had been over a year since the incident. Unprepared for this call, he stuttered.

"Sir Rupert, are you there?"

"Mr President, yes Sir, I am. I must confess, I have no further news on the matter. I shall need to speak to the Home Secretary about this and get back to you."

"Very well then, I expect to have better news say by the end of the week, Sir."

"I will do my best, Mr President."

The phoned clicked to a dead tone.

"Sir Rupert, you look flustered. What did he want?" Elizabeth asked as she put a mug of black coffee on the table on a coaster.

"Thank you for the coffee. I could really do with it. He was asking for an update on that incident in Leeds about a year ago. Why now I don't know. Lizzie, could you get me Bob Tessington, the Home Secretary, on the line please?"

"Yes Sir."

Elizabeth pressed one of the buttons, asked for the Home Secretary and passed the receiver to Sir Rupert.

Abdel's hope his father would speak with him was dashed as Papaji left the house early. He did not return by the time Abdel was about to leave in the afternoon for his journey back home. Sadly, for him all hope had faded away.

"*Amii*, I am going to go. I see you have prepared some food for me."

"*Puttar*, I could not let you go without you eating your favourite chicken tikka, *sabzi, roti* and rice. I have packed some for you so you can take it with you and freeze some of it. It will come in handy when you're feeling hungry."

"*Amii*, you are so good to me. I do have a housekeeper that cooks for me."

"Well, it can't be as good as my food; besides, what are mothers for? I hope you will remember me with fond memories in time to come, unlike your sisters, especially that Allia. She was a devil, I tell you."

16

Abdel chose not to respond to the last remark. He sat down at the table to eat. After finishing his meal twenty minutes later, he hugged *Amii* and bid her farewell. As he left, he handed two white envelopes to her.

"What is this?" she asked.

"Here, take it; one is for you, *Amii*, and one for Papaji. It will help."

"*Puttar*, what is this?"

"Don't worry about it; just take it please."

Abdel sat in his sports BMW, started the engine and revved it for a few seconds causing some neighbours to lift their curtains to see what the noise was as he zoomed off, his car tyres making a screeching sound.

Raazia spent the morning mulling over the dilemma. The more she thought about what to do next, the more confusing the situation became for her. She was in a real tight spot about this. She picked up the phone and spoke to Allia first. After listening to her sister telling her about what she had heard, Allia expressed she was not a least bit surprised. Her opinion was that Raazia should report it to the police. She advocated seeking revenge for Saleena. Raazia knew Allia would be unforgiving of her parents and this might be an opportunity for her to get even with Papaji. She wondered if Allia had thought it through. Raazia thought her approach was predictably biased.

Next, she spoke to Sameena who expressed her reservations in making a hasty decision in going to the police straightaway without carefully thinking through the implications first. She asked Raazia if there was any risk of harm involved to anyone. Sameena accepted that it was by no means an easy decision to make for anyone in that situation but her advice was to exercise care. Sameena, however, pledged her support provided her sister discussed the decision with all her sisters before acting upon it.

Raazia agreed. That seemed fair to her as a decision to report could have possible impact on all of them. Her sister's worry was the unseen, perhaps, catastrophic consequences that could result here. This was important. To her, it was not a question of divided loyalty. Papaji had simply been a figurehead who had not been a loving father to any of them. Raazia had been like a mother to all her sisters, a friend too and, more importantly, someone who had showed a stronger loving bond than Papaji ever did.

"Bob, hello, old chap; it's Rupert from Kampala. How the devil are you?"

"Hello, Rupert; I am good, thanks. I heard Hilary was not too well. Trust it's nothing serious? Is this a social call, Rupert, or official business? Only the PM has called a meeting, and I have to leave in five minutes."

"It is official business, Bob."

"Oh my, doesn't sound too good to me, old boy; I can tell from your grim tone."

"Well, Otambu called me today. He wanted an update on that case just over a year ago, you know, the Leeds one. Some sort of burglary, and two occupants, a black chap and an Indian woman, were hacked to death?"

"Bob, I know the one you mean. Afraid I have no update on it. My understanding was it was wrapped up as a cold case. What is his interest in it?"

"In the interest of justice, he said. The two victims were Ugandan Citizens."

"Rupert, I will have to get more on it, if I can, from the Chief Constable and get back to you, that okay?"

"I guess, but don't leave it too long; I need to get back to him with something as he had left an urgent message for me on this one. I don't think he will be too happy to hear it's been shelved as a cold one, if it has been."

"Stall him, and I will get back to you tomorrow. I have to go, otherwise will be late for my meeting."

"Righty-o Bob."

Chapter 2

Amii, whilst shopping for some clothes on Green Lane, popped into Fly Safe Travel Agent to enquire about flights to Pakistan. She had the £5,000 Abdel gave her which she could use for any travel as she intended to keep the money a secret from her husband. She had left the other envelope for Faizali on the mantel in the lounge. *Amii* was dying to get away from home. Faizali's business with Nawaz had caused arguments between her and Faizali. Unnecessary grief for her, she thought, not to mention tremendous tension in the house. The arguments about it seemed unending to the point of separation.

Being a woman, she did not know how her husband would react if she said she was going to Pakistan on her own. She knew he would object; she was his wife, and could not go abroad without his permission. *Amii* had become exasperated with all the arguments with Papaji. It would be an opportunity for her to see her sons back home too, but she would wait, pick the right moment when the time was right.

"Did you find the envelope Abdel left for you on the mantel?" *Amii* asked.

"Yes. Why has he left exactly £5,000?" he asked.

"You counted it? Your son isn't stupid, you know. He must have overheard our conversations about Nawaz asking for £5,000. He has plenty of money so he has helped you out. So, it isn't a big deal, is it? Just pay the man and be done with it. I know Raazia was in the kitchen tidying up that night. I hope she did not hear our conversation."

"I know Raazia too well. She will not put herself in danger. She knows her place too!"

"Danger *baba*, what are saying? You are worrying me, Faizali."

"Nothing, my dear, but she is too wise to cause any mischief."

"Aaakh, you talk in riddles sometimes, and I don't know what to say anymore," *Amii* said in a sharp tone.

"You look after your stuff, and I will take care of this matter myself. That is my final word on the matter, *samjee*?"

"What about Abdel?"

"What about him? You meddle in my affairs too much," he retorted in a sharp tone.

"Faizali, I am not meddling. It has everything to do with me, unless you have excluded me from being part of the family, huh? You will need to speak to Abdel. He is your son. You cannot continue to ignore him like this. *Wo toh bachaa hey; kaafi tadap rahaa hey saara din aur raat beychaara. Bus inteyzaar ker raha hey key aap ek din unkey sath kuch alfaz mey baat kaarengey. Bolo naa kiya*

19

mushqeel hey bachey say baat kernaa? Maafi chaiye? Wo tayar hey. Aap kaa betta hey naa? Ek betta hey. Zindaagi ka kiya bharosa. Ek din tow janna hey ooper. [He is a kid pining for you to speak to him. He is waiting for you to speak to him even a few words. He is prepared to apologise to you if you wish. He is your son. Who knows one day, God will call us up.]

"Look how caring he is. To ease your burden about the money situation, he left £5,000 for you, did he not? Shows he cares very much about you, and so you don't have to worry. Don't you think it is about time for you to make up with him?"

"Nawaz is a dangerous man. Today it's £5,000 *kee dhamki dey raha hey* [he is demanding as blackmail]; tomorrow it will be more. We have to be careful with him. Raazia, I am not too worried about her. I shall have to think on what you said about Abdel. I cannot forgive what that boy did, but he will need to show me that he is repentant. Get rid of all the *haram* money first."

"You speak like you are a perfect Muslim man without any stain of a sin on you. We are all human, and to forgive is human too," *Amii* said.

"I just told you, I will think on it. Now go on with your wifely duties."

Amii made a tsk sound with her tongue and rolled her eyes before leaving the room.

Chief Constable Hathaway's schedule for the day was a busy one as he sat down with a strong cup of black coffee trying to prioritise the day's work when the phone rang.

"Morning, Chief Constable, it is Bob Tessington here, the Home Secretary."

"Morning, Sir. Yes, I know who you are. What can I do for you, Home Secretary?"

The conversation seemed official in tone though cordial. The Home Secretary was not exactly someone Hathaway respected due to some past unfinished business.

"Could you dig up a file for me and update me on the Leeds case; the man and Asian woman, Christmas 1997, killed during a burglary?"

"Hold on, Sir, let me call it up on the system."

There was a long pause. A rhythmic tapping sound, like a pencil, could be heard at the other end of the line. It seemed to get louder as the Home Secretary waited. Hathaway took his time.

"Sorry to keep you waiting, Sir," Hathaway said in a particularly slow tone, almost as though he relished keeping the Home Secretary waiting.

"Quite all right, Hathaway. Yes, what was the outcome?"

"The case was closed, Sir, as a cold case."

"Why?"

"Lack of evidence, Sir, I was advised, not to mention resources, Home Secretary," Hathaway said with some glee in his voice.

"I want you reopen the case, you hear."

"Why? There is no further new evidence. What would be the point? I had two of my best people on the job. I could not afford to tie them up nor the other resources when they were so desperately needed elsewhere. Besides, the police have had to make do with the hard cutbacks the HO has imposed err so..."

"Look, Hathaway, I don't need a lecture. I have briefed the Prime Minister about this case. We have discussed this matter for reasons I cannot go into. The Prime Minister himself, yesterday at our meeting, simply stated the case must be reopened. It may be expediency for the force, but I am afraid it is a political decision whether you like it or not, and this is a direct order from the PM."

"Very well, Sir," Hathaway said as he slammed the receiver on its cradle.

Sherlock and Kiki were summoned for a meeting in the afternoon to his office that day. Though somewhat inconvenient with the Chief's tight schedule, the meeting had to be squeezed in along with pressing matters already pencilled in his diary. It seemed extra work the Chief could have done without, especially as the reason for reopening was unclear.

It was a short, brief meeting. Chief Constable Hathaway did most of the talking. Simply, he gave the instruction without giving any reason to reopen the case, something that Kiki had been eagerly waiting for. She was not exactly interested in the 'why' but was thrilled to hear the investigation was to be reopened even though the previous investigation team would not be reassembled. It was just the two of them this time round with the proviso minimum resources allocated, namely just Sherlock and Kiki.

"I don't understand why suddenly after over a year, the case is to be reopened just like that. Don't get me wrong, Sir. I am very pleased it has...no, actually relieved that we get the opportunity to reopen as we had months of painstaking work done on this case. It was a shame that we had to close it off without a chance to get a result," Kiki said.

"The reason, my dear Kiki, is neither our concern nor of any significant importance. If I am honest here, what we have, dear DI Slater, is a second chance now, so let's give it our best shot aye?" Sherlock said.

"It's just the two of us on the case; we don't have the backup team this time, Sir, which will make life difficult, harder for us to investigate on our own."

"Maybe, maybe, let's go get the boxes from archives first, shall we?"

"Lizzie, would you get the President on the line for me, please?" asked Sir Rupert.

"Sir."

"Mr President, I trust you are well? It's the British ambassador here."

"I know who you are, Sir Rupert, thank you. What news do you have for me about what we talked about the other day?"

"Mr President, I am afraid I do not have much news for you, but I do know the investigation continues into the incident."

"This for me, Sir, is most disappointing. Let me tell you, Sir Rupert, the British police, Scotland Yard are the best known for their excellent reputation for crime solving. I have to say, though, I am displeased to hear that there have been no arrests. This is no justice for my countryman and woman who died so tragically in your country, Sir. They are my fellow citizens, not to mention the families of the two victims who have suffered so greatly their loss, Sir."

"I am on it, Mr President. I will vigorously pursue this now that you have brought it to my attention."

"I stress to you, Sir, this matter is important to me. I hope the British are not stalling me."

"The relations between our two nations have been most cordial, and the Prime Minister would not have it any other way, Mr President. So, I assure you, I will pursue this vigorously. I had no idea this was an important issue for you."

"Very well, Sir Rupert, please keep me posted. Goodbye for now."

"Goodbye, Mr President."

"I wonder what is so important about this case to him, Lizzie. I get the Ugandan citizen bit for his man, but the woman was a British citizen and not, I understand, from any particular standing as such. I wonder if the chap's family is influential. Can you get Gary Tughe to make some enquiries about the chap? Tell him to be very discreet."

"Yes, Sir Rupert, leave it with me."

A week went past. Raazia was in turmoil about what to do. She had signed off work on account of feeling unwell. The twin girls were worried about their mother's state of health. They knew their mother was a strong woman. Suddenly, after their aunt's *barsi*, she had been ill complaining of headaches as well as been off work which was unlike her as she loved her teaching job. It was getting to a point they did not know what they should do apart from worry about their mother. They spoke to Akeel one morning in the car on the way to school. Later that night, Akeel thought it time to address the matter with his wife.

"Raaz, the girls are very worried about you. You need to lighten up with them. Meesha never complains but today she discreetly told me you were snapping at them for no reason. You're going to have to sort this business out soon, Raaz. You cannot go on like this. It's making you ill. More importantly, it is affecting the girls too."

"Akeel, it is not easy. In fact, it is the hardest decision I have ever had to make."

"Well, what did you hear exactly that night? Tell me again."

"Papaji said that Nawaz was demanding payment of £5,000 for taking care of the Saleena business. He said, 'Our involvement must be kept between us.' Why would he say that? What involvement? Akeel, I tell you they had some hand in her murder. It was to save Papaji's honour."

Akeel appeared stunned at this statement. He was unsure if it was an honour killing situation; not that he disbelieved his wife, but now he could see the bigger picture surrounding this. He wondered if it was to save not only Papaji's honour but Nawaz's too as Saleena had instigated divorce proceedings which, if made public, the domestic violence Saleena had endured for years being married to Nawaz would all be out in the open. If this went public, the family, including his, would be exposed to an intrusive enquiry, even the community making it into a public discussion. This would put a lot of pressure on him and his family which he was not ready for.

Akeel stayed quiet looking decidedly quizzical.

"Akeel, what are your thoughts? You are the man of the house. I will go with the decision you make, as long as we discuss it with Allia and Sameena," Raazia said.

"Since when have I made decisions on anything?"

"Akeel, don't joke around. I am serious."

"Well, as I see it, this must be the first then, Raaz!"

"Akeel." Raazia tutted.

"All right, all right, but I will add that any decision I make will be from my own thinking. Well, as I see it, if you were to say nothing, then it shields those who are guilty of this hideous crime, but it may protect us from exposure to the world, not to mention any danger that it may put my, err…sorry, our family in. If you go to the police, it will become public. This will cause ripples in the water, maybe exposing us to some danger too. So I don't know which I prefer. I do not know which one is the lesser evil of the two choices we are faced with here, Raaz."

"Danger did you say, Akeel? What sort of danger? This worries me."

"I see that the issue is much bigger then I first thought it to be. The unknown scares me. We have a family that we need to protect."

"I never thought of it like that, Akeel."

"Raaz, I have not finished."

"Sorry, Akeel, go on."

"It is a tough one. There is no easy solution. I have not ever thought about being educated like you, Raaz, as I always just wanted to follow my father's footsteps: be a simple shopkeeper, have a wife like you and children. I have all that. I thank Allah as he has blessed me with all I need and got in this life. As a simple guy, never did I think I would face such a difficult decision in life. But I do. My wife is asking and I have to be her knight in shining armour!"

Tears began to run down Raazia's cheeks. Akeel fished out a tissue from a box from the side table and wiped her eyes.

"I am so sorry, Akeel. You are good, decent human being, and I love you as much as I love Meesha and Shakeela."

"This means a great deal to me, you saying those words directly to me. I have been longing to hear those words from your lips, Raaz. Finally, I have, and I know you do. I always knew you did! You will not know how happy it makes me feel to hear you say that. My life is complete," Akeel said holding both Raazia's hands as tears filled up his eyes.

Raazia paused, sat as still as she could. Akeel seemed deep in thought trying to process the information in his brain. A spell of silence descended. The conversation had been emotional. Akeel gathered himself together quickly and regained his composure.

"I need a couple of days to think this over, Raaz."

The next day, Kiki drove down to Leicester from Leeds to see Raazia in person. Though it was a two-hour journey, she felt it was important to meet her face to face. An individual's body language and facial reactions can often convey important signs or tell a story that would not be picked up over a telephone conversation. It was early afternoon. Raazia was in the house simply tidying up, at the same time collecting her thoughts together on her profound conversation with her husband the previous night. She dwelt also on her conversations with Allia and Sameena about a week ago on the dilemma of what to do. She happened to be in the hallway at the time when she spotted through the two layers of glass someone approaching the house. Her view was not clear as the internal hallway glass panel was translucent with white netting curtains covering the panels which masked the view. She was not expecting any visitors. Raazia went to the door hearing the doorbell ring. Recognising DI Slater at once, Raazia seemed a little startled to see her. For one thing, she was not expecting the DI coming to see her, and secondly, it seemed coincidental.

"Hello, Raazia, DI Slater. You remember me? I am sorry, it is an impromptu visit, but it really is important," she said holding up her warrant badge.

"I do, I do remember you. What brings you all the way here from Leeds, DI Slater? Has there been something new on the case?" She asked two questions one after another in quick succession. "What brings you here today?" was a third one before DI Slater had a chance to say anything more.

Raazia stood in the porch collecting her thoughts, at the same time waiting for responses to her questions. Some seconds passed. Both stood where they were momentarily, Kiki outside, Raazia in the porch surrounded by an assortment of shoes on the floor. Kiki paused waiting for Raazia to invite her in. Kiki was smartly dressed. She had a dark-coloured jacket on with a matching skirt and polished black shoes. She was in her thirties, dressed in civilian clothes. She looked nice as she had a moderate amount of makeup on, which nicely displayed her lovely smooth dark, slightly olive skin. Holding under her arm, she had a black leather executive-styled organiser case. The scattered array of shoes in the porchway seemed a sign, perhaps a telling sign, for visitors to take their shoes off before stepping into the house. As she waited for Raazia to invite her into the house, the DI felt a little uncomfortable not knowing whether she would be invited in or even should she remove her shoes before entering the house.

"May I come in please? I am happy to take my shoes off! I really do need to speak with you. It is very important."

"Yes, of course, I am so sorry. Do come in, please. You can leave your shoes on if you feel uncomfortable leaving them in the porch; it's fine," Raazia said trying to put her guest at ease.

"No, I am happy to leave them here. My mum back in South Africa had a strict rule of not wearing shoes in the house at all. I can see you have the same rule here, which is good," Kiki said as she stepped into the porch proceeding to slip her shoes off using the front of her left shoe placing it behind the ankle of the right to slip it off then using the big toe placing it behind her left ankle to slip the other shoe off. She bent down, picked them up before putting the pair neatly by the side of the door.

They sat down in the living room as Kiki looked around surveying the surroundings of the room. The room was nicely decorated. Pleasant, it had a current modern feel to it. Laura Ashley maroon and white striped wallpaper smartly covered the room walls. Pictures of flowers hung on walls with an arrangement of family pictures neatly arranged on a side wall. There were house plants in every corner making it feel homely.

"You have a nice house, Raazia."

"Thank you, DI Slater. May I get a hot drink for you?"

"That would be lovely. Black coffee, please, no sugar."

Raazia left the room for five minutes returning to the lounge holding a mug in her hand which she handed to DI Slater. Raazia was tense. She wondered why the officer was here. Her mind was full of questions. *Was it coincidence? Had the police got some evidence about what she had heard at* Papaji*'s house? Or was it something else?* She was filled with trepidation about the sudden impromptu visit.

"Thank you. Raazia, first and foremost, the reason I am paying you this visit is to inform you personally that we are reopening your sister's case. I drove all this way to let you know that as I know you would not have been happy with the case being closed unsolved. It must have been distressing for you and your family when the police closed the investigation last year. The second reason why I am here is for you to run through the information you gave us at the time shortly after the incident a year or so ago. This is important as I want to see if we have missed anything at all, if there were any missing gaps or we had missed something the first time round," Kiki said taking out an official-looking piece of paper after unzipping the leather organiser which she placed on her lap then laid the A4 size paper on top of it. "Raazia if you could run through with me what you stated, I can crosscheck on here."

As she recounted the story, memories of the awful incidents, all the abuse Saleena was subjected to upset Raazia to the point tears started to run down her cheeks. Kiki comforted Raazia by slowly patting her on her back. She stood up and went into the kitchen returning with a glass of water which she gave Raazia. It took Raazia a few minutes to gain her composure. Raazia was in a fragile state of mind.

"I am so sorry to put you through this. I can imagine how painful and upsetting it must be for you. You know, Raazia, I grew up in Soweto, an area heavily populated with poor blacks. My father was a junior police officer serving white people's dirty political jobs of catching blacks and putting them in prison indiscriminately. This was at the height of the political problems in South Africa. He had four children, one boy and three girls. I am the youngest of the four siblings. South Africa was going through a terrible political time. There were anti-Apartheid activists involved in riots every single day. The police hunted and killed thousands of people. The country was on the brink of civil war when my father sent me to UK. My brother Jonah and sister Evelyn were activists in the ANC. Raazia, believe me, it was a struggle of massive proportions.

"Jonah was coming home one day when a white police patrol Jeep stopped him. A white police officer just shot him with his gun at close range. The same afternoon, they came and ransacked our house, beat my mother with a stick and arrested Evelyn. They took her to some prison where she was beaten everyday by the guards. My father was finally able to locate her after six years searching for her. She is at home now suffering from Post-traumatic stress disorder. She sits there all day in the house like a vegetable, barely says a few words. My mother passed away two days after she was beaten up. She died of a broken heart, just could not bear the trauma of her only son being killed. The same week, we lost two members of our family, my brother and my mother. The same day we buried my mother and brother. Can you imagine how we had felt that day, that week?"

Kiki paused, closed her eyes as she pulled her body all the way back resting her head on the sofa. In a flashback, she could picture the hauntingly terrifying moments in her mind, back at home in South Africa as it all came flooding back to her. Few seconds later, she opened her eyes which had filled with tears of pain as she continued:

"We were completely helpless as we could do nothing. My elderly father and my other sister Karabo now look after Evelyn. I miss my brother and mother and my family too. When I joined the police force, I vowed to myself that I would not let guilty people who kill others go unpunished. So, you see, I understand your pain. I know what it is like to lose a family member."

Raazia had tears in her eyes by the time Kiki finished telling her story, as did Kiki. Raazia hugged her. Raazia's pain she continued to suffer resonated with Kiki. It was something Kiki rarely talked about. Talking about the painful moments helped both women as it seemed to be of comfort to them.

"I am so sorry about your family," Raazia said as she wiped away the tears. She picked up the tissue box and handed it to Kiki.

"Life is tough enough, Raazia, but when tragedy strikes it can debilitate you completely. I know what you have gone through. Sometimes, it feels almost like going to hell and returning back."

Raazia took some minutes to contemplate on the sad story Kiki had related to her. She almost opened up hearing this story. Kiki felt Raazia was about to speak about something, and then suddenly, Raazia paused. She remembered that Akeel had not yet decided upon the matter. It would not feel right to speak about it now as it was his decision. Her sisters had to be consulted too. So it was not the right moment.

"Have you any new information on the case?" Raazia asked.

"No, not yet. But we intend to leave no stone unturned this time round. The lifeline came from the Chief when he simply asked me and DCI McLean to reopen the case this week. Listen, my gut instinct always told me there was something different about this case. I firmly believe this killing was an honour killing. When I was a police officer in South Africa, I had seen similar cases. I was a very young cadet officer in those days, completely inexperienced in such high-level crime of this sort. What I do know is they are the hardest cases to prove. We have to be super-meticulous, look at every possible clue, every angle covered however small. So do you have anything more to add or have a view on this case yourself that could help us?"

"Erm…I have thought about it, but I am not sure about it, just yet."

"Does that mean you have information that could help us, Raazia? Please, this is important."

"Yes."

"Tell me what you know?"

"Like you, I ran it through my mind a billion times. I feel convinced Nawaz could have done it. He is certainly capable of extreme violence, and Saleena had started divorcing him. He hated the fact a woman could do that to him. From some of the horror stories Saleena had related to me about him, I am sure he is a dangerous and violent animal. I wondered if he had anything to do with it. He either did it to exact revenge for sending him to prison or he was a man and it hurt his stupid honour. Only thing, I do not have any proof that would stand up in court."

"To me, what you say is important as you share my gut instincts. That is good enough for me for now, a basis, a start, you know, from which to go forward with my enquiry. I came here to hear this from you personally, to see what your reaction was. Your reaction has confirmed my suspicions. I also think your father may be involved too in this. You are not just a female family member, but someone who cared deeply about Saleena. I know that too well. Some families have terrible secrets, and I wanted to know if you knew anything about this honour killing business which, I must confess, is not only bugging me but is niggling me. I am pretty sure either Nawaz or your father or both had something to do with the murders. I did not want to waste my time if I was barking up the wrong tree, so to speak. I wanted to be sure, you know? We can talk again soon. I thank you for your time and your hospitality. The coffee was good."

Gary Tughe was in his late thirties, a rugged-looking man originally from South Africa. He was a white African. Though affiliated to the South African Secret Service, his loyalty lay with whoever made sure his bank account stayed healthy. He had reported back that Calvin Lenton was the President's nephew. His sister Ophelia had three boys; Calvin was her middle child. Sir Rupert could see clearly why the President had an interest in this case.

Chapter 3

The Foreign Secretary, James Cassidy, waited in the arrivals lounge at Gatwick Airport on a cold but sunny day in February 1999. It was 2:35 in the afternoon. His brief was to receive President Otambu at the airport. Ugandan Air Force Boeing jet was due to land at 14:47 that afternoon. Cassidy waited patiently, having arrived a little early but made good use of his time finishing some urgent calls. He asked his secretary to brief him fully on the Leeds 'murder' case. The President's visit was not an official state visit. As Augustus Otambu was the head of state of a former colony, it was unwritten protocol that he be met officially at least by a government minister, if not the Prime Minister himself, recognising the status that he was President of a country.

"President Otambu, welcome to UK, Sir. It is good to see you, and I trust you had a pleasant journey. The Prime Minister asked me to meet you on his behalf."

"Mr Cassidy, I thank you for coming to meet me. It is very good to meet you as I believe I have not had the pleasure."

"Likewise, President Otambu. Please come with me; we have a limousine waiting to take you to your hotel. We can talk on the way."

"Akeel, have you made a decision? DI Slater has called me about six times today, and each time, I end up stalling her. The more I think about it, the more I feel I want to tell DI Slater what I heard. Then it is up to Allah as well as to them to decide if they want to probe into it more."

"Why?" Akeel asked.

"Why, Akeel? My beautiful sister Saleena lost her life needlessly. I cannot forget that. My mind is filled with anger. I want vengeance."

"You mean revenge?"

"Yes," Raazia said forcefully without hesitation. "What do you think?"

"Raaz, but the Christian Bible says, the Lord said vengeance is mine and mine alone, I think."

"Akeel, you are beginning to annoy me with this stuff. What, you Christian now?"

"No, just saying. Well, I was all confused in my mind too, just like you. It is not something you can make a decision upon just like that. My head said, *Don't*. One night, I happened to be sitting downstairs with Meesha. She seemed engrossed in a history book. I did not know why she was so engrossed in it until I asked her. She said, 'Dad, I am doing a history project at school. I chose Turkish history, the start of the Ottoman empire with Osman I.' She told me Osman was the youngest son of a brave warrior called Ertuğrul who faced many challenges in his life. You should read some of the stuff. It is fascinating, thirteenth century. I went to the local library and read a lot about him."

"Akeel, what has all that history got to do with our issue?"

"Exercise a bit of patience, Raaz; it will fall in place in a few minutes."

Raazia made a tsk sound then rolled her eyes, seemingly losing patience with Akeel, not quite wanting either a Bible lesson or a history one on Turkish history at this moment in time. Akeel continued:

"Raaz, this man was amazing. I have total respect for him. I will not bore you with some of the details I read about him, fascinating though they were, but I had no idea that this guy firmly stood for what he believed in, resolutely!"

"Seriously Akeel, you amaze me. 'Resolutely'? You have either been speaking with Allia or you have swallowed a dictionary, I swear. Just hearing you using words I have never heard you use before, I am gobsmacked. You are trying my patience though."

"Raaz, just be patient and listen, please."

"Indulge me," Raazia said in a strict tone.

"Whenever this guy was in a real mess, and I mean in a real mess which was dire, like life and death situations, he turned to Allah for guidance directly or through men of religion. I am taking about life and death situations. If you imagine what it must have been like in thirteenth-century Turkey. Christians were fighting Muslims on one side, the other side hordes of Mongols keen to invade lands, plundered, pillaged, terrorised, raped and killed people if they were not ready to be subjugated. Every single situation of potential danger to him and his family was a knife-edge situation. What did I read now?" Akeel paused for a moment, scratched his head, and then he continued. "Let me get this right. He truly believed in…yes, that's it, Allah's justice above everything else, amazingly ready to sacrifice his family, even, if it meant God's justice prevailed."

Raazia sat on the bed, her right elbow resting on her knee, index finger on her lips, the rest of the fingers buttressing her chin, quietly listening to her husband with undivided attention now, as he regurgitated history with passion. Never had she seen him like this before, knowledgeable, passionate, paraphrasing what he had read in the history books in the library.

"The man followed this principle completely. It is thought he believed if you did not believe in this highest form of Allah's justice then life was not worth living. After I read all this stuff, I went to see this guy Professor Edmunds at Oxford University today. He teaches history, Raaz, but he was brilliant. Not like Sheikh Ahmad; no disrespect to him, but he knows nothing more than Papaji does. This guy, not only has he studied most major religions of the world but is thought to be a scholar versed in Islam as well as a leading scholar of history. I asked him about this concept of Allah's justice and to put it in some sort of perspective for me as it was important. Do you know what he told me?"

Raazia just shook her head in disbelief with half her jaw dropped down. She was not only speechless but completely mesmerised by the information Akeel had imparted upon her. She was surprised by her husband's unusual interest and display of intellectual ability. It was simply incredulous.

"Raazia, the professor told me Ertuğrul guided his whole life by the concept of truth and Allah's justice. If whatever it was did not fit the path of Allah, he would fight it. He would fight it in the name of Islam. That professor cited loads of verses from the Koran. I can only remember the one which was *Surah An-Nisa* chapter 4, I think. I looked it up, Raaz, it says: '*O you who have believed, be persistently standing firm in justice, witness for Allah, even if it be against yourselves or parents and relative. Whether one is rich or poor, Allah is more worthy of both so follow not [personal] inclination, lest you not be just…*'

"This man stood for justice, truth and protection of right against wrong. He was fearless in the face of extreme dangerous adversity, never faltering in what he believed in which was the path of God. Raaz, like I said to you, I am a simple guy. I wanted to take the coward's way out until I realised all this, and it made me think. Saleena would be disappointed…no, angry with us if we did not speak up. What justice would there be for her, huh?"

"Wow, Akeel, I did not know you would research it so well. Whatever your final decision, I have to say, to me it is a reasoned decision. So you are saying we go to the police?" Raazia asked with a slight hint of fear in her voice.

"I am convinced the right thing to do is follow the path of justice for Saleena. We would all be failing in our duty if we did not seek justice for your sister for she was a wonderful human being, Raaz. Look at her personality. She went all the way to some African country to look after orphans. Who would do that? I could not do it. It would take someone very dedicated to do that. You know, Raaz, I read somewhere, Alexander the Great said something like, '*In the end, when it's over, all that matters is what you have done.*' Don't you see, Raaz, you have the chance to seek the truth."

"Akeel, I am so choked up at all this! I don't know how you even thought about all this fine w…"

"Shhh, Raaz, it's okay. Don't you see she was my sister-in-law too? Saleena was to be admired for who she was, yet she unfortunately had a bad deal in life. Papaji failed in his duty as a father to protect his daughter as a proper father would have done. I would give my life for my two girls. Papaji was and still is, basically, a twat. To him, it's all about some damn tradition, respect and honour which is all crap, which means nothing to me when the gift of life has been taken away from a beautiful, almost perfect, human being."

Raazia was in tears hearing her husband as though he was giving a eulogy for Sal, choked at all those fine words of reasoned explanation of why she should do what, to him, seemed the right thing to do. Akeel hugged his wife, wiped the tears off her cheeks. He continued:

"Life for her has gone, cut short tragically. You can't bring her back, Raazia. I cannot be more certain then I am now. You need to do the right thing. Follow the path of justice. Papaji deserves what he gets if he is guilty. Look how he has shunned Abdel out of his life. What for? Abdel has not done anything wrong to deserve this, this horrible treatment the poor guy is having to suffer. In my eyes, he is not a proper father worthy of your protection anymore."

Raazia sat on the bed next to Akeel, tears streaming down her cheeks like water cascading downhill, emotional yet uplifted by a feeling of elation, at the same time, full of admiration for a simple green grocer husband of hers who had gone out of his way to strive for a perfectly reasoned answer for his wife's terrible dilemma.

"Akeel, I am so very proud of you."

President Otambu paced up and down in his plush Presidential Suite at The Dorchester Hotel for near enough twenty minutes seemingly restless. His security aide David Mutembe came in to check on the President. The President's aide was thirty-five, six-foot-tall, dark skinned, clean shaven, muscular and dressed elegantly in a dark Versace suit. He was someone who cared how he looked; he took pride in looking the part of the President's aide, and at the same time, loved dressing suitably, very much conscious he was in the United Kingdom. He knew the English had a long tradition of sartorial elegance.

"Mr President, why are you so restless today, Sa? I take it your meeting with the British Foreign Secretary did not go too well, Sa?" David asked in his distinct African accent.

"It did not, David. I tell you, these British think I am stupid and they can stall me. David, I want you to get for me all the information about all the members of Saleena's family, especially information on that deviant husband of hers. That man is not innocent, I tell you."

"Yes Sa, I will get on it straightaway, and get it for you as soon as I can."

"Good. Remember to be discreet. We are in a foreign country. I do not want to arouse too much suspicion as this may cause us some diplomatic issues with the British government. They know already why I am here, but I do not want to be seen to be meddling in their police investigation. This would be risky as well as dangerous for us too"

During a short briefing the following day, DI Slater and Sherlock discussed the progress of the case. Kiki reported nothing of significance, but she had this gut feeling, she shared with Sherlock telling him she knew from talking to Raazia, from her reaction that she knew something. Kiki had sensed there was something sinister preventing her from opening up. Maybe she was frightened. Sherlock knew himself this may be an important lead, even though it was a mere gut feeling at this stage.

"Kiki, it may be wise to persevere with Raazia; see what happens. Don't lean on her as she may need time to open up to us. You know it is imperative there is a break in the case and soon!"

Kiki went back to her desk, picked up the receiver and dialled Raazia's number. There was no answer, so she left a message asking Raazia to call her back.

Raazia arrived home after finishing work at the school. She picked up her messages, listened to Kiki's message first. The second seemed somewhat cryptic. It alarmed her. The caller had a foreign accent; she could not exactly make it out. He simply stated it was important and that he would call back. She remembered her profound conversation with Akeel the other night. Akeel had mentioned the word 'danger'. This had caused alarm bells to ring in the back of her head. *What if this was the danger Akeel had alluded to,* she thought. She reserved her thoughts for the time being. She returned Kiki's call.

"Raazia, hello, hope things are good, and thank you for returning my call," Kiki said.

"My husband and I had a very long chat after your last call. I have something more. Would you come and see us, please?"

"Yes, brilliant, how about after 6:00 p.m. tomorrow? DCI McLean will probably accompany me this time, that okay with you?"

"Is he the detective who was working on the case before?"

"Yes, he is my superior."

"Okay, we will see you at around 6 p.m. tomorrow."

As soon as she put the phone down, Kiki punched her fist in the air and at the same time screamed out, "Yhessss!" She stood up and walked over to Sherlock's desk. "Guess what, Chief?" Kiki said.

"What is it?"

"We may have something. The sister, Raazia, has agreed to see us tomorrow at six."

"Ah superb, let's hope it is the break we need. Good work, DI Slater."

"Thank you, Sir."

That night the family settled down for their evening meal. Raazia had made chicken *handi* with *rotis* and plain rice. She let the family know the police would be arriving tomorrow at around 6:00 p.m. Akeel should be there, she insisted. As the twins had dance classes, aunt Allia would pick them up and take them to hers first. The girls would eat at Allia's. Raazia had arranged it all with her sis. She knew they would be famished after their dance class so it would be better they ate over at Allia's, then she could drop them home around 8:30 p.m. assuming the police would be done by that time. Raazia insisted she would not be preparing any food at home as she did not want the house smelling of curry. During the conversation, she avoided mention of the cryptic message purposely as it would have alarmed the girls. Both of them were aware the police were coming though were not exactly sure why they were, except it was to do with aunt Saleena. The phone rang interrupting the family meal.

"I'll go pick up. You can finish eating, you lot," Raazia said as she stood up hastily to get to the telephone.

"Hello, Maleeka, how are you. It is good to hear from you."

"Hello, my dear, I am good, thanks. Raazia, this may be nothing but I had a very strange call today from someone who did not quite identify himself properly. It was a man with an African accent. He said it was important, that he wanted to meet me. Seemed a bit like, you know, cloak and dagger stuff. The reason I am calling is to ask is if you have had a call from him too."

"Yes, I did, but I was at work. I assume it must be the same person. He left a short message saying he would call back. I thought it was a strange message, to be honest. It did unnerve me a little. Also, come to think of it now that you mention it, yes, it definitely was an African accent, but I did not pick up on it at the time when I listened to it. All he said was he would call back some other time. What did he say to you? Who was he?"

"Well, I don't know, my dear. He wanted to meet with me to speak about Saleena, said it was important. I have agreed to meet him, as it happens, tomorrow actually. He said he will explain when we meet. Like I said, it was very cloak and dagger stuff, my dear, but I was intrigued by it all. I don't know if there is some connection with her murder from these *kaley* people. You don't know, do you? I really do think there is more to Saleena's murder than meets the eye. I shall, if I can, try to get to the bottom of it."

"Maleeka, be very careful. You don't know if you could be in danger."

"I am meeting him at McDonald's right in the centre of Manchester. So no chance he can attack me there. I will take Anisha with me too. I know she is no bouncer, but safe in numbers aye," Maleeka said with a cackle.

"Okay, Maleeka, and can you call me after the meeting to let me know what it was about. I also want to know who exactly this guy is."

"Sure, I will, my dear. Goodbye for now. By the way, hope the family are all okay."

Raazia felt insecure, almost frightened, unsure exactly why there was this sudden interest in Saleena's death after all this time not just by the police but some stranger from a foreign country. It all seemed eerie. She counselled herself to act with prudence at the same time best to be reserved with the information. She did not let on to Maleeka that she was meeting the police the next day.

Chapter 4

Amna, Abdel's housekeeper, normally arrived at 7 a.m. every morning. She often saw Daniel, the security guy, at the front iron gates, leaving the estate heading for home from his night shift. They would often wave at each other. Amna always arrived promptly on time, letting herself in with her set of keys to the house. She was a middle-aged Muslim woman, always wore her housekeepers uniform, black slacks, green top with a dark green short sleeved overall. Her jet-black hair was neatly tied back in a ponytail. She wore comfortable flat black slip-on smart shoes. A single parent, she completely relied on this job supporting her two teenage sons. The boys' father had been killed in a car crash a few years back. Amna was determined to see her boys through university education no matter what. She was a hard worker. Abdel knew her sad story, often paying her a generous bonus twice a year, at Christmas and Eid. She knew he was a good man, and she enjoyed working for him. She treated Abdel like a son, aware he was estranged from his father which often made her emotional as she knew too well how much her own children missed their father.

Her first task in the morning was sorting the boxes of fresh roses and lilies which had just been delivered that morning, making sure old ones were discarded, the vases cleaned and new ones arranged in all the rooms before the master of the house was up. Abdel loved the scent of fresh flowers, roses, lilies pervading the house which reminded him of his truly memorable stay at The Dorchester hotel. He met Philip there. He always remembered the scent of roses which hung in the air and it reminded him of happy times, perhaps distancing his mind from the troubles of the mind and heart. Amna had worked as a florist's assistant one time in her career and was good at arranging flowers, arranging them just as her master liked which pleased him.

Abdel had decided to spend a quiet day at the estate. He sent a text message to Philip on his Blackberry first thing in the morning, as he did every day, whilst enjoying breakfast Amna had made for him eggs on toast with strong sweet Indian tea. His text message read:

"Hi Philip, how are you today? x"
"I am good my friend, and you?"
"Getting ready for work."
"Oh, I am at home chillin."
"It's all right for sum! That is gud Abdel. Ill catch you l8r if ok hav to rush. xx"
"Bye for now, x"

Abdel's gregarious nature had got him into a habit of always messaging his old friend Philip, a habit Philip cherished very much. Their friendship had endured over time, first as lovers, then as good friends from the moment they met at The Dorchester hotel. After breakfast, he walked over to the stables. His main passion was Arabian stallions. His collection stood at ten in number. Sparing no cash in the purchase of horses, his prized Arabian thoroughbred's value stood at nearly £2.5 million. He was a proud owner of Antoninus, a beautiful chestnut-coat Arabian stallion who had a Cheltenham Gold Cup and Epsom Derby wins to his name. Not surprisingly, Antoninus was Abdel's most cherished and prized possession.

He owned three grey coats, one black coat, one roan, one bay and four chestnut coats including his favourite one Antoninus. The stallion was smart, intelligent and a powerful horse known for his speed and enormous strength. When Antoninus ran in races, he ran like a dream. There was a bond between the horse and his master. Antoninus could always sense his master's presence whenever Abdel was on the stud farm or in the stables. Whilst the horse had a sensitive side to him, he had a temperamental disposition too. There was the same bond between the horse and Jacob Jens, the stable hand, one of Abdel's employees.

The stable workers were Jacob Jens, Ben Straw and Susy Appleton. All three worked for Abdel on the stud farm looking after the horses. Daniel Doran was his security night watchman who normally worked a twelve-hour night shift usually starting at seven in the evening working through the night to seven the next morning. The employees were young from nearby villages who loved horses either having grown up with horses on farms or someone in their family had worked as a stable hand for other known race horse owners in the vicinity. Abdel had hired them for their passion for horses, and they seemed trustworthy wanting to pursue careers to do with horses. Ben had an ambition to be a jockey. He was 18 years old, as was Susy.

Jacob was twenty-two, trustworthy, intelligent and a young man who had built a strong bond with Antoninus, which Abdel admired. Jacob always accompanied the horses when transporting them to races. Abdel had a soft spot for Jacob too which he kept to himself; after all, he was an employee. Jacob had blond hair, was handsome looking, with a strong stature and blue eyes; he reminded Abdel a little of his friend Philip. Jacob lived on the estate in the small cottage attached to the stables which had adequate living quarters.

"Good morning, Jacob."

"Morning, boss, it is a lovely morning today. Shall I saddle up one of the horses for you?" Jacob enquired.

"Yes, Jacob, I will ride Antoninus this morning."

Jacob hesitated, not quite sure how he would convey to his master the horse's temperamental disposition this morning. He stood there looking quizzical.

"Jacob, is something the matter with Antoninus?"

"Oh, he errr…shall we say, is in a temperamental mood today, boss."

"What is wrong with him?" Abdel asked in a concerned tone about his favourite horse.

"The vet came yesterday, said he was fine physically."

"Then what is wrong with him?"

Jacob smiled unsure exactly how to express Antoninus' problem.

"Jacob, what is it?"

"Oh err…shall we go see him boss? He needs a release."

Abdel looked puzzled, pulling an odd face at Jacob, wondering what Jacob was talking about, why he was speaking in riddles, clearly slow to catch on his drift.

"Ermm…Boss shall we say you will need to find a nice Arabian filly for him soon or have him gelded!"

"Oh Lord, that? I see. I was going to speak to you, Jacob, about that after my morning ride, but it seems nature is something we cannot control or predict. I am aiming to book our flight out to Dubai to look at some Arabian thoroughbred fillies out there that I want to buy and bring over. Can you accompany me as I would value your opinion, please? You will be looking after them anyway so I value your input. Have you got your passport ready?"

"Dubai, boss! Really! I have never been abroad, let alone on a plane. Where will I be staying, boss?" Jacob asked looking a little concerned about the trip; his main worry was not the flight but where he would be staying in a foreign country.

"Don't worry about that, Jacob. Just make arrangements to get ready to fly Monday or Tuesday next week. I will need your passport. Do you have one?"

Jacob seemed surprised but nodded.

"Good," Abdel said as he walked into the stable to see for himself. Jacob followed.

Antoninus was agitated. He snorted repeatedly neighing in between making snorting noises, moving about undulating restlessly in his pen. Abdel could see Antoninus was not going to be in the mood for a ride this morning as his mind was elsewhere. He could see he was aroused.

"I don't think it is a good idea going into his enclosure today, boss. I'd let him calm down first, and he will; give him time," Jacob said.

Abdel went close up to the enclosure gate, stretched out his arms reaching out to pat Antoninus. He moved backwards bumping his rear into the stable wall, and then lunged forward making fierce snorting noises as if to signal to his master that he was not happy with him. The horse was known for his unpredictable characteristic and disposition. The mood the horse was in did not bode well for riding him that morning. He heeded his employee's advice of exercising care, as probably, if he did ride him, Antoninus might well throw him off anyway.

"My God, Jacob, I did not know he was this agitated; he seems almost wild today. I suppose he is a young horse and it's all that built up testosterone he has, I dare say. He could expend it with a good run, but I guess he is in a different kind of mood! So I shall have to leave him be today, Jacob. Can you saddle up Gustiani for me? You can ride Zeus. Those two stallions need a good run this morning as well. We need to get them ready for the next race in a few weeks' time."

"Sure boss, so how many fillies are you thinking of buying, if you don't mind me asking?"

"Three for now, then I can see how things pan out later on," Abdel responded.

"Are you planning on breeding the horses?"

"Yes, that is the plan, Jacob. You are part of the plan too. I want to get a good number of thoroughbreds here in England, as well as keeping the stallions satisfied too at the same time, if you know what I mean!"

Jacob smiled. He seemed happy to hear that he was part of the plan for breeding the horses at the stud farm where he enjoyed working.

"I look forward to it boss."

"I mean, look at Antoninus, though he may be impossible to ride when he is like that, just imagine the sheer strength he has, the power that horse possesses. He is a fine thoroughbred, and I bet he has some good genes for him to produce another fine thoroughbred."

"I guess Ben and Susy will be busy too for some time to come. Ben wants to train to be a jockey, boss, as you know."

"I do. I hope he will stay with us here and train. I am also trying to source some good training for him as, if you all stay with me, I think there is an exciting future ahead for all of us," Abdel said.

"That is good news, boss. Both Ben and Susy will be ecstatic to hear this. I know Ben will be really happy."

"Yes, that should be good news to announce, but for now just keep the information to yourself until we have the fillies here. The news may be premature in case we aren't able to get the fillies. I will speak to the staff myself at the right time. I think I have good loyal employees worth investing in."

Both laughed out loud.

Later in the evening, Abdel was at home relaxing, unwinding thinking about the conversation with Jacob in the morning about breeding horses. The strong scent of lilies hung in the air in the billiard room. Abdel lay on his favourite red leather sofa in the billiard room. He had his headset over his head covering his ears listening to The Corrs' song *Runaway* when his mobile rang. He did not hear it ring but felt it vibrate. Abdel fumbled around trying to look for it then as he got hold of it, grabbed the phone from underneath him, the screen displayed 'Raazia'.

"Abdel, hi, it's Raazia here, how are you?"

"I'm fine, sis; I know it was you. What's up?"

"The police have reopened Saleena's case; I thought I'd let you know just in case they get in touch. I have let Allia and Sameena know as well so they are not caught by surprise, in case they get in touch with them. Has anyone strange been in touch with you, Abdel?"

Abdel sat into an upright position hearing about the case being reopened, then jumped up from the sofa and walked over to the billiard table, picked up one of the balls and started to gently roll it on the table.

"Why have they done that, sis, after all this time, do you know?" Abdel asked with a touch of alarm in his voice.

"No, I just wanted you to know they have, that's all. I do not have any more information until I speak to them. There are two detectives coming to see me this evening."

"What's this about some stranger?"

"I don't really know. All I know is some guy with an African accent left a message on my answerphone saying he will call back. He spoke to Maleeka, and apparently, she has agreed to meet him."

"Wow, be careful, sis. African accent you said?"

"Yes, do you know anything about it?"

"No sis, but I am just thinking Saleena was in Uganda, and it may be someone from there."

"If they get in touch, be careful, and let me know as I am worried about this."

"Okay, sis. Bye for now."

Abdel paced up and down in the room in an agitated state. "Why would they resurrect the investigation," he said to himself aloud.

Raazia felt nervous as she spent hours cleaning the house that day making it look spick and span tidy. Fresh bunches of lilies were strategically placed in the hallway to give the house that fresh homely feel. Presentation of her house to guests was important to her. Any lingering smell of curry odour would be unacceptable. She could still remember the stale smell of curry odour that always lingered around in Papaji's house. She remembered also at school, English kids turning their noses away as their school clothes had the same smell. She was determined not to create that impression of Indian houses smelling of curries, so a fresh bunch of yellow roses mixed with some white carnations with green foliage, she arranged and placed in the lounge area on the narrow side table, then a final tidy up, puffing up all the cushions on the sofa, neatly piling them in a concertina arrangement. It was approaching time as she waited anxiously feeling nervous. She continued tidying up to the last minute as it helped keep her mind occupied. Sure enough, they were on time. It was 6:00 in the evening; the front doorbell rang. Akeel got up off the sofa, to answer the door.

"Good evening. You are Akeel, aren't you?" Sherlock asked.

"Yes, I am, err…"

"I am Detective McLean, and this is my colleague DI Slater."

Both police officers had their warrant cards lifted up in front of them with arms stretched out. Akeel shuffled his head closer to have a good look at the identification cards before inviting them in.

"May we come in?" Sherlock asked.

"Yes, of course, Raazia is in the lounge expecting you. I see you are on time?" Akeel said tongue in cheek.

"Well, laddie, never let it be said, you know, that the coppers are always late!" Sherlock said grinning at the same time.

Akeel did not know quite exactly what to say or respond, nor whether he should even respond but only nodded in acknowledgment simply raising both his eyebrows simultaneously. As they entered the hallway, a strong scent of roses hit them; it was a pleasant scent. Kiki proceeded to take her shoes off, hoping she would not have to remind her superior to do the same.

"Err…Boss, you couldn't leave your shoes here in the porch, if you don't mind terribly, would you, Sir?" Kiki said.

He looked at her, slightly amazed.

Raazia got up to greet the two police officers recognising both of them at once.

"Please come in, come in. DCI McLean, it's quite all right, you can leave your shoes on. Come in and sit down. May I get you a hot drink?" she asked them before they had chance to sit down.

"Black coffee and no sugar for me, please?" Sherlock said.

"Black coffee with one sugar for me, please, Raazia. Shall I give you a hand?" Kiki asked.

"No, no, no, you sit please, DI Slater, I won't be long. Akeel would you like a drink?" Raazia asked.

"Usual tea for me please. Thanks, Raaz," Akeel replied with a tiny grin on his face.

Akeel sat down on the long sofa. The two detectives sat at the other end on the single seat chairs each one positioned at the other end of the sofa.

"Shall we start?" Akeel enquired.

"Let's wait for Raazia to get back before we start, shall we?" Kiki stated.

"Yes, that would be a good idea," Sherlock responded as he looked around the room surveying it.

The scent of fresh flowers, lillies, pervading the room was pleasant for the guests. It gave the house a homely feel to it. The décor impressed Sherlock. He commented how the house had been tastefully decorated. Akeel prided himself receiving the compliment and taking credit for it. No reason why he should not, either, as all the work was done by him. He started telling Sherlock and Kiki how he had done all the work after Raazia had picked the wallpaper and the paint colours. He hung the wallpaper, painted and decorated the house himself. His flow was interrupted by Raazia returning into the lounge holding a tray with three mugs on it, shaking slightly, but managed to disguise her nervousness by steadying the tray, holding it tightly with both her hands once she closed the door behind her.

The situation reminded her of the time years gone by when in the summer of 1972, she had been summoned by Papaji into the sitting room after she and her sisters had come home from the park. She could feel the knots in her stomach making it churn, though this time, it was not Papaji she feared; it was something else, something unknown. A fear of the unknown she could not explain, possibly maybe dangers that may be lurking ahead Akeel had talked about.

She tried to keep calm, just as she did that day when Papaji had summoned her in 1972. The police officers were here in her house. It was about Saleena, Papaji, and this ugly honour killing business. She hated it all. But it was out of her hands as there was nothing she could do about it. The situation was as it was, she thought to herself. If she had the power, she would have given her right arm for the situation to have been different, to change it all: her sister alive and well, Papaji in his own little world. But sadly, she did not have the ability to change things. The two officers were there at her house for a purpose, to try catch her sister's killers, for her new evidence she said she would give them. She decided to deflect the negatives in her mind; to concentrate on a positive outcome from this hideous mess. She directed her mind to Akeel's words:

'Saleena would be disappointed in us if we did not speak up. What justice would there be for her then?'

Those powerful engaging words helped calm her. She reigned in all the strength required of her to be brave for her sister. Difficult as it was for her, she was determined to get this difficult task at hand over and done with as quickly as possible.

"Now Raazia, when we spoke last on the telephone, you said you had something new to tell us that could help with our enquiries going forward. Is that right?" Kiki asked.

"Yes, I do," Raazia replied.

Kiki proceeded to open her bag taking out A4 size pieces of papers. There was something printed at the top.

"My colleague will take down what you say in a new statement, if that is all right with you, Raazia. May I call you Raazia?"

Raazia nodded

"Then once finished with your statement, we will ask you to read it carefully, if you agree with the contents, to sign it, that okay?" asked Sherlock.

A deafening silence descended in the room for a minute. If someone had dropped a pin, you would have heard its sound as it made contact with the floor. A formal statement would be in writing with her signature attesting the contents. It would have her words in it that could very well mean a prosecution of her father. He may go to jail. Raazia paused. The presence of two senior detectives in her house brought home the reality of the seriousness of what was facing her. The gravitas of the meeting was a little daunting for her. She simply did not know what lay ahead for her and her family. Raazia began to shake quite visibly. Akeel moved closer to his wife as she sat down on the sofa. He put his mug of tea down on the side table on a mat, held her hand providing support.

"Raaz, there is nothing to worry about. We have talked about this. It is the right thing for you to do. Remember this is for Saleena," Akeel asserted.

Raazia was naturally in an emotional state as tears rolled down her cheeks. Kiki stood up, walked over to the television and fished out a tissue from a box on top of the TV handing it to her. Raazia wiped her tears away.

"Thank you. I am sorry but I can't help it; every single time I think of my poor sister, her tragic life, it just makes me so emotional. I feel helpless."

"You don't need to feel helpless anymore, Raazia. Look, unfortunately you cannot change things. You know that. What you can do for her is seek justice which is the only way you will get closure on this or come to terms with it," Kiki said reassuringly.

"I guess you are right." She paused to catch a big breath, and then she began telling her version. "Well, I was at my parents' house for the *barsi*, which was a first anniversary remembrance service…"

Chapter 5

It was early evening. McDonalds in Manchester City Centre was crowded with customers. Maleeka walked into the restaurant with Anisha close by her side. It was a good public place for a meeting, Maleeka thought. She was eager to meet David. There was something intriguing about him. To her, he was a stranger from a foreign land come to speak with her on an important matter to do with Saleena's murder. That fact alone intrigued her. She was a woman in her forties with not much going in her private life. She loved reading mystery novels; in particular, she was an avid fan of Agatha Christie's *Poirot* novels. She had watched all the movies too.

Anisha, on the other hand, was filled with trepidation, not looking forward to meeting the stranger at all. The whole business of meeting a stranger, to her, sounded bizarre and risky. It was not like Maleeka to do this, she thought. Maleeka was in the business of rescuing women who were victims of domestic violence, not putting women in danger. David could turn out to be one of those horrible men who enjoyed inflicting gratuitous violence on women. The more she thought about it, the more she became fearful as he could turn out to be a killer possibly. The strange thing was, the more she dwelt on it, the more frightened she began to feel.

As they waited for a table, she shared her thoughts and fears with Maleeka. Maleeka brushed it off saying to her she was being silly; they were secure amongst the hustle and bustle of the busy restaurant. The crowd, she knew were oblivious to this important rendezvous. Soon a table was about to become vacant. Anisha spotted it; it was in the corner by the window where a young English couple were picking the rubbish after they had finished eating. The two women raced towards it to secure it before it was taken up. A young lad came over with a spray bottle and a cloth. He sprayed the table with liquid before wiping it with his blue-coloured cloth. Seemed like a sixteen-year-old probably working part-time to earn a bit of cash. As soon as he was done, he moved on to clean another table which had just become vacant. They had a good view of the restaurant from their seating position.

"Maleeka, do you not feel scared about meeting a total stranger like this here? I feel so nervous that I feel my bladder is about to give way!" Anisha said as she continued to feel anxious.

"Oh Anisha, look at the place; it is so busy. What can possibly happen here? Relax a little; I know we are safe here," Maleeka responded trying to reassure her friend.

"I don't know, Maleeka. I have a bad feeling about this *kala* stranger."

"Just think, Anisha, you and I, we could be important in this matter of international espionage. I have never met a high official from a government department before. I am excited. Aren't you?"

Anisha gave Maleeka a strange look implying Maleeka was crazy. "But he could be part of some sort of mafioso from a mafia, you know," Anisha said with a little tremble in her voice.

"Anisha, shush will you. Just keep your eyes and ears peeled open and see if you can spot him."

A tall African chap, six-foot-tall, dark-skinned, clean shaven, muscular, grade one styled haircut, dressed casually in jeans and a dark green jacket with dark glasses came through the front swing doors. Anisha looked directly at Maleeka. With her eyes, she signalled his presence. He saw two middle-aged Asian woman together, assumed it was them he was meeting and began walking towards their table when Maleeka waved at him which confirmed it was them.

"Are you Maleeka?" he asked speaking with an African accent.

Maleeka stood up to greet him. She shook hands with him. "Yes, I am pleased to meet you err…"

"David is my name, Maleeka, please stay seated. And who is your companion?"

"This is my friend, Anisha."

Anisha just nodded at him avoiding shaking hands. Mutembe's height, his dark sunglasses seemed enough characteristics for her to shrink away from him as she moved closer to her friend wanting to shield herself just in case he attacked them. She was not used to meeting black men let alone black men from a foreign country. Being perceptive, David detected the fear in Maleeka's friend.

"Please ladies, I assure you I come as a friend of Saleena. Let me first go get a drink as I am very thirsty; then we can talk. What can I get you?" Mutembe asked.

"Pepsi will be fine for both of us," Maleeka responded.

David walked across to the counter to place his order.

"Maleeka, he looks terrifying to me. *Kala hey naa*? What does he want from us?" Anisha whispered as she leant closer to Maleeka.

"Shush Anisha, stop being racist. He will see you whispering. I want to know what all this is about, so I don't want to give him cause to treat us with suspicion. Let's have an open mind, shall we? I think he looks friendly. He's a friend of Saleena, he said; that's good enough for me. Besides, look at this place. It is crowded. We should be fine. He has agreed to meet in public, hasn't he? If there was anything shady going on here, my dear, I dare say he would not have agreed to meet us here in a crowded place. I am sure of that." Maleeka reassured her companion.

Anisha stayed alert, however, not letting her guard down not even for one second. David returned five minutes later with a tray full of food and cups of fizzy drinks on it. He put the tray down on the table.

"Pepsi for you ladies as ordered," he said as he handed each of them a cup with a straw. "I am starving. Would you like something to eat?" David asked courteously.

Both Maleeka and Anisha shook their heads.

"All this fast food, my dear, is not very good for you," Maleeka said.

"Oh don't worry, madam, I don't normally eat this stuff. I have to be on a strict diet at home, so please don't tell anyone. I have to say, though, I am going to enjoy my burgers today; have an off day as you English might say," David said as he took a big chunky bite with his mouth into one of his cheeseburgers.

"No doubt, my dear, no doubt, you seem to be strong like Saleena's friend Calvin. I dare say, you do have to be on a strict diet," Maleeka said with a shrill laugh.

Anisha gave Maleeka a strange look of disapproval. Maleeka simply bobbled her head seemingly acting flirtatiously with David as she continued to smile at him. David had a mighty nice physique, she thought in her mind without saying it aloud. Maleeka was in her late twenties when she had been forced to leave her husband. Being forced to abandon her home, taking refuge at a friend's house, and then occupied with creating and running the women's refuge had eaten away all her time – time lost unable to spend in a man's company or seek satisfaction for her womanly desires. She undoubtedly found David to be an attractive man.

"Thank you, madam, I try to keep fit as it is my job."

"What is your job?" Maleeka asked directly.

"My job is not of importance, though I will say this much. I work for the government in Uganda."

"Really, my dear! That must be an exciting job? Now then, my dear, I am intrigued, where did you get my contact details from?"

"Saleena had a pocket address book we found at her flat in Soroti. It had your details."

"Ah, I see. I am also very intrigued by your request to meet with me, not least your cloak and dagger approach about why you are here. So tell me what is this all about?" Maleeka demanded softly.

"First, I must ask that you keep our meeting here today confidential including our discussion," David said as he wiped his hands with a white serviette then put a hand in his jacket pocket about to take something out.

Anisha flinched backwards in her chair wondering if he was about to pull out a handgun or something as she suddenly stood up trying to excuse herself wanting the ladies room desperately. Her bladder apparently was causing her grave discomfort. The urge to pee was quite genuine as it was also now urgently unavoidable for her as she rushed off towards the toilets.

David thought it a little amusing, Anisha's peculiar behaviour. "Is she always like this, your companion?" he asked pulling out a pocket-size handheld recorder from his pocket similar to ones reporters usually carry with them. It was a small blue-coloured device which had 'OLYMPUS' embossed in silver on the front of it. Maleeka had been reasonably relaxed unlike Anisha who displayed some obvious signs of fear.

"Yes, I am afraid so. Please do excuse her. She was, unfortunately trapped in a domestic violent marriage, as all our rescued woman who are at our women's refuge, just as Saleena was, tend to develop nervous dispositions when around men, you know, it is very difficult for us women to then re-establish confidence in men."

"I see. I am sorry to hear about it. Not all men are wife beaters, but I can understand how she feels. Anyhow, I hope you don't mind me recording our conversation as it is easier for me."

Maleeka nodded

"As you know, Maleeka, our President was very fond of Saleena and her friend Calvin. I believe you met Calvin before he was killed?"

"Yes, he was a charming man. I met him a few times here in Leeds. He was a gentle, kind person. Saleena and Calvin were close. They were, I believe, intending to get married as soon as Saleena had divorced that brute of a husband of hers, Nawaz. He refused to give her a divorce."

"So talking of the devil, Nawaz, please tell me what you know about the man. I would like to know from you all about him and Saleena," he said as he clicked his Olympus recorder on 'Record'.

"Well, I first came across Saleena when I visited her in hospital..."

Time flew past. An hour had gone just like that by the time Maleeka finished telling her friend Saleena's woeful story. She had tears in her eyes. David seemed somewhat moved by this story too. He asked how he could get in touch with Nadine Nugent and Nawaz. Maleeka scribbled down on a piece of paper some details before handing it to David.

"I thank you for meeting me today. I realise it must have been daunting for you to meet a complete stranger like this. I salute your bravery as it must have taken lots of courage to do this. It can't have been easy for vulnerable ladies like you. I too understand for your safety why you picked a public place to meet. I am a friend, believe me, not a foe. You have helped catch Saleena and Calvin's killers, that I promise you."

"Will you be speaking to Raazia?" Maleeka asked.

"Yes, I will. I have her telephone number so I will call her. Goodbye now. Thank you again. You have helped a great deal."

They shook hands. Even Anisha shook hands with David, surprisingly, as they parted.

Later that evening, Maleeka spoke to Raazia about her meeting with David. The first thing Raazia asked was how he got the contact details. They had found a pocket address book at her flat she advised amongst Saleena's things where he got the details from. She allayed any fears Raazia might have had, encouraging her to meet up with him to tell him her side of the story. "He comes as a friend to help find Saleena's killers." Maleeka, being slightly odd, had some nagging doubts; she was still convinced there was something odd about the whole thing, *"Daal mey kuch kala hey,"* she put it. She confessed she could not quite place her finger on this stranger's involvement. For her, where government officials were involved, particularly from another country looking into the murders which happened in England, there had to be something more than met the eye. To her, a high official of Ugandan government looking into the deaths was unusual and smacked of some sort political espionage. It was all very suspicious. Who knows, she thought, it might be connected to Calvin or even Mafioso involvement. Maleeka was still peddling her suspicion to Raazia. It unnerved her rather than put her at ease. Maleeka stated that Raazia should not be put off meeting him as David appeared to be a friend. What she said about her suspicions was just her. Raazia did let Maleeka know this time round that she had met with the two police officers, that she had given a further statement though she did not share with her what she had said in her statement. Maleeka was pleased she had the courage to give a new lead to the police that might lead to some arrests.

David Mutembe's next stop was to see Nadine then Raazia afterwards. Even though it was getting late in the day, David was determined to press on. Nadine was more than happy to spare the time to provide information as she was eager to see justice done for Saleena. Following a phone call to Raazia, though very late, David travelled to Leicester to meet Raazia and Akeel. Raazia was filled with trepidation about a stranger visiting her very late at night. He was some official from a foreign government which had worried her. There was some comfort about him being friendly from Maleeka who had met him which did help put her at ease in meeting him. Akeel would be there. She aptly remembered Akeel's words about the courage of the warrior Ertuğrul which helped maintain courage to carry on.

Jacob was nearly dozing off in his comfortable business class seat on board a flight to Dubai when Abdel came over to check in on him. The British Airways 747 aircraft was cruising at 33,000 feet in the sky above the clouds. Apart from the chatter from other passengers, he could hear the smooth whirring sound of the four giant engines propelling the jet in the sky cruising at a subsonic speed of five hundred and seventy miles an hour. Jacob could not hide his excitement about the trip. It was his first time on an aeroplane. What amazed him as he looked out from his tiny window was the clouds were below the aircraft which he had never seen before. It was something new as well as exciting for him. Neither had he seen before passengers being pampered by the in-flight crew attendants much to Jacob's amusement, who were busy rushing around the plane 'servicing' their needs. A particular passenger, seated in the opposite seat to his was a middle-aged man, dressed smartly in a suit and tie had his leather briefcase open resting by his side seemed to be concentrating intensely examining his paperwork. What made him smile was the passenger kept downing lots of glasses of champagne. It amused Jacob. He could not help notice his finger was constantly on the small white button on the side of the seat calling for attention. Soon an attendant would appear holding a bottle of champagne to top up his glass! The aircraft crew soon got used to him and seemed to keep him happy.

"Hello, Jacob, how are you doing? I was just stretching my legs. Thought I'd check in on you make sure you were okay," Abdel said as he knelt down on the floor of the plane as Jacob, seeing his boss, was about to get up from his seat.

"No, it's fine don't get up; stay where you are, Jacob."

"I am fine, boss."

"Good, good. I wanted to make sure you were all right."

"Boss, I could have travelled economy; you didn't have to book me in business class travel."

"I know, Jacob, but I know it's your very first time flying so I wanted to make sure you had a comfortable flight. It's a seven-plus-hours flight. We have one day's rest then a long day after that travelling to Sharjah. We will be visiting two different breeders. I want you to help me choose the best fillies. Once we have chosen the right ones, I want you to get all the paperwork organised with the authorities then for you to travel with the horses back to England ensuring they get to the stables safely. Besides the return flight with the horses may not be so comfortable! I know you have not done this type of thing before, but I am sure you will get it all done for me, Jacob; you are a very intelligent young man."

Jacob paused for a moment, then simply acknowledged with a nod.

"I will, boss, don't worry," he said.

"I am not worried. I trust you Jacob, you have that trained eye in looking for the best in horses. You are well organised as well as meticulous with all your paperwork on the horses at home. The paperwork on all the thoroughbreds, especially the vet's medical records are well organised. It is impressive. Now you know why you are here."

"Thank you, boss, I will not let you down."

"Good, I trust your judgment. Now rest up."

"See you later, boss."

Jacob moved his body as far back as he could in his seat making himself comfortable resting his head on a pillow and covering his legs with a blanket. With a smile on his face, happy at hearing the nice words from his boss, confidence boosted, the twenty-two year-old closed his eyes to try and get some sleep.

Chapter 6

David returned back to the President's suite at The Dorchester in the early hours of the morning with the information he had gathered so far. He went into the room to see if the President was awake. Finding him asleep, he decided to wait until the morning before briefing him. It was at breakfast that he had the opportunity to brief the President. They were both of the shared opinion that it was highly likely there was a conspiracy between Nawaz and his father-in-law to murder Calvin and Saleena with Nawaz taking the lead.

"Sa, I do know that the police are looking into the honour killing theory, Mr President Sa. The women, Saleena's sister Raazia as well as Maleeka told me about that."

"Let's listen to the tapes first, shall we? We can then see if there is anything more we can do here or it may be, I think, that we have achieved our purpose for now. I believe the journey has been fruitful. Do you not agree?"

"I agree, Sa."

David put the Olympus recorder on play then placed it upright on the side table turning the volume up to high as both of them listened carefully.

"I believe, no I am convinced, that it was the husband and the father who killed our people. The only problem is if we interfere in the ongoing investigation, the British will not be happy. David, when you return back to UK, I want you to pay that *kumamayo* [motherfucker] husband a visit. David, we should fly back home today. Get my jet ready for the departure in the afternoon. I will telephone the Prime Minister and let him know we are leaving in this afternoon."

"Sa."

Immigration at Terminal 3 Dubai International airport was a fairly smooth affair for the two travellers. Abdel was used to travelling. Jacob, on the other hand, was a novice. It was all new to him, first time abroad. Dubai looked like a vast country with tall skyscrapers everywhere. Jacob looked around him from the limo windows surveying some of the breath-taking scenic views as the limo travelled down Sheikh Zayed Road. There were road signs everywhere on the highway. They went past a sign which read 'Jebel Ali/Abu Dhabi'. He seemed mesmerised as he stared out the Limo windows sometimes turning around to look at the unusual tall architectural buildings all around. Abdel smiled. Jacob reminded him of his own first experience being chauffeur-driven in a limo in London the day he picked up his lottery cheque. He smiled looking at Jacob as it took him down memory lane with a feeling of déjà vu. After a thirty-minute ride, the limousine pulled up outside Grosvenor House hotel. The concierge opened the doors to the limo allowing both of them to disembark. The bellhops scrambled to get the luggage out of the boot as they took care of the luggage.

Jacob was enjoying being pampered. Back home, he would be cleaning out the stables, he thought. This side of how the other half in the world lived, like his wealthy master, seeing the rich people how they lived was something attractive than being a stable hand. A slight feeling of envy enveloped him. He pretended to be one of their wealthy guests, feeling happy not having to carry the luggage. It was a great feeling being treated as a rich guest. Jacob began to dream. He would love to be living the life he saw people lived there. It was a beautiful day, nearly thirty-degrees temperature as the sun beat down with sunrays bouncing off some of the tall glass buildings shimmering across the vast horizon. The hotel was plush. Jacob looked around climbing some steps to the huge foyer. The high ceiling had huge chandeliers hanging from it beaming down tons of light. The hotel, located on Dubai Marina promenade boasted its five-star rating offering simply luxury as well as panoramic views of Dubai. The hotel foyer was busy with guests milling around. Hotel staff were busy pandering to the needs of their wealthy guests.

Meesha and her sister were getting ready for school when the telephone rang. It was 8 a.m. Meesha picked up the phone. It was *Naaniji* Fauzia. She began screaming unintelligibly down the phone in Urdu. Meesha pulled the handset away from her ear attempting in English to try to calm her down. *Naaniji* was not having any of it. Meesha thought something had happened to *Naanaji*. She tried again to calm her down, but Fauzia continued ranting in Urdu screaming at the top of her voice. Meesha put the handset down at the side of the phone on the table.

Raazia was upstairs getting ready for work when Meesha called her, shouting at the top of her voice.

"Mum, can you come? *Naaniji* is on the phone ranting in Urdu. I can't understand what she is saying."

Raazia quickly came down and picked up the receiver. She barely had chance to say 'hello' when this volcano blasting down the phone receiver forced her to pull the receiver away from her ear as the decibels Raazia's ear was being exposed to was excessive. Raazia had known Fauzia had a dark side to her but had never before heard her use so many expletives in Urdu all fired at her in quick succession. Raazia hung up the phone as it was well-nigh impossible to understand her. The woman was having a rant.

"Meesha, Shakeela, I will drop you off at the bus stop today so you can get off to school on time as I will need to make a detour this morning, call in at *Naaniji's* house first see what the mad woman was ranting about on the phone. Is that okay, girls?"

"Yes Mum, that is fine with me, sure Shak be okay too. Mum, *Naaniji* seemed to be in a panicked state to me. Was she okay?" Meesha said.

"I don't really know, Meesh. I've got to go see what is going on otherwise I will be the one to get it in the neck from them, you know what both of them are like, not to mention I'll be in a right state all day if I don't find out what is going on. It will eat away at me."

"Okay, Mum, but you should not be made to feel like that. It is not right."

"I know, baby, I know. Let's go now; love you, sweetie."

"Love you too, Mum."

As soon as Raazia got to the house, the front door was flung open. Fauzia was inside the room by the front door. She nearly ripped Raazia's head off immediately, verbally attacking her first then attempted to strike her with a chapatti rolling pin. Raazia defended herself by putting her handbag up to block the rolling pin. This brought back memories of the time when she and Allia had been assaulted with a rolling pin many years ago when they were children. Fauzia continued shouting at the top of her voice most of it expletives mixed with rambling sentences about Papaji being arrested by the police. Fauzia continued waving the rolling pin wildly in the air.

Raazia tried to pacify her, but Fauzia was having none of it. What she had gathered was Papaji had been arrested by the police. They had taken him away under arrest that morning. Fauzia said something about all of it being Raazia's fault not to mention embarrassing for them as the neighbours were all watching when her father was taken away with his hands in handcuffs. The audacity, the shame Raazia had brought onto the family, how was she going to restore the family's honour which she had irreparably damaged.

Raazia was not prepared to listen to anymore of her demented nonsense that morning, so she left the house slamming the front door shut as some neighbours looked on from their front room windows. Raazia walked at a fast pace as she hurried to her car, got in, locked the doors from the inside as she tried to catch her breath. Her nerves were all on edge. She hated ugly scenes like that. Akeel was not answering his phone when she tried calling him on the mobile phone. Raazia sent a text message to him to saying: *'Could you call me as soon as possible,'* before driving on. Some neighbours must have heard the commotion. As Raazia pulled away, one or two nosy ones lifted their net curtains to peek at her from their windows.

Raazia, although all too aware at some point the police would be calling upon Papaji, she had not anticipated such a dramatic scene from Fauzia, maybe from Papaji but not her. She pulled up her red-coloured Toyota Corolla hatchback in the school car park feeling jaded and mentally exhausted. Akeel still had not called her back or sent a message via text. Feeling a little frustrated, she dialled Akeel's number with no luck again. Raazia left a frantic message on his network messaging service to call her back immediately, that it was urgent.

"Oh Akeel, where are you? I really need you right now," she muttered to herself. Unable to reach him, she had no choice but to carry on with her day. She rushed into the school as she was running late. The school head Mrs Susan Crombie observed Raazia's lateness. Mrs Crombie was small in height, slightly plumpish, middle aged with light brown hair neatly tied in a bun. She wore a light grey suit, skirt and jacket. Her crisply starched blouse stood out from all her dress wear. It was white, buttoned to the neck, with pleated cuffs neatly protruding elegantly at the end of the jacket sleeves. A gold brooch of a beetle was pinned on the left lapel of her jacket. She was, as one would expect, a typically proper school head. Raazia stumbled as she rushed to her class in the long corridor of the primary school where she worked, dropping the stack of children's books taken home for marking. Raazia became even more nervous as she saw Mrs Crombie approach her.

"Mrs Khan, you look to be all in a bother. Whatever is the matter?" she asked in a serious tone. The Head knelt down to the floor to help Raazia pick up the notebooks detecting something to be wrong as Raazia looked completely flushed.

"Oh Mrs Crombie, I am ever so sorry. There was a domestic issue at my father's house this morning. I went to see if everything was okay, but my mother was in a frantic state as my father had been arrested by the police."

"My dear, that is awful. Just go to my office, and wait there for me. I shall be along shortly once I have sorted your class out."

"Thank you, Mrs Crombie."

Five minutes later, the Head returned to the office. On a side table in her office, there was a portable kettle which she turned on.

"I shall make us a nice cup of tea first, then we can sit and talk."

Nawaz and Papaji were both under police arrest. Papaji was initially taken to Charles Street Police Station in Leicester, then later on in the afternoon, he was transported to Salford Police Station where Nawaz was being held. As soon as they had been arrested, both Nawaz and Papaji complained vehemently of police harassment as they were innocent citizens. The police paid little attention to their complaints. Both were later taken to Leeds police station for questioning.

Papaji as usual wore his traditional *shalwar kameez*. His hair was all ruffled, looked quite shabby with his greys protruding out from under his shabby old *topi* he had worn for years. He looked old, tired and frail. Papaji's hair was almost all white. As usual, he carried in his hand the blue-coloured *tasbee* passing each bead between his fingers repeating the words "*Allah hu akbar*" [God is great] all the time.

In the police interviews at the station, he refused the assistance of a duty solicitor, insisting he had done nothing wrong and so would not need a lawyer. Kiki and Sherlock asked him questions in a formal recorded interview asking him about the conversation Raazia had heard on the evening of the *barsi*, but he denied it. When asked about honour killings, again he declined to comment, adding he knew nothing about it.

Nawaz stood firm, resolutely denying any involvement to do with the allegation of killing his wife or her *kala* boyfriend. He launched a scathing attack on the police threatening to sue them for wrongful arrest and false imprisonment, muttering words in Urdu alleging the police were making wild allegations which amounted to slander as they had no proof.

Sherlock secured an extension from his superiors extending the legal arrest time from twenty-four hours to thirty-six which would be the maximum time they could hold them at the police station unless further extensions were authorised by the courts. The lack of time did not deter him. Both the detectives were determined to charge them if they could, despite struggling with sufficiency of evidence to formally charge them.

Transportation for Abdel and Jacob to travel south to Abu Dhabi from Grosvenor House hotel had been arranged by agents. They travelled in a 4x4. Part of their journey was by road, part travelling through desert on the sand dunes. The journey by road was normal. The driver stopped to let air pressure out of the tyres making them flatter for the rest of the journey before driving on the sand dunes. The ride on the sand dunes was incredibly bumpy. Both Abdel and Jacob enjoyed the thrilling ride. As they stepped out from the 4x4, they felt the intense heat which was dry and stifling. It must have been over thirty-five degrees out there. There were flies everywhere. Neither Abdel nor Jacob was used to the afternoon desert heat as the sun was as high as could be in the sky as it beat down making it hot and sultry.

The first stop was at a place which had a large marquee where he met the owner of the horses. First, the owner's servant served customary black tea then was a tour around on the desert enclosure which had a pack of horses roaming around. He had some marvellous Arabian Stallions. Jacob did a closer inspection on the fillies that were being sold. He examined their legs by running his hands along the front legs first followed by the hind legs, patting each horse on the head as he went along closely trying to get a feel of the fillies, at the same time making sure not to spook them. Jacob was not a vet. Abdel could tell from Jacob's reaction he seemed not happy with any of them.

"Jacob what do you think? You did not seem excited when you looked at the fillies closely?" Abdel asked.

"Boss, I am unsure about them, to be honest. I can't see anything wrong with them though; it's only a gut feeling, I don't think Antoninus will take to some of the fillies we looked at just now. I don't know, boss. I just got this feeling. Like I said, it is only a gut feeling. Did you like them?"

"Jacob, I will go along with your gut feeling. I am not sure either."

Abdel thanked the owner for his kind hospitality and politely bid him farewell by shaking his hand advising him he would be in touch through his agent in Dubai.

Following a late lunch and refreshments, they headed north in the direction of Sharjah, a forty-five-minute journey in the car. Jacob seemed quiet. Maybe he was admiring some of the scenic views. He could see vast areas of desert for miles as far as the eyes could see. It was an amazing sight Jacob had not before seen with the naked eye. Soon they travelled back through Dubai. The tall modern skyscrapers came into their view.

"These must have taken years to build." Jacob commented.

"Just look at them, they are monstrously tall works of architectural geniuses, I'd say," Abdel responded.

"It seems to be a rich country with lots of money here, boss, and a haven for wealthy to come live here."

"You would like to live here?"

"Well, I don't know, seems to have a lot to offer."

"Jacob, the grass looks greener, but it isn't always the case! I love England: beautiful seasons, even though it rains all the time, plenty of nice things to do. Besides our families are there, you know. If you were here, you would be homesick and miss them. Like I said, the grass is not always greener on the other side, Jacob."

"I know, boss. I don't think my dad would miss me."

"Jacob, who knows what the future holds." Abdel wished he could have said something more positive about that to make his young employee feel a lot better. He said nothing more as he was in the same situation as Jacob. It was something that resonated with Abdel. He did not know quite how to respond to such a delicate as well a sensitive matter.

Their driver took them towards Sharjah which was their next destination. Upon arrival, they were met by Sheikh Azim Bin Hallawaji, a breeder of fine Arabian thoroughbreds. His palace was impressive. Jacob had never seen anything like it before, having grown up in a sleepy village of Mickleham which quietly nestled in the Mole Valley in Surrey. Though the village had its historic scenic attractions – delightful period properties, attractive woodland areas, cosy little quaint pubs and area popular with equestrian lovers where Jacob grew up being with horses all his life – this was something else. The land that the Sheikh owned was no comparison to anywhere in Mickleham. It was simply a vast area of land separated by desert, his palace and manmade lush green areas of land. Part of it looked like a ranch lifted out from somewhere in Texas.

Sheikh Hallawaji was in his early thirties, had a short designer beard, smooth olive skin, wearing a long white *thobe*, *keffiyeh* worn on his head which was held firmly in place by an *agal*, Armani sunglass and a smart IWC gold watch. His English was perfect, manner polite. It surprised Jacob a little as he greeted them both by shaking their hands welcoming them to his estate. The Sheikh drove them in his 4x4 Mercedes Benz M-Class through the vast estate. Like Abdel, he, the Sheikh, had a passion for not just owning the most beautiful thoroughbreds but racing them. Pack of beautiful horses roamed freely on his land. What a sight Jacob thought it was. Something he would not likely forget easily for a long time nor had he seen anything like that in England. The Sheikh owned some of the finest Arabian thoroughbreds.

News of Papaji's arrest spread to other members of the family fast. Aliya, her husband Sajjid, their children Rabbiya and Abbas, Sameena, her husband Faraz and their two daughters Sara and Salena gathered at Raazia's house in the evening much to her delight. The moral support was much needed by Raazia. It was essential for the family to gather to discuss the situation. They had all joined

Raazia's family for an evening meal. Allia was dressed in modern western clothes, smart black trousers, blouse and jacket, neat jet-black hair tied in a French braid. It suited her. Sameena, on the other hand, was dressed in traditional clothes, *shalwar kameez*, *dupatta* and a scarf covering her head.

"Have you been in touch with Abdel to tell him about Papaji's arrest, Raazia?" Allia asked.

"I have tried to call him, but he is not picking up his phone, so I sent a text message to him."

"He must be abroad somewhere. What about Sara?" Allia said.

"I don't know as Abdel is not easy to get hold of these days. You know what he is like. He hates being asked questions. I called Sara today to let her know but she said she was too busy to come over. 'I hope the police throw away the keys after they have locked him up,' she said to me when I spoke with her!"

"I am not the only one who hates him then!" Allia said with a slight snigger.

"Allia, c'mon he is your father. Have a little compassion for him. He is old. Can you imagine how it must be like for him stuck at a police station somewhere in the country all alone?" Sajjid said to his wife.

"Well, he deserves it. I am not going to feel sorry for him at all if I am honest, doesn't matter how old he is. Can you imagine if it's true, this honour killing business; he deserves what he gets, I say," Allia stated sticking, firmly to her guns.

"I thought the police had closed the investigation due to lack of evidence, Raazia. So what suddenly made them decide to reopen it, any idea?" Sameena asked.

"DI Slater came to visit me here. She had travelled all the way from Leeds to tell me that. It was completely out of the blue. She said they had reopened the case; quite why, she did not say. Either she did not know or the police wanted to keep the information under wraps. Curiously though, she asked me for a further statement which I have given to them now. I had to following Akeel making the decision to make a statement. Sameena, I am sorry; I did say I would consult you and Allia, but there was no time."

"It's okay, Raaz, it doesn't matter. I would have supported the decision anyway. I am more concerned about if there are any dangers ahead for us," Sameena said.

"Thank you, dear sis; I have been advised by the police not to say anything more at this stage to anyone. Whilst I know you would not say anything to anyone, but for good reasons, I will not reveal what I said in my statement. As for dangers, well, I will let Akeel explain."

"Raazia is right. It is for the best we don't say much at his stage as the police have said not to. It is hush, hush because we think there is another angle to it," Akeel said.

"What do you mean another angle to it?" Allia asked.

She seemed annoyed with her sister and brother-in-law, paused for a while, and though silent, momentarily displayed unequivocally disapproval only by her body language by folding her arms tightly. Raazia sensed from her sister's demeanour she was either about to explode and say exactly what was on her mind or have an argument with them. Sameena, on the other hand, remained calm. The atmosphere got a little tense.

Raazia did not want the kids to witness any unpleasantness between the adults nor hear what was about to be said, so she asked them all to go upstairs. She told the girls that Meesha and Shakeela had some pictures taken of a dance routine they did recently at a show they took part in. She asked her twins to show them their routine they had performed. "It was really good," Raazia said to all the children. They should all see it and to take Abbas with them upstairs too. Once the children were out of the room, Allia offloaded what was on her mind.

"Raazia, you need to share information with us. This is not fair. We are here as part of the family and, more importantly, to support you. We need to know what is going on. We used to share all the secrets at one time, remember? Or have you forgotten? I feel like being excluded from the family again," Allia retorted in a sharp tone as the tension in the room began to rise.

"Allia, we are not excluding you. We are trying to protect you," Raazia insisted.

"From what?" she asked sharply.

"Allia, we are dealing with a delicate situation here. This honour killing business is something we all know exists, but you don't expect it would happen to you or your family. We don't exactly know what ramifications it has for the family. If Nawaz was involved, we all know what a monster he can be. We don't know if he is capable of threatening us to back off. Coincidentally, something else too is we don't know if there may be some other dangers that put ourselves and the children at any risk." Akeel intervened.

"Akeel, now you have got my undivided attention, and I want…no, insist you tell us what is going on," Allia demanded.

Akeel looked at Raazia directly and nodded his head as if to signal to her that Allia was right.

"Allia, we are only protecting you, sweetie! If you remember, I mentioned to you on the phone that this chap had come to see me. He is some high official from the Ugandan government. We are not sure what his involvement is here. He says he comes as a friend of Saleena but Akeel and I, and Maleeka, think there's more to it than meets the eye. Maleeka said she was convinced there was something odd about the whole thing, '*Daal mey kuch kala hey*,' she said. Do you remember how everyone talked about how Saleena's funeral had been taken over by those people? Although there was nothing sinister about that, we don't know if all this involvement by them is to do with Calvin. We do not know anything about him, who the man was and exactly where he was from. Maleeka keeps talking about espionage which frightens me," Raazia insisted.

"So how is Maleeka involved, and how does she know more than we do?" Allia asked.

"Well this *kala* chap his name was David, some high official from Uganda's government. Not exactly sure who he is, but he came to see Raazia here at home. Maleeka had told Raaz on the phone that he had been to see her. They met at

55

McDonalds in Manchester City Centre. He stated he would be calling on Nadine too. Maleeka thought there was something sinister going on." Akeel began to explain as the atmosphere got tenser.

"Akeel, what do you mean *sinister*?" Allia asked abruptly.

Allia pushed her body all the way off the sofa. It was unlike Allia to become all tensed up like that and anxious. It seemed fear had crept into her. She had children to worry about. She sat there silently deep in thought. No one said anything for a while. It was one of those 'edge of the seat' moments when watching an absorbing film or a drama where the *genre* you are watching gets you on tenterhooks not knowing what was next.

"I'll go make us all a hot drink. Some nice sweet coffee will do nicely, I think; what do you say everyone?"

"Oh yes!" A resounding yes from everyone including Allia.

"I will come help you, *Baji*," Sameena said.

"Akeel go on," Allia asked.

"Ah well, yes, *she* thought so anyway. I think Maleeka is a bit odd, you know. Nice lady. But what if she is right about her gut feeling? It's all to do with Calvin or that there was some international espionage going on or a mafia involvement that Calvin may be mixed up in, you know, something criminal, is what she said to Raaz."

"Oh Akeel, I see what you are getting at," Allia said.

"Let's just wait for that coffee. I could do with a drink, you know," Akeel said.

Allia got up and went into the kitchen leaving Akeel, Sajjid and Faraz to chat.

"So Raaz, is Papaji involved with Nawaz, you think, in Sal's killing?" Allia asked.

"Sameena, would you get the cups from the cupboard please? And Allia get the trays for me, will you. I made some chocolate cake this morning; how about a slice for everyone aye? Allia, could you do the cake please, it is in the fridge. There is single cream in the fridge too; if you could plate it for me, sweetie? We can take some up for the kids; they will love it," Raazia said changing the subject, hoping Allia would forget the question she asked.

"Oh wow, chocolate cake with cream and coffee, lovely. Let's all tuck in," Akeel said as they helped themselves to the cake and coffee.

Raazia's diversionary tactic was just the ticket to get the tense atmosphere removed from the room as well as her attempt to get Allia to forget her question she asked in the kitchen.

"Look, we did not want to say all this as we knew it would alarm everyone. It is quite worrying as we all have kids. But I am glad we have talked about it because now you know. I suggest we all take precautions for the time being. Keep an eye on the kids as far as you can. Drop them off. Pick them up from school and any activities, just to be on the safe side," Akeel advised.

"Akeel you said Mafia did you?" Sameena asked.

"Look, I was only telling you what Maleeka said to Raaz. I think, personally, Maleeka probably lives a drab life, poor lady, and my feeling is she was letting her imagination run wild. But we better be careful."

"We want to know more about this guy from Uganda," Allia said.

"Well, all we know, he came here one night; it was late. He introduced himself as David but did not mention his second name. He was a big African guy. He said he was a friend of Saleena and Calvin. He would help, he said, get Saleena and Calvin's killers. How he would do that, he did not explain," Akeel said.

"What did he want from Raazia?" Sameena asked.

"Just a statement, apparently, which he recorded on his little pocket recorder; seemed strange but that was it."

"So what did you say, Raazia?" Sameena asked.

"I talked about us as a family, about Saleena, how she was trapped in domestic violence and an awful marriage, you know, just background stuff that the police would ask. The police came to see me, and then out of the blue, this *kala* chap. What I do know, and I am so happy to say, is the police have reopened the case. I want to see justice to be done. Saleena was our dear sister. Look how she met her death. I don't really know if Papaji had a hand in it or not, but I am going to see this through now. I promise if Papaji had her killed because of his stupid reputation business, I am going to see him go to prison for a long time. He will pay for this. I dare say he will probably die in prison," Raazia stated feeling melancholy.

"And Fauzia, what about that bitch?" asked Allia.

"What about her?" Raazia replied.

"I wonder if that bitch was involved in Saleena's death too. I wouldn't put it past her. She never liked any of us. The bitch was always jealous of Saleena's beauty," Allia said.

"Allia, you have locked yourself in a Tardis of hate and thrown away the key. You need to let go at some point. Just move on, my dear. You can't change history. Live your childhood through our beautiful children," Sajjid said pleadingly.

Allia sniffed, looking away resisting the temptation to respond. The advice tendered seemed quite fair. Sajjid had always advocated some sort of reconciliation with Papaji, at least, if not Fauzia. It was not the first time he had said that to her. Allia remained resolute on the issue. This new situation with Papaji and Saleena was, for Allia, the last straw. Any notion of reconciliation was non-existent anymore.

Chapter 7

It was 10:00 a.m. DCI McLean and DI Slater following a call to Leeds Magistrates' Court rushed off to court to make an application for a three-day lay down as the 36-hour time limit to detain Papaji and Nawaz approached fast.

"Sir, have you rehearsed the application?" asked Kiki.

"Yes, I have, Kiki. I don't want to take any chances here as we will only get one bite at the cherry. Release would be catastrophic as for sure the old guy will exercise undue pressure on our key witness. I fear she will back off. If that happens, our case will be out of the window," Sherlock replied.

"Okay, Chief, good," Kiki said apprehensively.

"Don't worry, we will be okay. I feel the stars are shining upon us today," Sherlock said optimistically reassuring his nervous colleague.

Leeds Magistrates' Court was busy that morning with lawyers, some smartly dressed in suits, carrying leather brief cases, others simply carrying folders of papers wandering around looking for their clients. Ushers seemed busy registering attendees on their lists attached to their clipboards, whereas security staff were mingling around the court area ensuring the safety of those attending court.

Magistrate Hathern sat in his rather small chamber, looking comfortable in his cosy brown leather captain's chair behind his oversized oak antique desk which had a green leather top, looking officious. Sherlock looked around, habit of being a policeman, observing. He looked at the shelf behind the magistrate spotting a black hardback book with 'Blackstone's' written on the spine stacked against three red bound books which had 'Archbold' written on the spine. He had seen lawyers and crown prosecutors use those books before. The books created the ambiance of a legal institution. DCI McLean had been familiar with this particular magistrate from past search warrant applications he had made before him. He knew he was not going to be a pushover lawyer. The DCI collected his thoughts before making his application for a further seventy-two hours extension. The reasons took some fifteen minutes to convey. Magistrate Hathern did not interrupt his flow but made copious notes.

"Detective, I can see this is a difficult case for you. I am for that reason sympathetic, but I cannot allow officers to detain citizens if it is a fishing exercise. You have interviewed them. They have either denied any involvement or said nothing so far to incriminate themselves. So what will the further time achieve?" Magistrate Hathern asked inquisitively.

"There are three very good reasons, Sir. One is the Principal Crown witness is protected from interference from the father who lives in the same town as the witness. She is, in fact, his daughter. Secondly, we are still conducting further intelligence enquiries, and thirdly, we do need time, Sir, as keeping them in police custody may be beneficial to see if one of them will crack as it were and give a statement," DCI McLean replied.

"Your first two reasons seem compelling. I am unsure about the third reason which is not a good reason, detective. On balance, I have heard what you have had to say, and I shall grant you the three days you seek. After that, if there is no progress, you must release them, understood?"

"Yes Sir, perfectly, thank you."

"Thank you, detectives, good day."

"Thank you, Sir."

Kiki let out a huge sigh of relief as they stepped outside into the corridor. Sherlock smiled at his colleague feeling elated. Later, she expressed relief as the detectives travelled back to the Station in Sherlock's car. Sherlock in his usual casual manner stated, "Sometimes you have to hold on to faith, for it pays off in the end." They both smiled.

Abdel finally picked up the messages left on his mobile phone learning of Papaji's arrest. He rang Raazia from the hotel straightaway.

"Raazia, what is going on? Why has Papaji been taken into police custody? I am really worried about him."

"Abdel, the police have reopened the murder case. It's a long story. I will explain when I see you. There is some new evidence which points to his involvement in Saleena's murder. Where are you, Abdel, as the reception on the phone is very bad?" asked Raazia.

"I am in Dubai; business trip, Raazia. Look, I will fly back home as soon as I can," he replied.

Abdel could not think straight afterwards. *How could* Papaji *be under arrest,* he thought to himself. He could not understand how it could be so. For him, no matter what, he still loved his father. *Nawaz,* he thought, *was a likely culprit, but no way would* Papaji *do anything like that.* He felt the urgent need to get back home. The purchase for the fillies was important too as he had nearly sealed a deal on them with Sheikh Hallawaji.

The night seemed long for Abdel. He tossed and turned trying to sleep. The harder he tried, the more difficult it was to sleep. It was no good. Papaji in police custody played on his mind constantly. He thought about nice moments in his life in early years as he was growing up in Leicester. It was still no good; he couldn't sleep. Then he began to think about how nasty Papaji was to him. What had he done that was so wrong or bad that he had thrown him out like he was a piece of trash? Maybe his father being incarcerated might be the jolt needed to wake him up from his stupid stubbornness. Abdel was a son in the Rehman household, and as such, he had rights too, he thought. It was not for Papaji to answer for his sins, it was for him ultimately to do that. The situation was unfair being treated by his father as an outcaste.

Abdel turned on the light, walked across to the window to look outside. The darkness of the sky was peppered by hundreds of twinkling stars, shining brightly perhaps millions of miles away. The moon shone brightly amid the darkness of the night. He looked down surveying the city from his thirty-third-floor penthouse suite. Street lights lit the roads on which he could see sparse traffic. Cars looked small, yellow taxis dotted about seemed to be keeping some roads busy. Who would be travelling at 3:00 a.m. in the morning, he did not know. Maybe it was workers who started their shifts early. It was a city that never sleeps. Abdel drew the curtains back then at a slow pace slowly walked to the fridge in his room, took a bottle of orange juice out, unscrewed the top and gulped down its contents in one swoop. He could not believe how thirsty he was. Returning back to bed, he switched the bedside lamp off and tried to sleep. He couldn't. All he could hear apart from the faint sounds of motor car engines outside was his bedside clock ticking away. Abdel's mind was in turmoil thinking about his Pa treating him badly. He must have barely slept two hours that night.

Pleased to see daybreak, Abdel rolled out of bed. No sooner had he opened the curtains, the sunlight flooded into his luxury suite in abundance. He slowly made his way to the bathroom. He stood there for a few moments in front of the large rectangular bathroom mirror staring at himself feeling weary not just from the long sleepless night but the unfair treatment meted out by his father. As he looked at himself, he could see huge bags under his eyes. He ran the cold tap, joined his palms together collecting water in it then splashed heaps of cold water on to his face. The cold water felt good. Before stepping into the shower, he called room service and ordered his breakfast, tea and scrambled eggs on toast.

As he sat eating his breakfast, his agent rang on his Blackberry to give Abdel the good news he had waited for. He advised Sheikh Hallawaji had not only accepted his offer of 340,000 AED for the three fillies but the medical checks had been done, and clearance certificates would be issued in a day or so ready for the fillies' transportation to England. Very pleased at hearing the good news, Abdel hurried in eating his breakfast, then as soon as he was done, he could not wait to tell Jacob the good news. He knew he would be ecstatic. Abdel was buzzing with excitement. As the adrenaline began pumping, he forgot the feeling of listlessness he felt earlier. He walked along the long corridor with a huge smile on his face, whistling away. He took the elevator to the next floor up. Jacob was in room 3406 one floor above. Abdel knocked on the door rapidly. Jacob didn't hear the continuous knocking on his door as he was in the shower. As he turned the water tap off, he heard the knocking sound. He put a towel round him and still dripping, rushed to the door to answer it. Abdel stepped into the room as Jacob opened the door.

"Jacob, we got the three fillies! Isn't that wonderful?"

"Yes, wow boss, that is really good news."

Abdel was so excited he was a little tempted to get hold of Jacob and hug him. He stopped just in time. Jacob was his employee; besides he only had a towel wrapped round him. Things might get awkward in the excitement of the moment.

"I really could not wait to share the good news with you, Jacob. I was sure you would be pleased."

"What's the next step now, boss?"

"Well, we need get the fillies back home as soon as possible and safely. I have spoken to the agent. He is going to get the necessary paperwork ready as soon as he can. Could you stay behind and travel back with our extremely valuable cargo, please?"

"Yes sure, boss," Jacob responded, hardly in a position to say no!

"I have to get back to England today as something urgent has come up. I need to get back as soon as I can."

"Okay, boss. I hope all is well, boss."

"It's my dad. He has been arrested by the police and is in custody, so I need to get there as fast as I can."

"I am so sorry to hear that, boss. Hope it turns out all okay for him."

"Thanks, Jacob. Keep it to yourself, the information about my dad when you get back, please."

"Sure, boss, don't worry."

Chapter 8

Papaji had been in police custody for near enough sixty hours. The incarceration was taking its toll on him. He had refused to eat food apart from having water and had a couple of slices of bread in all that time. The food was not halal for him, he kept muttering to the officers who did not understand what he meant by it. His cell was 8' x 7' and it stank of urine. There was no way Papaji could eat in such conditions had the food even been halal. He felt the conditions were atrocious for him. Kiki had not expressed any concerns about Nawaz. She did keep an eye on Papaji as he seemed unusually lethargic at the last interview where he had refused to say anything except responding, "No comment," to questions put to him. He could barely get those words out of his mouth. In the last interview, he did request a cup of tea and some paracetamol tablets. Later, Kiki checked his custody record card kept at the central desk in the custody suite noticing comments recorded: 'Only ate bread slice and had bottle of water.'

Papaji sat in the small police cell, feeling hungry, decidedly looking pathetic and beginning to feel traumatised. He wondered what he was doing there in a stinky cell. He was baffled, not exactly sure why he had been brought there and being held under arrest. For him at the age of sixty-six, the experience of being locked up in a police cell seemed unreal for he was innocent. He was missing home, all the home comforts, home cooked food and his dear wife Fauzia who was all alone at home. Curiously, what would happen next was not a worry to him. He believed in Allah. The faith he had in the Almighty was not only strong but greater than anything on earth. Faizali placed his fate in the hands of Allah for he knew that his God would protect him ultimately. It was sad that he had not been permitted to have his *tasbee* with him as chanting *Allah hu akbar* as he twirled the beads between his fingers brought comfort to his troubled mind. Despite the conditions of his cell, worn, grimy with graffiti writing everywhere, words such as 'fuck' etched on the walls, 'Sam waz ere '88, 'fucking pigs they stink', a drawing of a phallus and the unbearable disgusting smell of urine were transitory for Allah the Almighty would see him free soon enough.

Nawaz surprisingly had put up very little resistance. He slept most of the hours he was incarcerated in his cell. When interviewed, he simply replied, "No comment," to every question put to him during the formal recorded interviews.

"Sir, I am worried about the old guy," Kiki said as her boss contemplated the next move in the case.

"Why?" he asked her.

"I checked his custody record. He has only had a few slices of bread and some water."

"What, hunger strike?"

"Sir yes, I don't think it's intentional in a sense, but I don't know. We need to look into it."

"Kiki, what's happened to plain English. You are talking in riddles?"

"It's a religious issue I believe. He claims the food served to him is not halal."

"What does that mean?" he asked exasperated.

"Sir, like Jewish people eat kosher meat, Muslims eat only halal food. The old guy is labouring under a belief he is being fed food that he would not be permitted to eat."

"Can't we get, err…what was that word you called it…"

"Halal, Sir"

"Yes, *that* food for him, surely we should be able here in Leeds?"

"Even if we did, Sir, might be too late now. The trouble is he may be old school. White officers serving him food will not make any difference. He has conditioned his mind into thinking that he will not be permitted to eat the food served, either that or he will think that it's *haram* food or worse still, he will be suspicious of them feeding him food that he is not permitted to consume."

"May I enquire how you know all this stuff, Kiki?"

"Education, Sir, I have a nice Muslim couple who live next door to me, very religious family."

"What the hell is, what did you say, *haram*?"

"Prohibited, Sir."

"Wow. What has he had to eat in the last few days then?"

"Bottled water and bread pieces or bread rolls with butter."

"My God, why wasn't I told about this?"

"I don't think the police officers are trained to pick up on such esoteric issues. They would not know."

"Can we not get—"

At that very moment in time of the discussion, a middle-aged officer popped his head round the door.

"Gov' you best get down to the custody suite. One of your detainees, the old guy I think, has collapsed. The custody Sarge has called the medic chap, but it looks like he may need an ambulance."

"Oh Jesus Christ! C'mon Kiki, let's move," Sherlock said as they dashed to the custody suite.

Papaji was examined by the police surgeon on duty. British doctor, 29 years of age, blonde hair, had a round face with round gold-frame glasses firmly sitting at the top of his nose. He had a stethoscope hanging round the back of his neck. His shirt at the back untucked into his trousers, he was kneeling on the floor by Papaji examining him.

"Doctor, what's the matter with him?" Sherlock asked.

"Appears he has fainted. Seems weak to me, dehydrated. The worrying factor is his hypertension. It is elevated. 175/105 mmHg. This is dangerously high. He needs to be moved to the ICU at the hospital, Detective McLean. I understand he has not had much food to eat in the last two/three days whilst in custody which has not helped his condition."

Papaji was just about coming round beginning to regain consciousness.

"Mr Rehman, you need to stay still for the moment. I am a police doctor. My name is Andrew Proctor. You had fainted."

Doctor Proctor continued to speak to his patient trying to keep him awake. Papaji made some faint inaudible sounds at first, waving his hands in the air. Then he was heard to murmur, "I should not be here. I have done nothing wrong. Where is my wife?"

"Mr Rehman you are at Leeds Police Station being held here until the investigation is completed," Dr Proctor said to him.

The doctor stood up and asked to speak to the two detectives outside the cell.

"In my opinion, it would be best for this prisoner to be moved to the local hospital ICU. His BP is dangerously high, not to mention low on sugar, dehydrated too. His vital signs indicate to me a possible risk of heart attack or even worse a stroke."

"Very well, Doctor, seems we have no choice here. He is still under arrest, so I need two police officers to go with him," McLean said.

Exhausted from his long haul, nearly eight-hour flight back home from Dubai, Abdel was anxious not to waste any more time. He caught a taxi back home from Heathrow. After a couple of hours sleep at home, he showered and then phoned *Amii* to get an update on Papaji's condition and to ask where he was. *Amii* had been advised that he had been moved from Leeds A&E unit to Manchester Royal as there were no beds in the ICU at Leeds. Abdel hurried making tracks headed for Manchester driving his black Porsche north on the M1 first then M52 to get to Manchester. *What am I going to say to him? What if he shuns me at the hospital, what shall I do?* he thought to himself. It seemed like a grim journey for him thinking about the strained relationship. It reminded him of the times when he had travelled back home to Leicester on occasions when the same thoughts had crossed his mind. He shook his head, opened the middle console, fished out a Corrs CD from his collection, inserted it and turned the volume up trying to cast the negative thoughts out from his mind, eventually reaching Manchester Hospital.

Abdel slowly approached the room as he got to the Intensive Care Unit. Papaji seemed sedated, sleeping, as he came into his view. The top part of his chest had round white pads stuck around his nipples area with wires connecting the pads to an ECG machine which was tracing his heartbeat. Next to his bed, slightly elevated on the side of his bed was a cardiac monitor making a beeping sound displaying Papaji's heart rate rhythm. A slender aluminium pole had two inverted plastic bags hooked on to it. A drip line ran from the bags to his left hand above his wrist which had a butterfly cannula feeding him intravenously. He slowly approached his father's bedside with tears in his eyes. He touched his father's right hand then gripped the palm of his hand. Papaji did not respond nor reciprocate. This was the first time in ten years he had made physical contact with his father. A nurse came in to check on him.

"How is he doing?" Abdel asked the nurse quietly.

"He is stable. We are monitoring him closely," the nurse replied. "There isn't much you can do for now as he has been sedated and will be out for a few hours I would say. So may be a good idea for you to go have coffee and get some rest as you look tired. I take it he is your father?"

Abdel nodded his head. It felt good some stranger stating the patient was his father. He had missed that. The connection had been absent for many years. He stepped outside in the corridor then made his way into the waiting area. He rang *Amii* to let her know he was there at the hospital. She was frantic at first but soon calmed down. She said on the phone she would ask if Akeel would drive her to Manchester but thought it might be intruding, difficult as the family were not on speaking terms.

"*Amii*, look, just get a taxi and I will pay for it. I can drive you back to Leicester afterwards."

"Thank you, *puttar*, I think that is best as Raazia puts the phone down every time I call her."

"Don't worry, *Amii*, just get here as quickly as you can. Papaji needs you. He will be happy to see you when he wakes up."

The hospital was a hive of activity. It was like worker bees in a beehive. Patients being attended everywhere, some by doctors, some by nurses, others being wheeled around by hospital orderly staff being transported from one place to another. This was, apart from his birth at Leicester Maternity unit, the first time he had stepped into a hospital. For him it was not even a memory as Begum gave birth to him there. *Amii* and his sisters brought him up. He always regarded his stepmother as *his* mother as he never had the chance to know his real mother, Begum. He had not thought about her before. It was being there, in the hospital environment, suddenly made him think about his mother. Hospitals are places for sick people that jog your memories about bygone days, family and loved ones.

Abdel began to reflect on his real mother, *what was she like?* It would have been nice to know her, his biological mother. He had seen, by way of a fleeting glance, one photograph of her which Allia had kept hidden in her room from *Amii*. She took it with her when she got married to Sajjid. So what his mother even looked like was a faded memory to him. He began to imagine, create a picture of Begum in his mind. *She must have been a good-looking lady, no doubt, in her prime days of life,* he thought. After all, she had given birth to Saleena, one hell of a good-looking girl, and of course Abdel who was some handsome guy too. Apart from that he thought about how different things would have been at home had she been around to care for her own children. It's not the same being brought up by someone who did not have those natural maternal instincts. Life would definitely have been different at home had Begum still been around.

Abdel walked across to the hospital waiting area, thoughts about Begum firmly fixed in his mind. He spotted a vending machine and decided to get a can of Coke, Caffeine would help him keep awake, he thought. He hung around there by the vending machine in the corridor mostly making essential calls from his Blackberry to principally while away the time waiting both for *Amii* to arrive and Papaji to wake up. He spoke to Philip first, had a long conversation with him talking about the current state of affairs telling him Papaji had been arrested ending up in hospital and was in ICU. Abdel spoke to Raazia after he spoke to Philip briefly. Raazia seemed unconcerned hearing Papaji was in hospital which puzzled him. He had asked her if she would be travelling to the hospital. All she said to him was it was not a good idea then hung up the phone.

Feeling hungry, Abdel decided to wander off to see if he could go somewhere to have a bite to eat. He followed some signs for a cafeteria. As he did, he dwelt on the brief conversation with his sister. Raazia always was the first one to take charge of a situation especially one like this where a member of the family had been taken to hospital. He remembered conversations at home about how she rushed off to deal with Begum's emergency, then how she got Akeel to drive her to get to the hospital in Manchester when Saleena was taken to hospital after being nearly battered to death by Nawaz. He thought it odd that Raazia was behaving differently, but tiredness from his long journey made him feel confused, emotional and he had the feeling of life being way too complicated to figure out. Abdel was someone yearning for a simpler life without having to think of all this baggage he seemed to be carrying around. But he knew deep down that was never going to happen. He stood in the line to be served. *Good,* he thought, *that you could choose your friends. Shame you couldn't do the same with family.*

In the cafeteria, a young man in his early twenties, English, was serving from behind the long glass counter which had displayed cold food items, sandwiches, drinks of all different makes and sizes. Further on, an aluminium hot food cabinet with aluminium deep trays, some covered and some not, had inviting hot meals. They had labels at the front of each one. It smelt good. Abdel asked for a portion of chips with a fried egg with baked beans and a strong cup of coffee. The young man obliged handing him his order on a tray.

Abdel looked for a free table as the cafeteria was busy. He spotted one in the far corner where he sat down. He put his tray on the table, grabbed a few chips popping them in his mouth, then took a sip of coffee. It was hot. A young English doctor came over holding a tray in his hand. On it was a prepacked triple ploughman's sandwich and a cup of coffee. He pulled the chair out, sat down letting out a big sigh. He looked to be in his mid-twenties, probably newly qualified, ruffled brown hair, round baby face and a stethoscope hung round his neck.

"I beg your pardon, please excuse my bad manners," he said immediately. "I should have asked if the place was free."

"Yes, please do sit. You look tired. Hard day?" Abdel asked.

"Hard is an understatement. This place is always busy whatever time of day or night. I am starving. I should have been on my break some two hours ago. The A&E is heaving with patients. I could do with a break. I am hoping to get a full hour's break, but you never know in this place. My bleeper could go at any time. I best crack on eating my sandwich," the doctor said as he ripped open the packaging taking a huge bite of the sandwich which made Abdel chuckle a little.

"Hey take it easy, Doc; you don't want to end up getting indigestion! You seem to be newly qualified?" Abdel asked.

"Doctor Oliver Tanner, I am a junior doctor here, my first-year internship; Oli to my friends, by the way. Pleased to meet you err…?" he said as he wiped his right hand on the napkin then extended his hand over the table to shake hands. He had a tight grip.

"Abdel Rehman," he said as he reciprocated shaking his hand with a similar tight grip.

Oli had a warm tight grip as they shook hands. Both continued shaking for a few seconds more before letting go.

"You staff here or visiting?" he asked.

"Visiting, I am afraid, have driven from down south to see my father; he is in ICU."

"Oh, I am sorry to hear that. What's wrong with him?"

"High blood pressure, collapsed I believe. He was sedated and sleeping is why I came down here, thought I would come down here, get a cup of strong coffee and something to eat."

"Touché."

They both chatted for the rest of his break. The doctor was most definitely relieved he was not disturbed for the whole hour for a change.

"Listen, I best head back. Thanks for the chat, I truly enjoyed the company. It was nice to sit, chat to someone easy to talk to for a change. Thank you for that."

"Likewise, it was my pleasure, Doc," Abdel replied.

He was about to walk away but returned back. He took a white napkin he was holding wrote his number on it, folded it and placed it on the table.

"Get in touch if you need any advice or help with your father or anything." He smiled before disappearing through the double doors of the hospital cafeteria.

Abdel put the napkin in his coat pocket then headed back to the ICU unit. He sat in the waiting area for *Amii* to arrive. Sitting down there a couple of metres away was a white middle-aged woman. She had a brown mac on and her brown hair tied back. She sat in a slumped position, her legs stretched out in front of the chair one on top of the other. She looked as though she had dozed off to sleep. He put his hand in his pocket, took the napkin out then opened. It had a mobile number written on it. *Wonder why he gave me his number,* Abdel thought to himself. Maybe it was out of genuine concern for his father, after all he was a doctor.

The English woman suddenly woke up. She made a funny odd sound as she did.

"Oh," she said.

"Are you all right, lady?" Abdel asked.

"Yes, thank you," she responded.

"Tiring isn't it, just waiting?"

"Yes, it is very. You have someone in ICU?" she asked.

"My dad; he was brought in earlier today."

"I am sorry to hear that. How is he doing, do you know?"

"I don't know; he was sleeping last time I looked in on him. I am just waiting for my mother to arrive. She is travelling from Leicester."

"Oh, that is a bit of a distance to come. You and your Paa live here?"

"No. we are from Leicester, long story to explain. How about you?"

"My mother, Doris, is in the ICU. She collapsed yesterday. She is in her eighties. I am not sure she will make it. Hope my sister Emily is able to get here on time to say goodbye. I am Carol, by the way."

"Abdel; pleased to meet you. Where is your sister?"

"Pleased to meet you too, Abdel. She is in Australia. It is a long way for her to come. I hope your Paa gets better soon."

"Thank you, likewise, your mother too, Carol."

"Oh, I think it might be time for her. She has been pining to be with Dad for years now. Albert, his name was. Dad passed away must be coming up twenty years. She lived on her own over Eccles Way.

"I don't know Manchester at all, but my sister Saleena used to live round in that area."

"She used to, did you say?" Carol asked.

"Yes," Abdel responded reserving information about Saleena, exercising a bit of discretion.

"Your sister wouldn't be a very pretty Indian lady, Saleena Khan would she? She used to visit my mother two/three days a week and used to keep her company. Mum used to love her company. Often, she would tell me excitedly on the phone that Saleena was coming round to keep her company for a bit. Mum would bake a Victoria sponge cake especially for her. Lovely, kind-hearted lady Mum used to say. Saleena was her dear friend, she would say with delight. Then one day, she stopped coming. Mum was really distraught as she did not know what happened to her. I think Mum said her husband – can't remember his name, she thought it was *Nader* or something – not a nice man, used to beat her up. I am from Leeds; I had heard on the news that she had been murdered with a friend of hers. I did not tell Mum the grim news about her dear friend as she would have been deeply upset. Sorry, I did not mean to. I have gone on a bit too long. But Saleena was your sister?"

Abdel stayed quiet, unsure what to say, how to respond as he had no time to process the information conveyed to him in that conversation he just had with a total stranger. It was someone who knew Saleena indirectly. What were the chances, Abdel thought, of meeting someone by chance like that in Manchester, at the hospital, who actually knew of his sister Saleena? It was *quaint* he thought, continuing to maintain silence.

"Oh dear, I am so sorry dear, did I say something to upset you? I am sorry if I have. I didn't mean to," Carol said with definitive regret in her tone.

"No, no, it is quite all right. Yes, she was my sister. She had that kind nature in her personality which everyone loved except her husband Nawaz."

"I truly am sorry about your sister. I hope your Paa recovers soon," Carol said changing the subject quickly.

Amii walked into the waiting area at that very moment. Surprisingly, she looked fresh, nice clothes on, *shalwar kameez* with a long dupatta hanging off her shoulder, her jet-black hair brushed back tied with a hair clip, not a single grey hair in sight on her head. She had heavy makeup on her face; her bright red lipstick stood out a mile. The scent of her strong sweet perfume pervaded the waiting area. Carol looked up as she made a sniffing sound to see who was wearing that perfume. Abdel stood up off his chair and rushed towards her to greet her. Glad to see her, he gave his *Amii* a big hug.

"Where is your Papaji, Abdel? How is he?" she asked seemingly concerned.

"He was sleeping last time I looked in on him," Abdel responded.

"Well, let's go see him," *Amii* said.

"I wish the best for your mother; hope all goes okay," Abdel said turning his head round looking at Carol.

"Thank you, dear. I take it that is your mother? Hello. I have the same perfume; Elizabeth Arden, isn't it?" Carol asked.

Amii simply nodded with a smile. She was not in the habit of speaking to perfect strangers, much less someone who she had met literally two seconds ago who knew exactly what perfume she was wearing. She thought it odd that a stranger would comment straightaway about her perfume.

Papaji was awake as the two got to his room, happy to see his wife, he lifted his hand slightly in the air, beckoning her to approach him. She responded by rushing over to his bedside knelt over as she held his hand. Papaji had tears in his eyes as he reciprocated squeezing his wife's hand tightly. Abdel stood quietly on the other side of his bed standing about a foot away.

"Look who has come to see you, *meri jaan*. He was the first one to get here but you were sleeping. See for yourself; none of the girls are here, Faizali," Fauzia said.

Papaji turned his head towards Abdel. For the first time in many years, Abdel could not see the same hatred on his face but a faint smile which pleased Abdel. He had longed to see that change in his face, to touch him, to feel the closeness to his father. Abdel came closer touching his *Abbaji*'s hand, squeezed it at first then lifted it slightly towards him. Abdel curved his body, and his black hair fell in front of his forehead, his face almost covering Papaji's hand then he kissed it. Papaji squeezed Abdel's hand. It felt good. Tears ran down his cheeks. *Amii* pulled a few tissues out of her handbag, handing one to Abdel, the other she wiped Papaji's tears from his eyes. She made a sniffing sound too joining in the emotional reunion but her eyes were completely dry! Papaji did not say anything to his son, but for Abdel, the warm response was enough for now.

"*Aray*, what happened at the police station, Faizali, why have you ended up in hospital like this? Did they mistreat you? The police everywhere are the same. Even in Pakistan they beat you *salley kaminey, buttemeez log hey naa*? They must have mistreated you in police custody is why you here, no? And they are still here! There's a policeman outside in the corridor. Why is he here, Faiz?" Fauzia asked.

"Nothing, nothing, nothing my dear, I could not eat their food, my cell smelt of *peyshaap* [urine] which made me feel sick; my blood pressure tablets were at home, so I fainted."

"But you have been brought into ICU, things must be serious *naa*? You are not dying are you?" Fauzia asked.

Abdel thought it a strange thing to say to her husband.

"Insha'Allah I will recover. Give me time. Now let me talk to my son for I have missed my *puttar*. How are you, son?"

"I am good, Papaji. It has been a long time."

"Yes, it has. Come here son give your Papaji a hug, *puttar*," he said as tears rolled down his cheeks. Why have you been away for so long from me? You did not even call me."

"I called a number of times, but *Amii* said you were not around. I thought you were angry with me about what happened. You stopped talking to me. I came home for my eighteenth birthday; do you remember?"

Abdel by now was in his father's embrace. It felt so good. The two continued to hold each other in a tight embrace not wanting to let go, both emotionally charged, tears cascading down their cheeks.

"You are younger than me, *puttar*. It is your duty to forgive your elders. I was stubborn thinking I could bring my children up the way I was. I failed. I failed miserably at that. I did not realise how different it would be for you children to have grown up here, a different country to where *I* was brought up. I should have listened to Malik when he told me to let go of the old traditions; I should have let go too," Papaji retorted almost crying loudly.

Hearing him sob, a nurse came in to the cubicle to check if all was well. "Gosh, the sobbing was a bit loud. It frightened me. I thought you had left us," she said in northern Mancunian accent. "Looks like a family reunion," she added. She smiled and left.

"I have many times, Papaji. I have forgiven you. How can I not do that to you, Papaji? I ask for your forgiveness now."

"I do, *puttar*. I do. It does not matter now anymore. You have made a life for yourself. Are you married yet?"

"No, Papaji, I am waiting for the right moment," he said.

"Shall we make a new start? I did not want to die without making up with you, *puttar*. I thought this was it for me when I ended up in hospital. A sudden wake-up call for me, this is, you know. You only realise life is short when you are at death's door. We forget we are mortals. To end up here in ICU reminded me when I went to see Begum for the final time. I remember she was as still as anything, just sleeping. Ending up here reminded me of your mother. I thought my time had come too, to meet your mother Begum."

Fauzia rolled her eyes looking away momentarily but stayed silent.

"I think that is a good idea, Papaji. Start again, I mean, a clean slate."

Papaji ran his hand through Abdel's hair, still holding him tight in his embrace.

Fauzia smiled seeing the reunion between father and son. Papaji expressed he felt better seeing his wife there with him too. Fauzia whilst elated at the development was not keen on staying at the hospital though she may not have had a choice in the matter. Papaji wanted her to stay at the hospital with her. She was his wife. It was her duty. Abdel knew the hardship she may endure staying at the hospital. He told her, if she wanted, he would book a hotel room for her nearby. She should let him know so he could arrange it.

Abdel felt ecstatic. He took the A34 Princess Street towards the city, then turned right on Portland Street. He pulled into the car park for Mercure Manchester Piccadilly hotel, parked up, then checked into the hotel. As soon as he was in the room, he dumped most of his things on the bed, took his shoes off and jumped on to the bed with his feet up on the bed. Feeling very excited, he started to dial his old friend Philip's number. The phone battery was running low; he took the phone charger out of his bag and plugged it in to charge his Blackberry. He was buzzing, excited, adrenaline flowing fast through his veins.

"Abdel hi, how are you? Good to hear from you. Where are you?"

"I am really good, Philip."

"You sound cheerful?"

"I have some good news to share, Philip. Papaji is in hospital here in Manchester. I went to see him, and he not only spoke with me but hugged me. We both cried! It was an emotional moment for both of us. Oh my God, I couldn't believe it. It was so surreal. I thought he was going to be his normal self and reject me. It surprised me, I have to say."

"That is wonderful news, Abdel. I am happy for you he finally gave way and did the right thing. It was well overdue if you ask me. I am truly happy for you. What is going on, Abdel? What was he arrested for?"

"He was arrested along with that twat Nawaz, allegations of conspiracy to murder apparently."

"Are you serious, Abdel?"

"Yes, I am."

"Really, wow, I did not expect your old man to be involved in something like that, Abdel."

"Philip, I don't know if he did or he did not. It is an allegation at this stage."

"I don't really know what to say, my friend. It's a shock to me. Have they been charged?"

"No, not yet."

"What will you do? You can't stand by him if has."

"I'd rather leave that problem to a later stage, Philip, if I am honest. I'll cross that bridge when I come to it, you know. In my eyes, he is innocent until proven guilty."

"I suppose you are right. What else is new? You seem to be grappling with problems all your life, hmm?"

"I travelled to Dubai and picked up three Arabian fillies. You should see them. They are absolutely beautiful."

"Are you thinking of breeding horses then?"

"Yes, that is the plan. Antoninus was getting aggressive. Jacob thought if I got his carnal desires sorted then he would run like a dream."

"Jacob? Who is he, Abdel?"

"Philip, he is my employee, and I was taking about my prized horse, Antoninus, not Jacob. You have a dirty mind."

"I bet Jacob is gorgeous."

"He is a bright young guy, very good at his job. He loves horses."

"Does he ride them well?"

"I am not even going to answer that!"

"I shall come by, Abdel, to yours and shall see for myself."

"I need to check on Dad, so speak soon ay?"

"Sure, speak soon. Take care."

"You too."

Jacob was at the Heathrow Airport cargo area waiting in the lounge. The horses had to be unloaded then transported to the quarantine area. They had to be checked and carefully inspected by Customs Officers. Paperwork was the next step before releasing the cargo into his custody. He was pacing up and down in the waiting area when his phone rang.

"Boss hi, the cargo is safely here at Heathrow. I am just waiting for the officials to complete the paperwork. They were a little agitated on the aircraft, but I managed to calm them down."

"Well done, Jacob. Any issues at customs?"

"No. I am keeping my fingers crossed nothing arises. All the paperwork in Dubai was A1"

"You are a star, Jacob. Make sure they get to the stables safely. Call me when you are there."

"Yes boss, I will. Goodbye."

Abdel woke up after two hours' deep sleep feeling hungry. It was 6:30 p.m. He got up, showered, got dressed in fresh clothes. Anxious to get back to the hospital, he hurried out of his room, stopping at a halal burger place on the way back to the hospital. He pulled up in the hospital car park polishing off his own cheeseburger and French fries first in the car, before heading back to the ICU. Papaji had been moved to a normal ward. Papaji was famished. He ate the burger and fries pretty fast. *Amii* took her meal to the waiting area to eat there. It was his first good halal meal in days. He thanked his son for the appetising meal. Papaji would be discharged tomorrow, *Amii* informed Abdel. As Papaji was in a normal ward, she could not stay the night with him and needed a place to stay the night. She travelled back with Abdel to the Mercure Hotel where he checked her into a room. He sat with *Amii* chatting about the reunion with Papaji until about 11 p.m.

Back in his hotel room, Abdel got a can of Coke from the drinks bar from the fridge. He looked out from his room on the ninth floor. The night in the city seemed vibrantly lively from what he could see, reminded him of London, a city that never sleeps. His instinct was to take a walk around and see if he could get something to eat. Excitement was making him feel hungry. As he put his coat on, a napkin fell out on to the carpet. Abdel picked it up. The young doctor's number was written on it. Abdel dialled the number.

"Hi, this is Abdel from the hospital cafeteria, remember me?"

"Of course. How is your father?"

"He was moved from ICU to a normal ward, fingers crossed, due to be discharged tomorrow."

"Ah, that is excellent."

"I was wondering, err…are you still on duty?"

"Nope. It's my night off and day off tomorrow too. What have you in mind?"

"Something to eat; I am hungry and fancied some good company."

"Where are you?"

"Mercure Hotel."

"Okay, meet me in fifteen minutes at the top of Canal Street. It's not far from where you are."

"Okay I will find it."

Abdel walked to Portland Street, turned right onto Minshull Street, walked down the street three hundred yards pass Bloom Street; next one on the right was Canal Street. The street was busy, vibrant, with a mix of people mostly young guys, some standing around chatting, others busy walking around enjoying the liveliness of the evening. The street seemed to have some kind of marvel attraction to it. The place was really busy, much to Abdel's surprise. It had an array of shops, bars, restaurants and clubs. Abdel stopped by a wall, nervous as hell. The place was somewhat too overt for him, but he was in a good cheerful mood. Oli seemed like a good friend to have for company in a strange city, to sit down with, talk and enjoy some food. To hide his nervousness, he stood there pretending to text on his mobile phone. As passers walked by, some glanced at him.

"Hi stranger, you look nervous!" a voice said from his left side. Abdel turned around quickly to look to see who it was as the voice startled him.

"You all right, Abdel? Sorry, I did not mean to make you jump. So you found the place okay then?"

"Yes, it was easy. Your directions were perfect. I was not expecting you from that side."

"I am glad your dad is fine, by the way."

"Thanks."

"I am starving; the last time I ate was when I sat down with you in the hospital café."

"Really, Oli, you are serious, aren't you? That was ages ago. You must be very hungry."

"You could say that," Oli said as he smiled making contact with Abdel's arm. Oli then extended his arm, placing his hand on Abdel's shoulder. "Let's walk this way." He pointed to the direction he wanted them to walk. "I finished my shift at seven, went to my place and just crashed out. I was so exhausted, I could not be bothered to eat. There is a nice place here, Canal 1. Let's go there and have something to eat."

After a long journey from Dubai, finally the Arabian fillies were settled into the stables, much to Jacob's relief. The vet advised he would call in the morning to inspect them. Jacob called Abdel to let him know the fillies were safely home. Abdel's excitement continued as he received more good news from Jacob about the fillies. He could not stop talking about them to his newly found friend as they settled down to eat.

Chapter 9

Back at Leeds station, Sherlock and Kiki were in a terrible quandary whether to charge Nawaz and Faizali or to place them on police bail. They were exasperated, having worked hard getting to where they were so close to charging the two suspects. It would not be right to charge the old guy at this time, Sherlock thought. It may prove to be counterproductive. They both agreed, after discussing the issue, to delay charging them. "Does not hurt to be prudent," Sherlock put it. Truth was they had little choice. CPS would not have agreed to charging a sick man. Kiki telephoned Raazia to let her know the bad news that the two were being released on police bail. Kiki assured Raazia there was nothing for her to worry about as they would be keeping a close eye on them. Should anyone approach her, she should telephone Kiki at once which rather than reassure Raazia unnerved her.

Amii rarely left the house so the ride from Manchester to Leicester in Abdel's Porsche was nice for her. Surprisingly, she said very little through the journey, rather sat in the back seat of the Porsche seemingly enjoying the ride watching cars and the English countryside that she could see from the side of the motorway. Papaji was looking forward to getting home after his harrowing experience being locked up at the police station. He talked in some graphic detail about the cell he was locked up in: the smell of urine that constantly pervaded the room, the horrible smell from the toilet bowl, dirty walls with disgusting writing on it, never mind the food which he did not even touch owing to it being *haram*. Papaji talked in disparaging terms about the criminal justice system in the country.

Once he had finished speaking on that subject, he turned his anger to Raazia. He slated Raazia completely about her disrespect for him. "How dare she?" he exclaimed in his conversation angrily. "She was solely responsible for my arrest." It was as though he couldn't wait to get home, go see her, confront her to give her a piece of his mind about what she had done to him.

Abdel advised Papaji to be cautious. He was on police bail so he should not do anything to jeopardise his liberty.

"*Betta*, thanks for bringing me and your *Amii* back home. It is really good to be home. I hope you will stay for dinner, but I need to go sleep as I am exhausted."

"Papaji, I need to attend to some urgent business at home. I really need to get back. I promise I will come over and visit at the weekend."

He embraced his father first then *Amii* before leaving. The urgent business was the fillies. He dared not tell his father about his passion for horses as he

75

knew it would be met with clear disapproval. Worse still, it would put his renewed delicate relationship with his father in jeopardy.

Abdel drove mostly in the fast lane southbound on the M1 anxious to get home as quickly as he could. Traffic was light. His speedometer often touched nearly ninety-five miles an hour, though he was unaware he was doing that sort of speed. He could not contain his excitement. The adrenaline was pumping in his veins. The feeling of happiness was almost a feeling of being intoxicated. Abdel was on cloud nine. He was not keeping an eye on his speed as the state of euphoria had completely taken over him. His Papaji embracing him bringing to an end the long period of estrangement coupled with the happiness of the horses arriving safely was such a good feeling, it was indescribable. The thrill of seeing the Arabian fillies was completely overwhelming. As he got closer to home, his feeling of excitement intensified many folds.

It was early evening after the two-hour drive home to Oxshott. He parked the car, changed his clothes and rushed over to the stables. Jacob had settled the horses in the stables for the night. Abdel slowly walked into the stables at a slow pace not wanting to spook the new ones. Antoninus immediately sensed Abdel's presence. He neighed as he approached the gate of his pen, his head rose up then down acknowledging his master's presence. He continued moving around in his pen undulating his head as Abdel approached him. The synergy between the two was inexplicable.

"Hello, Antoninus, you beautiful creature. I think you know, don't you?" Abdel patted him.

Antoninus snorted gently once. Jacob stood at the entrance of the stables quietly watching his master bonding with his prized horse. Abdel beckoned Jacob towards him. Forgetting momentarily that Jacob was his employee, Abdel hugged him. It was to thank him for the enormous task of ferrying the fillies home safely. Jacob was taken by surprise but did not flinch. He hugged his boss back.

"Thank you so much for bringing the horses back safely from Dubai, Jacob. You don't know how terribly nervous I was about them being transported safely to Oxshott. I really appreciate what you have done. Thank you. You did an excellent job. How was the flight back home for you with the fillies?"

"I missed my business class travel home, boss. The flight was okayish."

"Are the horses okay?" Abdel asked as he moved away to a distance of about a metre from Jacob.

"They are fine. Seem to have settled in well, boss, after that very long journey. It was a tiring journey for them as they, like me, had not travelled on a plane before. It must have been an odd feeling for them. I am sure they could sense it. The chestnut one was the most stressed. I sat with her for part of the journey, just calming her down."

"Has the vet been to check them."

"All done, boss, and he was happy with them. No issues flagged up."

"That is good news. I wonder which one of the three Antoninus is going to fall for?"

"Well, boss, he seems to have a choice from the three, but you never know; he may well have a harem here, boss."

The two laughed as they walked to the stalls where they were. Jacob had put them in separate stalls but next to each other. They were absolutely beautiful, one chestnut, the other black and the third one a roan coat. Jacob approached them first patting each one. The chestnut neighed then snorted. Antoninus become agitated; he neighed too.

"C'mon boss, might be a good idea to leave them for the night. Let them get used to the place first. Tomorrow they can have a good run in the open area. It will be strange for them at first, but they will settle down in time. I want to see what Antoninus is going to do."

"Do you think he will be ready for the Cheltenham Gold Cup?"

"Oh, the big one. He is physically fit and has the power to run fast. He is ready. I will get Ben to ride him tomorrow, and we can see what speed he is running at."

"What do you think about getting him introduced to the chestnut filly before Ben races him?"

"I don't know, boss, part of me thinks he knows the fillies are here. I think to hold back the introduction, make him wait."

"Seriously?"

"Yes, seriously, boss."

"Okay. I have a good friend of mine coming over tomorrow to watch him run, and I want to show off the fillies, so make sure they are groomed."

"Sure, boss."

Chapter 10

Two weeks later, Papaji had almost recovered. He was feeling much better. He felt good about making up with Abdel. Erasing out history was something not quite an easy thing for him being a man of the old school, though relations were cordial. They were both warm towards each other when they spoke on the telephone. Sadly, Papaji's enjoyment of life was short-lived. A brown envelope with Leeds Metropolitan Police stamped in red on the front dropped through the post box next morning could not have come at a worse time as it dampened his good mood. Papaji did not open it straightway. He left it on the mantle with the intention of opening it after he returned home from his *Zohr* prayers at the mosque that afternoon. As he prostrated in the *sajdah* during his prayers before Allah, he asked Him that he hoped the letter carried good news for him.

Back home from afternoon prayer, he sat down in his old worn-out chair holding his *tasbee* in his right hand, as was his habit, head resting back, quietly chanting, "*Allah hu akbar.* [God is great.]" He repeated the words as he twirled each bead between his fingers. He mustered up the courage an hour later and slowly ripped the top of the envelope with a sharp knife, reciting as he did, "*Bismillah hir rahaman ir Rahim* [in the name of Allah, the most beneficent, the most merciful]," believing that opening it in the name of God would deliver good news as it was done in His name.

The letter stated his attendance at Leeds Police Station was required on 9 April 1999 at 2:00 p.m. Papaji was aghast at the bad news; he dropped the letter on the floor. He began hyperventilating as his breathing became erratic clutching his chest. At that moment, Fauzia walked into the room. She noticed the letter was lying on the floor. Her husband seemed to be distressed. Quickly, she hurried to the mantle, picked up a medicine bottle, unscrewed its top, and inverted the bottle taking out in her palm a nitroglycerin tablet which she handed Papaji to put it under his tongue. The medicine worked in seconds.

"Faizali dear, what does the letter say? Is it not good news?" she asked.

"I don't know if it is good news or bad. The letter says I have to report to Leeds Police Station on 9 April."

"What do you think they will do? Surely, they can't charge you. You are not well. Look at your condition," Fauzia said displaying some concern with her body language as she put her hand on her mouth.

Papaji did not respond. He closed his eyes and sat there still as a statue. Fauzia sat down on the sofa waiting for him to respond, but he looked as though he had dozed off to sleep.

Fauzia telephoned Abdel to let him know the grim news Papaji had received in the day. The shock had set off his angina. Abdel said he would call back later when Papaji was awake. Abdel had set aside the day to sort out a pile of paperwork, but hearing the news, his concentration waned away. He sat in his study for a while simply staring at the pile of paperwork in front of him. He paced up and down in the room for a while, then took a walk in the garden. Troubled by the news, Abdel picked up the telephone, dialled the home number.

"Hello, Papaji, it's only me. How are you? *Amii* called me earlier but you were sleeping."

"Hello, son, I am not good, you know. How are you, son?"

"I am good, Papaji. It's nice to speak with you."

"*Amii* tell you about the letter?" Papaji asked.

"She did, Papaji. What does the letter say exactly?"

"The letter states I have to attend at Leeds Police Station on 9 April 1999 at 2:00 p.m."

"I am sure it will be all right. The Police know you are not in the best of health, and I don't see what they would gain if they did take it further. They don't have any evidence anyway, so I wouldn't worry."

"I hope you are right, *puttar*. It is easier said than done though."

"You will see, Papaji, it will be fine. I will take you in the car, so don't worry about getting there. I will get a good lawyer for you, so don't worry."

"Okay, son, I am happy you are with me."

"Sure, Papaji, please don't worry. I am sure we can sort this out."

Abdel felt less concerned after the conversation. He wondered if it would do any good if he spoke to Raazia about this mess with the police. Unsure if he should, Abdel turned to his friend Philip for advice. Philip counselled his friend not to do anything that the police might view as interfering with a prosecution witness which Raazia clearly was. If he did, that would potentially put Abdel in peril were Raazia to report the contact to the police. He urged him not to do it.

Abdel had not quite thought it through himself about the possible consequences. It was good to have a confidant to turn to in times of difficulty. Raazia was his sister. Surely, she would not dob him to the police. She had reported Papaji and so it would be wise to sleep on it, he thought, make a decision later on.

It was about 9 in the evening. He was about to call it a night, mentally exhausted from all the thinking when the front doorbell chimed. It was Jacob. He called in to report one of the fillies was unwell.

"What is wrong with the filly, Jacob?"

"I am not exactly sure, boss. She has been lying down for the last four hours. I have been keeping an eye on her, and from this morning, she has lost her appetite too as well she seems to have a temperature. I tried to get her up. She refuses to. I have called the vet; he is on his way. I also made some cold flannels and put them on her body to try cool her down."

"Good, let me get changed first. Come inside, Jacob; wait here for me."

Abdel rushed upstairs, changed into appropriate clothing quickly and came down in a real hurry so he and Jacob could get to the stables as fast as possible.

"What about the other two fillies, Jacob, how are they?" Abdel asked as they walked at a fast pace.

"The other two are fine, boss. I have kept my eye on them all day."

"I'm lucky to have you, Jacob. I hope it's nothing too serious or complicated with the filly. They cost me a lot of money."

"It will be fine, boss, don't worry. It might be just the change of weather."

"I hope you are right."

It was timely, as they got to the stables, Harry, the vet, arrived at the same time. He was a locum veterinary surgeon not the usual vet. James was the usual vet who was on vacation. Harry was middle aged, wore round gold-rimmed spectacles and had a slight podgy belly. Abdel greeted him and showed him over to the stables.

"So Jacob, what symptoms is the horse displaying?" he asked.

"Loss of appetite, temperature, lethargic; I tried to get her up but she refused to."

"Hmm…let's go look at her. Where is the filly from?"

"Dubai. They arrived over here about two to three weeks ago," Jacob responded.

"May I ask how many did you bring over?"

"Three."

"Are the other two okay?"

"Yes, they are fine. James, the regular vet, examined them and gave them the all-clear."

"What about the rest of the pack?"

"They all seem fine. It is just the one filly."

Harry spent some time examining the horse. Abdel was pleased as he seemed thorough with his examination. Harry also examined the other two fillies whilst Abdel and Jacob waited for the vet's prognosis on the sick filly.

"They are fine horses, Sir. Arabian fillies are strong and powerful. This filly has a common cold. It's down to the change of weather I suspect. They have come from a hot climate, so it isn't surprising at all to me. She is a beautiful strong young filly. She will recover, but I am afraid being female she is going to need some TLC. Jacob, you need to increase the level of her fluid intake immediately with lots of cold flannels over her. That should do it. If you think the temperature is not going down, call me on my mobile. In fact, I wouldn't be surprised if the other two went down with it. Keep them apart if you can. Other than that, there is not much can be done."

"Thank you so much. I appreciate you coming out straightaway. Daniel, the security guy, will see you out," Abdel said.

"No problem at all. In fact, I wouldn't mind betting a bob or two on that one winning a race and even having a foal this time next year! Goodbye for now; remember, if you need me, just call," Harry said as he walked towards his white Range Rover. He gave Daniel a nod to show him out.

"What a relief, Jacob. I was kinda worried about them thinking there might be something serious. Thank God it is only a common cold," Abdel said relieved.

"Let's try and get some fluids down her like the vet said boss. I'll take care of the water buckets and the flannels. Boss, do you have cartons of apple juice in the house?"

"Yes, I think so. I will go get them."

"Sure thing, boss. Have you thought about names for the fillies yet?"

"No, no yet, I need your help with appropriate names."

"I am honoured, boss; sure, I'll be happy to choose names with you."

Jacob fetched buckets of cold water with flannels immersed in them over to the pen. He took out one wet flannel at a time, squeezed the water out and placed it on the filly, changing them every ten minutes. Abdel went to fetch cartons of apple juice from the house. Gradually, as the temperature came down, she responded by taking in the apple juice, lapping it up from Abdel's palm at first, then he poured it into a plastic funnel, letting the horse take in a little at a time as he moved his finger away from the tip of the funnel letting the juice trickle out into her mouth. She liked the juice as she did the tender loving care from her new master.

Both Jacob and Abdel laughed as the filly began feeling better. They had not worked together like that before nursing a sick animal. Soon she began making snorting noises.

"Good girl," Jacob said as he patted the horse gently several times.

Abdel patted his valuable asset too.

"I will get some blankets from the rooms and bed down here for the night, boss, stay with the horses."

"Okay, Jacob, thank you. Can I get you a cup of tea?"

"No, no, boss, let me get it. How do you like your tea?"

"Thank you, Jacob, white, milky with two sugars."

Abdel continued drip feeding the filly apple juice as she seemed thirsty and carried on taking in the juice without stopping. Jacob returned a few minutes later holding two mugs of tea in his hand, and then put the mugs down on a bale of hay.

"How is she doing?" he asked.

"Seems to love the apple juice, not stopping drinking it so I am going to continue until she has had enough. So Jacob, how about if we think about names for them?"

"I was thinking Lady Sharjah, Electra and Misty Rose."

"Good names, Jacob, I like all three. Lady Sharjah seems appropriate for this one."

"She is Antoninus' favourite, did you know?" Jacob said.

"She is?" Abdel responded.

"Yes, he seems to have taken a shine to her. She was playing hard to get in the fields earlier today, typical female. I was watching them. I guess she was not feeling well so maybe she did not respond to him. Things might be different when she is up to it, I hope. Boss, the tea is getting cold."

They both bent down and stretched over to pick up the mugs of tea simultaneously. They sat down on the bale of hay and began chatting about Jacob's future aspirations as well as his family. Jacob wanted one day to own a farm and have horses that he could breed. Abdel learnt Jacob had three siblings, two brothers and a sister, all younger than him. His mum had passed away a few years back from breast cancer. His dad was a farmer and lived on the family farm with his new partner Laura. Jacob had a falling out with his father, not about Laura replacing his mother so soon after her death, nor about his dad's relationship with her but an inheritance issue. Abdel felt terribly sad hearing Jacob's story, an all too familiar tale as he knew how he must have felt. It was a story close to his heart he knew so well.

"You need to make up with your father, Jacob, no matter what it takes."

"I don't know if I can, boss, I grew up on the farm. My mum worked hard for years on it, working her fingers to the bone on that farm. I found out dad had made a will leaving half the farm to Laura, the other half to his four children. He probably has cut me out now altogether, I dare say, as I have fallen out with him."

"Is there anything I can do to help?"

"You are very kind to me, boss, but I don't think so. Dad is typical old style, very headstrong. He doesn't like strangers. Will probably resent you getting involved, so thank you for that nice thought, but I don't think it will do any good. I look up to you, you know, boss. You are like my mentor, my dad!"

"Hey, cut it out boy, I am only five years older than you," Abdel said ruffling Jacob's hair then putting his hand on his shoulder. Jacob moved a little closer to his boss. Abdel, feeling sorry for him, wanted to be close to Jacob but he resisted the moment. Abdel stood up off the bale and walked over to the pen to check on Lady Sharjah.

"You keep in touch with your brothers and sister?"

"I see them once a week after school or when Dad is at the farmer's market once a week."

"Good, lad, bring them to the estate sometime, they will love the horses; they can help you scrub them!"

"Oh, thanks, boss, I am sure they will love that."

"She seems comfortable, Lady Sharjah. I am going to go catch some sleep. Good night, Jacob. Thanks for being here; you are a valued employee to me."

"Sure, no problem, boss. I love being here. This is home for me," Jacob said wiping a tear off his face quickly. Jacob decidedly felt a little embarrassed displaying emotion like that at his age.

"Good, Jacob, home is important to have. I am glad you think of this place as home."

Abdel winked with one eye then nodded before he walked away, soon disappearing out of Jacob's sight as Abdel closed the stable door. Jacob felt good after that. It gave him a sense of belonging.

The last two weeks had been painfully unbearable for Raazia. She had been on edge most of the time worrying about contact from Papaji. Concentration for her both at work and home was difficult. In fact, it was at its lowest ebb. Each day that went by, her nerves got worse. She was sure he would call her. She knew him too well. It was only a matter of time before he did, she kept thinking to herself. Akeel had issued strict instructions to the family not to pick up if he or *Amii* called. The number would come up on the screen as he had caller- display facility. Papaji did not to call his daughter fearing arrest. The putrid smell of the cell in which he was confined for many hours was still fresh in his nostrils. He did not want to return back there.

"He has not called, Raazia; I am surprised. I've been checking the phone for messages every day. Nothing on the previous numbers either," Akeel said.

"I am surprised, Akeel, I have to say, as it is very unlike Papaji. I don't know what must have happened at the police station. It must have been something horrid for him to be scared. DI Slater had called to let me know he had been taken to hospital in Manchester, and then a few days later, they released him. Apparently, Abdel brought him back from hospital. Abdel has not said anything to me either, not that I have spoken to him much in the last couple of weeks."

"I saw *Amii* walk past the shop a couple of times, but she did not come in. Isn't that weird?" Akeel said.

"Well, that is good. They must have been warned by the police to keep away."

"Have you heard anything more from Maleeka?"

"No, I have not. This is all making me feel very uneasy Akeel."

"Raaz, just hold tight, will soon know what will happen. Something has to happen."

Chapter 11

The journey to Leeds was strange, a quiet one, conversation sparse. Papaji hardly said anything on the journey to Manchester. His lifelong companion, his *tasbee* was with him; he continued twirling the blue beads between his fingers. Abdel tried to reassure Papaji.

"I have hired Andrew Stanton to meet us at Leeds Police station, Papaji. He is from a large city firm of lawyers and is, I am told, renowned for being a sharp lawyer in criminal law, very skilled."

"Criminal law, did you say, *puttar*?"

"Yes Papaji, he practises criminal law."

"I am not a criminal. Why would I need a criminal lawyer?" Papaji retorted.

"Papaji, the police deal with crimes. You need a lawyer who is an expert in that area of the law. He will take care good of you. I don't want you to go through the distress again like you did the last time. The lawyer will ensure they don't keep you in the cells."

Papaji went into his usual quiet mood, twirling the beads on his *tasbee*. After that, he just simply closed his eyes. Abdel assumed he had gone to sleep. Abdel could not put any music on to while the time away on the long journey. He tried to think about his plans for Antoninus and Lady Sharjah. He planned it all out how Jacob and Ben would fit in with his plans. He spared a thought about Jacob's predicament with his father. The estrangement from his dad, which he knew all too well about, must be hard for Jacob, as it had been for Abdel all these years. *Families, who needs them,* he thought, *but you cannot do without them.* It was a terrible thing for a twenty-two-year-old to deal with.

Staff at the station knew Sherlock and Kiki were buzzing with excitement that morning. Both arrived at the station a little earlier than they did normally to make sure all the paperwork was in order. Sherlock was keen to finalise the details with Senior Crown Prosecutor Carlie Singer who had taken charge of this case at the Crown Prosecution Service end.

"Morning, Detective McLean, it's Carlie Singer here. How are you today?"

"Oh, fair to middle, you know how it is. It is a good morning though. I trust you are well? Both DI Slater and I have been looking forward to this day. It has been a long time coming. It has taken its time, and I firmly believe it is the right time. It's now or never, you agree?" Sherlock asked.

"Yes, I do agree with you, Detective McLean. So did you receive the paperwork I drafted up for you?"

"Yes, I have, thank you. We cannot go higher on the charges, can we?"

"No, it would not be wise in my opinion to do so, as the realistic prospect criteria may be compromised for the Crown."

"Very well, we will go with your recommendation, Prosecutor Singer."

"What time are the defendants due at the station?"

"Nawaz Khan is due in at 12:30 p.m., the other chap, Faizali Rehman, for 2:00 p.m."

"Good, let me know if you need me for any last-minute issues."

"Will do, indeed, but we should be fine; thank you for your assistance, Ma'am."

The afternoon did not go as planned. Kiki paced up and down in the office. Sherlock sat in his chair, unlit pipe in his mouth, swinging his chair side to side. It was 12:45. She picked up the phone and rang downstairs to the main reception area to enquire if Nawaz had answered to his bail.

"What did they say?" Kiki asked.

"Negative Gov. The bugger didn't turn up. Shall we give him another fifteen? If he is not here by 1:00, I am going to send a squad car out to his place."

"Yep."

The telephone rang on Sherlock's desk. He picked up.

"Turned up, has he?"

"No Sir, there is a solicitor here, an Andrew Stanton, wishes to speak with you?"

"I don't recognise the name. Whose brief is he?"

"Mr Faizali Rehman, Sir."

"DI Slater and I shall be down shortly. Just ask him to wait."

"Sir, what's the latest?" Kiki asked.

"Apparently, the old man has got some highfalutin London brief with him. He is asking to speak to us."

Faizali sat in the police station waiting area with Abdel whilst the solicitor spoke to the two detectives. He was quite a while in the office with the two officers. Papaji appeared to be in deep thought, looking down at his feet mostly, as he twirled each bead of his *tasbee* slowly between his fingers. It was not at his usual pace the beads passed his fingers; this time it was much slower. Abdel noticed but did not comment. It was as though his faith in Allah had begun to wane. In the car travelling to Leeds, he had mentioned he had opened the envelope remembering Him, but it did not do any good. There are times when humans question the level of their faith in Allah, other times, it will be a strongly held belief that humans are responsible for their own misery, not God; it's no good blaming Him, and as a consequence, hold on tightly to the rope of ones faith in good and bad times.

The reception area was busy with people. There was a group of five white young men with their lawyers in one corner waiting. The lawyers were dressed smartly in dark suits. The young men all seemed to be between eighteen and twenty-five years old. Abdel looked at one English guy with short designer stubble, decently dressed in T-shirt, jeans and a short leather jacket. He looked at Abdel and stared at him for two minutes. Abdel averted his eyes unsure about the eye contact. Was he curious? Was he attracted to Abdel? There were fleeting glances exchanged between the two. At one point, the stranger had his eyes fixed on him for a good minute without blinking, then winked at him. Abdel smiled feeling sure the exchange was attraction between the two but averted his gaze as Papaji was sat next to him. A loud chatter sounded more like a disagreement at first then suddenly erupted into an argument between the group and the policeman at the reception desk when the guys started speaking in raised voices.

"Quieten down, lads, or you will all get arrested, I am telling you," the policeman at the desk shouted out.

Abdel heard something about Chester Football Club being mentioned and something about a night out a week before which had resulted in a fight between a group of people and players.

"C'mon, lads, keep it down. There are other people in the station here." The police officer repeated his warning.

"Can you hurry up? We were here on time and haven't all day, you know," one of the guys retorted back in a Liverpudlian accent.

"Keep it down. The officers are doing their best to get you guys processed soon."

No sooner the contretemps ended, a group of officers came through one of the heavy wooden doors which had a security lock on it, the type you punch code numbers to open. The group all stood there with their lawyers in a line about to follow the officers through the same door. The young guy that had winked at Abdel turned round once more, winked and walked off.

"Thank Allah, those rowdy boys have left," Papaji said with a trifle fear in his tone. "I was beginning to feel uneasy with them there. They seemed intimidating. One of them kept staring at us Abdel, did you see? This is the problem when you are in a strange area where people are not used to seeing us here."

"Err…no Papaji, there are Pakistanis living here in Leeds, you know," Abdel said anxiously, at the same time keen to change the subject fast. "I was wondering why Mr Stanton is taking so long."

"I hope this lawyer can persuade the police to leave me alone for I have done nothing wrong."

"He is a good lawyer, Papaji. Don't worry, he will help; I am sure he will."

The Solicitor, Andrew Stanton, returned into the reception area a while later. He stated that he had vehemently objected to the course of action the police were taking due to the lack of evidence against Mr Rehman. He had stressed to them that they would not be able to discharge the burden of proof required in law. Additionally, it was not in the public interest to prosecute a sick old man. Despite his protestations, Papaji was charged with conspiracy to murder Saleena and Calvin. Papaji was bailed to Leeds Magistrates' Court for the first hearing to take place on 16 April.

Nawaz was not at the house when the police made a forced entry. The house was in an absolute chaotic state. Strong smell of cannabis pervaded the house. The search for him was negative.

"God, look at this place; it is like a pigsty. The smell of drugs is overpowering. Where the bloody hell is he?" Sherlock wondered.

"Do you think he might have skipped the country, Sir?"

"I hope not Kiki. If he has, then out goes our case," Sherlock said with a worried look on his face.

"Sir, we have worked so hard to get this far."

"I know, I know. We will find him. He is a junkie, can't have gone very far."

"I hope you are right, Sir."

Kiki telephoned Raazia to inform her of Nawaz's disappearance. Her father had been charged with conspiracy to murder and been bailed, she informed her. Raazia should be careful, she advised, and certainly keep away from the area where her father lived and not to answer the telephone if he or his wife rang the family.

Somewhere in the Yorkshire Moors, Nawaz sat on a wooden chair, his hands tied with plastic ties and a paper bag covering his head. He had no idea where he was or why he had been brought there. Nawaz could not hear any sounds in the room. It was a deserted rundown property.

"Who are you? What the fuck do you want from me?" Nawaz shouted angrily, but there was no response from anyone.

He began to struggle to try to get free. Then he heard a sound as someone walked into the room.

"Who are you? What do you want from me?"

"How does it feel being helpless, Mr Khan?" a voice in an African accent asked him.

"Who are you?"

"A friend of Saleena and Calvin, do you remember them?"

"No. What the fuck you want from me?"

"How does it feel to be helpless, you fat ugly fuck? You made Saleena's life a misery. Now I want you to have a taste of your own medicine."

Nawaz needed the toilet. His bladder was full. Captivation and fear of the unknown made the urge to relieve himself become more urgent.

"I need to piss," Nawaz pleaded with his captor.

David ripped open his fly with a sharp knife, cut one of the plastic ties to free his left hand, and stuck a bottle up his crotch. Nawaz, not normally known as someone who would easily be frightened, for the first time displayed fear. David stood behind him. A pointed end of a sharp knife was firmly embedded in the first layer of his skin. Nawaz relieved his bladder in to the bottle. As the bottle filled up, urine began dripping on him.

"Who are you? You are hurting me."

David did not respond. The pointed edge of the knife dug in a little more into his skin with pressure being applied causing it to bleed slightly. He applied a little more pressure. Soon blood began to drip down from the cut in his neck down the side and onto his torso wetting his T-shirt. Mutembe withdrew the knife and pretended he had left the room by opening and closing the door.

"I have asked you hundred times, who are you? What do you want from me?" Nawaz continued asking aggressively.

Mutembe's response was deliberately to stay silent to see if Nawaz would change his tone. The silence began to get to Nawaz. It became eerie. Not being able to see with a bag on his head slowly began to add to the fear which was starting to take a grip on him. Suddenly, a sharp pain to his crotch made him jump as he was not expecting it. After emptying his bladder, he was unable to cover himself. His privates were at risk of harm. David slowly applied pressure. The pressure eased as Mutembe picked the full bottle of urine and threw it out of one of the windows. The sound of the bottle hitting the ground, shattering into pieces was heard seconds after it went out of the window. Nawaz guessed he was on a first or second floor of a building somewhere remote. He could not hear sounds of any traffic. The pointed jagged edge of the knife returned back. David dug the knife deeper on his testicles exerting pressure from the top of the knife turning the knife sideways to the point Nawaz could bear it no longer. His pupils were fully dilated; his breathing became heavy. He pleaded with his captor to ease the pain from the knife. David removed the paper bag allowing him to catch a breath of oxygen, at the same time eased the pressure on the knife.

The sudden exposure to the light from two burning candles in the room caused Nawaz to squint hard. His pupils constricted; the room looked blurred to him at first. Hardly having had time to adjust to the light from the candles, Nawaz looked around quickly. Gradually, the eyes began to adjust to the light. There were two candle lights by the window. He tried to get a better view of his surroundings before the paper bag went back over his head. It looked like a rundown, perhaps deserted, remote place devoid of human existence apart from him and his captor. The ceiling had big cracks in it. Some floorboards had been lifted up creating gaps in the flooring. Windows seemed boarded up apart from one window. He began to twist his head round anxious to get a glimpse of his captor. Nawaz wanted to know what he looked like.

"Stop right there, mister, unless you want your head separated from your neck," his captor warned. "Now you appreciate what fear is, my friend. What a ridiculous pathetic creature you are, Mr Khan. Can you imagine what it was like for Saleena to have been married to you? All that power you wielded on an innocent woman, tut, tut, tut…abusing her day in, day out. Can you imagine now how you made her feel living in fear eh? She could not wait to get away from you. You don't look mighty to me now, Mr Nawaz Khan, do you? You killed those two innocent people just like that, you bastard."

"I had nothing to do with it, I tell you; it wasn't me."

"Tut, tut, tut, Mr bastard. You still deny it, do you? You must think I am a fool?"

David twisted the edge of the knife into Nawaz's scrotum as blood began to flow staining his trousers. The stench of his urine was overpowering.

"All right, man, I'll do what you want. Just stop."

"Looks to me you rather keep your balls intact aye? Wise man, I'd say, so here is the deal." Mutembe eased the pressure off the knife, moved from behind

Nawaz and for the first time faced him. Nawaz flinched seeing Mutembe's dark eyes staring directly at him. "You tell me the names of the people who entered the flat that fateful night killing Saleena and Calvin. If you do not, I am going to slice your balls off you."

"Yes, err…I only know the name Tom. I don't know his second name, white guy, tattoos all over his body. He has one distinct tattoo on his upper arm, err…hammer and sickle, I think. All I know is he lives near Leicester somewhere. That's all I know."

"Okay, Nawaz, I am beginning to feel you understand me very well, which is good for you. I like a man who cooperates. So now what you have to do is simple. You will go to Leeds Police Station tomorrow after you have cleaned yourself up and surrender yourself. Don't fuck this up, understand? If you do, man, I swear I will come and find you. Next time, Mr Khan, see this knife here, will slice your balls clean from your body; afterwards, well, your life will be over. So if you value your manhood, you will do as I say," Mutembe threatened.

Mutembe threw a bucket of water over Nawaz. The mixture of blood, urine and water turned into a dark-coloured liquid which ran down Nawaz's legs then on to the wooden floor. The water had washed some of it away, but the stench remained. Mutembe untied him first, allowing Nawaz to fix his torn trousers enough to cover his privates before walking him down the dark staircase. A torchlight Mutembe was holding guided them both down the dark staircase. The floorboards creaked as they slowly descended. Some made a sound as though they were about to give way. Much of the flooring was either rotten or had fallen away. Descending them was a little tricky; with the weight of both men, it had to be a slow exercise. It was like crossing a rotten wooded bridge between two mountains where you had carefully to dodge the rotten panels, crossing over the gaps carefully to prevent falling through them. David was right behind Nawaz holding his top gripping it tightly.

Once on the ground floor, they walked through a hallway to the front door both stepping outside one after another. A rented Vauxhall Bedford Midi van was parked about a hundred yards outside by the front door. David tied Nawaz's hands and bundled him into the back of the van. Before he did, Nawaz surveyed the surroundings, trying to figure out where he was if he could or at least try to remember the area. It was difficult as the place was in darkness. Low clouds covered the sky so the light from the moon was dim. There were trees all around. The place was unfamiliar to Nawaz, and it seemed remote, deserted. Probably miles away from Manchester, he thought to himself. It seemed like an hour's drive getting back to Manchester.

Nawaz got into the house from the rear as the front door was boarded up. He secured the back door by locking it then stacked up a bunch of chairs against it. It was déjà vu. He remembered how his late wife used to stack up a chest of drawers behind her bedroom door barricading it to keep him out. This time it was Nawaz trying to keep Mutembe or anyone else out! After showering, he attended to the wound in his neck and then delicately to the knife wound to the scrotum. He bunched up sheets of toilet paper, drenched it with brandy, and then applied pressure to the wounds which made him flinch. It hurt like hell as he let out a huge puff of air from his mouth. His breathing became heavy as he dropped to the floor of the bathroom. He stayed still crouched down on the floor breathing heavily letting out puffs of air in quick succession. The stinging pain subsided after a while. Using some surgical Elastoplast, he taped the tissues to his neck. Unable to move from the pain to his scrotum, Nawaz lay on the bathroom floor unable to move.

He passed out waking about three hours later; the pain had subsided a little and hunger pangs dictated an urgency to get up off the floor to get something to eat. He slowly stood up holding his private area applying a little pressure to prevent it bleeding, opened the bathroom cabinet and grabbed a bottle of paracetamol. He unscrewed the cap, popped two out in the palm of his right hand and swallowed them. He threw the bottle on the floor, opened the cold water tap and bent down to drink water straight from the running tap. Slowly he hobbled to the bedroom, managed to change his clothing and made his way down the stairs and into the kitchen. As he opened the fridge door, the light from it lit up the room. There was a leftover doner kebab in the fridge from a day or two before. He took a sniff at it before he stuck it in the microwave for a minute, took it out before hobbling over into the lounge. He carefully sat down on the sofa, ate the kebab as he sat in darkness in the living room with a cricket bat beside him.

Nawaz woke up the next morning feeling like a truck had hit him. His head, neck and scrotum felt very sore. At around 2:00 p.m., Nawaz walked through the front entrance of Leeds Police Station. He stood in front of the reception desk silently staring into thin air. It was as though he had seen a ghost. The sergeant on duty recognised him from the previous day's events and immediately placed him under arrest.

"Gov, you won't believe what the cat has dragged in through the front door," the sergeant said after picking up the phone speaking to Sherlock.

"It's not Nawaz Khan, is it?" Sherlock asked.

"Bingo Sir! Come down and see for yourself!" the sergeant responded with a laugh.

The two detectives rushed down to the foyer of the building. The sergeant had cuffed Nawaz who was sitting down on a chair in the waiting area. They were both surprised to see him. Nawaz did not utter a word. When Sherlock asked why he failed to report yesterday, Nawaz made no response. A police surgeon was called up to see him.

"So Doctor, what is the verdict on Nawaz Khan?" Sherlock asked.

"I am not sure, you know. He has a deep wound in his neck which I have cleaned up. It required stitching so I have sutured it. Didn't explain how he'd got the wound when I asked him. He seemed uncomfortable also with possible pain down below, kept holding his privates making sounds indicating feeling of pain. I asked him about that and offered to examine him there, but he refused. My opinion is though he looks a little withdrawn, I can't see anything wrong with him mentally to prevent him being interviewed. You want to interview him, do you?"

"No, not really, we just want to charge him now, Doc. He has not been cooperative before, exercised his right to silence every time."

"I don't see why you can't do that. The issue of capacity to understand the charge will be a matter for his lawyer to deal with, I'd say in my opinion," the doctor said.

"Very good, Doc, I think we will go with that line, thanks.

"Shall we go down and charge him, Sir? Kiki asked.

"Let's go, my dear Kiki, and do just that. We will hold him on remand. Produce him to the mags court for tomorrow," Sherlock responded.

Chapter 12

It was Saturday. Jacob was up early. Lucy and Ben had arrived early. Antoninus had to be prepared for the day ahead. Jacob attended to Antoninus, Ben to Lady Sharjah. Both horses were being prepared for the race at Cheltenham that afternoon. Ben would be riding, for the first time, Lady Sharjah in the Queen Mother Champion Chase, a two-miles-long race. Antoninus had been entered in the Prized Cheltenham Gold Cup. The horses were taken for an early morning ride to start off the day. It was misty. That did not deter either of them as they both ran fast. Following both horses being cleaned after the run, they were groomed then fed before the three stable hands attended to the other horses. By the time Abdel came to the stables, much of the work had been done.

"Morning, boss," all three greeted him.

"Morning all, great work, guys. Thanks to the three of you. Have the horses been exercised?"

"Big day today boss! Yes, both the horses ran fast. It was a good run even though it was a bit misty. Antoninus did not seem to mind the morning mist," Jacob said.

"Ben, you ready for your first race this afternoon?" Abdel asked.

"Yes boss, I am. She rides like a dream. The power she has is phenomenal, boss," Ben responded.

"You think she can beat Antoninus?"

"I am not sure, boss. He is one powerful horse. This morning when Jacob and I were riding the horses, there seemed to be some display of competition between them!" Ben stated.

"Really?" Abdel asked with some surprise. "That is very interesting."

The same morning just after 10:00, over in Manchester, a short hearing before a single Justice at Leeds Magistrates' Court was taking place. Detectives McLean and Slater attended to ensure things ran smoothly. Nawaz did not have a brief. A duty solicitor at the court, representing Nawaz, made a bail application for him to be remanded on bail as his co-defendant, Faizali Rehman, had been bailed from the police station. The Crown objected to bail as he was likely to fail to surrender having already failed to attend the police station once, as well as the Crown argued there was a flight risk. The Justice remanded Nawaz in custody for seven days to tie his case in with the hearing the following Friday on 16th when Faizali Rehman was due to appear before the court.

Cheltenham Racecourse, Prestbury Park was a busy, crowded place. Abdel had secured a ticket to sit in the royal enclosure rubbing shoulders with the rich and some famous people. He had asked Philip to come, but it was his mother's birthday so he could not be there with Abdel.

Jacob walked through a dense crowd of people to Antoninus' box to see him before the race. Jacob knew the horse, understood what he said to him. He gave him a pep talk before the big race, rewarding him with pieces of apple as he stroked him whilst talking to him.

"Antoninus, you are the best horse I have ever seen. I know you understand me." The horse blinked his eyes, put his front leg forward and brought his head down, at the same time moved his head up then down letting out a snort. "See, I know you understand what I am saying. Your lady is racing today too. I guess you know that, don't you? She knows your power, your speed. She knows you want to win her over. Well, Antoninus, here is your big chance my creature friend. She will look up to you, a strong fella like you. Do your master proud. He wants you to win today, so don't let anyone of us down especially your lady. She will be looking to see how good and powerful you are. Go out there today and do your thing, mate."

Abdel was dressed for the occasion. He was wearing the full gear, topcoat with tails and grey trousers, light blue pressed shirt, blue tie and a top hat with polished black leather shoes. If Philip saw him today, he would comment on his sartorial elegance. A young English guy looked about Abdel's age, dressed in a Gucci suit sat next to Abdel.

"Nice day for a race," he said.

"It sure is," Abdel responded.

"It's nice to be in the royal enclosure."

"Yes, it's lovely, my first time in the enclosure. I have two horses running today," Abdel said.

"Ah really, that is marvellous. You are not here just spectating then? I've not seen you here before? Oliver Osgathorpe, pleased to make your acquaintance," he said extending his hand out towards him to shake hands.

"Abdel, likewise I am sure," he said as he reciprocated shaking hands.

Oliver had a tight grip. It took nearly thirty seconds before he released his grip. "Your horses are named what?"

"Antoninus and Lady Sharjah."

"I have put hundred quid on Lady Sharjah. 7/3 to win or each way. I hope she wins. I wondered who the owner was. I presumed the filly was owned by you-know-who."

"You mean the ruler of Dubai?"

"Yes, he runs quite a few in the races. He breeds the finest stallions and my goodness, they are the best as well as always very competitive horses. HRH hates losing, you know."

"Hmm…yes, I know. My filly is from Sharjah."

"She is, really?"

"Yes, really."

"Well, here's to Lady Sharjah then, Abdel," he said raising his drink. "Abdel, it's good to make your acquaintance. Here is my card, call me sometime."

Both horses ran like the wind in their respective races, Ben did well coming second riding Lady Sharjah, but the Queen Mother's horse Sir Roger-Cripps just beat her by seconds. The main prize, the Cheltenham Gold Cup went to Antoninus who won the race by twenty seconds ahead of all the other horses beating the Queen's horse as well as the ruler of Dubai. Abdel was extremely proud as his horse who suddenly sprang into the world of fame. Philip sent Abdel a text message congratulating him. The son of the ruler of Dubai, HRH Sheikh Abu Zaha went over to Abdel. He shook his hand first then a pat on his back. "Well done, well done, indeed," observing that he was the owner of a fine Arabian stallion and making history by beating his father's fastest stallion. The Prince handed Abdel a business card stating if he was in Dubai or London that he should be sure to give him a call as he had a keen interest in horses. Abdel was almost beaming with happiness. Two rich and handsome guys had given him their cards. Not only had he rubbed shoulders with the rich, the famous as well as royalty and aristocracy, he had acquired status and a reputation to be proud of.

Abdel could not wait to get to Antoninus. He dashed from where he was over across the field to where Jacob was tightly holding Antoninus' reigns. He waded through a crowd of people who were all clamouring around Antoninus. A huge number of photographers surrounded them both furiously clicking their cameras, taking the winner's picture for the next day's front-page news. Abdel, all of a sudden, stopped in his track standing completely still before he reached Jacob and Antoninus. The camera flashes reminded him of that day at The Dorchester hotel and the next day when his picture was splattered all across on the front pages of national newspapers. That day came alive in his mind. It was as vivid as the day it all happened. It was a dreadful feeling of déjà vu. *Papaji will see the pictures of me,* he thought. This was not a good idea, a bad omen. He phoned Jacob on his mobile and told him to pretend to be the owner. He would explain the 'why' later on. Jacob and his jockey Andy Forbes were basking in glory. Jacob enjoyed the moment so much it was surreal for him – a moment completely unforgettable. He felt honoured to be asked.

Later that evening, back at the estate, Abdel hurried to get to the stables. He put his arms round Antoninus' head, and then patted him continuously. "Well done, Antoninus, you beautiful horse." The stallion acknowledged his master's presence by neighing continuously at the same time moving his head up then down as though he was expressing a celebratory win by undulating. He then did the same to Lady Sharjah. Jacob came over once he had completed his tasks at the stable securing the horses to join his boss.

"Boss, I am intrigued why you wanted me to pretend to be the owner. I didn't do that, boss, as I did not feel it right."

"What did you say?"

"I told them that the owner was unwell and that he would be making a statement when he was feeling well enough."

"Good thinking, Jacob. I guess I owe you an explanation!"

"No boss, you don't. It sounds like a private matter."

"Thank you, Jacob. For someone so young, you seem quite aware of things in life. Jacob, I will tell you why, but I want you to keep it to yourself, you know, don't discuss it with the others here. Some luck came my way when I was seventeen years old; fortunate, some would say. I was stupid enough not to choose to remain anonymous though. My immaturity led me into something I did not appreciate at all at the time. The dazzle of the limelight drew me in. You can imagine the publicity, the youngest lottery winner in UK. My pictures were plastered all across the front pages of all the main national newspapers. My dad saw them. He broke all relations with me afterwards."

"What, are you serious? He did that to you? One crazy guy, I would say. I would have been all over you…err…figuratively speaking, boss."

"Yeh, you may ask why, and this is the difficult part to explain. Well, I am a Muslim. Buying a lottery ticket was gambling. My father is a proper Muslim. To him, my win was an anathema, against our religion, you know. So is horseracing, Jacob. They are seen in exactly the same terms. So whilst I was dashing across to see Antoninus, I suddenly had visions of those days and I suddenly froze. That is when I called you. The estrangement with my father that followed, killed me, Jacob. After a long period of estrangement, he has made up with me very recently but the relationship is fragile. I did not want to do anything to cause my relationship to be affected adversely."

"I see, boss. I also see why the other day you were concerned about my relationship with my dad hmm…" Jacob responded. "I think Antoninus was making a point to his lady, you know. I am pretty sure she knows he was showing off his strength and prowess."

Ben and Daniel walked into the stable at that point. Both congratulated their boss on the great achievement of the day.

"Aye, aye, boss. How was today? Great win we hear; and where are the champagne bottles then, boss?" Daniel asked.

"How about a celebratory meal out Sunday night in Central London? It will be my treat. I am planning on taking you all out for a nice celebration. I want you all to enjoy the evening; it's on me. Can you get someone to cover your shift tomorrow night, Daniel?"

"Aye boss, I can, thanks."

"Ben, you did superb coming second. How was it for you, Ben, riding on her ladyship?" Daniel asked.

"It was surreal. I cannot explain it in words. The experience was just out of this world."

"Well, congrats to you, boy. I saw part of the race on telly; you was good on that filly, you really was mate. She ran like the wind, she did. And for Antoninus, he was like a bloomin' bullet," Daniel said, making them all laugh.

Abdel's Blackberry rang as he walked to the house. Philip congratulated him on the win. They chatted about the race first. Abdel could not contain his excitement as he continued to speak fast about the whole day's experience without taking a breath. Abdel asked about his mum's birthday and how was it. Philip had treated his mother to a West End show *Les Misérables* which she always wanted to see but never got round to it. She loved it. Philip said he and Abdel should go see it one day soon. Abdel asked what it was about. Philip explained:

"It was set in nineteenth-century France, a French peasant Valjean, served nineteen years in jail for, would you believe it, stealing a loaf of bread for his little nephew. Nineteen years in jail, Abdel. Valjean was on parole, but after a tremendous act of mercy shown by a bishop, it inspires him to break his parole, but he is relentlessly tracked down by police inspector Javert. Valjean as well as others are swept into the French Revolution in that time, where a group of young idealists attempt to overthrow the government." Philip highly recommended the play. That would definitely be a date for the two they agreed.

His next conversation was with Papaji:

"Abdel, how was your day, *puttar*?"

"Papaji, nothing much happened, just an ordinary day. As it was a Saturday, I was at home." It was an awkward question he avoided answering.

"So how is your wife, Abdel?" he asked.

"Papaji, I am not married yet."

"Oh, I thought you were?"

"No Papaji, I am not married. I will once your case is over. There is a lot of time to do that, Papaji, later on. How is *Amii*?"

"She is fine. It is good to speak with you, *puttar*."

"Likewise, Papaji. Are you all right? You sound down to me."

"I am fine, *puttar*. Don't you worry about your Papaji. I am getting old and ready to be with my Begum now."

"Papaji, don't worry. I have booked a good barrister for the hearing, so don't worry. He is really good."

"Okay, *puttar*, I was waiting for you to call. I think I will go to bed now as I am feeling very tired today, so *khudda hafiz*."

"*Khudda hafiz*, Papaji."

It was an amazing day for Abdel and his employees. The win had put him in a cheerful mood. The conversation with Papaji dampened the cheery mood as his father seemed down in the dumps. He toyed with the idea of postponing the celebration arranged for the employees for the next day and thought he'd visit Papaji instead. Something told him to do that wasn't right. Abdel would be letting down his employees badly who had earned the celebration as they not only had worked so hard for the win, but the excitement of the celebration was well earned. His conscience would not allow him to ruin the moment for them.

Chapter 13

Raazia finished clearing up that evening after the family had their evening meal. The twins helped her tidy up the kitchen. She sat down at the dining table and was about to start making her shopping list for the family's weekly shop the next day when the front doorbell rang. Akeel and the twin girls were watching television in the family sitting room having settled down to watch *Midsomer Murders*.

"I'll get it, Mum," Meesha shouted.

There was a young Asian woman at the front door. Meesha did not recognise who it was. The woman stood holding on to the doorframe swaying a little. She looked as though she was dizzy, her face bloody, clothing torn and hair ruffled. Meesha screamed as loudly as she could, and as she opened the door, the woman collapsed in front of her. Raazia had flashes of her daughter being in danger causing her to sprint to get to her as fast she could, so did Akeel and Shakeela. They all saw a woman had collapsed to the ground. Meesha stood still by the door completely frozen.

"Meesha, darling, are you okay, sweetie?" Raazia asked as she hugged her daughter making sure she was okay first. Meesha looked terrified as she had never seen anyone in a traumatic state before.

"Akeel, go dial 999 quick. Get some help. Girls, let's try and pull her inside the house so we can close the door. Shak go get a pillow from the sitting room."

"Hello, hello." Raazia gently patted the woman on her cheeks. "Can you hear me? What happened to you? Have you been mugged?"

"The ambulance people said it could be up to half hour as they are busy tonight, Raaz. Here, see if the smelling salts will work to bring her round," Akeel said as he handed the bottle of smelling salts to her, then put a blanket over her.

"Akeel, she looks very familiar, but I can't tell with her face being like this," Raazia said as she began to cry.

"Hey, Raaz, don't upset yourself. Whoever she is, I am sure she will be okay," Akeel reassured his wife.

Raazia remembered the time when Saleena had called them out that awful night when she had been attacked by Nawaz. "Akeel, do you remember that day when we rushed off to Manchester to see Saleena? My heart tells me this woman is a victim of domestic violence. Why would she come to our door? Akeel, go check the road to see if she has not been followed."

Akeel had a good look around outside as he walked up and down the road making sure there was nothing strange going on, no sinister looking strangers were hanging about the quiet cul-de-sac road. There was a car with its engine

97

running. Akeel was brave enough to walk past it. As he did, he tried to see if he could make out who the occupants were. He could not as it was dark. Akeel walked a few steps then turned back to have a second look. As he came to the car, the driver wound his window down.

"Excuse me, we dropped a lady off on this street; we gave her a lift like, you know. My girlfriend and I wanted to just make sure she got there safely wherever she was going," a white male sitting in the driver's seat said.

"Oh yes, she is at my house. You don't know who she is, do you?"

"No, sorry. We gave her a lift. She asked to be dropped off here. She needs to go the hospital, mate."

"Thank you so much for being a Good Samaritan. I have already called for an ambulance. Thank you and good night; safe journey home guys."

"Raa…z, it…it's…me…" she stumbled in getting the words out.

"Mum, it is Auntie Sara! Oh my God, Mum, what shall we do?" Meesha said frantically.

"Meesha, go inside the house; go and get a glass of water. Baby, it will be fine. Sara baby, I am here, please wake up, sweetie." Raazia had tears streaming down her cheeks by now.

It was déjà vu for Raazia, history repeating itself. It was much too much for her. She began feeling sick, she could feel the knots tightening in her stomach as she began having flashbacks of Saleena being hit by Nawaz. Now her younger sister had fallen victim to domestic violence, just like Saleena.The burden of it all, family issues coming all at once, was far too much for her to cope with. Papaji's probable involvement with the death of Sal, some foreigner, a *kala* guy, working in the shadows lurking in the background, not knowing much about his real angle in all this, and now her younger sister was lying on the floor of her house semi-conscious right in front of her. Was this the danger Akeel had talked about and was the *kala* something to do with all this? She wondered. She tried to cast it all out from her mind. She couldn't. She continued her efforts of trying to talk to Sara.

Raazia began feeling traumatised with yet another situation being sprung upon her. It was one thing after another. She just sat by Sara's side sobbing. Some moments passed as Sara returned to some consciousness as she began to mumble words. The darkness of the night was changed to flashing bright blue lights outside her house. Akeel rushed out to greet the ambulance crew as they pulled up outside the house. The ambulance crew alighted, greeting Akeel as they walked to the house. The crew were both white, a youngish pair; they looked to be in their late twenties.

"What has happened?" the young male enquired.

"It's my wife's sister. She arrived at the house I'd say about half hour ago. As my daughter opened the front door, she collapsed on the floor and has been semi-conscious since then," Akeel explained.

The female crew member seemed like a paramedic. She had a green-coloured jumpsuit type-uniform on. She had a bag with her that she put on the floor next to Sara as she crouched down on the floor.

"Hello, can you tell us what happened, please," she asked.

"I was hit by my partner earlier on at my house in Frisby. I left and got a lift from some kind strangers and came here to my sisters' house," Sara explained in clear language.

Raazia was pleased to see Sara was fully conscious. Talking was a good sign though her face was all bruised. She wiped her tears away to gain composure.

"John, I think we can ferry her across to hospital and get her checked by a doctor, what do you think?"

"Okay, sounds good to me as she will need to be cleaned and checked for any concussion as she had passed out."

"We are going to take you to the A&E at the Royal, okay, just to make sure you get properly checked by a doctor. You might be concussed, so best to get you checked aye?"

"Raazia, will you come with me, please?" Sara asked.

"Yes, of course I will, baby," Raazia reassured her.

The blue flashing lights had attracted some curious locals from the neighbourhood who had gathered some distance away from the house wondering what was going on. Raazia's immediate next-door neighbour approached the house to ask if he could assist.

"We are fine here, Sir, there is nothing to worry about. Please would you give us the space here for the patient, thanks," the paramedic advised.

"Yes, sure, I had only come to see if everything was all right," the neighbour said as headed back to his house.

"Sara baby, what happened to you?" Raazia asked.

"*Baji*, I will tell you later; it's a long story. Do I really need to go the hospital?" Sara asked.

"We need to get you to the hospital, get that head stitched up and get you looked over. You have been subjected to some trauma. It's important you are checked over by a doctor. Also I have to call the police given what you have said. It's procedure."

"Akeel, can you get the girls over to Allia's, then get to the A&E at the Royal after, please? I will travel in the ambulance with Sara, if that is okay?" Raazia enquired.

"Yes, that is fine," the paramedic responded.

"Yes, okay, I will meet you there, Raaz."

The twins knew about their aunt Saleena, what had happened to her. Now it was their Aunt Sara. The girls were very anxious to find out why men were so brutal towards women. They had never witnessed any violence at home as their parents had been protective of the girls. They were full of questions in the car about the incident.

"Whoa, girls, whoa, I will tell you the full story in good time. Let's get this bit about Aunt Sara over and done with first. Okay?"

"Yes Dad, okay, but we need to know why this is happening to our family. It is really scary for us," Meesha stated.

"I will need to tell your Aunt Allia what's happened. She is going to go up the wall. You know what she is like."

Shakeela dialled Allia's telephone number on her dad's mobile phone.

"Hello, Akeel, you don't usually call me on my mobile phone, is everything okay?" Allia asked assuming it was him.

"Auntie Allia, it's Shakeela speaking, not Dad; he is driving."

"What is wrong?" Allia asked.

"Don't panic, Auntie. We are on our way to your house though. Dad is driving, and he is dropping us off before going to hospital, Auntie."

"Oh my God, it's Raazia, isn't it? Give the phone to your dad; let me speak to him."

"Auntie Allia, Dad is driving, but it isn't Mum, it is Auntie Sara."

"What has happened to her? Where is she?"

"We will be at yours in about five to seven minutes. Dad will explain when we get there."

The few minutes wait seemed like a long time for Allia. She waited by the lounge window looking out for her brother-in-law's car. As soon as Akeel pulled up the car in the long drive, she ran to the front door. She ran to the car next as Akeel parked up. Sajjid followed his wife to the car. Rabbiya and Abbas waited by the front door. Akeel got out of the car, then explained in detail what had happened. Allia insisted she wanted to go to the hospital with Akeel. Sajjid took the children into the house.

Saturday night was busy at Leicester Royal A&E. Some parents with young children waited in the waiting area. There was a young man holding his arm in a makeshift sling. Another who looked to be in his early twenties had a bloody face; he was holding what looked like a T-shirt to a wound on his head. At the far end of the waiting area, an elderly couple sat there. The woman was reading a book; the elderly gentleman sat next to her had his eyes closed, head slightly dropped on one side. Raazia met Allia and Akeel in the A&E waiting area.

"Hello, Allia, I thought you might be coming with Akeel. Sara is in a cubicle being attended to by a doctor stitching the wound on the side of her head."

"Blimey, that was quick. How is she?" Allia asked as the two hugged each other.

"She came in by ambulance so some sort of priority I guess. She is bruised all over, but thankfully, she is fine."

"What do you mean stitch her up? How bad is she?"

"The doctor said it looks worse than it is. He said it was a superficial wound though it needed a couple of stitches."

"Raazia, what happened to her? Really strange we did not hear from her for ages, then suddenly she turns up just like that all battered at your house."

"I know Allia. I know. It reminds me of Saleena. She has not said what happened exactly. From what was said back at the house, she has a *gorah* boyfriend who apparently hit her. The ambulance crew have reported the assault to the police. Sara refused to give the ambulance crew any details about him, so I expect the police will be calling on her soon."

"Bloody hell, Raaz, Sara should get the bastard arrested."

"Allia, there is a lot going on at the moment with Papaji's case, that *kala* business and now Sara and her boyfriend. I really am losing my mind. I just don't know what to do. Thank goodness for Akeel being here."

"Saj has never laid a hand on me. Why do these men think they can beat women up and get away with it?"

"Allia, when Saleena was taken to hospital that is exactly what I said to Akeel until I met Maleeka who opened my eyes to reality – victims of domestic violence in this world. You and I have been lucky in life – our husbands are gems – and have very much been sheltered from these horrible things that happen out there. You should hear some of the stories I have heard from Maleeka, Nadine, about her friend Grace. I worry about our girls, Allia. It is so depressing."

"What we going to do about Sara?" Allia asked.

"One thing I am sure about is I am not letting her go back. She will stay with me. This must stay quiet also. Papaji or Abdel must not find out about this otherwise she may well be in danger. DI Slater is convinced that Saleena's murder was down to honour killing. She told me about instances she knew about in South Africa. It's frightening. I really did not think it would affect us in this way. How wrong was I? But when I dwell on the past, do you remember our conversation the night Papaji announced my *rishta* to Akeel?"

"I do, Raazia. I remember your words. God, they were ominous words, now when I think about it. They did not mean much at the time as we were so young. It was like a premonition, and they have come true. I remember Sal talked about running away. You said if you fight against them, you will not win as you will bring dishonour to the family. They will protect this honour with their lives. You said something about dishonour was a curse. I now know what those words mean exactly. You were only sixteen at the time, Raaz, when you said those words."

"Premonition, Allia? You always had a way with big words. That's one of the things I liked about you," Akeel said jumping into the profound conversation between two sisters.

"I think Akeel has been following your footsteps with big words too!" Raazia said.

"What do you mean?" Allia asked looking quizzical with furrowed lines on her forehead.

"What was it now, erm…oh yes 'resolutely' was the word he used which surprised me. That was not all, Allia. One night, he came out with all this stuff about twelfth or thirteenth-century Turkish history. He talked about some warrior. He had looked into the Bible, and to top it all, gone to some *gorah* history professor at Oxford University!"

"Wow, Akeel, good on ya, bro. I bet Raazia was gobsmacked," Allia responded looking at Akeel.

Akeel stood there proud of himself with the display of knowledge he had demonstrated then to his wife and felt elated that his wife was sharing the information with his sister-in-law. At that moment, Sara walked into the waiting area holding her head. The blood had been cleaned up. Allia ran towards her, hugging her tightly as tears ran down her cheeks.

"Sara, I am so happy to see you, not like this, I mean, but happy to be with you. I have missed you so terribly. Come and stay with me, Sara. We can catch up on all those years missed being together. My Rabbiya would love to have you around."

"Allia, I'd like that very much, thank you. My head is really sore right now."

"Oh baby, what happened?" Allia asked.

"Not now, my dear sisters, you can have that conversation later on. Let's get Sara home first." Raazia intervened.

Abdel had booked a table at the Tamarind in Central London for the celebration meal. Hassan the head waiter had become well acquainted with Abdel as over the years, he and Philip had dined at the restaurant. Hassan knew it was an important celebration for Abdel and his guests tonight. He greeted Abdel's guests as they arrived, seeing them to the reserved table ensuring they had drinks until the full party had arrived at the restaurant. Jacob, Ben, Susy, her boyfriend Andy and Daniel sat at a rectangular table which had been set for them. Abdel arrived some minutes late delayed by Sunday night London traffic.

Abdel greeted Hassan at the entrance. The two had a short chat before Hassan showed Abdel to the table. The restaurant was busy. Some familiar celebrity faces were there that night – Charlie Hunnam, Hugh Grant, Stephen Fry. The restaurant's strict privacy policy for celeb patrons was to be observed, no photos. Susy recognised them all and she could not stop talking about them to her boyfriend Andy.

"Hello everyone, it is good to see to see you all," Abdel said as he approached the table. "Sorry, I am late; London traffic tonight is horrendous." Abdel went round shaking hands with everyone.

"Evening boss," they all greeted him as Hassan pulled a chair out for Abdel.

"Hello, err…you must be Andy, Susy's friend, right? Pleased to meet you Andy, glad you could make it," Abdel said as he shook hands with him.

"Likewise, Mr Rehman, thank you for inviting me. This place looks great," Andy responded standing up to reciprocate shaking hands.

"It's Abdel, Andy; Mr Rehman makes me feel like a school teacher; besides we don't stand on ceremony here, so just Abdel will do."

Andy was twenty, just a few years older than Susy. He was five foot nine in height with a crew-cut hairstyle. He was smartly dressed, wearing white polo-necked shirt and black trousers. He seemed like a guy who visited the gym three–four times a week with his toned muscles and bulging biceps hugging the short sleeves of his polo-necked top. Abdel thought to himself, if he had to hazard a guess, Andy looked the type to be a member of the armed forces. It later transpired Abdel was half right. Andy was in the British Navy and was away most of the time aboard a submarine. Daniel asked about Amna as she had not arrived. Abdel informed everyone Amna, unfortunately, could not make it as both her sons had exam revision to do. She did not wish to leave them on their own. She had, of course, sent her apologies and wished everyone a wonderful time.

Philip made a surprise appearance. Abdel had talked to him about the evening on the phone earlier in the day and must have forgotten about the invitation he had extended to him. He came over to the table, greeted Abdel with a tight hug. Abdel tried to disguise his embarrassment by introducing Philip to everyone straightaway.

"It's a very pleasant surprise, my friend, to see you here tonight. Please do join us. There is a vacant place for you," Abdel said.

"Thank you, Abdel, I will. Now where is that champagne?" Philip asked as he picked up a glass from the table.

Jacob stood up to oblige and filled up his glass. Jacob looked at Philip in a certain way then turned his gaze away. It reminded Philip of that innocent but quaint shy look Abdel had given him as he tried to fix his tie for him at The Dorchester.

"Shall we start by having a toast to Abdel, mark this wonderful win at Cheltenham as I understand he beat all the royal horses? Let's face it. It must have been something extraordinary for him, an outsider taking the crowning glory aye? Everyone, c'mon raise your glasses to mark this superb occasion for him. Congratulations, Abdel, the win was well deserved; Antoninus is a fine horse. You must be a really proud owner of him," Philip said standing up holding a glass of bubbly.

"To our boss," everyone at the table said as they all stood up too, raising their glasses to Abdel. He was overcome with emotion as the crowd waited for a speech. Abdel raised his glass of orange juice and lemonade acknowledging the praise received.

"Thank you all very much. I am not one for making speeches. The win was a team effort. All of you, Jacob, Ben and Susy, I raise my glass to you for the hard work you three put in which I completely appreciate, Daniel for watching over the horses with your life every single night of the week. Philip and Andy, thank you both too for being here with us to celebrate the win. Let's enjoy the food as it's on its way now I can see, and please, everyone, have fun. Thank you all so much."

The evening was thoroughly wonderful and enjoyed by all his guests. Jacob was the worse for wear having consumed lots of champagne. Philip offered him a lift back home which he accepted.

It was around 2:00 a.m. Akeel returned back home following dropping Allia and picking the children when at the same time a police car pulled up on the road outside the house. Two police officers, a male in his late thirties and a young female officer in her mid-twenties alighted from the police car. Akeel finished locking the car and asked the twins to go inside the house.

"Good morning, Sir, I am Police Officer O'Malley, and this is my colleague WPC Foster. We were called earlier this evening to this address, but when we arrived here there was no one at home. We are sorry for the lateness of the hour, is a Miss Sara Rehman here at this address?"

"Yes, she is, officer. Please come inside the house," Akeel responded.

"Thank you."

As both police officers entered the house, Officer O'Malley had a preconceived notion expecting smell of curry to pervade the house. His preconceived stereotypical attitude changed when he was met with a fragrance of fresh roses in the hallway. As the two officers were led into the sitting room, a different fragrance of fresh lilies hung in the air, which was a pleasant surprise for him. This soon dispelled his seemingly racist, stereotypical notion, he had attributed to an Asian house.

Sara was resting on the sofa lying down in a foetal position, Raazia was in the kitchen. Seeing police officers at that time of night was a surprise. Neither of them was expecting to speak to the police as it was late. She had not long been home from the hospital either. The police officers apologised for the lateness of the hour. They asked if they would be able to take a statement from Sara. She refused at first. Raazia persuaded her it was best if she did. She explained that domestic violence was a cancerous disease which needed to be excised from society. She reminded Sara of how their dear sister Saleena had suffered dreadfully at the hands of Nawaz. She urged Sara she must not allow this disease to go unchecked. The eloquence with which she spoke without an Asian accent was another surprise for the officers as Raazia was wearing traditional Pakistani clothes. The two white officers had assumed, as it happened quite erroneously, she would be speaking in broken English with a heavy Asian accent.

"Thank you, err…" WPC Foster said.

"Raazia Khan, I am Sara's sister."

"I am WPC Foster. I would like to take a statement from you. It will enable us to hopefully arrest the person who assaulted you," the officer said as she looked at Sara.

"Well, I was at home when Tom, that's my boyfriend, came back from the pub. He had run out of money," Sara stated.

"Sorry to interrupt you, can we have Tom's full name?" WPC Foster asked.

"Tom Ford," Sara responded.

The two officers looked at one another. It was as though the name seemed instantly familiar to them. "Not Tom Ford the infamous, ex-prisoner from HM Prison Strangeways, Manchester?" Officer O'Malley asked.

"Yes, he has served time," Sara responded.

"Oh my God, sweetie," Raazia said, letting out a gasp.

"Anyway, Tom found out that my brother Abdel was a rich man, and he wanted me to ask him for some money. I said no. He got angry and he slapped me. I slapped him back, and then he attacked me with a kitchen utensil hitting me on the head. He then punched me three times on my face hard. I began to cry. He asked me for a beer from the fridge, but I walked out through the back door. I kept walking until I reached the main road from Frisby to Leicester. I had walked maybe a mile when some stranger gave me a lift in his car. His girlfriend said they should take me to a hospital or a police station, but I refused. I said I wanted to get to my sister's house first, so they kindly dropped me off at the top of the street even though it was out of the way for them." Sara began choking up the tears, as she explained a rather too familiar story to the police.

"Oh sweetie, why did you not call me? I would have picked you up," Raazia said.

"I did not have my phone or any money. I just ran out. It's not the first time he has hit me. Afterwards, he apologises, and I end up forgiving him. This time, I just had enough of it. This is the second time I've had to leave home without taking my belongings. I feel so sad and awful. Look what has happened. I should have stayed home. By leaving, I thought I'd be free, but life is cruel for women. I don't know what to do now."

Akeel confirmed he had spoken to the driver of a car at the top of the cul-de-sac who had given Sara a lift. The driver had expressed that she should be taken to hospital as she needed medical attention.

"Did you thank them, Akeel?"

"Mm…I did, Raaz. They seemed like nice people."

"Sara sweetie, you don't have to worry. You can stay here for as long as you want. Allia said you can stay with her too. We will take care of you, my sweet, so don't worry," Raazia said as she fought her tears back, wiping her nose with a tissue at the same time. She wiped Sara's tears off her with her thumbs from underneath her eyes.

"Thank you, *Baji*."

"Sara you don't have to thank me, you are family."

"Is there anything you wish to add to your statement?" officer O'Malley asked.

"Yes, I do. Please be careful. He has a gun in the house. What happens now?" Sara asked.

"We will arrest him, interview him and see what he has to say. I hazard a guess that if you keep to your statement, he may well be charged with ABH. He is a known dangerous person to the police. I expect armed officers will be called to arrest him with a gun in the house."

The two officers thanked Sara and Raazia apologising once more as it was so late at night. As they left, they advised they would keep her updated once he was arrested.

"Sweetie, how did you get mixed up with such a man?" Raazia asked.

"Raazia, I was his Probation Officer when he was released from prison. He really charmed me. I, unfortunately, fell in love with him. What I did not know, had no idea, in fact, but only got to know last week, was that he knew Nawaz. He had met him there whilst Nawaz served time. Raazia, I tell you there is something sinister about him. I hope they send him back to prison."

"What do you mean sinister?" Raazia asked with a dreadful worried look.

"That's it, I don't know, but something odd about him, it niggles me, as he seems to know quite a bit about our family when I have never spoken to him about the family at all. I told him I was an orphan brought up by my aunt."

"Oh sweetie, I am so sorry. We will need to be very vigilant. I have quite a lot to tell you too!"

Chapter 14

Papaji woke up early the morning he was due for his first appearance at Manchester Crown Court with his body aching all over, in particular, his arthritic knees which were very troublesome. Gradually, he managed to get himself out of bed. He got himself together managing to offer the morning *fajr* prayers, getting some breakfast after taking a plethora of tablets for his hypertension, arthritis and ibuprofen for the pain to get him through the day. As he struggled on, he began feeling sorry for himself. *How could Raazia do this to an old man?* he thought to himself. *Only if she knew how difficult things were for her old Papaji, she might feel differently, even sorry.* He felt the need to get her to change her mind about all this Saleena business. The question was how would he do it?

Fauzia was keeping a low profile for fear of more arguments between them. Papaji had become short-tempered with her. She claimed to be unwell and would not be accompanying Papaji to the hearing that day. She seemed uninterested in getting involved in his affairs anymore. Papaji poured scorn on her attitude towards him, decidedly being unsupportive just like his daughters; this allegation, Fauzia resented completely.

Abdel arrived at court with Papaji in good time to meet his barrister for a conference before the hearing listed for 10:30 a.m. Jeremy Peggs-Green QC was a criminal lawyer renowned for his sharp reputation in the field of criminal law. He was fifty-four years of age, five foot nine tall in height, leathery skin, clean shaven and crow's feet by his eyes with pronounced glabellar lines on his forehead when he made facial expressions. He was dressed in smart striped trousers, white starched wings with tabs and barrister's black gown with a wig which sat, seemingly, uncomfortably on his head as he kept adjusting it with the left palm of his hand frequently.

Papaji did not notice it or say much except that he insisted he was not guilty of the charge laid against him. It was an absurdity to suggest he had a hand in his daughter's murder. Not saying much, Papaji seemed content sat there in the interview room twirling his *tasbee* beads between his fingers. He displayed his frown lines looking angry. Counsel advised Papaji that he must not adopt such a posture before the Judge. Looking calm, maintaining ones decorum was one key important appearance of a defendant in court. "It was all about making impressions in court." He expressed with confidence that the Crown would not be able to prove the charge. The conference meeting did not take long. Abdel and Papaji sat in the public waiting area with their solicitor Andrew Stanton waiting for his case to be called on in court number 3.

The courtroom was an old-style building, with court corridors that looked endlessly long, each leading to different courtrooms. Public notices on brown boards in the main foyer displayed the day's business in various courts. Ushers mingled with court staff, lawyers dashed about looking busy as did some counsel who seemed comfortable strutting about in their wigs and gowns holding papers with pink ribbons tied round them. It was a busy court. There were people everywhere. Nawaz walked past them with his lawyer without stopping to say hello. He simply walked on. A group of young men who were at Leeds Police Station were standing in a bunch together in one of the corridors. The young man, who had winked at Abdel, recognised him as he walked past with a smile. Abdel needed to empty his bladder after the long drive to Manchester. It was getting uncomfortable holding it any longer. He excused himself advising his father that he was going to the toilet. As he got to the gentleman's toilet, the young chap was drying his hands under the hand blow dryer. He looked at Abdel and smiled. Abdel smiled back.

"You were at the station some weeks back. Are you from Leeds as I am pretty sure I have seen you before somewhere?"

"No, I am from London."

"So what brings you to court today? I am Jason by the way." He extended his hand to shake.

"Oh, good to meet you. I am Abdel. It's my father. He is here on a conspiracy charge," Abdel responded, holding his hand back from shaking with the stranger as they still seemed wet.

"Blimey, conspiracy sounds heavy," he responded as he wiped the residue of the water on his trousers.

"Sorry, my hands were a bit wet. They are clean now. What are you here for then?" Abdel asked shaking his hand.

"On a charge of affray but we are all pleading not guilty. We didn't do it. The police fitted us up, our brief says. We are going to fight it. Is your dad pleading guilty?"

"Not guilty."

"Good, I hope your brief gives the prosecutor hell."

"Thank you, Jason."

"No worries. I play football for Chester United. Here is my number; give me a call sometime buddy, okay? See you soon."

"Sure, I will, good luck with your case."

"Thanks, don't forget to give me a call. Bye for now."

Abdel walked into courtroom number 3 with Papaji. Huge oak panels, high ceilings with chandelier lights hanging down from them made an impression of awe. Papaji was directed to sit in the prisoner's dock by the usher next to Nawaz. Abdel sat in the public gallery as did detectives McLean and Slater. Papaji acknowledged Nawaz's presence with a nod but Nawaz ignored Papaji. He sat down next to him feeling uncomfortable and began to twirl through the rosary beads between his fingers, silently repeating the words, "*Allah hu akbar.*"

The clerk of the court ordered the two defendants to stand up.

"My Lord, the next case is for plea and directions. This is the case of R v. Nawaz Khan and Faizali Rehman. Now, it is said that you conspired jointly to murder Saleena Khan and Calvin Lenton on 19 of December 1997 contrary to section 1 of The Criminal Law Act 1977. How do you plead?"

"Not guilty," replied Faizali.

There was no response from Nawaz. The clerk asked him to respond as failure to respond would mean a 'not guilty' plea would be entered.

"My Lord, may it please the court."

"Yes, Mr Griffidam."

"My Lord, I represent Mr Nawaz Khan. My client enters a plea of not guilty."

"Mr Griffidam, is your client, Nawaz Khan, unable to speak for himself?"

"He does My Lord, but he is somewhat overawed by the proceedings."

"Very well, I direct the court to enter a not guilty plea," the Judge said.

"Mr Peggs-Green?" the Judge asked.

"My Lord."

"Do you wish to make any applications?"

"No, My Lord."

"Are there any applications from the Crown?" the Judge asked addressing his question to the Crown Prosecutor Mr Ravenstone. "I take it the disclosure papers will be ready to be served on the defence in six weeks?"

"My Lord, yes, that can be done, and I am grateful to My Lord, there are no applications for the Crown," responded Mr Ravenstone QC.

"Very well then, I direct the Crown to serve the defence with the disclosure paperwork setting out the Crown's case together with all unused material by 31 May, the defence to serve the Crown with a list of witnesses they wish to call by the same date. I reserve the case to my list for the first available date for ten days after the first week of June. What is the bail situation?"

"My Lord, both defendants are on conditional bail," the clerk advised.

"I remand both you Nawaz Khan and Faizali Rehman to stand trial in respect of the charges you face on bail subject to the same conditions which will be on your bail notice. Be warned any breaches will result in your arrest. I will not tolerate any breaches. Should you come back before me, you will be remanded in custody as the charges are serious, understood?"

With a nod from the prisoners' dock from the two defendants, the case was adjourned.

Chapter 15

Time had ticked on fast that summer, in 1999, which came round quickly. The trees were in full bloom with lush greenery everywhere displaying the splendid time of the season. It was mid-June. Raazia had a call from Kiki putting her on notice to be ready for attending court at short notice as the Crown Prosecution Service had been in touch to say that that the case had been entered in 'the warned list'. The impending attendance at court made her anxious, not to mention the anxiety caused at the prospect of facing her father in court giving live evidence against him which was a daunting prospect for her. Though her family, Maleeka and Nadine would be there supporting her, she would be seen as a traitor by Papaji, betraying her culture, the traditional role of a woman in an Asian family and above all, her father. She knew she was not a traitor nor was she turning her back on her culture. This was about the truth. He had to face the truth just like the people in the past, in history, have someday all had to face the truth of their actions one way or another. Therefore, her mind was clear, so was her conscience. She did not have to feel afraid. The community was the problem not her. She knew he would not see it in the same way but that didn't matter to her. Raazia was not seeking revenge. She had not turned her back on traditions.

Abdel arrived early at the house to pick up Papaji to drive him to Manchester on the morning of the trial. Papaji was dressed in his normal traditional Pakistani clothes. He wore a dark sleeveless waistcoat over his *kameez* top and his old *topi*, which must be some forty years old, covering part of his near normal bald head. Abdel tried to persuade him to wear smart English clothes, shirt, suit and a tie, but he refused saying, "What is wrong with our traditional Pakistani clothes?" It was the first day of his trial so Abdel dropped the subject straightaway choosing not to start any arguments with him recognising that he may be as nervous as hell about going to court. The last thing he wanted on an important day was to get Papaji in a bad mood. That would make the long journey uneasy for both of them.

The trial began on Monday 14 June 1999, eighteen months after the tragic deaths. Sir Christopher Norrington QC, a High Court Judge, was the presiding trial Judge on the case. He was a son of a miner, grammar school educated. In the legal circles, he was known for his excellent academic skills. He was a brilliant lawyer, a principled man who was known for his firmness in court and belief in absolute fairness and justice.

DCI McLean, DI Slater, Raazia, Akeel, Allia, Sara, Maleeka, Nadine were all there. Apart from the Crown witnesses, they all sat in the public gallery. The two detectives, Raazia and Maleeka were seated in the waiting area outside

Courtroom number 1 at Manchester Crown Court. For Sherlock and Kiki, getting the case to court at long last was a real relief for them. It had been an uphill struggle getting the case to court. The public gallery inside the huge courtroom was nearly full. David Mutembe was there too. He was dressed in a Ugandan Army Captain's uniform. Nadine sat there quietly thinking about her friend Grace. For Nadine, it had been painful enough the first time round sitting through a gruelling trial of her friend Grace murdered by her husband. It was déjà vu, sadly, the second time she had to sit through a criminal trial again another friend Saleena tragically murdered. Abdel sat next to Nadine in the public gallery. Akeel sat next to Abdel. Allia, Sameena and Sara sat next to each other all in the same row. Four reporters, three men, one woman were tightly huddled in the reporter's box with their notebooks and pens poised ready for taking notes of the proceedings.

Whilst the jury seemed evenly balanced gender-wise, six women and six men, it was glaringly noticeable all, except one member, were white. The token juror was a woman of West Indian origin.

Mr Daniel Ravenstone QC Counsel for the Crown stood up to open the case. He stood facing the jury to his left.

"Ladies and gentlemen of the jury, I state at the very outset that whilst the charge of conspiracy to murder is not in any way unusual, I confess the case I shall be presenting in this court will be. It is a case that is not one which we hear about every day, but it is a case which has all the hallmarks of an honour killing. Yes, members of the jury, you heard me right, it is a case of honour killing.

"Whilst the facts of the case are simple, what lies behind it, the Crown will show you, is something extraordinarily sinister, members of the jury. Let's get to the facts first, some of which are undisputed. It was approaching Christmas in 1997, a time of year people look forward to very much so as it is a time of the year for joy, celebration for the birth of our Lord Christ, a time most people would be looking forward to spending with family. I will take you now to a flat in the Woodhouse area of Leeds. It was early hours of 19 December 1997. It wouldn't have been any different, I expect, for Saleena Khan and Calvin Lenton who were no doubt looking forward to celebrating Christmas, either together or with family. It was noted by the police there were lots of toy gifts found in their flat which would indicate preparation for this celebration. They were both asleep in their flat, when sometime in the night, there was an apparent break-in. Later when the police attended, they found two bodies at the flat. It seems the occupants had been disturbed by whoever broke into their flat and one concludes that the occupants must have confronted whoever had made the illegal entry into the flat.

"What followed, ladies and gentlemen of the jury, was a frenzy of violence inflicted on the two victims. They were bludgeoned to death. Not something, I suppose thankfully, usually found in an ordinary domestic burglary. A grizzly and a grotesque crime scene awaited the police. It was a horrendous crime scene where two people were lying in a pool of their own blood. The victims were a man called Calvin Lenton and a woman Saleena Khan. The female victim was the separated wife of the accused Nawaz Khan and the daughter of the accused Faizali Rehman. You will hear evidence from Saleena's sister Raazia Khan that Saleena, following her arranged marriage by the accused Faizali Rehman to the accused Nawaz Khan, had become trapped in this forced marriage, enduring nine years of brutal abuse and domestic violence at the hands of her husband until following hospitalisation in 1990, helped by a women's refuge, she finally managed to escape the brutal life at home. It is sad story of a woman who lived her life, it seems, on the edge on a daily basis and sadly a life full of misery.

"Her escape from her brutal life was not, the Crown would say, an audacious act but, members of the jury, a very courageous act for a woman having to flee home for her own protection and prevention of perpetration of further violence upon her body. Taking refuge at a women's refuge, cannot be an easy thing to do for anyone. Saleena was one remarkable lady, I tell you. She worked for a number of charities including the well-recognised charity the Red Cross. Her charitable work she involved herself in was from days when she was a teenager. She was not only praised by all her colleagues but by no less than President Augustus Otambu of Uganda. What did she do out there to earn this wonderful accolade, you may be wondering? Well, she worked out there in a foreign land at an orphanage looking after children. These children, some very young, were tragically orphaned by the catastrophic spread of HIV virus and AIDS epidemic which had ravaged Uganda's people. There were some two-hundred children at the Raffiki Centre where she worked and helped look after children of Uganda. This sums up the person in question. She was a woman who selflessly performed laudable acts of human kindness one would say. She devoted her life in looking after these orphaned children.

"As I said, her work was praised by no less than the President of Uganda. The parliamentary report of the day when Saleena Khan attended parliament at the invitation of the President reported as follows and I quote:

'We welcome a special guest to the House today. Saleena Khan, we are indeed honoured by your presence today in the House of Uganda's parliament. I can tell you the House is united in not only welcoming you, madam, for the important work you have undertaken in Soroti but helping my people of Uganda, the children who are the future of my country. The children talk about you fondly. I hear they call you 'Mama' as you are like their mother, might I add, with great fondness too. You love them like your own. Well, ma'am, Uganda loves you too. I salute you. Centa sana mama Saleena'*

"This remarkable lady had the ultimate accolade and recognition of her contribution by the highest office of the Country, and let me tell you, she received a five-minute standing ovation from the House. The measure of success for this woman was so remarkable it earned her a seat on the Board of the Raffiki Centre charity immediately after receiving that praise.

"Whilst working at the Centre, she met and befriended a young African man Calvin Lenton who worked for the same organisation. You will hear evidence that she had returned to England to obtain a divorce from the accused Nawaz Khan. But for an Asian woman, this was not easy. Was the accused going to give her a divorce? It seemed unlikely. Why? It was seen as an anathema within the Muslim culture. She was from a male-dominated culture where women were unequal to men. They were expected to be completely subservient to them. What Saleena had done was seen to be against their culture, values, traditions built up over many generations, even possibly centuries. So much so that what she had done was seen to be inflicting significant harm to the family reputation or honour. This was unacceptable. A married woman should have known her place, asking for a divorce first then having the audacity to marry a man of a different colour; a man of her own choice would not be acceptable to her father and husband. This was the ultimate dishonour upon them brought about by a woman.

"So members of the jury, the issue to do with subservience of women may well be disputed by the defendants but the women from such culture have a very familiar story to tell. I would say that so far what I have presented to you is undisputed. What is disputed is that the defendants were involved in a conspiracy to murder. The Crown will prove that that the two accused made a verbal agreement to eliminate Saleena who had become a thorn in their side. The evidence presented will point to their guilt. They had motive. This was the preservation of the perceived honour of the husband Nawaz Khan and father Faizali Rehman."

Papaji and Nawaz were hearing information for the first time of what Saleena had been doing following leaving Nawaz. Counsel had painted a picture in the minds of the jury, one which was that she had been trapped in a terrible marriage with Nawaz, then following her departure had led a happy and independent life free from the shackles of her culture. During Counsel's opening statement, Papaji had stopped twirling the beads between his fingers as he listened with undivided attention as did everyone in court. David Mutembe had listened proudly to his President and Country being mentioned in good light in a British courtroom.

"Mr Ravenstone, it is very nearly approaching lunchtime. I think we can break for lunch?" the Judge said.

"My Lord, yes, I feel lunch would be good," Counsel responded.

"Very well, I will rise for lunch. It is 12:30 now so I would like you all to return here at 1:45 pm."

"All stand," the court's usher bellowed as his voice echoed through the courtroom.

Abdel took Papaji away from the court for some fresh air to nearby Piccadilly Gardens Park. They walked there via Aytoun Street. The area seemed familiar to Abdel. He remembered the area as it was around there somewhere he had met Oliver, the young doctor from the local hospital, for an evening meal. On their way to the park, he stopped at a local sandwich shop to grab some food. Abdel bought cheese and tomato sandwich for Papaji, ploughman's sandwich for him with two chilled orange-flavoured Fanta bottles and a water bottle. It was a pleasant summer's day with the temperature about twenty-one degrees. The sun was out. It felt very pleasant sitting on the bench in the park having a bite to eat for lunch. Papaji ate his sandwich in no time. He sat back on the bench feeling the cool summer's breeze on his face, twirling the beads between his fingers.

"How many times in a day do you say *shookher* [thanks] to Allah then Papaji on that *tasbee*, do you reckon?"

"Five, six hundred times, maybe more; I don't count, but it is good to say thanks to Allah for the life and all the bounty he has blessed us with. He blessed me and Begum with you after many years of trying for a boy," Papaji said with a quaint smile on his face as he turned his face towards Abdel and smiled at him. This made Abdel feel good. He had longed to hear some nice words from Papaji's mouth. The words felt sweet.

"Did you know Saleena had gone to Uganda and was working there after leaving Nawaz, *puttar*?" Papaji asked.

"No, I didn't, Papaji. I was not in touch with my sisters."

"I had asked Raazia many times to tell me where she was, but she kept saying she did not know where Saleena was. I will find out if that was so when she gives evidence."

"Papaji, what would you have done if you did know. She made her decision to go."

"I don't know, *puttar*, but I would have done something to get her back home where she belonged."

"Nawaz was bashing her about, Papaji. I am not surprised she had left him. Nawaz is a creepy guy; you must admit that. I never liked him. In any case, what would you have done?"

"I would have talked to her. She was a woman who had to go back to her husband. It was not befitting for her to have run off like that, certainly not going off to a foreign country being with that *kala*. Can you imagine what people would have said? I could not get over all those *kaley* people coming to her funeral like that. They intruded at the funeral. I had to avoid questions when people asked me later on what was all that about. It was very embarrassing for me even when *Maulana* Ahmed asked me after the funeral when we got back to the mosque why they had attended Saleena's funeral."

"Papaji, you are being a little bit racist, aren't you?"

"What do you mean racist?"

"I think it was nice for the President of a country to pay his last respects to Saleena."

Abdel could see the disapproval of what he had just said on Papaji's face so he chose to change tact and be diplomatic. The subject seemed delicate anyway, so he decided to change the subject, choosing not to engage his father in the same conversation any further."

"Why did *Amii* not come to court, Papaji?" Abdel asked.

"I don't know, *puttar*. It's best she did not come as she really does my head in with her petty comments."

That seemed a sign to Abdel of some cracks surfacing in Papaji's marriage to *Amii*. "I think we best be getting back to the court, Papaji, as it will take us ten minutes to walk back."

114

The case received national coverage in the media. Philip sent a text message to Abdel to ask if he was at the court. Abdel replied he was. He warned him that the Prosecutor's opening statement had been reported on all the main channels at lunchtime so it had attracted media interest. The public's interest had been captured. Philip reminded that they would soon discover he was there, and with his past, it may generate more interest. Philip thought it would be better for his friend to be careful.

Papaji and Nawaz returned back to the dock for the afternoon session. There seemed to be about a dozen reporters now, four of them seated in the area reserved for the press, the others sat in the public gallery. The Judge walked to his seat as everyone stood in the courtroom.

"Good afternoon, everyone, please do sit down, and Mr Ravenstone, please continue," the Judge said.

"Thank you, My Lord. As I said before lunch, members of the jury, the motive was Saleena was a thorn in the side for the two accused. She had to be stopped. Now I recognise that traditions, values and culture can be important, a source of enrichment, in one's daily life. However, to take one's culture to extreme levels which involves commission of a crime is wholly unacceptable, member of the jury. Taking or participating in a conspiracy to kill one of your own is simply egregious. To do it in the name of honour it is an insult to a word which connotes 'highest respect' or 'regarding great respect'. The actions they engaged in are not only abhorrent but criminal. I will now call Mrs Raazia Khan for the prosecution."

The usher went to fetch Raazia from the waiting area. Raazia was feeling nervous enough as it was; being in a courtroom setting with so many people was nerve racking for her. As she walked into the packed courtroom, she immediately felt overawed. The sheer number of people there, literally so many barristers all wearing wigs and gowns, looking like a sea of wigs to her, senior counsel were all there with their juniors besides them, the Judge sat high behind a long elevated oak bench wearing a red robe, a wig with a coat of arms plaque above him with the words: *'Dieu et mon droit'* hung high at the top behind the judge. Not only did she feel the knots in her stomach beginning to churn almost to a point they hurt, but all sorts of things went through her mind at that very moment.

Immediately, she remembered the day in summer 1972 when Papaji had summoned her into the sitting room when she began feeling sick. It was a similar feeling of dread she was experiencing now as she did then. *I have to be courageous for Saleena.* She repeated the words over and over in her mind to overcome the fear she felt. She rubbed her hands together as her palms began to perspire slightly. She surveyed the crowded courtroom. There were so many people there. *Oh my God, I am going to have to speak in front of all these people*, she thought to herself. It was good to see all her family there. Akeel nodded at her. Akeel closed his eyes and rested his right arm on his chest, a coded message to his wife to stand resolute just as the warrior Ertuğrul did in the face of adversity.

"Can you please take the oath, Miss?" asked the usher. "It's the Koran, isn't it?"

Raazia nodded.

"And can you read the words from the card, please?"

Placing her right hand on the Koran, she read the words: "I swear by Almighty Allah that the evidence I shall give will be the truth and nothing but the whole truth."

"Mrs Raazia Khan, is that right? And what is your profession please?"

"Yes, I am, and I am a primary school teacher."

"Mrs Khan, you are the oldest of the six siblings in the Rehman family, and Saleena, your sister, was the fourth sibling, is that right?"

"Yes," she responded quietly.

"I know this may be very difficult for you, but you must speak up so everyone in the court can hear you. My Lord, the Judge over there, is making notes of the evidence, and so he needs to hear what you say. I don't wish to lead you, may I call you Raazia?"

Raazia nodded.

"Now, can you start by telling the court about Saleena, your sister, so the jury has a picture of what your sister was like?"

"I am the oldest, and then after me, Allia, Sameena, Saleena, Sara and the youngest is a boy Abdel. My sister was bright, very good looking. By the time she was sixteen years of age, there were a lot of young men who wanted her hand in marriage. Saleena had this dream that she would marry someone she chose as her partner, and unlike all her sisters, she would not be forced into an arranged marriage. She used to say to me, 'I will run away and no one will find me if they do this to me.' She was wrong. Papaji and *Amii* chose Nawaz for her. She was not happy and wanted to run away, but she could not."

"Who is *Amii*?" Counsel asked.

"She is our stepmother, Fauzia."

"Your father was remarried?"

"Yes, he was. Mother died a few days after giving birth to Abdel. I was nearly sixteen at the time, and my sister Saleena would have been eight years old. Papaji – I mean my father, we call him Papaji – went to Pakistan in the summer of the same year my mother died, married Fauzia and returned back with her to England."

"Can you tell the court what happened?"

"Saleena was not happy about marrying Nawaz Khan at all. She was only sixteen. He was twenty-eight, much older than her. Saleena hated him from the very beginning. He was ugly, massive like an elephant, my sister used to say after Papaji said yes to the proposal from Nawaz."

The observation made some people, including some jury members, burst out in laughter. The Judge did not seem to be amused as he kept a straight face. He looked in the direction of the jury looking serious with his half-moon eyeglasses perched slightly below the bridge of his nose. All the barristers found the comment funny but laughed in a control way seeing as the Judge did not find the observation funny.

"Go on, Raazia."

"Well, she had no real choice in the matter. It was tradition so she was forced to marry him."

"What do you mean tradition?"

"Girls had marriages arranged by their parents. They would choose the boy for you to marry. Sometimes the arrangement is sealed shortly after the birth of the children as it was in my case."

"Please explain what you have just said as it needs some explanation."

"Yes, some parents will make a promise to another family member or a friend that they will give their daughter in marriage to their son as soon they were of age, usually sixteen. In my case, my father had promised my hand in marriage to his friend Malik Khan. At the age of sixteen, I married my husband Akeel, Malik Khan's son."

"Did you have a say in the matter?"

"No, I did not. My father announced it on my sixteenth birthday. There was a gathering arranged in the evening. I thought for the first time in my life I was going to have a birthday celebration. It wasn't. It turned out to be my engagement. Don't get me wrong. My husband is a one in a million. He is a kind, lovely man, but I did not want to marry when I was still a child."

"How is the marriage?"

"I was lucky. My marriage has been wonderful. I have two beautiful twin girls."

"Your sister Saleena was not so lucky, was she?"

"No, Mr Ravenstone, she was not so lucky. Nawaz, from the very start of the marriage, demanded having sexual intercourse with her every night, even if Saleena had sometimes gone to bed or was tired. He did not care. It was his God-given right he would say to her as she was his wife, *his* property and there was nothing she could do about it. Saleena hated his sexual demands on her. Nawaz had duped my father and Saleena. When he came to see Saleena at our house before they married, he told my father he was a businessman. Well, he was not. He lied. Papaji liked the fact that he chose a son-in-law who was a businessman. He was impressed by him. My sister, after the marriage, found out he was a self-employed taxi-driver. He drank alcohol which was *haram*, I mean prohibited for a Muslim to drink. He also smoked cannabis and dealt in drugs."

"My Lord, I object. The Crown witness cannot introduce that sort of prejudicial evidence against my client," Mr Griffidam said rising to his feet.

"My Lord, this witness is simply setting out factual information from her own knowledge which is relevant to the case," Mr Ravenstone responded.

"Mr Ravenstone, I am afraid I agree with Mr Griffidam. Yes, the remark is prejudicial, though relevant. The jury will disregard the last remark and it will be stricken off the record."

"Thank you, My Lord," said Mr Griffidam.

"So Raazia, Nawaz Khan was a perfidious individual who had, shall we say, told a bit of a white lie, in other words misrepresented himself to your father and your sister, to put himself in a better light deliberately to be a worthy candidate for marriage to your sister?"

"Yes, he did. My sister had many proposals, and he knew that too. Mr Ravenstone, we were, very unfortunately, brought up to believe certain things are the way they are and you do not question them. We were told by our elders that it has always been a tradition in our culture for parents to find marriage partners. They do that for girls at a very early age. Women have their place in our culture, and there is a red line, if you like, between men and women. It is not permissible to step outside or cross that red line. If you do, the honour of the family is damaged and this brings enormous shame to the family and the family's reputation. Saleena went through the marriage ceremony as there was nothing else she could do. Her marriage to Nawaz was a disaster. Nawaz was a violent man. He assaulted her virtually every night. The violence was at its worst when he was drunk. All my sisters are very close to me and to each other. We are all best friends and confide in each other about everything in life. Not a day goes by without us speaking to each other."

"Did Saleena leave Nawaz at some point in her life?" Mr Ravenstone asked.

"Yes, she did. One night it was late. I was asleep when my phone rang. All I could hear was muted coughs from the other end. I knew it was Saleena. I tried to speak to her, but she could barely speak. I called an ambulance out to her address. Then I got Akeel, my husband, to drive me from Leicester over to her house in Manchester. The journey took us two hours to get there. I could not get into the house. There was no one there so I made enquires with some neighbours."

"What did you find out?" Mr Ravenstone asked.

"My sister had been taken to the hospital. Nawaz had been arrested by the police for domestic violence."

"Objection, My Lord," Mr Griffidam stated.

"What do you want me to say, Sir? When I got there, Nawaz had been taken away by the police. It is a fact," Raazia said as quickly as she could.

"Just hold on please, Mrs Khan. Mr Griffidam, I will hear you now," the Judge said.

"My Lord, I believe it would be appropriate for an application for a *voire dire*. At this stage."

"Mr Griffidam, I will hear your application in the morning. It has been a long day today. I suspect the *voire dire* will take some time. It is approaching 3:45 in the afternoon. It seems an appropriate time to adjourn."

"As Your Lordship pleases, I am obliged, My Lord."

The court adjourned for the day with Raazia being advised by the judge not to discuss the case with anyone, including her family, as she was under oath. As soon as the Judge stood up, the reporters made a dash out of the court to file their reports for the next day's papers.

Abdel had arranged hotel accommodation at the Mercure Piccadilly for him and Papaji to stay over the duration of his trial. Back at his hotel room, Abdel put the television on at around 6:00 pm and stepped into the shower as it had been a long day for him. Sitting in court listening intensely to the day's proceedings had worn him out. Feeling refreshed after his shower, he opened the window to the room letting a gentle breeze in, and then made some calls as he sat on the bed. He spoke to Jacob first. Everything was well at the estate, the horses were all fine. Philip was next on his list of callers to discuss the day's events. He thanked him for the media report warning. Next he called Oli, the doctor he had met at the hospital. Oli did not pick up, so Abdel left a message for him on his messaging service to let him know he was in town and staying at the Mercure and asked Oli to message him back if he was free at any stage so they could go have a meal somewhere.

The volume of the television was low, so he turned it up exactly at the time when a report of the trial came on. He sat back to listen:

"At Manchester Crown Court, the trial began of the two men, Nawaz Khan and Faizali Rehman today. The two men are charged with conspiracy to murder Saleena Khan and Calvin Lenton. The victims were found dead when the police attended their flat in the Woodhouse area of Leeds on 19 December 1997, days before Christmas in 1997. The accused Nawaz Khan is the husband of Saleena Khan and the second accused Faizali Khan, her father. They are accused of conspiring jointly to murder the two victims in a case of honour killing.

"Opening the case for the Crown on the first day of the trial, Mr Daniel Ravenstone QC prosecuting said this: 'Ladies and gentlemen of the jury, I state at the very outset whilst the charge of conspiracy to murder is not in any way unusual, I confess the case I shall be presenting in this court will be. It is a case that is not one which we hear about every day, but it is a case which has all the hallmarks of an honour killing. Yes, members of the jury, you heard me right, it is a case of honour killing.' Something he described as extraordinarily sinister.

"He went on to describe how the couple Saleena Khan and Calvin Lenton were looking forward to spending time with family, celebrating Christmas, either together or with family. But the two victims were found in their flat bludgeoned to death when the police later attended the scene. He described the scene as 'A grizzly and a grotesque crime scene.' The female victim was the separated wife of the accused Nawaz Khan.

"He went on to say in his opening statement that Saleena Khan fleeing domestic violence was not an audacious act, but a very courageous act for a woman having to leave home. He told the jury of six men and six women, Saleena was one remarkable lady. Her charitable work she involved herself in from when she was a teenager was not only praised by all her colleagues but by no less than the President of Uganda Augustus Otambu, an accolade very few receive. She returned to UK to obtain a divorce from her husband Nawaz Khan so she could marry her friend Calvin Lenton. The Crown's case is that the two accused made

a tacit agreement to eliminate Saleena who had become a thorn in their side. The motive for the crime was protection of their 'family honour'.

"Today, much of the day was taken up with court procedure and Crown's opening statement. The Crown did call their first witness Mrs Raazia Khan, the sister of Saleena. She gave evidence to the court setting how she and her sisters were forced to marry at the age of sixteen by their parents. The marriages were all arranged by them. She told the court her sister Saleena did not want to marry Nawaz Khan but had been forced into marrying him. Nawaz was described as a man of perfidious character. That is as far as she got with her testimony to the court as an application was made by Mr Josiah Griffidam QC for legal argument he wished to put before the Judge trying the case, Judge Sir Christopher Norrington QC finished the day at court when he adjourned the case to listen to legal applications the following day. The case continues. Reporting for BBC News this is Sean Denton at Manchester Crown Court."

Abdel turned the television off with the remote control, got up off the bed, changed from a bathrobe into jeans and T-shirt and walked to Papaji's room to see if he was ready to go out to eat. Papaji opened the door with a grim look on his face. He was not in a good mood, he confessed that night. Apart from the fact that his arthritis in the knees was playing up something rotten, sitting in one position most of the day had not helped. He'd rather prefer not to go out as he did not feel like eating out. Abdel would not settle for that response from his Papaji as hotel rooms can be terribly lonely, so he forced him to join him for a meal as he did not fancy eating by himself either. Abdel drove to the Royal Nawaab, a splendid Indian restaurant out on Stockport Road. Both avoided talking about the case that evening whilst they enjoyed the good food there. The conversation was dull, mostly discussing the weather and the food they liked to eat. For Abdel, the subject matter of the conversation was not important. It really did not matter to him what they talked about; the important thing was he was with his Papaji spending lost time.

Day 2 at the Crown Court. It was 10:00 a.m. The usual court formalities completed, everyone was seated. A hushed court waited for Mr Griffidam to rise to his feet to make his application. He waited for the Judge to indicate his readiness to hear him.

"Good morning, Mr Griffidam. I will hear you in a moment." The Judge turned sideways looking directly at the jurors. "Members of the jury, Counsel Mr Griffidam wishes to make an application on a legal issue and has requested what is called a *voire dire*, which is a trial of an issue to be decided within a trial. In other words, if there is a matter of law to be decided upon in a trial, it is my job to deal with that matter, not you. I am going to ask you members of the jury, therefore, to step out to your jury room for me to deal with the issues raised by Counsel. Usher, can you lead them out to their room, please?"

As the jury members were making their way out, it provided a momentary break for everyone. There was some chatter in the courtroom. Some started fidgeting and moving about even though it had not been long people had taken their seats. The public gallery had no vacant seats left today. Last night's national news gave the case wide publicity. It had attracted interest from others who had come in to the courtroom to listen to the case. Some people were standing at the back of the courtroom, others were simply crouched down on the steps just in front of the public gallery area. The courtroom fell in complete silence as the hushed court waited for counsel to make his application. Raazia sat in the witness box looking perplexed. She sat and listened.

Mr Griffidam rose to his feet.

"My Lord, the disclosure material has Mrs Khan's two section 9 statements, one taken in 1997 and another one taken recently this year which no doubt His Lordship has read."

The judge nodded

"She discloses the fact that my client, Nawaz Khan, had been arrested and goes on to disclose his convictions. If the jury were allowed to hear his previous history, My Lord, that I believe may have a significant prejudicial effect on the fairness of the trial. His Lordship is aware that he has pleaded not guilty to the instant charge. He denies the charge. Were that information to be introduced to the jury, they may well feel that the man has 'form' which inevitably may lead to, shall we say, 'colour' their minds. I therefore make an application that any reference that this prosecution witness has to state any information connected to my client's previous convictions and any predisposition to violence not be permitted to be mentioned in court for the jury to hear. I make the application under Section 78 of the Police and Criminal Evidence Act 1984 in that the admission of such evidence would have such an adverse effect on the fairness of the proceedings that the court ought not to admit it. I would consequently ask that His Lordship exercise his discretion given the circumstances of this case and the gravity of the charge facing him not to admit his past record. Thank you My Lord."

"Thank you, Mr Griffidam. Mr Peggs-Green, before I hear Mr Ravenstone, perhaps I would like to hear your position which will then give Mr Ravenstone opportunity to address your issues, if any."

"My Lord, thank you. Whilst I concur with my learned friend's application entirely, my client Mr Rehman does not have any previous convictions or any arrests prior to the instant charge of conspiracy. Though I say that as the two accused are related, father and son-in-law, I venture to think perhaps the admission of such evidence may indirectly affect my client's position, Your Lordship. That is all I have to say on the matter. However, I do, My Lord, have another application to put before His Lordship."

"Yes, Mr Peggs- Green?"

My Lord, the application is for His Lordship to consider a no case to answer. It seems a convenient time for me to make this application and that is for the case to be dismissed as there is no case to answer against Faizali Rehman. The evidence relied on by the prosecution is purely circumstantial. There is absolutely no cogent or indeed sufficient evidence, in my view, sufficient to discharge the required burden of proof in criminal cases. The evidence falls far short of the standard of proof required to prosecute in this case."

"Well, Mr Ravenstone, both applications prima facie appear to be valid applications," the Judge stated.

"Thank you, My Lord. Well, the accused Nawaz Khan without a doubt has a predisposition to violence. Saleena Khan had been so violently assaulted by him in 1990 that she ended up in hospital. Raazia over there travelled to see her sister following a desperate mayday phone call to her from Saleena the night she had been assaulted. The police had been called and indeed he had been arrested. Subsequently, in fact, Saleena had gone to court on the day of his trial for assault occasioning actual bodily harm. Nawaz had previously pleaded not guilty, My Lord. Upon seeing his wife at court to give evidence, he changed his plea to guilty. How is Mrs Khan here going to know or, indeed, avoid telling the court the factual information which is within her knowledge? I accept that she can be told not to mention any convictions when giving her evidence. Nevertheless, it is a fact, that he was arrested by the police. That information, My Lord, is not only pertinent but probative to the fact and charge. This accused had a predisposition to violence such that he battered his wife and put her in hospital. It was not just one occasion, he had assaulted the victim Saleena Khan, My Lord, but on numerous occasions. My application is that the case undoubtedly raises an issue of predisposition to violence, such extreme violence in point of fact, that the two have a close nexus, so close that one cannot escape it."

"My friend Grace was killed by her husband and the law did nothing about it. There is no justice for women," Nadine shouted from the gallery. She had tears in her eyes as she said those emotive words.

"I will not have any outbursts in my courtroom from the gallery, do you hear? Otherwise you will be removed from the court. I understand the case raises emotions but the emotions cannot cause distractions in my court, understood?" Judge Norrington stated firmly.

He nearly used his gavel to strike on the wooden block but resisted the temptation as he could see the woman having the outburst was not just emotional but a white female in her fifties dressed impeccably. She had reminded him of his late mother who had participated in the suffragette movement.

"Mr Ravenstone," the Judge said.

"My Lord, thank you, as I was saying, there is such close similarity in the type of violence used in the earlier case when Mrs Khan ended up in hospital; the weapon there was a cricket bat, and it appears a blunt heavy object was used in the Christmas incident. I am not saying he is guilty of murder, but Your Lordship will hear evidence from this Crown witness of a conversation she overheard that there was an agreement between the two accused to conspire to kill the two victims which will be probative evidence the Crown would say would prove the charge. In addition, my learned friend will have seen in the bundle of evidence, telephone call records from the home telephone line of Nawaz Khan to Mr Rehman's landline. Several calls were made just prior to the victims being killed in suspicious circumstances. There would have been no reason for those telephone calls as Saleena had left her husband several years ago and was seeking a divorce from Nawaz Khan. There is *prima facie* sufficient evidence to prove the charge, My Lord, given the circumstances of the case, especially there being a strong indication of an honour killing."

"Thank you, Mr Ravenstone. Anything further either of you would like to add by way of response? Here's your opportunity to say so before I make my decision."

"No further observations from me, My Lord," said Mr Griffidam.

"My Lord, whilst I hear the argument articulated by my learned friend Mr Ravenstone for the Crown, the evidence against Faizali Rehman falls well below the required standard of beyond a reasonable doubt. All they have is a conversation his daughter overheard and a few phone calls, nothing else."

"I shall rise now and we will break for lunch for one hour as it is very nearly 12:30 p.m."

"All rise." The usher's voice reverberated in the courtroom as everyone stood up from their seats as did the reporters who as usual dashed out of the courtroom at speed to follow up on their stories.

Abdel and Papaji went for lunch to the same park as yesterday.

"Did you follow what was going on in the court today, Abdel? I had switched off after a while as my knees had begun to hurt something rotten. They felt frozen as I could not move them. All I could do was silently sit there in pain and twirl my *tasbee* remembering Allah. I tried to make eye contact with Raazia whilst those barristers were talking in their legal language, but she would not even look at me once. I am an old man. Surely she can't put me through all this. Can't you speak to her, Abdel?" Papaji groaned as he massaged his left knee with his hand whilst they sat on a bench in the park conversing with each other. The park was busy as usual as it was a beautiful summer's day. The sun was shining bright. The warm air mingled with a slight cool breeze made it a pleasant afternoon.

"Papaji, she is a witness for the prosecution. I cannot interfere with a witness as I would get arrested by the police."

"Speak to Akeel then; he will listen to you."

"I will try, Papaji, but I can't promise anything."

"Well, at least speak to him, and see if he can talk to his wife."

"Nawaz has convictions and his barrister does not want the jury to know that he has been in trouble with the police before so he has asked the judge to direct Raazia not to give evidence about that, as if the jury hear that he has criminal convictions, they may draw their own conclusions about that which might not be good for you as you are jointly charged with him. As for your barrister, he has asked the judge to dismiss the case against you as there isn't enough evidence against you for the conspiracy charge. He is doing his job, Papaji. Andrew Stanton said he was a good barrister; that is why I have hired him for you."

"I am placing all my faith in Allah. He will look after me."

Papaji had a triple ploughman's sandwich today. He must have enjoyed eating it as not only he ate it quite fast but was picking the crumbs from the packaging and popping them in his mouth too. Next, he gulped down his can of

Coke pretty fast. They walked back to the court at a slow pace after finishing their lunch in the park.

"Mr Peggs-Green, to my mind, there is a prima facie case to answer. I therefore refuse your application for no case to answer. Mr Ravenstone and Mr Griffidam, I will allow admission into evidence of the arrest but not Nawaz Khan's previous convictions for now. Should he choose to give evidence and should he happen to attack the character of Crown witnesses, then it may be a different story. Now we continue with the evidence of Raazia Khan who has patiently been waiting to continue. Mrs Khan, the court apologises for having to keep you waiting, but now that the legal arguments are out of the way, would you please continue with your evidence to the court."

All three barristers stood up and acknowledged the Judge's decision with a bow. The jury returned back into the courtroom as Mr Ravenstone waited for them to take their seats before continuing. Once seated, he rose to his feet and continued with his examination-in-chief.

"Please continue, Raazia," Mr Ravenstone said.

"We were strangers in the city. After seeking directions, we got to the hospital. When I first saw Saleena, my heart sank. I thought she was going to die. A bandage was wrapped round her head, which had a dry blood stain on the side of her head. Her face was severely bruised. My reaction was I burst into tears when I saw her. 'Oh my God, what has that bastard monster done to my sister,' I said to my husband. 'Just look at her, Akeel, she looks as though she is going to die,'" Raazia said as her eyes filled up with tears.

Then she began to sob uncontrollably. The judge indicated by his hand motion to the usher to assist her. In a hushed courtroom, all you could hear was Raazia sobbing. The court usher went across to Raazia to hand her a box of tissues.

"Mrs Khan, I am sorry to see you so upset. Would it help for you to have a short break? Maybe you can have some refreshments. Courts aren't the most wonderful places to be in when you are giving evidence of the type you are giving."

Raazia nodded as she wiped her tears away then blew her nose. The judge ordered a short recess. The court usher helped her to the court cafeteria where Raazia got a cup of tea. She soon gained her composure and was ready to proceed.

"Thank you, My Lord, for the break," Raazia stated.

"Very well, Mrs Khan. Are you ready to continue?" Judge Norrington asked.

"Yes, I will continue. Thankfully Saleena recovered. A very kind doctor, I believe her name was Dr Katherine Chang, treating her at the hospital had made a phone call to a local women's refuge organisation. The doctor had strongly advised that Saleena remove herself from home otherwise she would end up a domestic violence statistic on the Home Office records. A woman from the refuge, Maleeka, came to see Saleena at the hospital the next day. The refuge was marvellous. They helped Saleena enormously and she managed to get away. Saleena moved to Leeds sometime later. With the help of the refuge, she got a place in Woodhouse and a job. Initially, she worked at a school as a TA, teaching assistant, for a while, then she got a job with the Red Cross. An opportunity to work at a children's refuge in Uganda came up. She told me on the phone she was so excited about it that she accepted it without giving it a second thought. 'I will be far away from Nawaz. I will be safe,' were the words she used."

"My Lord…" interrupted Mr Griffidam.

"I know, whilst technically the words are hearsay, the words are of a deceased individual, Mr Griffidam, and as the words are within the knowledge of the witness giving evidence, I am inclined to allow it. You may note it down for your appeal if there is to be one."

"My Lord," Mr Griffidam acknowledged.

"Please continue, Mrs Khan, remembering not to say what in evidence what someone else has told you," the Judge directed.

Raazia was even more confused now. Her train of thought had gone right off the rails as she could not think straight. Her stomach began to churn. She knew that was not a good thing.

"Well, err…like I said, Saleena had made up her mind to go to Uganda. When she got to Kampala, she rang me to say she had arrived there safely. I told her to call me every day if she could to let me know how she was doing. She phoned me when she could."

"What did she do there, Mrs Khan?" asked Mr Ravenstone.

"Saleena worked for an orphanage, called the Raffiki Orphanage Centre in a small town called Soroti. My sister Saleena was one outstanding person with a good heart. There she worked at a refuge for children. From her teenage years, she loved doing charitable work. From the age of about ten, she busied herself raising money for different charities. After school had finished, she would often visit elderly folk nearby where we lived in Leicester, particularly at Christmas time. Oh, she was full of life, vibrant; she would help anyone in need. She helped out at the local Christian church serving soup in winter months to the homeless and hungry. Even after she got married, she joined Elmwood Church Centre. The lady who runs it, Mrs Nadine Nugent is over there in the public gallery, the lady who spoke out earlier. Her best friend, Grace, was killed by her husband; she was victim of domestic violence. Anyway, Nadine will tell you how she loved working at the Centre in Manchester. This was escapism for her from her tattered marriage and ruined life with Nawaz.

"The violence she experienced at the hands of Nawaz was phenomenal. To avoid getting beaten up, she would barricade her bedroom door with a chest of drawers. Every night she went to bed, she bolted the door from inside first, and then she would empty the drawers, drag the chest of drawers' carcass behind the door to barricade it in attempt to prevent Nawaz getting in. He would often come home late at night, drunk as a skunk and demand sex. If Saleena refused, he would beat her up. The night she called me, Nawaz had forcibly entered her room breaking the door down with a bat, then smashing my sister with it. She ended up in hospital. I swore on my dead mother's grave I would never let her return back home to that *kuta*."

"What does that mean?" the Judge asked.

"Dog, your Worship, I mean My Lord. He was an animal. My father, Papaji, made several attempts to try and get information from me about her whereabouts so that he would put pressure on her to return back home to Nawaz. I refused to give any information to him. Wild horses could not have dragged it out of me. I wanted to protect my sister from harm. My father was relentless. He phoned every single day to ask where she was. I said to him I did not know. All he cared about was his honour, his reputation. 'What will the people in our community say,' he would say all the time. 'Families stick together no matter what. It is our culture; wives should stay at home with their husbands where they belong.'"

"You knew? And you lied to me, Raazia? How could you?" Papaji stood up as he shouted the words from the dock holding his right hand up in the air with his blue *tasbee* between his fingers, waving the *tasbee* about. "*Wallahi!*"

"The defendant in the dock will remain quiet. I have warned a member of the public about outbursts in my courtroom. Any more outbursts or interruptions, I shall have you removed from the court. You, Mr Rehman, if you do not remain quiet will sit in the cell downstairs for the duration of the trial, understood?" the Judge warned him sternly striking the gavel three times on the wooden block looking cross.

Mr Peggs-Green went up to the dock and whispered something to him which was inaudible.

"Mr Peggs-Green, I take it there will be no more outbursts from the accused?"

"I have spoken to him, My Lord, and there will be no more outbursts from him," Mr Peggs-Green responded.

"Before we go any further, I want to know the meaning of the word or phrase the defendant just used," the Judge demanded.

"It means 'I swear to God' My Lord," Mr Ravenstone responded.

The courtroom fell into silence. The Judge was in deep thought. Counsel looked at one another and waited for the Judge to speak. The Judge looked at Mr Rehman and let another twenty seconds or so go by. The silence was eerie. The room was that silent that a pin could be heard drop. Raazia sat there in the witness box looking nervous. Papaji had called her a liar in front of the jury. What would they think of her now and about her evidence? Would they not believe her? She knew he would do something like that in court. The court waited for the Judge to speak. There was a long pause.

"Mr Peggs-Green, I am unhappy with your client. He appears to have made a threat in open court to a Crown witness. We will take a break now, and I would like you to take instructions from him and understand first the context of the phrase or words used before we go any further.

"Yes My Lord." Mr Peggs-Green responded.

"All rise," the usher stated loudly.

Raazia could not speak to anyone as she was still under oath. Papaji had unnerved her to the point she needed words of wisdom from her husband to carry on. She couldn't. Those were the rules by which matters had to be played. Now she was on her own.

As the court reconvened, Mr Peggs-Green rose to his feet to address the Judge.

"My Lord, I have spoken to my client and taken instructions upon the matter His Lordship has raised. The word *'wallahi'* loosely translated means something like 'I swear to God', and here it was not used in the literal context, he assures me. In other words, it was not in any way a threat to Mrs Raazia Khan, he tells me, but in the context of everyday usage that a religious Muslim man would use. He tells me that he also uses other phrases like *Insha'Allah* which means 'God willing', another would be *astagfirullah* which translates 'I seek forgiveness in Allah'. He says he uses these phrases all the time. They are Arabic phrases which have become accepted usage in their language, and it was simply a turn of a phrase similar to, for example, some would use a phrase like 'you are toast' but it is not intended to be used in the literal sense, rather the use of the phrase is in the form of common parlance."

"Very well, Mr Peggs-Green, I will accept the explanation this time round. I warn your client however, that anymore similar outbursts in whatever language will not be used or tolerated."

"I am obliged to His Lordship," Mr Peggs-Green said.

"Mrs Khan, you may now continue," the Judge said.

Raazia was still in a state of contemplation about being called a liar in open court. Lost for words, she looked at the Judge first, then at the row of barristers who were all looking in her direction. Next, she looked at the reporters who had momentarily stopped writing. The public gallery was next as she surveyed the courtroom. She worked through the people seated in rows until her glance became fixed on her husband. Akeel could see his wife had gone blank and was searching for help for what to do next. He knew her mind well. The silence was a distress call. Without being too obvious, Akeel lifted his right arm up to his chest and rested the flat of his palm there. It was a sign. He was there and she needed to show courage in the face of extreme adversity. She remembered what he had said to her that night when Akeel had explained in detail his reasons why she should go ahead with helping the police prosecute Papaji and Nawaz. Raazia became emotional. To Raazia the words used by Papaji inferred a threat of some kind. Being called a liar in open court was disingenuous. She was not happy and could not utter another word.

"I feel given the distraught state of the witness, we better adjourn for the day. Mrs Khan, I remind you that you are still under oath, and so you cannot discuss the case with anyone. We will reconvene tomorrow at 10:00 a.m.," the Judge announced.

"All rise," boomed the usher's voice.

Abdel put his sunglasses on with a white peaked baseball cap covering his face then tried to exit the court quickly with Papaji. Papaji could not walk fast on account of his arthritic knees. They were stiff, and he could not walk even at normal pace as they were hurting him badly. A horde of reporters waiting outside with cameras approached to try and obtain snippets of information with photographers clicking their cameras at a fast pace. The flashing bothered Papaji and he became angry at them asking them to stop pointing the cameras at him. As Raazia exited through the door, they all rushed towards her. Akeel simply said, "No comment," as they walked away.

Abdel and Papaji, by this time, were safely inside a taxi on their way to the hotel. Papaji said he wanted to catch up on his prayers, and then have a snooze as he was very tired, advising Abdel to do the same as it was important Allah is not forgotten in such testing times of difficulties. Abdel put the news on in his hotel room to listen to the day's report. He turned the TV on mute as his mobile phone rang. It was Philip checking on how his friend was doing. They had a chat about the day's events at court. Abdel then spoke to Jacob to ask if the horses were all okay.

Raazia called the twins from the hotel room. They were staying with Sajj who was looking after them with his two children. Akeel spoke to them afterwards telling them he loved them a lot and missed them very much. The twins were in tears as they spoke to the parents. Akeel was on the telephone speaking to them for nearly thirty minutes reassuring them as they had seen the news that day. Later that evening, he decided he was going to take everyone out to an Indian restaurant to cheer them all up after the way things had ended in court today. He light-heartedly complained everyone looked so glum, telling them it was not the end of the world. Nawab's restaurant turned out to be just the place to go for a relaxing meal. It was fairly busy and lively which helped take Raazia's mind off the day in court. Akeel asked for a table for six people. A waiter showed them to their table, handing each one a menu. Once seated, Akeel took charge in ordering the food and drinks. A young Asian waiter stood just behind him with a little notepad writing the order down as Akeel worked through the menu ordering six poppadom's, eight naans, rice, a lamb curry, a chicken tikka curry, aubergine with *aloo* curry and *aloo gobi*. For drinks, he asked the waiter to bring a jug of water and three jugs of mango *lassi*.

"Restaurant is nice, isn't it guys?" Akeel said hoping to get rid of the glumness.

"It is lovely. My husband and I have been here before. The food is excellent. Akeel, you have ordered too much food. Gosh, who is going to eat all that food," Nadine responded.

"Oh, don't worry, I have a big appetite, besides we can always take a doggy bag with us, can't we?" he joked.

"I am worried it did not go too well today. Papaji broke my train of thought when he called me a liar in front of the jury. How am I going to recover from that? It was a gruelling day for me in that witness box. I cannot say I am looking forward to going back to court tomorrow!" Raazia shared her thoughts aloud.

"You better brace yourself for the cross-examination love," Nadine said.

"Raaz, Nadine, it is better not to speak about the case as the judge said. They will ask you if you have discussed it with anyone. I don't want you to stumble. Say it with confidence that you haven't," Akeel advised his wife.

The evening whiled away as the group engaged in small talk. Everyone including Raazia enjoyed the meal. The food was so good they finished it all by the end of the evening as they chatted. Allia, Sameena, Sara and Maleeka were keen to know about Nadine's friend Grace so she regurgitated the story. She told the story in exactly the way she had to Saleena some years ago, as she had done countless times over the years. Apart from Akeel, none of the women had dry eyes when Nadine finished telling the chilling story of her friend Grace, though it helped while away some of the time that evening. Meanwhile, the case was reported on the main news channels:

"It was the second day at Manchester Crown Court for the trial of Faizali Rehman and Nawaz Khan who face a charge of jointly conspiring to kill Saleena Khan and Calvin Lenton. The morning began with legal applications from barristers' details of which we are unable to report due to reporting restrictions placed by the judge. Sir Christopher Norrington QC, the presiding judge, did rule that the case must continue against the two as there was a prima facie case to answer.

"Once the arguments were decided upon by the judge, the principal Crown witness Mrs Raazia Khan was asked to continue with her testimony. She first talked briefly about how her parents had arranged a marriage for her at the age of sixteen, then she talked about her sister's life with Nawaz Khan at length. Tragically, Saleena's marriage was marred throughout by domestic violence and abuse. After she ended up in hospital on one occasion, she sought refuge at a women's refuge organisation in Manchester. She worked for the Red Cross, picking her life up and grabbing an opportunity to go to Uganda to work for Raffiki Orphanage Centre in Soroti looking after children who had lost parents as a result of HIV and AIDS disease which had ravaged the country when many thousand lost their lives during the epidemic.

"As the witness gave evidence about Saleena Khan's life, at the time, neither her husband, Nawaz Khan, nor her father, Faizali Rehman, had known her whereabouts. As she continued with her evidence, there was a sudden outburst from her father, Faizali Khan, accusing her of lying to him when he had asked her where Saleena was and she had apparently told him she did not know. The witness did say that she kept Saleena's whereabouts secret from him as she was protecting her sister from interference from the family. She feared he would put pressure on her sister to return back to her husband which she did not want. The day ended by the witness apparently being unnerved by the outburst. The Judge adjourned the case as the witness apparently could not continue. The case continues tomorrow. This is Sean Denton for BBC News at Manchester Crown Court."

It was late, around 1:00 a.m. Abdel could not sleep. Something was occupying his mind. The two gravest decisions he had to make were whether or not he should claim the lottery jackpot and then afterwards whether to return home to Leicester given Papaji had been furious with him. There was now another dilemma. It began eating away at him. Should he tell Papaji the truth or should he keep quiet for now. At that moment, it was just after 1 a.m. when his phone vibrated which diverted his mind. He wondered if it was Jacob calling him at that time.

"Hello."

"Hello this is Oli, you left me a message. Sorry, I couldn't get back, been working some long hours, weird shifts at the hospital. How are you? Is everything okay with you and your dad? I saw you on telly, on the news, coming out from Manchester Crown Court."

"Yes, everything is fine. I rang to let you know I was staying in Manchester for a few days, same hotel as before. My dad's trial is ongoing at the Crown Court."

"Gosh, I know. He looks frail to me. What has he done?"

"Long story, Oli, but in a nutshell, he has been charged with conspiracy to murder my sister and her boyfriend, jointly charged with my brother-in-law Nawaz Khan."

"You are joking. Oh, it's been dubbed as the honour killing trial by the media. Everyone in the hospital is talking about it. I did not make the connection Abdel, too busy with my work, you know. It must be terrible for you. Sorry to hear, buddy. I guess troubles on the mind preventing you sleeping aye? Listen, I am a great listener. I have a day off tomorrow; I can come over if you like. You don't drink alcohol, do you? Otherwise, I could have brought a bottle of wine. I tell you what, I will grab a pizza and soft drinks and come over. Text me your room number; I will be there in forty-five minutes."

"Good, I will see you then."

It was Day 3 at court. The weather forecast for the day was thunderstorms. The sky looked overcast. Grey clouds covered the sky. This did not bode well for Raazia. Just as the weather seemed ominous, she feared the grey clouds were gathering over her too. Still feeling disjointed in her mind by the previous day's events, it was a day she did not look forward to being in the witness box. The court corridors were wet as people walked in with wet shoes. Water droplets from wet umbrellas dripped on the polished floors. The weather had turned. The courtroom was full. All seats had been taken. Raazia nervously made her way to the witness box. She did not look up towards the dock as she walked past it. She slowly climbed one step up into the witness box safely making her way into position. She began to breathe slowly just as Akeel had advised. Judge Sir Christopher Norrington QC walked into court shortly after her.

"Good morning all. Now that we have the Crown witness here, we need to get moving as we are in the third day of the trial. Mrs Khan, I take it you ready to continue?" Judge Norrington asked her.

"I am, your Worship," Raazia responded nervously.

"It's My Lord, not 'your worship'. Please continue with your evidence."

"When Saleena went to Uganda, she became mother to those orphan children, some of whom were babies. She told me to keep it a secret about Calvin and her. Calvin had proposed to her, and she had accepted to marry him."

"How did you feel about that? He was not someone from your own community. He was different," Mr Ravenstone asked.

"Saleena had had a very rough life. I was happy for her. To me, it did not matter what colour Calvin was. My sister for the first time in her life was happy. That meant a lot to me. Saleena knew without a divorce she could not go ahead with her plans of remarriage, so she flew back to England with Calvin. 18 December was a perfect day for them. Both of them made a trip to London on the train Christmas shopping. She told me on the phone before they went. That was the last time I spoke to Saleena."

Raazia paused. She had tears in her eyes. Judge Norrington waited for her to compose herself.

"I am so sorry, but I cannot help getting upset every time I think about my sister. The next morning, I had been up early as I had lots to do. I wanted to tidy up the house, get things ready for Christmas. I have twin girls, and they were looking forward to Christmas. When we were little, Papaji would never let us celebrate Christmas, not even allow us to be up late to watch television. There were no birthday celebrations for us girls either. For a boy it was different. He had big celebrations planned for Abdel. We wanted to be children, Mr Ravenstone, but we were not allowed to be children. We used to sit there in the sitting room all huddled together under a blanket trying to keep warm in winter months. A small paraffin heater burning on low heat kept us warm. At Christmas time, we would fight for the *Radio Times* magazine to circle with a pen the movies or programmes we wanted to watch over Christmas holidays when schools were closed. As kids, we were excited to be at home looking forward to watching the programmes on television. Papaji would not let us watch anything. There were no celebrations for us, no presents or a special meal. My sister Allia would beg Papaji to at least let us stay up to watch television. She was the toughest of all the siblings, and she would argue with him about how stupidly strict he was. But it did not do any good. My father ruled the roost with an iron rod. There were no birthday celebrations either ever as I recall. The first time that I thought he had arranged a birthday party for me was on my sixteenth birthday."

Raazia's eyes filled up as she wiped those tears away. She blew her nose into a tissue which she crumpled up and put in her coat pocket. To describe her as being emotional would be an understatement. Still fighting back those tears held back of bygone memories, hurtful memories, she decided to carry on giving her testimony to the court. All sorts of words were just swimming around in her brain. Silently she whispered to herself, *Mera dil dookh raha hey mey ini logo ko kiya batawoo. [My heart aches, how could I explain that to them.]*

"I was expecting, for the first time in my life, a birthday present from Papaji, a birthday party. Instead, he announced my engagement on my sixteenth birthday." Again, wiping away those tears, bravely she continued. "I have twin girls. They look forward to Christmas every year. We celebrate Christmas, Mr Ravenstone. I encourage my children to have a full life as children. It gives me joy to see them having fun as children. It helps me relive my childhood through them. They love the dance classes my husband and I have joined them to. We have always had Christmas celebrations in our house now from when the twins were born. I do not see any harm in that. Akeel and I had bought presents for them, and I wanted to wrap them up to put them under the Christmas tree. When I put the radio on, I heard that a man and woman in Woodhouse area of Leeds had been attacked. My heart sank at that point. Something told me it was Saleena. I sat on the chair in the sitting room praying it was not my sister. I later found out it was."

"I am sorry, Mrs Khan, would you like a glass of water? Are you able to continue?" Mr Ravenstone asked.

The testimony given in open court was not just testing but emotionally draining for her. She nodded accepting the kind offer as the court usher walked up to the court clerk's desk to get a glass of water. Raazia had poured her heart out today. She harked back in time in her mind to the day when she wanted to complain in 1972 about her father making her do all the work but Begum had stopped her with the raise of her *chappal*. Today, there would be no such force restraining her. People were amazed hearing a story that would maybe jump out in a Dickensian storybook, not in the twentieth century.

The silence in the courtroom was intense. The sound of the second hand on the clock in the courtroom could be heard ticking away loud and clear as the only sound in a hushed courtroom. The ticking noise seemed to get louder as the seconds ticked by. The women jurors had tears in their eyes, as did many in the public gallery. Nadine fought back her tears too. Judge Norrington QC had been sitting leaning forward as he took notes from time to time of her testimony, leant back at that poignant moment, into his chair. Mrs Khan's evidence had, he could see, reached a point, an emotional crescendo of sadness. The court was suddenly in a dramatically emotional mood. The Judge silently collected his thoughts as he pushed his body as far back into his chair as he could, composing his own thoughts for a minute or two. Then the loud noise of a sudden lightening thunderstorm outside broke the deafening silence of the courtroom as the lights overhead in the courtroom flickered.

"I knew where she was," Raazia said with some gusto in her tone. "Yes, I knew. She was safe there." She maintained her forceful tone, just like the force of the thunderstorm outside, as she leant her body forward. "I was ecstatic for Saleena. She had told me that she wanted a divorce. The proper thing to do was to get a divorce in England. I agreed with her, and I was looking forward to seeing my sister as I had missed her so much. I wanted her to see my twin girls too as they were growing up fast. My sister then decided it was right to return back to England to formally sort out her divorce, and at the same time she could get some presents for the kids at the orphanage centre in Uganda. The kids would love presents, especially from UK. After that, she would be returning to Africa to resume her work with the charity. She and Calvin planned to get married there.

All the time Papaji constantly kept pestering me and all my sisters for her whereabouts and contact details, but we had sworn to each other we would keep it a secret. I know Nawaz had telephoned Papaji many times asking where she was. I will never forget the day when she died. I picked up the phone, dialled her number with trepidation. My heart was beating fast. I knew it was her when a policeman answered the phone. My Saleena was gone." Raazia sobbed loudly. The judge called a short recess.

"Mrs Khan, I am sorry you have to go through this, but it is really important. Can you tell the court what happened about a year later? It was your sister's anniversary of her loss," Mr Ravenstone asked.

"I know it is important, Mr Ravenstone, that is why I am here. It is hard for me. No one can imagine how hard it is for me to be here, but here I must be. That is the will of Allah. Being here talking about the painful moments in my life is like someone driving an arrow through my heart. It hurts. It was a small memorial service for Saleena we had at Papaji's house. We call it 'barsi' in Urdu, a remembrance event on the first anniversary of her death. After everyone had gone, I was in the kitchen tidying up before going home. The door leading to the dining room was ajar, so was the door from the dining room to the sitting room where they were, Papaji and Amii. I heard some raised voices between them. Abdel, my brother, was upstairs. It was, I think, only those two in the room. At first, I took no notice. It's not unusual for couples to argue. I had just about finished all the cleaning up, so I stepped into the dining area. I heard Papaji say, 'Nawaz has been touched. He is asking for the money, £5,000. Where am I going to get that sort of money?' 'Why?' Amii asked him. He said, 'Sorting out the business to do with Saleena.' Amii told him to keep his voice down as I was in the kitchen cleaning up and I might hear them. I could not believe what I had heard. I was so disgusted, I left through the back door without saying bye. I was in a daze, to be honest with you."

"Did DI Slater contact you at some stage?"

"Yes, she did. I was surprised because my understanding was the case had been closed. There were no suspects, no evidence to go on so they closed the case and marked it as a cold case."

"Please continue," Mr Ravenstone said.

"Well, I was in two minds whether to tell the police about what I heard or not for fear of repercussions from the family, especially Papaji. He has been a powerful figure in the family, dominant. We were all scared of him. I have a family now, and I did not want to put my family at any risk."

"What made you change your mind?"

"My husband, Akeel, persuaded me; DI Kiki Slater was very persuasive as well. It was a terrible dilemma. In the end, I had to make a decision. I wanted justice for my sister Saleena. She was a beautiful human being. Her life was cut short so tragically. She did not deserve to die so young. I also want to move on with life; I have a family and am yearning for closure."

"What is *your* understanding of family honour system, Raazia?" Mr Ravenstone asked.

"Well, if you are a girl born in a family led by tradition and culture like ours, you do not have rights. Go against those long-established traditions in any way at all, you get trampled on. The price you may pay would be your life if the family is shamed, and that is not acceptable to the men of the family. What I do know is it is something particular to our culture as you do not hear about it in any other cultures."

"Mrs Khan, thank you. Just wait there, please," Mr Ravenstone said.

Mr Peggs-Green rose to his feet to cross-examine the Crown Witness. He adjusted his wig, then his gown. With both his hands, he took hold of the side lapels of his gown and pulled it down. He stood for a second or two silently looking up at the ceiling of the court. He turned towards Raazia.

"Mrs Khan, were you forced into an arranged marriage?" he asked.

"Yes, I was," Raazia replied.

"You were forced into it and you were not happy about it, that is right, isn't it?"

"That is correct. I was sixteen years of age. In fact, it was on my sixteenth birthday that Papaji announced my marriage without asking me or letting me know first. I was not ready as I was still only a child, and I wanted to carry on with my education."

"That was cut short by the forced marriage?"

"Yes, it was."

"And so, you were very bitter about it? It vexed you?"

"Yes, I was. I did not have a proper childhood. I am not vexed. I have a wonderful husband and twin girls. They are my world."

"What was it you said, let's see now…aah, yes, 'He did not let us have fun as kids.' Christmas time, you and your sisters could not stay up to watch television. No birthdays even. So, you harbour a grudge against your father, don't you, and now you have an opportunity to get even with him, isn't that so?"

"No, that is simply not true."

"It would seem so. You are consumed by anger, and you want to seek vengeance for that, don't you?"

"No, that is not true."

"In any case, if certain things are the way they are, as you put it, and in your culture, it is accepted, or shall we say expected that girls are married off early, why would that have been a surprise to you? Surely you would have expected it to come?"

"I thought it would be different as we live here in England now."

"But it was not, was it?"

"No."

"You were and still are very bitter about it and harbour a grudge against your parents. So much so, that it is fair to say that you want to get even with them now?"

"No, that is not so. I want justice for Saleena. She did not have to die so young."

"When your sister left her husband, she took flight from the matrimonial home. You testified that you knew where she was all the time, that is correct, isn't it?"

"Yes."

"Your father asked you many times, did he not, if you knew where she was, and you said you did not. That is correct, isn't it? But you were not telling the truth were you, as you knew where she was?"

"I wanted to protect my sister, and like I said before, not even wild horses would have dragged that information from me. I made a promise to Saleena that I would keep her whereabouts a secret. There is a difference between telling a deliberate lie and keeping information for a good reason, Mr Peggs-Green."

Akeel smiled. He loved the answer his wife had just given. He continued smiling.

"Let's get to the night you were in the kitchen when you apparently heard raised voices coming from the sitting room area. First of all, how far is it lengthwise from the kitchen to the dining room would you say?"

"Seventeen feet or something like that. I don't know exactly."

"So, you were away about seventeen feet; there are two walls in the way, that is the kitchen and the dining rooms, is that correct?"

"Yes, but both the doors were open to the rooms."

"I did not ask you that. I asked you there are two walls there, yes, or no?"

"Yes."

"Was the television on in the sitting room?"

"No."

"Are you sure about that? Because your father says he had put the television on that evening after everyone had left the house. You were in the kitchen. Your brother, Abdel, was upstairs in a bedroom. You still maintain you clearly heard their conversation, despite the two walls between you and them and the television being on?"

"Yes, the television was off."

"Okay, Mrs Khan, here is what you said, and I quote: 'I heard some raised voices between Papaji and Amii. Abdel, my brother was upstairs, I think, it was only those two in the room. At first, I took no notice. It's not unusual for couples to argue. I had just about finished all the cleaning up, so I stepped into the dining area. I heard Papaji say 'Nawaz has been in touch. He is asking for the money, £5,000. Where am I going to get that sort of money?' 'Why?' Amii asked him. He said, 'Sorting out the business to do with Saleena.' Amii told him to keep his voice down as I was in the kitchen cleaning up and I might hear them. I could not believe what I had heard.'

"You used the words 'I think' so you were not sure it was just your parents. Is it possible that you say that because the television was on?"

"No."

"I put it to you that the TV was on and you are not sure about that."

"The TV was not on."

"So, you remember clearly word for word as you have said, do you?"

"I have been thinking about nothing else but what I heard that night, Sir."

"This honour issue is a figment of your imagination, is it not? This is a perfect opportunity for you to punish your father for taking your childhood away from you and your education too."

"No, it is not. That is not true."

"Thank you, Mrs Khan. I have no further questions."

Mr Griffidam rose to his feet for his cross-examination of the Crown witness. He stood straight, arms behind him, his left-hand fingers locked together with his right-hand fingers.

"Mrs Khan, what do you think about your brother-in-law, Nawaz khan?" he asked.

"What do *I* think of him? Raazia asked.

"Yes, that is my question."

"I hate him. He is a scoundrel and a bastard. Please excuse my language, Judge," Raazia responded.

"You hate him? Those are the words you just used. Emotive words, Mrs Khan. So, you want to exact revenge, do you? This trial is all about getting even with him, isn't it?"

"No, my aim is to get justice for Saleena. The evidence is there. Why would he keep contacting Papaji all the time after Saleena had left?" Raazia asked.

"I am asking the questions in cross-examination of your evidence you have given to this court. You are in the witness box to answer *my* questions, not the other way round, Mrs Khan. What is the evidence? Your recollection of telephone calls between the two defendants in which you don't know what they talked about, do you? Unless the line had been bugged by you? What else? Oh yes, your recollection of the conversation on that night when you were in the kitchen. You used the words 'I think' they were alone. So, you are not sure about your evidence, are you? Have you any cogent proof or is it a hunch you have?"

"He has my sister's blood on his hands, I tell you."

"That is pure wild speculation on your part," Mr Griffidam retorted.

"No Sir, it is not. I know the type of animal he is, and he would do anything to get his hands on drugs and money. If you had seen my sister that night when she was black and blue, you would know what an animal he is. Who would do such a horrible thing to a woman?"

"You have described him as 'an animal', so you are yearning for him to pay for what you think he has done to her?"

"Yes, I do, to be perfectly honest, and I do stand by my opinion of him as being an animal."

"So, you are motivated by hate and anger and your profound desire that he should pay for being, perhaps, a bad husband?"

"No, that is twisting things. He is guilty. He has had a hand in killing her, I tell you."

"You are trying to play God here aren't you, Mrs Khan? Vengeance shall be mine sayeth the Lord. Thank you, Mrs Khan. That will be all."

"Do you wish to re-examine your witness, Mr Ravenstone?" Judge Norrington asked.

"Yes, I do, My Lord," he said rising to his feet, adjusting his wig with the palm of his hand.

"Raazia, I have just one question, you are one hundred percent clear about what you heard that night?"

"I am, Sir."

"Thank you, Mrs Khan. Does My Lord have any questions?"

"No, I do not have any questions. Mrs Khan, you will be pleased to hear that you are done, and madam, you are excused. We are adjourned for the day. We will have a prompt 10:00 am start tomorrow," the Judge said as Raazia stood up and made her way out of the witness box, relieved it was over.

"You are no daughter of mine, such shameful behaviour," Papaji shouted at Raazia as she walked across the courtroom towards the public gallery. The Judge pretended he did not hear the remarks.

Later that evening, Abdel returned to his room after having had a takeaway evening meal with Papaji in his room. Papaji was unusually quiet. He kept rubbing his knees continuously. Abdel expressed to him that he would try to find a specialist for him after the trial was over to see if he could get some relief from the excruciating pain. He said he knew a doctor at Manchester Hospital so would make enquiries. Papaji wanted to be left alone that evening. He said he wanted to have a private conversation with *Amii* so Abdel left the room. He took the elevator then walked along the long hotel corridor leading to his room admiring some of paintings that were hung on the walls. Some were paintings of flowers, others displaying themes of the four seasons which brought a slight smile to his face.

Abdel took his T-shirt and jeans off once inside his room. He grabbed a bathrobe from the shower room, put it on, then jumped on to the bed and grabbed the TV remote from the side cabinet. His phone rang. It was Oli.

"Hey doc, how are you?"

"I am good, thanks, Abdel. I popped into court today for an hour. I had to stand as I could not get a seat. The place was crowded. The case seemed interesting though. Did your dad do it then?"

"Oh, I did not see you. You are right, the place was crowded. No, he did not do it; that is why he pled not guilty."

"Wow, seems there were some heavy guns in there."

"Heavy guns, Oli?"

"All those QC's, you know. My dad was a QC. He died a couple of years back. He wanted me to be a lawyer like him, but I chose medicine, much to his dislike. My father was good buddies with guy called Lord Osgathorpe. He was a bigshot barrister, retired last year, loads of money. His son Oliver was at university with me. He is a real character that lad. He is into horseracing bigtime, makes heaps of money, good-looking guy and very much into good-looking young guys too."

"Oliver Osgathorpe, did you say?"

"Yes, do you know him? He is from your neck of the woods, somewhere rural in Leicestershire."

"I don't know him really. He bumped into me at Cheltenham race course in April, gave me his card."

"Well, my boy, there is a reason why he gave you, his number! A word of warning though, be careful. He is helluva shrewd businessman; some of his methods, shall we say, are a bit questionable. He is cunning and ruthless at the same time."

"Okay, thanks for the warning. Oli, I don't mean to change the subject, but would you by any chance know a good rheumatologist at all? My dad has terrible arthritis in his knees. He seems to be in excruciating pain a lot of the time. The tablets he takes are no good anymore."

"What's he takes?"

"Prescription medication called indomethacin and 400 mg of ibuprofen daily."

"Okay, let me speak to colleagues, do some digging around and I'll text you the details. I am back on duty at the hospital tomorrow, so I'll give you a call in a couple of days' times, okay chap? Take care of yourself. Bye."

Abdel had missed the news so he skipped channels on the remote to find BBC 24-hour News channel. He pushed his body back on the bed, plumped all the pillows behind him and waited for the report to come on. He toyed with the idea of calling Oliver Osgathorpe but decided against it remembering Oli's words to be cautious. He just wondered about the racing interest side of it. It would also be good to see his horses. He put his phone on the bed and turned the volume up to listen.

The news on BBC channel was reporting on the NATO-led United Nations peacekeeping force's joint operation entering the province of Kosovo in the Federal Republic of Yugoslavia. Thabo Mbeki had been elected President in South Africa. The channel reported on the first European election to be held in United Kingdom where the country had used proportional representation resulting in 87 members being elected from the UK. The result was also remarkable as the Conservatives had won double the number of seats than they had in the previous election.

"In other news let's go over to Sean Denton in Manchester. He is covering a conspiracy trial where Faizali Rehman and Nawaz Khan have been accused of conspiring to murder Saleena Khan and Calvin Lenton whose bodies were found at a flat in Woodhouse area of Leeds in December 1997. The two accused are father and husband of one of the victims Saleena Khan, and the case has been dubbed as honour killings trial. Sean, tell us what happened at court today."

"Thank you, Fiona. Yes, as you said there, the two accused in the dock are Faizali Khan who is the father of the victim Saleena Khan and Nawaz Khan who

was her husband. They are jointly charged with conspiring to kill Saleena Khan and her male friend Calvin Lenton. They deny the charge. In the witness box giving evidence for the Crown for the last three days has been sister of Saleena, Mrs Raazia Khan. She finished giving her evidence for the Crown today. The witness continued describing the sad state of affairs not just her growing up in a strict house but for her sister Saleena too. She described how difficult it was for them when they were children as her father Faizali Rehman would not permit them to celebrate Christmas; they were not even be permitted to stay up to watch Christmas programmes or films on television. It sounded like a grim tale of children in Victorian times being banished to their rooms.

"She told the court in Uganda, Saleena was much happier. She had met Calvin Lenton there. The only reason she had returned to UK was to obtain a divorce from Nawaz Khan. As she was in UK, she wanted to buy Christmas presents for the children at the Centre where she worked. The witness described how she was busy preparing for Christmas for her family on the morning of 19 December 1997. She said 'When I put the radio on, I heard that a man and woman in the Woodhouse area of Leeds had been attacked. My heart sank at that point. Something told me it was Saleena. I sat on the chair in the sitting room praying it was not my sister. I later found out it was.' The witness fought her tears back. It was an emotional few moments in the courtroom. There were some women, including some jurors who were in tears too. The few moments of intense silence were broken by the sound of the thunderstorm outside as it poured down with rain.

"She described how a year later, after a memorial service held for Saleena at the house of Faizali Rehman on her first anniversary of her death, she was finishing off cleaning that she heard raised voices. She overheard a conversation between her father and his wife about Nawaz Khan had been asking for £5000 to sort out the Saleena business. She told the court that is when she knew that her father had been involved in the death of her sister. As for Nawaz, she said she knew he had been telephoning the house when he had no cause for it.

"She was asked about her understanding of the family honour system. This is what she said: 'Well, if you are a girl born in a family led by tradition and culture like ours, you do not have rights. Go against those long-established traditions in any way at all, you get trampled on. The price you may pay would be your life if the family is shamed, and that is not acceptable to the men of the family. What I do know is it is something particular to our culture as you do not hear about it in any other cultures.'

"Mr Daniel Peggs-Green QC for Mr Rehman and Mr Josiah Griffidam QC representing the two accused were not long on their feet. The cross-examination was short and to the point. Mr Peggs-Green for Mr Rehman under cross-examination asked her directly that as she had a very unhappy childhood coupled with being forced to have an arranged marriage at the age of sixteen that she was vexed. She wanted to get even with her father. She was seeking vengeance and that was the principal reason why she was there and not because of the conversation she heard that night. Testing the witness's credibility, this is

what he said: 'You were and still are very bitter about it and harbour a grudge against your parents. So much so, that it is fair to say that you want to get even with them now?'

"'No. That is not so. I want justice for Saleena. She did not have to die so young.' She denied that her motive was to get even with her father though Mr Peggs-Green maintained she was still bitter against him. Mr Peggs-Green asserted that she had not told the truth to his father when he asked where Saleena was she lied to him.

"Similarly, Mr Griffidam for Nawaz was equally brutal in his cross-examination of Mrs Khan. He asked her if she hated Nawaz. The reply was an unequivocal yes from her. The witness called him an animal. Asked if she wanted revenge, she said her aim was to get justice for Saleena. She alleged he had a hand in her sister's death. There was no cogent evidence to prove that, Mr Griffidam asserted. Mrs Khan stood by her answer. He suggested to the witness that it was a hunch on her part, some wild speculation, accusing her of trying to play God, seeking vengeance, and he concluded before he sat down with the words: 'Vengeance shall be mine sayeth the Lord.' The case continues. This is Sean Denton at Manchester Crown Court."

Day 4 was Thursday. The storms of the previous day had passed. Though the sky was still grey, it was cloudy but dry. The temperature in the morning was around 15 degrees Celsius. Papaji struggled to get ready for court today. Abdel went to his room in the morning to give him a hand to get ready for court.

"I cannot believe what that girl said in the witness box about me, such a shameful girl. I cried in my bed all night last night, saying to Allah that I am old now, I have seen enough. I did my best to bring up all the children. I have been thinking, Abdel. You left a bag of money the following day when you left the house. It was exactly £5,000 in the bag. How did you know about it? Did you hear the conversation I had with *Amii* about the money as well?"

Abdel sat on the floor by his father massaging his knees. He sat in silence not really sure what to say. Was it the right time to confess to him or should he ride it out, he thought, as Papaji's barrister was confident that the jury would not convict on the evidence?

"Abdel, did you hear what I said?" he said sternly.

"Papaji, no I did not hear your conversation, but I left £10,000 that day. I gave £5,000 to *Amii* too."

"*Bhen chod*, she did not tell me you had given her money."

"Papaji, I wanted to leave some money for both of you as a gift that day as I thought it was right to give you some, you know, just in case you needed it for whatever. I thought *Amii* had always looked after me and a little gift would be nice to show my appreciation."

"It still does not make sense to me. I am very hungry this morning. Let us go have breakfast, then see if you can get a taxi, *betta*, as I am struggling to walk today. I am not sure how I will be able to sit in court all day. Now can you get my medication for me, please?" Papaji said.

There were a myriad of different drugs and topical creams in his medication bag. Indomethacin for his arthritis, blood pressure tablets as well as ibuprofen for the pain in his knees. Papaji managed to just about get into the dock slowly, before the Judge walked into the courtroom, though it was a struggle for him to stand. With his left hand, he constantly massaged both his knees. With his right, he had his blue coloured *tasbee* twirling the beads between his fingers continuing to chant, whispering, "*Allah hu akbar.*"

"The Crown calls Ms Maleeka Akbar to the witness stand," Mr Ravenstone QC announced.

Maleeka walked in to the courtroom holding her head up as she shuffled across the courtroom making her way to the witness box. She was a small porky lady who gave the striking appearance of someone who was looking forward to doing this. It was like she was going to be the centre of attraction for all those barristers assembled in court. For her, it was like being on stage for a performance she had rehearsed or at least had that air of theatrics about her. Maleeka was perhaps, sadly, someone who had a dull life, and today, the centre stage would be hers. Undeniably, she would make the most of it. As usual, she had heavy makeup on; bright rose-pink lipstick stood out as her main feature with her jet-black hair tied back, brown-coloured short sleeves chiffon dress which stretched up to below her knees, wearing a heavy necklace made of ivory beads round her neck. Not stunning in anyway but suitably dressed for court. It made David Mutembe smile seeing Maleeka make her way to the witness box. She looked towards the public gallery which was heaving with people eager to follow the day's events. There seemed hardly any room to stand in the courtroom. She smiled at David, who had taken a seat high up in the public gallery so he could be seen clearly. He was wearing his captain's uniform as he did on previous days, which stood out. Recognising him, she acknowledged his presence with a nod. He reciprocated.

Maleeka slowly walked past the dock slightly turning her head towards the two defendants simply throwing a cursory glance from the corner of her eyes before getting to her destination, the witness box. *I hope you regret having a brush with me outside the Magistrates' Court now,* she thought to herself remembering how Papaji had verbally assassinated her character then.

"Will you take the oath on the Bible or the Koran or do you wish to Affirm?" the usher asked.

"I shall Affirm," she said in a clear loud voice looking at the Judge with a beaming smile.

Judge Norrington QC maintained decorum. He stared at the witness maintaining his position of authority. The judge glanced towards the row of Counsel who all seemed to be focusing on the witness's apparent glamorous-style entrance seemingly amused. Mr Ravenstone was on his feet ready for his examination-in-chief of his second witness.

"I Affirm that I shall tell the whole truth and nothing but the truth," Maleeka stated.

"Your full name is Maleeka Akbar?" Mr Ravenstone asked.

"Yes, it is, my dear."

"If you wish to address me, Ms Akbar, my name is Mr Ravenstone. Now can you tell the court how you were acquainted with Saleena Khan?"

"I founded and run a women's refuge called the MWRC which stands for Manchester Women's Refuge Centre. It is a place of refuge for women who are victims of domestic violence. Dr Chang from Manchester hospital one day called me. It would have been the tail end of summer 1990, August, I think it was. She asked me to pop by to see a woman who had been admitted there for treatment. She stated she was a victim of domestic violence. I went the next day. I met Saleena. Her sister Raazia was there; I met her too."

"Go on, Ms Akbar."

"Please call me, Maleeka, my dear, I meant Mr Ravenstone. Well, Saleena was in a right state. She was black and blue that day I saw her. I assumed at the time when I saw her it was bruises acquired from when that husband of hers had bashed her. Saleena confirmed it when she gave a statement to the police afterwards. I have seen some terrible bruises on women who are victims of domestic violence over the years taking in women subjected to domestic violence. Anyway, Saleena had a bandage wrapped round her head with a dried blood stain on one side of her head." Maleeka touched the side of her head pointing where the stain was.

"Saleena could hardly speak, she looked that bad. I spoke to Raazia, her sister, about my organisation and said we could help her. The police were there too, two very young officers. I believe they wanted a statement from her. There wasn't a shortage of people around her wanting to speak to her, to help, I guess. That lady over there from the Church, Nadine, was there too. Saleena was discharged a few days later, and she came to the refuge to stay with us there. I accompanied her to her house to collect some of her belongings. Nawaz was still held by the police so it was safe to go there."

"What was the state of the place like, Ms Akbar?"

"It was a real mess. It was like someone had thrown a grenade there and it had exploded. I remember the door to Saleena's room was broken in two bits, the top half was hanging by a thread, looked as though it was about to fall off. There was debris everywhere. It was really in a mess. There was a blood stain on the carpet in the bedroom, and the telephone was on the floor. I said to Saleena she would do well to be out of there as the place looked really creepy to me."

"Continue please," Mr Ravenstone said.

"Well, Saleena stayed with us for some months. She was a star. It was like finding gold dust. She was a smart, good looking girl. Her previous experience working with charities was invaluable to us. She expanded the facility so we could have more women in. She managed to persuade the Council somehow to give us a grant so we could have an extension built. I had been trying for years and the Council kept saying no every time we applied for it. We were really pleased. Everyone at the Centre was happy, and people working there with me were full of praises for her. She devised a computer system for us making administrative and financial jobs efficient and easy. Previously, we had done

142

them manually which was laborious to say the least. I was glad to have her. She became a close friend to me also. I liked her very much, Mr Ravenstone." Maleeka had tears in her eyes as she recounted the historical facts about her friend. Her mascara began to run making vertical black marks on her cheeks as it ran down her face. "I am so sorry, Judge, I need a tissue please."

"Would you like a short break?" he asked.

"Yes, please, your honour. Look at me, my mascara is all over the place. I need to use the restroom, Sir," Maleeka said as by now much of her mascara was close to running off her face. She looked as though she had poked her face in a chimney full of soot.

"We will have recess for ten minutes," the Judge said.

Maleeka rushed to the lady's room to fix her makeup on her face. Raazia wanted to go help but Akeel stopped her. He reminded her she was under oath. Raazia knew how Maleeka felt for she had been put through the same mill having given evidence already. The last thing he wanted was defence making allegations and suggestions of some sort of 'collusion'.

"Thank you, your honour."

"Ms Akbar, you will address me as 'My Lord'. Very well, please continue."

"I am glad Saleena did not listen to her folks, especially her father and go back to that monster husband of hers."

Nawaz was about to say something. His Counsel could hear a growling noise coming from the direction of the dock. This was the second witness who had made a reference to him being a monster in open court. He turned his head towards Mutembe and stared at him. He turned away restraining himself from any outburst, by which time, Mr Griffidam had gone over to the dock to speak to Nawaz. Whatever he said was inaudible but it did calm him down.

"Can you be a little clearer about what you mean? By her folks, I take it you mean her father, do you?" Mr Ravenstone asked.

"Am I able to say where we were?" Maleeka asked looking quizzical.

"Where did this encounter happen, Ms Akbar; we are all intrigued?" Judge Norrington QC asked her.

"We were outside Manchester Magistrates' Court. Saleena was with me with other women from MWRC. Mr Rehman over there," she said pointing towards the dock, "came over and pushed me hard on my shoulders. Then he said, and I shall always remember what he said to me, 'You women are an affront to our culture poking your nose into other people's affairs. You should mind your own business and stop corrupting my daughter to your nasty ways. *Sharram honi chayey na?* You should be ashamed. Why don't you stay at home with your husbands?' I just walked away without rising to an old man's rantings. He had no clue about victims of domestic violence, I dare say."

"So, what happened to Saleena, did she stay at the MWRC? Did she move on?"

"Saleena relocated to Leeds three months later. With some help from me and Raazia, her sister, she bought a small studio apartment in Woodhouse area in Leeds, close to Blenheim Primary School where she worked for a few months as a TA. Then I discovered her husband was making enquiries about her whereabouts. I let Saleena know about that and told her to be vigilant. She told me she was scared and hated living life on a knife edge. It was fortuitous that the opportunity to work in Uganda came up at that time. Oh, she was so excited about it. She did not give it a second thought. She knew it was her opportunity to get as far away from Nawaz as she could. Saleena packed her things and off she went. We wrote to each other all the time.

"It was the spring of 1997 Calvin had proposed to Saleena, she told me in a letter she wrote. She was ecstatic. Her happiness seemed almost perfect; she wrote. She was, unfortunately, still married to Nawaz, so she returned back to UK to get a divorce from him. So, the next time I saw Saleena was some years later when she flew into Manchester Airport with Calvin in December 1997. She looked wonderful. Her fella was a handsome man. I went to collect them from the Airport. She told me all about him and Uganda. The best bit was she had a standing applause in Uganda's parliament after their President made a speech about her. I could not be more pleased for her, I tell you. It was an amazing achievement for a woman who had gone out there in the wide world by herself getting recognised for the importance of women in society. I also remember Calvin said I was a star and a saviour of Saleena. It made me really proud of her. Her life had been saved.

"To be honest, Mr Ravenstone, it isn't every day something like that happens in a woman's life. Most of the time, sadly, it is a real struggle in life for us in society, especially ours. When something remarkable happens, it makes it all worthwhile, to celebrate such achievement in life. For me, the effort of saving women's lives is very important. But you know, Mr Ravenstone, what this lady Saleena Khan did was not only nothing short of remarkable but it was like icing on a cake, if you like, with double cream on it. I am glad she left Nawaz. I dread to think what would have happened if she had stayed at home as her husband and father wanted. I recommended a solicitor to Saleena. She lost no time in instructing him to file divorce proceedings. I know Saleena and Calvin had gone to London on the train Christmas shopping that day as I had spoken to Saleena on the telephone that morning before they left for London. Oh, she was so excited about buying pressies for those little kiddies in Uganda. Then…"

Maleeka suddenly began to sob loudly.

"Ms Akbar are you all right to continue?" the Judge asked. "Perhaps we should break at this point for lunch.

"All stand." The usher's voice reverberated around the hushed courtroom.

At lunch, Papaji and Abdel were in the park having lunch. A text message from Jacob sounded somewhat urgent. *'Boss if you have a chance, could you call me, Jacob.'*

"Papaji, something urgent has come up to do with work in London. I need to make a call to work. Stay there, I am going to walk for a bit and make the call, okay?"

"Yes, I have a lot on my mind anyway," he responded as Abdel stood up off the bench and then began to walk away from where Papaji was sat on the park bench as he dialled Jacobs's number on his mobile phone.

"Hi Jacob, what's up?"

"Hi boss. I just wanted to let you know some guy called Oliver Osgathorpe, spoke with a really posh accent, came by the estate today, said he was a friend of yours."

"Really, what did he say he wanted?"

"He just said he was in the area on business, called in to say hello. He asked if he could look round the stables. I couldn't say no as he seemed to be the boss's friend. I did not want to get into trouble with you. I hope that was okay, boss? He recognised Antoninus. Said we had some superb horses. He offered me a job as well to go work for him on his farm in Leicestershire. He would double what I was getting here."

"Jacob, what did you say to that?"

"I politely declined saying my folks lived in the area and I did not want to live miles away from them. I also tried getting rid of him saying I was busy as the vet was going to make his usual rounds at any time."

"Smart boy, Jacob, anything else he wanted?"

"No boss, as you were not around, he left."

"I don't know the guy, to be honest. He bumped into me at the horserace in Cheltenham, gave me his card. If he were to come back, tell him I am not around and he should call in when I am back."

"Okay, boss. Sorry if I disturbed you. I thought it was important."

"No, no, Jacob, you did the right thing calling me."

What a bastard, Abdel thought to himself. He was glad he did not call him last night which he nearly did. Abdel got back to join Papaji. As it was nearly time to head back, he urged Papaji to start walking back to the court. All the court users were ensconced back into their seats when the Judge returned into the courtroom.

"Ms Akbar, can you continue from where you left before lunch? You suddenly stopped, became upset," Mr Ravenstone asked.

"Then the next day I found out Saleena and Calvin had been slain. It was horrible. It was the worst day ever in my life. It was so painful to hear the sad news. Judge, I could not believe it. My heart stopped completely when I heard the news. The women at the Centre ran to me, calling an ambulance thinking I had suffered a heart attack. Oh my, I could not stop crying. I was so angry as well. *Why?* I thought to myself," Maleeka said as she wiped the tears from her eyes. "It was the most gruesome thing. I knew then those two idiots had something to do with it. They never left the poor girl be, bastards."

"My Lord really, I object, that is pure speculation on the part of this witness." Mr Peggs-Green protested.

"I concur with my learned friend's objection," Mr Griffidam said as he rose from his seat.

"My Lord, I believe the witness is referring to the instant charges the accused are facing before this court."

"Objection overruled. Ms Akbar what did you mean by your comment?" the Judge asked.

"Well, they are here in court, aren't they, facing conspiracy charges?" Maleeka said.

"Thank you, Ms Akbar, please stay there."

Maleeka took out a small round mirror from her purse and began to fix her makeup. She cleared the dark mascara marks from underneath her eyes, then as she was about to take a tube of lipstick out, Mr Peggs-Green made a sound like he was clearing his throat. Maleeka looked straight at him.

"Oh sorry, my dear, is it your turn now to ask me questions?" she said putting away the tube of lipstick.

"Indeed, it is, Ms Akbar. Thank you for allowing putting questions to you. Is it fair to say you are a feminist?"

"I suppose I am, my dear. Why shouldn't women have equal rights?"

"So, your views of cultures like my client's where men appear to be the dominant species would be what? I can guess but let's draw it out of you."

"I despise them."

"You despise them. Hmm…I see. So, you and Mr Rehman could never see eye to eye, I suppose. I mean agree on your opinions which appear to be, shall we say, miles apart, perhaps quite properly and apparently firmly held by both sides too I hasten to add."

"I don't suppose we would Mr err…"

"Peggs-Green. Well now, so the contretemps with Mr Rehman outside Manchester Magistrates' Court would not be unusual then?"

"What does that word mean, *contry* what?"

"A disagreement."

"No, I suppose not."

"Thank you, Ms Akbar, no further questions."

"Ms Akbar, you appear to have an axe to grind against my client Nawaz Khan. Do you?" Mr Griffidam asked rising to his feet at the same time adjusting his wig with the palm of his hand.

"No, I don't; why would I?"

"You have already made a derogatory reference to him alluding that he was…let's see…" He looked at his notes adjusting his bifocals. "Ahh yes, a 'monster husband' hmm?"

"You do not know what your client Nawaz is like, my dear. He had mistreated Saleena to such extent that he drove her away. Some of the stories she told us at the refuge were horrendously harrowing. He demanded sex all the time and often forced himself on her. She found him repulsive. One day she said to me when we were talking about Nawaz, 'I can feel that horrible man crawling under my skin.' My dear, it was lucky that she got away from him. Had she stayed, she would have been dead."

"I see. Very well as a confessed feminist then, your opinions are profoundly infected by misandry?"

Maleeka scratched her head. She was unsure how to respond. Counsel repeated his question. He rephrased it.

"Do you hate men?"

"No, not all men, only those that beat and abuse their wives." There was a roar of laughter in the courtroom at the remark. Maleeka paused. "Or their partners, and the worst thing is they think they can get away with it, Mr Griffidam. Calvin was a perfect gentleman; he was so sweet and—"

"Thank you, Ms Akbar, no further questions," Mr Griffidam interrupted Maleeka as he resumed his seat.

"Re-examination, Mr Ravenstone?"

"No re-examination, My Lord."

"Ms Akbar, you are excused. Thank you. Mr Ravenstone you have two more witnesses to call for the Crown. I was thinking, if we finished with the witnesses in the morning, then we may be able to get one defence witness dealt with in the afternoon before we break for the weekend, Hmm?" Judge Norrington QC asked.

"May his Lordship Pleases." All three barristers agreed.

"Good, we will adjourn for today."

"All stand," the usher said as the reporters as usual made a dash to the exit door.

The news report from Sean Denton covering the trial for BBC, reported that evening:

"It was day 4 at a packed Manchester Crown Court where Faizali Rehman from Leicester and his son-in-law Nawaz Khan from Manchester are both on trial jointly accused of conspiring to kill Saleena Khan and her lover Calvin Lenton on 19 December 1997. Mr Ravenstone QC for the Crown today called his second witness for the prosecution. She was a short but quite flamboyant woman Ms Maleeka Akbar. She gave her account of how she knew Saleena Khan. She testified that in August 1990 she had been called out to Manchester Royal Hospital where she first met her. Ms Akbar founded and runs a refuge centre in Manchester for women seeking refuge fleeing domestic violence.

"She described the state Saleena Khan was in when she saw her in hospital. 'She was black and blue from the bruises. She had a bandage wrapped round her head with a dried blood stain on one side of her head.' Later on, after Saleena had been discharged, she accompanied Saleena to the house to get some personal items. She described the house to be in a mess. 'It was like someone had thrown a grenade and it had exploded.' She said she remembered the door to Saleena's room was broken in two bits and described the house as a creepy place. She said to the court Saleena was smart and helped the centre expand, introduced a computerised system making it easier to perform administrative tasks. She became emotional at one point as she broke down. The mascara from her eyelashes ran down her cheeks with the tears running down her face.

"The Judge, Mr Norrington QC, granted her a short recess to put herself together. When she returned, she described Nawaz Khan as a monster. She went on to say she was glad Saleena did not listen to her folks, especially her father, and go back to that monster husband of hers. She said she had a brush-up with the defendant Faizali Rehman in September 1990 outside Manchester Magistrates' Court when she said Mr Rehman had accused her of interfering. She alleged he said to her, 'You women are an affront to our culture poking your nose into other people's affairs. You should mind your own business and stop corrupting my daughter to your nasty ways. You should be at home with your husbands.'

"Saleena had moved to Leeds, bought a studio apartment and had made a good life for herself until a few months later there came a point when Nawaz Khan started making enquiries about her whereabouts. That was the point where Saleena took an opportunity to go to Uganda to work at the Orphanage Centre as she would be far away from him. She met a man whilst working there who proposed marriage to her. Saleena returned to UK to obtain a divorce from her husband already instructing solicitors to do that immediately. The witness said she spoke to Saleena Khan in the morning on the telephone. The couple were planning on spending a day Christmas shopping in London. Maleeka Akbar went on to say, 'The next day I found out Saleena and Calvin had been slain. It was horrible. The worst day and Christmas I have ever had in my entire life. It was so painful to hear the sad news. Judge, I could not believe it. My heart stopped completely when I heard the news.'

"At this point, she broke down but went on with her testimony saying, 'It was the most gruesome thing. I knew then those two had something to do with it. They never left poor Saleena be, bastards.' Both Mr Peggs-Green QC and Mr Griffidam QC immediately rose to their feet to lodge their objections to the remark. Mr Ravenstone QC defended the remark his witness made stating that the witness was referring to the charges the two accused defendants were facing in court. The judge overruled the objection.

"Paying tribute to her friend, the witness Ms Akbar during giving her testimony said this: 'When something remarkable happens it makes it all worthwhile, to celebrate such achievement in life. For me, the effort of saving women's lives is very important. But you know, Mr Ravenstone, what this lady Saleena Khan did was not only nothing short of remarkable but it was like icing on a cake, if you like, with double cream on it.'

"Under cross-examination, she came under fire from both the defence Counsel accusing her of misandry, hating men owing to her feminist views, which were misplaced. When Mr Griffidam asked her the question if she hated men, she replied, 'No, not all men, only those that beat and abuse their wives or their partners, and the worst thing is, they think they can get away with it, Mr Griffidam. Calvin was a perfect gentleman; he was so sweet.'

"I understand from my colleagues in Uganda, the trial is being followed very closely over there by the media reporting in extensive detail the trial here in Manchester. The trial continues. This is Sean Denton for BBC News."

Abdel switched the television off. He wanted to call Oliver Osgathorpe, ask him directly why he was poaching his staff in such devious manner, but he resisted the urge as it might be a kneejerk reaction so he decided he would maybe tackle the issue some other time. He had more pressing matters to deal with right now. It did continue to bug him though.

Papaji's health was getting to a point where he was seriously struggling to get ready in the mornings for the trial. The routine of heaving to get up, get ready, get to court and sitting in the dock was taking its toll on him. Abdel wondered if he should ask Mr Peggs-Green to make an application to the judge for an adjournment until say Monday or Tuesday giving him time to recuperate from the gruelling regime of a trial which was incredibly stressful on him. He talked it over with Papaji who was keen in getting on with it. He wanted never to come back to Manchester ever again. Abdel reluctantly agreed.

Day 5 at Manchester Crown Court was another day where the courtroom was packed yet again. Papaji could visibly be seen struggling to get to the dock today. Mr Peggs-Green asked Abdel if his father was all right. Abdel said he was not due to the immense stress of the trial coupled with his arthritis in the knees had become excruciatingly painful. He had spoken to him about it. However, Papaji wanted to get today over and done with as he was looking forward to spending the weekend at home in Leicester. Mr Peggs-Green felt it his duty to bring the issue to the attention of the judge.

"My Lord, before my learned friend Mr Ravenstone calls his next witness, may I seek and ask the court's indulgence, in that my client Faizali Rehman is an elderly man. He suffers from painful arthritic condition in both his knees. I am advised he is in excruciating pain, My Lord, having to stay in one position is difficult for him. Add to that the stress of the trial has been immense on him. He has not instructed me, yet, to make any formal applications to the court, but it would be helpful for the man to have frequent breaks. Perhaps, it may help to stretch his legs as it were. His knees sat in one position are getting locked, I am told."

"I suppose that is a reasonable request, Mr Peggs-Green. I shall be cognisant of the fact as the trial continues on."

"My Lord, I am obliged."

"I call detective Benjamin McLean to the stand," Mr Ravenstone said rising to his feet.

"I shall swear on the Bible as I am a firm Christian believer," he responded in a strong Scottish accent when asked by the usher if he wish to take the oath or affirm. "I swear by Almighty God that the evidence I shall give shall be the whole truth and nothing but the truth, so help me God."

"You are DCI Benjamin McLean CID branch, are you not?"

"Yes, I am, My Lord."

"Can you take us through your investigation in this case, please?" Mr Ravenstone asked.

"I was called out, together with my partner DI Kiki Slater, to a flat in the Leeds area of Woodhouse. It was the early hours of 19 December 1997. Certainly after 2:00 a.m. At first, our investigation focussed on what appeared to be a burglary which may have gone wrong as the occupants of the flat had been disturbed. When we got there, my God, the scene I witnessed was a horrific one. Two bodies were discovered upon arrival at the property, a male and a female lying on the ground. It appeared some kind of weapon had been used, possibly a hammer, in what I can only describe as an orgy of violence where the victims Saleena Khan and Calvin Lenton had been repeatedly bludgeoned. There was blood everywhere in the small studio flat, arterial spurts of blood on the side walls of the flat. It was gruesome."

"Go on, Detective."

"I looked around as one does inspect the crime scene for clues, evidence. I took a look around and saw a window was broken which was used as the entry point into the flat. There were no fingerprints found as the intruder or intruders would most likely have worn gloves. Forensics were called, a thorough search of the area conducted, combing all the surrounding area. We carried on with the investigation for a while. My Lord, there was simply no evidence, clues or leads. The Chief Superintendent made the decision to close the case after some months. The team working on the case, much to their disappointment I hasten to add, were told the case was being shelved as a cold case. Some months later, completely out of the blue, the Chief calls me in to his office to discuss the case. I did. He advised that the case was to be reopened with use of limited resources. Naturally, my partner and I were delighted. We decided to go over all the information again to see if there was anything at all we had missed. We wanted to see if we could establish a line of enquiry."

"And did you?"

"My Colleague DI Kiki Slater went to see Raazia Khan to see if she could tell her anything she might not have before that could provide any clues or new leads."

"Go on, please."

"Well, it was a gut feeling really. We had to look and see if any members of her family could have had something to do with it. It was something we had not given a great deal of thought to before the first-time round. If they had, we would need to follow up that line of enquiry. This was something rather more difficult to ascertain to an untrained eye."

"You mean killings connected with family honour, Detective McLean? If so, this is intriguing," the Judge said.

"My Lord, yes, this was unfamiliar territory for me, I have to say. My colleague had a strong hunch that a possible honour killing could be the motive as she had come across something similar when she was a police officer in South Africa. I was sceptical at first until Mrs Khan made her second statement to us over a year later. We went back to the drawing board. We looked at telephone records for Nawaz Khan, and they show numerous telephone calls made around the time, especially before the killings. These are phone calls from his phone to

150

his father-in-law's number. The victim Saleena Khan had been gone for some years. Therefore, there would have been no particular reason or reasons for those calls. No obvious reasons at any rate. Why would a man contact his father-in-law after all this time? It was a very puzzling question. In this particular case, here was a husband who had a disposition to commit brutal acts of assault on his wife when they were married. Coupled with Faizali Rehman's obsession with his honour issues, it was a matter requiring a close scrutiny from the police investigation point of view. It was a lead for us that we could not ignore."

"Thank you, Detective McLean."

"Detective, now you say there was no evidence found of any sort at the scene of the crime in December 1997, is that correct?" Mr Peggs-Green QC asked rising to his feet as he commenced cross-examination of the witness.

"Aye Sir, that is correct."

"That remained so for some considerable time. There were no clues or leads and the Chief Superintendent decided the file must regrettably be closed?"

"Yes, indeed, Sir."

"Suddenly about a year or so later, completely out of the blue, he calls you back into the office and says you are to reopen the case without giving any reason why. The situation was just the same as when the decision was made to close the file, is that right? Did that not seem odd to you, Detective?"

"It did, Sir. He is the man in charge, Sir. If he is asking to reopen a case, who am I to disagree, Sir. He is the boss."

"Is it possible that there were some, shall we say, external pressures that could be the reason for reopening the case, if it was out of the blue?"

There was a pause there, as it was a good question, which had been on his mind too. David Mutembe began fidgeting. His breathing got heavier as the stress levels suddenly rose up causing him to perspire. He turned his body sideways, stretching his right leg outwards, fishing out a white handkerchief out from his pocket he then used to wipe the sweat off his brow. The chap sitting next to him, a middle-aged English fellow with a beard whispered, "It's hot in here, isn't it?" David simply nodded as Judge Norrington looked in their direction in a quiet courtroom which was waiting for Sherlock to respond to the question he was asked. David was extremely uneasy at that very point. Did he slip up somewhere? If he did, the President was not going to like that. Did this lawyer know something with his clever esoteric line of questioning or was he simply fishing? More to the point, did the detective know the case had been reopened at his President's request? How could he possibly know that? An uneasy few moments passed by for Mutembe as Counsel waited for a response.

"Err...Detective, why the hesitation?"

"Sir, that is a question for the Superintendent who made the decision to reopen the case, not for me, Sir," he responded.

Mutembe relaxed hearing the response, as his breathing started returning back to normal. He thought a break for refreshments would be very welcome. No sooner did he think that, Judge Norrington adjourned for a short refreshment recess.

He sat sipping his tea in the court cafeteria which was heaving with people vying for a drink. Maleeka walked with Nadine over to Mutembe.

"Hello, stranger, how are you, my dear. Do you remember me and my friend Nadine?" Maleeka asked as she began to prim her hair with her fingers.

"How could I forget you lovely ladies?" Mutembe said as he stood up from his seat.

"See Nadine, I told you he is a real gentleman. How do you think the case is going?"

"It is going very well, I think. Your evidence was very good, credible I thought. I am happy that you did not mention our little meeting in McDonalds. I think time is ticking on, ladies, c'mon we best get back into court before we lose our seats. We can talk over lunch."

"So detective, as I was asking you before recess, the decision came out of the blue to reopen the case, but once reopened, you focussed your enquiry on the possibility of family members having to do something with the killings. Why did you not consider this line beforehand when you started the investigation? Could it be that that line of enquiry was also a dead end for you rather than the explanation you gave which was, and I quote, 'This was something rather more difficult to ascertain to an untrained eye'?"

"No Sir, that is not the case."

"You conducted recorded interviews with Mr Rehman at the station, is that right?"

"Yes, My Lord, we did. He denied he had anything to do with it."

"Did you conduct a search at his house and did you find any evidence of the conspiracy?"

"No Sir."

"Did you find any money, say £5000, at his house?"

"No, we had not conducted a search."

"Thank you, Detective."

"After you arrested Nawaz, did you interview him?" Mr Griffidam asked rising to his feet from his seated position."

"Yes, we attempted several interviews with him."

"What did he say?"

"All the interviews were 'no comment'."

"How long in total, Detective McLean, was he at the police station in the cells?"

"A hundred and twenty hours, which included a three-day laydown from the Justices in Manchester."

"And you still did not obtain a confession from him, did you?"

"No Sir."

"You wanted to close the enquiry quickly as you were under pressure to do so, were you not?"

"Yes, we had a timeline, but I assure you, Sir, we had conducted our enquiries diligently."

"Of course, you did, Detective. My client continually and steadfastly denied any involvement as he had nothing to do with it. His wife had gone. She had left him. Why would he go to those lengths to enter into a conspiracy to have her killed? It is preposterous situation, isn't it?"

"No Sir, not as preposterous or fanciful as you think."

"Detective, let us look at the phone calls Nawaz Khan supposedly made to his father-in-law. You surmised that there would have been no particular reasons for him to call. That is simply speculation on your part, Detective, isn't it? You are guessing as opposed to having hard evidence. These phone calls could have been about anything at all, hmm?"

"I stand by the answer I gave earlier. For the record sir, the man's wife had left him. There was no longer a father-in-law and son-law-law relationship there. Why would he make, not one, but several calls to his house? That is highly suspicious."

"No Detective, highly speculative. No further questions, Detective, thank you."

"I feel it convenient for us to break for lunch before you call your next witness, Mr Ravenstone. I feel though it may be a tad early, I am minded to break now for lunch, also being cognisant of Mr Peggs-Green's observations from this morning," the Judge stated.

"All rise."

It was Friday today and Papaji was concerned about missing his important *juma* [Friday] prayers he could not attend. He blamed Raazia for this stating she will get the *gunah* [sin] for him missing Friday prayers. Abdel could not persuade him to go the park today; they ate lunch in the court cafeteria, instead, as Papaji wanted to perform his afternoon prayers. Abdel made enquiries with one of the court ushers who kindly found an interview room for him to use as it would be private.

David invited Maleeka, Nadine, Raazia, Allia, Sameena, Sara and Akeel for lunch. David hailed a black cab; it was a bit tight but all eight got in. Akeel sat in the front passenger seat. It was barely a three-minutes ride to Tariff Street. The taxi stopped; all eight passengers disembarked outside Taff Café. They stepped into the café. The place was getting busier as it was approaching lunchtime. Tariff Street was busy too with traffic. Some cars were honking their horns as some cars had stopped on double yellows lines others double parked blocking the road. It seemed a popular place for people, maybe workers, from nearby popping in for lunch. David asked everyone to go find a vacant table. He walked up to the front counter, placed an order for eight specials of the day, paid for it and returned back with a flag with number '9' printed on it in black. He placed it in the flower vase on the table. Akeel stood up to make an offer to pay.

"Don't worry, this is on me, Akeel," David said to Akeel as they shook hands.

"Thank you, but you don't have to, please," Akeel responded.

"It is an honour for me, I assure you, to be seated with our Saleena's family. Now sit please." Akeel sat down. "I know all of you here except these three ladies. I am David Mutembe, aide and security to President Otambu. You are?" he said in his African accent.

"I am Allia."

"I am Sameena."

"Sara."

"I am pleased to meet you all," he said as he shook hands with the trio. "You must be all—"

"Order for table 9," a loud voice bellowed from behind the café collections counter.

David went and fetched the tray of lunch with cans of Pepsi. He handed everyone at the table their lunch. It was cheese and beans toasties with salad in a small plastic tub all on a plate. He sat down too and tucked into his toasties which had steam rising from it.

"Oh, this food here is so delicious," he said taking a bite into the piping hot sandwich.

"How did you find this place?" Maleeka asked.

"It was by chance only. On Monday, I was walking around looking for a place to eat. I was asking the locals…" He took another big chunky bite into his toastie. It was hot so he began to blow air from his mouth to cool it down. It made everyone chuckle. "A young English man said to me, 'Try the Taff Café, it is good.' So, I have been coming here for lunch every day."

"My, you must be very hungry?" Nadine said.

"Yes, I am," he said as he tossed the last chunk of the first half of the toasties into his mouth licking his fingers.

"You are funny man. You must have an asbestos mouth shoving all that piping hot food in it," Akeel commented as he chuckled.

"Oh, I eat heat hot as well as spicy Indian food. I love it. Oh, I am so sorry ladies, where are my manners? I left my sentence halfway speaking to those ladies over there. I apologise. I was too hungry to delay collecting our order when it was ready. So, I was thinking, you three ladies must be Saleena's sisters, correct? I can see the resemblance."

"Yes, we are all sisters. We have heard about you and have to say we are, well, kinda intrigued about you being here. Don't get me wrong, we are delighted that you cared for our sister and it is probably down to you we are all here, I guess," Allia said.

"Ah, it is a real honour for me. Do you know how much our country appreciated Saleena? And what she did for our children was just amazing. We miss her terribly. We will make sure there is justice for Saleena. It cannot be right for her not to have justice."

"I am with you all the way," Nadine said.

"What about Calvin, David?" Maleeka asked.

"She is the one with an inquisitive mind!" Nadine said.

"How do you mean?" David asked.

"We are not sure about his family. No one is here for him. We were just wondering why that was. We thought someone might be here for him, my dear."

"Calvin was my brother. My mother is the President's sister."

Everyone at the table fell silent.

"Oh David, we are so sorry," Maleeka responded.

"If you are all finished eating, we must make our way back to the court so we can have seating space. This case has been widely reported here and in Uganda as well," David said, exercising restraint from being emotional.

"Thank you so much for buying lunch," everyone said.

It was a beautiful dry day; the sun was out. They walked down Tariff Street, turned left into Dale Street, walked all the way down the street then left at the end into Ducie Street, crossing Piccadilly into Minshull Street to the Crown Court. David briefly spoke to Sara as they walked about the bruises she was displaying on her face. Sara did not give much away though David was astute enough to pick up she was being bashed by her husband or boyfriend.

By the time they returned to the court, most of the seats had been occupied. They all had to sit scattered about.

"All rise," the voice of the court usher boomed in the courtroom ceremoniously ensuring Sir Christopher Norrington QC's entrance into his court.

"I call DI Kiki Slater to the stand," Mr Ravenstone said.

Kiki walked into the packed courtroom, surprised to see how full the court was. She knew from the news reports that the case had attracted national interest and she had observed from the waiting area outside where she had waited her turn to be called all week, people vying to get in, though seeing it with her own eyes took her aback slightly. She quietly walked across the courtroom making her way to the witness stand. Once ensconced into her seat, she stood again at the usher's request to take the oath.

I shall take the oath on the Bible," DI Slater said in a clear soft voice as she held the Bible in her hand. "I swear by Almighty God that the evidence I shall give shall be the whole truth and nothing but the truth, so help me God."

"Thank you, you are DI Kiki Slater from CID branch and you work with DCI McLean?"

"Yes, My Lord."

"We have heard the evidence of your colleague senior officer on the case; I suspect much of the evidence is likely to be the same. Can you confirm you were called to the scene in Woodhouse on the night of 19 December 1997 and that you have worked on the case from the start?

"Yes, My Lord, I confirm that to be so."

"Take us through from when the case had been reopened, Detective Slater."

"I was very pleased that the case had been reopened. It was a chance to see if we could do better in getting closure for the Rehman family as I know Raazia Khan was keen to get justice for her sister. For the police, it is always good to solve a crime too. I decided I was going to go see her, which I did. I talked to Raazia. I knew she knew something but it was not easy to get her to open up at first. Maybe she was frightened of her father. Certainly, when DCI McLean and I went to see her again she seemed readily willing to give us a statement, much to my surprise. When we took the statement the second time round, a different kind of picture emerged. Here was a family where girls soon as they tuned sixteen were forced to marry through arranged marriages. If they ran away, this would be seen to be an attack on the family honour. It could not be done. It was as simple as that. It would not be acceptable to do this. If it did happen, perhaps their life would be in peril."

"My Lord, is this really relevant evidence in respect of the charge, and is this witness professing to be some kind of expert in sociology and family affairs?" Mr Griffidam asked rising to his feet.

"My Lord, I am merely setting out what we as officers learnt as we went along investigating this particular case about the victim's family, and by the way, I do have a Bachelor's degree in Sociology qualification which I gained from Cape Town University when I studied there back home in South Africa."

"Mr Griffidam, you still object?" the Judge asked with a grin on his face.

"No, My Lord," Mr Griffidam responded as he resumed his seat.

"Very good, Detective, then you may continue," the Judge said.

"My Lord, thank you. Raazia was an interesting person who seemed to have divided loyalties between her parents and her sisters. In the end, she chose to go down the path of justice for her sister Saleena. She told us candidly what she had heard that night when she was clearing up in the kitchen. She is one hundred percent convinced that her sister Saleena Khan died as a result of what she was doing, getting divorced to get married to an outsider, which would ruin the accused's reputation and honour system. I believe that too. I was the one with the trained eye that spotted the motive and persuaded DCI McLean to take this line of investigation. I had seen it happen before in South Africa with Asian families."

"Thank you, Detective, please stay there."

"Detective, would you tell us what makes you think that these two accused were involved in the commission of this crime given the paucity of evidence relied on to support the charge of conspiracy?" Mr Peggs-Green asked.

"My experience, My Lord, Raazia's evidence and the telephone calls made by Khan from his landline to Faizali Rehman near the time of the killings. In addition, when you look at the system of honour killings, the history of violence inflicted by the accused Nawaz Khan upon his wife, it all adds up, and to me, it is as clear as daylight."

"Really detective? Your experience, Detective, is not evidence of the crime, is it?"

"No."

"Exactly, in fact there is no cogent evidence to support the charge, is there? The evidence is a sham."

"I beg to differ, Sir."

"No further questions.

"So, it was a hunch or a gut feeling on your part which led you to connect to honour killing, was it? Mr Griffidam asked once he was up on his feet adjusting his wig as the heat in the courtroom had become quite stifling.

"Yes, My Lord."

"The statement of Raazia Khan and the telephone call records are the two pieces of the jigsaw, are they?"

"Yes, My Lord."

"The telephone call records, they are mere data of calls made, not cogent evidence, agreed?

"Yes, My Lord."

"No further questions."

"No re-examination, My Lord."

"Very well, the witness is excused.

"The Crown has one Section 9 statement, My Lord, which is agreed and with His Lordship's permission I shall read it out in open court?" Mr Ravenstone stated at which the Judge nodded.

"My Lord, the Section 9 statement, is the statement by the pathologist who performed the autopsy on the victims. The statement is by Dr Craig Summers. He says in his statement as follows:

"My name is Craig Summers. I am a Home Office Pathologist. My qualifications are:

- *MSc Biochem, University of Edinburgh.*
- *MD, University of Edinburgh.*
- *FRCP, Internal Medicine and Pathology, Princeton University NJ (US)*
- *Clinical Professor and Chair, Dept. of Pathology and Biophysics, Royal London Hospital.*

In December 1997, I performed autopsies on a male and a female. The male was a black male in his late twenties and the female was Asian in her early thirties. Both the male and female had very identical and similar injuries which had led to their deaths.

Upon examination I performed on the bodies, they were found to have contusions and extremely deep lacerations to mostly the upper part of their bodies. The head and the skull, in particular, had received very severe and sustained blows from a blunt object, like a metal hammer. I describe the injuries to be as follows:

1. *The skull had a left parietal depressed skull fracture with underlying epidural haematoma of maximum 5.1 cm thickness, a right frontal open comminuted fracture with associated subdural haematoma of maximum 3.3 cm thickness, along with substantial blood collection within the subarachnoid space, both lateral ventricles and basal cisterns.*
2. *The wrists of both victims exhibited deep linear ischemic dermal abrasions which could only be caused by a tight constrictive device that strangulated blood circulation to the skin immediately underneath the constrictive device.*

3. *The time of death, I confirm, was between three and four a.m.*

In my opinion, death would have been within minutes of the attack and the blows from the injuries described above would have led to death within minutes. I think it would have been highly improbable for the victim's to have survived for much longer than maybe 5–10 minutes following the blows to the head and skull

Dr Craig Summers."

"That is the case for the Crown, My Lord."

"We will adjourn now. We will resume on Monday morning at 10 a.m. for defence Counsel to present their defence," Judge Norrington QC pronounced.

"All rise," the court usher stated.

David asked Akeel if he could drop by and see the family tonight as he wanted to make sure they were all going to be all right for the weekend. Akeel did not mind as he seemed a friendly fellow, besides it was an opportunity to treat him with a meal. Akeel wanted to thank him for lunch; besides, he was nearly going to be family. He never thought an African black brother could have been part of his family. He did not mind it at all if he had; he seemed like a nice guy. Papaji travelled back to Leicester with Abdel after the case finished for the weekend. Abdel put the radio on. Papaji was not in the mood to listen to the radio. He wanted to forget the case for the weekend.

"I made some enquiries with a doctor friend of mine, Papaji. He is going to source a rheumatologist we could go see about your arthritis."

Before Abdel could finish his sentence, Papaji was fast asleep snoring away, his head had slumped onto the side window. Abdel smiled to himself for he had not seen his Papaji asleep or heard him snore for a long time.

Heavy traffic on M6 made the journey time to Leicester longer than it would have normally taken Abdel to get to Leicester coming down M6 motorway, then exiting on to A50 at junction 16 towards Stoke-on-Trent. He had estimated roughly two hours for the journey, but due to heavy traffic, it took just over three hours. Papaji was completely zonked out throughout the journey. It must have been around 6:30 in the evening. Abdel parked up outside the house. He could see some nosey neighbours peering through their windows recognising his distinctive maroon-coloured Mercedes Benz. Some lifted the net curtains slightly to gain a better view making their presence by the window somewhat conspicuous.

"Papaji, wake up, we are here."

"What, where are we?"

"Home, Papaji."

"Fauzia, *mey aagia ger* [I am home]," he shouted as he entered the front door. There was no response. "I bet she is sleeping upstairs. Go see if she is, *betta*. Wake her up."

Abdel was about to rush upstairs when he noticed an A5-size note placed upright in a prominent position on the dining table resting against a vase. He picked it up. It was an A5 size paper folded in half with 'Faiz' written on the outside; the rest was in Urdu inside in the folded half.

"Papaji, there is note here for you from *Amii.* It's addressed to you," Abdel said as he handed the note to him.

Papaji read it. He paused for a few minutes then sat down in his favourite chair sitting on the edge looking very quizzical.

"Well, what does the note say?"

"She says she did not wish to spend life in England anymore, so she was flying out to Karachi for a few weeks possibly more. *Bhen chod*, I knew she was up to something when I spoke to her from the hotel room the other night. Never mind, she does my head in anyway, so good riddance I say."

"Oh Papaji, you will be on your own for the weekend. Would you like me to stay with you?"

"No *betta*, I want to be on my own for a little while. This is as good a time now to be on my own so it is a good opportunity, so you carry on with your business. You must be busy."

"I can stay, Papaji. You will need food. I can do all that."

"No, no, no, as I said, I want to be on my own. I can get Malik to get the food for me."

"Okay, if you need anything at all, you let me know. I will be here at around 6 p.m. Sunday. We will go have something to eat before travelling to Manchester."

That evening, David arrived at Raazia's house at about 8:30 p.m. Raazia introduced him to Meesha and Shakeela and the other children. David had with him six large boxes of Thorntons chocolate he gave to all the children. Akeel invited him to wash his hands and to come sit at the table which had on it a variety of delicious food. There were three types of meat curry dishes served in a tagine, plain naan in baskets, boiled rice, *samosas* and *pakhoras* all laid out on the table.

"Raazia, you must be a miracle worker cooking all this food after returning from Manchester. It looks so amazing. How do you do it? You Indian women are so versatile. Akeel you are such a lucky man."

"I'd love to take the credit, David. Sadly, I am afraid I can't. The truth is Akeel has some friends, Jamshēd and Chengez, who own a restaurant nearby on Green Lane, they made and delivered the food Akeel ordered as we were on our way back to Leicester."

"I am so happy to know you all. I feel you are part of my family so I very much appreciate this warm welcome to your house. I would very much like to get acquainted with the family of Mama Saleena. That is the name she was known by in my country. She was an amazing woman. You should hear some of the children crying every day, even now at the Centre. I visited the Centre after the tragic deaths and boy you could see how they are missed. They all miss her

159

very much, Calvin too. I miss him too. Let us all sit down and eat before all this lovely food gets cold. Sit, sit, sit, everyone, let us enjoy. It has been a tough week, especially for Raazia." David urged everyone.

"David, we are sorry to hear about your brother. He was a very brave and courageous man. I do pay tribute to him as he was here to protect my sister but inadvertently got in the middle of this family honour business. So, we are sorry," Raazia said.

"I appreciate your kind words, Raazia," David said as he put both his arms on his chest gesturing appreciation. "It means a lot to me. My father passed away after a long illness so he is not around, but my mother is very cut up about it. She cries every single day remembering her son Calvin. You should all visit her as it would mean a lot to her," David said as he had, for the first time, tears in his eyes which he quickly wiped away."

"Raazia, how about we plan go see her in September when all this is over? David what is your mother's name?" Akeel asked.

"You are going to make me emotional now, guys. I will let my mother know that you will be visiting her. She is going to be so pleased to meet you. You let me know your travel plans. I will send a limo to pick you up at Entebbe Airport. You will be VIPs, and you can meet the President also. My mother's name is Ophelia."

"I have never sat in a limousine before, so it will be something to look forward to," Akeel said with glee.

"Once I know your definite travel plans, I will notify the Director of Entebbe Airport that you are the guests of the President. You will be treated like foreign dignitaries, I promise you. You can visit Soroti and afterwards you can go to Chobe Game Lodge; it is our National Park. You will love it there."

"Oh, sounds very nice indeed. Sajj, how about us going with the kids too?" Allia asked.

"If you want to go, why not, but the kids will be back at school, Allia," Sajj said.

"Akeel any chance you could go in August whilst the kids are on their summer vacation?" Allia asked.

"We will see. We can, I am sure, work something out," Akeel responded.

David seemed elated. He was beaming with absolute delight hearing the conversation about Saleena's family planning to visit not just his mother but Uganda, more so hearing that the family would be visiting Raffiki Centre as Raazia promised she would be delivering all those presents to those children that Saleena could not give to the children herself.

"Thank you, David, we look forward to it. It will mean a lot seeing those children happy to finally get the presents Saleena wanted them to have," Raazia said as she began to be upset.

"Raazia Madam, do not upset yourself like this. Know this, your Mama Saleena's heart was in the right place. I am a Christian and I believe she is in heaven looking down with happiness for what we are all doing for her. She is in a better place, I tell you."

Raazia burst out crying.

"You know when Akeel came to propose to me, I cried because my mother, Begum, was not with us, David. You know what you just said, my mother-in-law *Amaaji* Farzana said exactly the same thing about her. I never thought someone else would be saying that to me in my lifetime. I feel so sad. How do you think the case is going?"

"Well, the two people are in court, that is the main thing. I have to say the evidence is not strong enough. The barristers representing your father and Nawaz are very clever. They have tried to focus on the credibility of the witnesses. Let us see what the jury decide aye? This food is so delicious. Akeel, you must pass my compliments to the chef at your friends' restaurant," David said as he tucked into the food.

"Sara, I heard someone say you work as a probation officer at one of the correctional institutes, is that correct? David asked.

"Yes, I do. How did you find out?" Sara asked looking quizzical.

"One of the secrets of my job is to find out things. That is what I do. So, you work with a bunch of criminals then?" he asked.

"The concept of rehabilitation of offenders is vital in society. I truly believe that. If we locked everyone up and threw away the key, what sort of society would we be."

"Bravo! I like you people you have good intentions, seriously, I do mean that. The philanthropic nature runs in the family. Tell me Sara, whilst I do not mean to pry, but I am curious about the bruises on your face you are sporting. You are not married to a man like Nawaz Khan, are you? I hope you are not as that man is one evil messed up guy."

"Ah, it is a long story," Sara said almost embarrassed.

"Auntie Sara has a boyfriend, Tom Ford, who bashed her face in the other night. Tell him what happened to you, Auntie Sara," Meesha intervened.

"Sara turned up at the house covered in blood. I did not recognise her at first until my daughter told me it was Sara. My heart sank at that point. All the bad memories about Saleena came flooding back. It was horrible. She is safe now. She will stay with me or Allia," Raazia stated.

"I don't know what kind of woman would put up with her man when they, let's face it, commit brutal acts of violence on their partners. I cannot understand it. So, Sara, are you able to tell me where you met this man, Tom Ford?"

The conversation at the table continued well past 11 p.m. David left the house, thanking his host for the wonderful hospitality extended to him as well with some vital information. He wondered why Sara, whilst suspecting something odd about her boyfriend the night Saleena was killed, an intelligent woman too at that, had not connected the dots herself about Tom. *Human nature perhaps,* he thought as he drove back to his hotel room in the town centre. It was an emotional evening for David, glad that he had spent time and become acquainted with the family of his brother's intended wife. He could not wait to tell his mother about them.

Abdel reached home approaching 9:30 in the evening, feeling completely bushed after over five-hours journey to get home as well as dropping Papaji off home in Leicester. The red light on his answer machine was flashing on the home phone. He walked over to the machine in the hallway and flicked one of the buttons on to listen. There were several messages for him, mostly unimportant, including one from Oliver Osgathorpe apologising for the impromptu drop-in whilst he was away. He said to give him a call as there may be a business proposition deal; they could work on. Abdel was hungry. Dealing with hunger pangs was a more pressing issue that needed taking care of first. He strolled into the kitchen to see if there was homemade food Amna had left for him. Sure enough, she did not disappoint her employer. Sitting on the smart grey marble worktop were three containers with a note next to them from Amna which read:

"The lamb sabzi was really nice when fresh, hope it still is when you get home. There is rice and some fresh rotis also which you will like, Sir. If there is leftover, could you kindly store it in the fridge for me, please. Amna. P.S. Sir, I hope you had a nice week."

Pressing matter solved, he followed the instructions storing the leftovers in the fridge. He took a can of 7Up from the fridge, switched the downstairs lights off, headed upstairs to his bedroom and put the television on before undressing, leaving his boxer shorts on being a warm night. Sean Denton's report came on exactly at the right time. Abdel turned the volume up, sat on the bed taking big sips from the can of 7Up.

"Well, today was the last day of the hearing before the weekend break at Manchester Crown Court. If you have been following my report all week on this case, you will remember the two defendants, Faizali Rehman and Nawaz Khan, who are related to each other – the first defendant Faizali Rehman is the father-in-law of the second defendant – are both charged with conspiracy to murder Saleena Khan and her boyfriend Calvin Lenton who were brutally bludgeoned to death at their home in the Woodhouse area of Leeds in the early hours of 19 December 1997. They both deny the charge. The Crown called its last two witnesses, DCI Benjamin McLean and DI Kiki Slater to the stand before closing its case. They were the main police officers who were the investigating officers from the very start giving evidence today.

"Both officers testified that whilst their initial enquires were focussed on a possible burglary that had gone wrong owing to there being no evidence or suspects found in the case, after some months it had been shelved as a cold case. Whilst they were disappointed the case had been closed, they were delighted when after a year, suddenly out of the blue, their Chief Superintendent decided to reopen the case. It was not clear the reason why it was reopened, but once they got the go ahead, they decided to go back to the paperwork and see if they had missed anything. It was by chance coupled with a hunch about honour killings that DI Slater had, that they both focussed enquires on the family, in particular Nawaz Khan who is the husband of the victim Saleena Khan.

162

"DCI McLean said this in court: 'Well, it was a gut feeling really. We had to look and see if any members of her family could have had something to do with it. If they did, we would need to follow up that line of enquiry. This was something rather more difficult to ascertain to an untrained eye.' The Judge, Sir Christopher Norrington QC, asked him, 'You mean killings connected with family honour, Detective McLean? If so, this is intriguing.'

"'My Lord, yes,' was his reply. He went on to say, 'This was unfamiliar territory for me, I have to say. My colleague had a strong hunch that a possible honour killing could be the motive as she had come across something similar when she was a police officer in South Africa.'

"Both detectives, under cross-examination by the defence lawyers, were asked, 'What makes you think that these two accused were involved given the paucity of evidence relied on to support the charge of conspiracy?' Detective Slater replied, 'My experience, My Lord, Raazia's evidence and the telephone calls made by Khan from his landline to Faizali Rehman near the time of the killings. In addition, when you look at the system of honour killings, the history of violence inflicted by the accused Nawaz Khan upon his wife, it all adds up, and to me, it is as clear as daylight.'

"'There is no cogent evidence to support the charge, is there? The evidence is a sham.' Mr Peggs-Green asked her. 'I beg to differ, Sir.' was her reply.

"At one point, there was an objection raised by Mr Griffidam, Counsel for Nawaz Khan, attacking Detective Slater. He asked her as to whether she was an expert in the field in following the honour killing line of enquiry, or was she simply following her instinct. In response, she said, 'My Lord, I am merely setting out what we as officers learnt as we went along investigating this particular case about the victim's family, and by the way, I do have a Bachelor's degree in Sociology qualification which I gained from Cape Town University when I studied there back home in South Africa.'

"She had gone on to explain: 'Raazia was an interesting person who seemed to have divided loyalties between her parents and her sisters. In the end, she chose to go down the path of justice for her sister Saleena. She told us candidly what she had heard that night when she was clearing up in the kitchen. She is one hundred percent convinced that her sister Saleena Khan died as a result of what she was doing, getting divorced to get married to an outsider, which would ruin the accused's reputation and honour system. I believe that too. I was the one with the trained eye that spotted the motive and persuaded DCI McLean to take the line of investigation. I had seen it happen before in South Africa with Asian families.'

"Mr Griffidam QC finished his cross-examination by stating, 'The telephone call records were mere data of calls made, not cogent evidence, agreed?'

"'Yes, My Lord.' The detective replied. There was no re-examination from Mr Ravenstone QC who then read out an agreed statement of the coroner Dr Craig Summers before closing the case for the Crown. The case resumes Monday morning when the defence will present their evidence to the court. This is Sean Denton for BBC News."

Abdel probably did not get to the end of the report. He fell asleep forgetting to switch the television off, sleeping through to the night right up to 10:00 a.m. Saturday morning. He rolled out of bed hearing some noises downstairs, put his nightgown on before going downstairs.

"Good morning, sir, sorry I did not wake you, did I? How was your week?" Amna asked two questions at the same time.

"No, Amna, it is fine. You did not wake me up. I needed to be up as I want to go to the stables. It was very exhausting. I have to go back next week again as the case has not finished. Have you been watching the news, following the trial?"

"I have, Sir. I feel sorry for you and your *Abbah* having to go through such a hard time; it can't be easy for you all. I hope there is a good outcome. Your sister Saleena seemed to be one remarkable lady."

"Thank you so much, Amna, for the food you had kept ready for me. It was delicious."

"I was pleased to notice you ate quite a bit which was good. You must have been very hungry. Thank you for putting away the leftovers in the fridge! Daniel asked this morning if there was any leftover. I looked and gave him what was there."

"That's good."

"What would you like for breakfast?"

"I will have some eggs with plain parathas. I am going to have a shower and get dressed first to give you time to prepare."

"Sure, I'll get on to it right away."

The stables had been cleaned by the time Abdel got down there. The horses were out lazily grazing in the lush green fields on a beautiful summer's day. The horses in the field made the place look picturesque like a postcard depicting some rural area of English countryside on a hot summer's day. It seemed a perfect day for exercising the stallions out in the countryside but Abdel was not quite in the mood for that. Ben was not feeling well that day, bad hay fever he was told, and the grass pollen had made it worse. Susy and Jacob were busy working hard getting the place finished off tidying up. Susy was anxious to get away as she was spending the rest of the day with her mum shopping.

"Hi, boss, it's good to see you. How was your week?" she asked.

"Oh, it was exhausting, Susy. I am glad to be home for the weekend. It is such a nice day too. I hear you are spending the rest of the day with your mum, spending her money aye?"

"Yes, Mum offered to take me into London, and I thought that's what parents are for!"

"I wouldn't know just yet until I have kids of my own."

"Oh, you'll find out how expensive we can be"

"I'm sure it's not that bad. You have your wages from here, so I bet it helps get by."

"Oh, I am saving all that for a nice holiday somewhere, or it will come in handy when I get married."

"You are so young to be thinking about that surely. Has Andy popped the question then?"

"No, not yet. Boss, I want to have kids and be a young mother. It would be nice to do things with the children whilst I am still young too. You have not thought about getting hitched then? I am off now, boss, as I have to rush off, mustn't be late, you know, and keep Mum waiting seeing as she is treating me!"

"I am waiting for Mrs Right to come along. That is a nice thought, having kids early; I like that. Have fun and enjoy your day. Do you know where Jacob is?"

"Not exactly, boss, he is out somewhere, maybe he is in the stables. Don't wait too long as Mrs Right may never come along, you know. Bye." Susy winked as she went off.

"Bye."

Abdel went into the stables to find Jacob. He wandered around to see if he could spot him in the stables. He was with Lady Sharjah hard at work spreading hay for the filly. The temperature in the stables must have been close to 32 degrees Celsius. It was hot working in the stables. Jacob had hung his T-shirt on the wooden gate to Lady Sharjah's enclosure pen. He had some hardy garden gloves on, denim jeans and boots. Jacob seemed hot and sweaty as sweat was dripping down his forehead onto his face and torso.

"Hello, Jacob, is everything okay? Bloody hell, it's hot in here!"

"Hello, boss, I thought you were going to rest up as I hear you have had a tough week?" he said picking up a bottle of water from the side shelf by the gate.

"Yes, it was exhausting. I have to be back again there next week, unfortunately, as the case has not finished. Everything here been, okay? How come Lady Sharjah is not in the fields today, Jacob?"

"Yes, well, a couple of things to report, boss. I am sure you will be very pleased to learn Lady Sharjah is pregnant. The vet came by for his usual inspection of the animals and he confirmed it."

"Jacob, that is marvellous news. Well, Antoninus is going to be a dad, the old dog. Wowee, that is great news! More work for you, bud. Speaking of which, you are going to stay, right?"

"Well, I could do with a raise, boss. But yes, I like it here. I don't really like that guy Oliver whatever his name is, seemed a bit creepy, close body contact and all that."

"Thanks, Jacob, for being loyal. I was thinking about giving you all a raise after the hard work all of you put in for the win at Gloucester in April. I have been so busy with other things; it's just escaped my mind."

"Boss, I was just kidding. I am happy here."

"Don't say I'm like your dad to you again, as I am not, you cheeky monkey. No, all of you deserve a raise. I will see to it. I will speak to the accountant on Monday."

"Boss, seriously, I only said it as a joke; I feel so embarrassed now," Jacob said as he shook hands. It was a tight grip.

"No Jacob, loyalty is important. It means a lot to me that you guys are all keen on staying with me. I feel so lucky, you know, to have you, Ben, Susy, Daniel and Amna. You guys are my family. Keep the raise to yourself. I want it to be a surprise to everyone. I was speaking to Susy about saving money just a few minutes ago outside in the yard; poor thing, she is saving up for a holiday. Jacob, you need a shower; you are spending too long with them horses. Did the vet say when the foal is due?"

"320 to 340 days, so summer next year, boss. Vet said she won't be racing in her condition."

"Yes, I know, Jacob."

David was up early. He grabbed breakfast at Ibis hotel restaurant where he was staying and then checked out. He phoned Raazia from his hired VW car. He asked her for Sara's address where she used to live, and said it was important that she not mention to anyone he had asked, not even Sara as he was just following up some enquiries. Raazia agreed. David had gained her trust. From the town centre, he headed out on the A607 towards Melton ending up in Frisby on the Wreake. David loved the quietness of the village as it looked like a quaint small sleepy village. He went into St Thomas of Canterbury Church. It was quiet in there, no one present. He walked in the middle aisle. On either side of him were rows of wooden church pews. The pews looked made of dark oak or were varnished dark. The grains of the wood were prominent, he noticed, looked rather attractive. He stopped a few metres away from the altar, knelt down, lifted his right hand to his face as he motioned his hand in the fashion of a cross reciting the words: "In the name of the father, the son and the holy ghost"

"Amen to that I say, son. It's lovely to see someone in the church so early on a Saturday morning," said the Vicar with a distinctive English accent.

David was taken a little by surprise with the Vicar appearing behind him suddenly without him sensing his presence. He had been trained to have eyes at the back of his head, being on the President's security team. It was one he would need to ponder over on. The Vicar looked to be in his mid-sixties, thin in stature, wore thick-lensed glasses, grey hair brushed neatly to one side of his head and loose leathery skin from his chin down his neck.

"Good morning, father. It is lovely to meet you. I have not been in a church since I was a teenager, I must confess. I used to go with my mother. She is a devout Christian. It is so peaceful here, almost serene, Father. It is nice."

"Yes, it is today, but we have a lot attending church on Sunday morning for the service. Where are you from, son? That African accent of yours sounds Ugandan."

"Yes, you are a clever man. Have you been to my country?"

"Yes, I was in Jinja for three years, preaching there. It is a nice place, Uganda. What brings you to England, my friend, and more particularly here of all places in England?"

"I am visiting some old friends of mine here from University days, one lady in particular, her name is Sara. She may be married now, I guess, I don't know. Sadly, I have lost touch with her."

"I must say your English is very good," the priest observed.

"Thank you, Father, I studied here for three years so picked up the language rather well. Oh, she was a charming lady, my friend Sara. She was at university with me. I was in Leicester meeting a university friend. I asked about her. He said all he knew was she lived in Frisby area somewhere, but he did not have an exact address for her. I thought I would drop by; if I could find her, I would surprise her."

"This is a small village; I know almost everyone here, but not quite everyone. There is an Asian woman, I believe she works in Probation. Lives with a white man, I assume he is either her husband or boyfriend. The couple seem to be a private family, the quiet sort, you know, not really mix much, so I don't know much about them."

"Do you know which house it is they live in?"

"Yes, you will find her living in one of the terraced houses near to the village post office on Main Street. Good luck in finding your friend. It was a pleasure meeting you. We don't often have strangers visiting Frisby, so it was nice to see you today, my son. Be sure to go often to church like you used to with your mother. Being near our Lord keeps us away from sin. It is good to have faith in Him. May He go with you, son. Goodbye now."

"Thank you, Father, I shall try my best. Goodbye and may the Lord's peace be upon you, Sir."

"Bless you, child."

David droves down from Church Lane into Hollow Lane, parked his hired VW car, and then walked on to Main Street. He walked past what seemed like a main grocery store. There were some terraced houses next to it just like the priest said. He knocked on the first door. A middle-aged English woman answered the door, seemed taken aback to see a black man in the village, and quickly said she was not interested in a buying anything or in any religion thinking he was perhaps a Jehovah's Witness or worst still an ex-con selling items door-to-door. David apologised for disturbing her but said the vicar form the church had directed him there. He was looking for an Asian woman called Sara. She said she lived next door, but had not seen her for some months. Her boyfriend, Tom, was there. Rather a ruffian. She said he was not a pleasant man. David thanked her and moved on the house next door. He knocked a few times, but there was no response. He knocked another couple of times. A young English man in his mid-twenties, tattoos on the left side of his neck and forearms, answered the door. A rancid smell of weed mingled with the stale smell of takeaway food wafted out of the door.

"What the fuck do you want?" he asked in an aggressive tone.

"Ah, I am sorry to disturb you; may I speak to Sara, please?"

"She ain't here. Who the fucks are you?"

"I am from the Probation office. We have been trying to get in touch with her as she has not reported for work for a few months. She has gone AWOL, and we are worried about her. It is not like Sara to be missing work like this. Do you know if she is okay? Do you know where I can get in touch with her? You must be Tom Ford, right?"

"No, I haven't a clue where she is, bud. She left a few months back, and I have not seen her since."

"Well, thank you for your time, Sir. If you do see her, can you ask her to get in touch with David? She has the number."

"Sure, no probs," were his final words as he slammed the door shut in David's face.

David smiled as he walked back to his car. *Part-mission accomplished,* he thought to himself.

Chapter 16

It was early evening. Abdel was about to settle in for a quiet evening at home relaxing when he got a frantic call from Malik Uncle.

"Abdel, it's Malik Uncle here. I am so sorry to disturb you, *betta,* your father has been taken into hospital a few minutes ago. *Amii* is not here. I have let Akeel know. He said to call you."

"Why? What happened?"

"He had chest pains. He called me as he could not get hold of anyone. I went down to the house. Luckily, the back door was unlocked. I found your father lying on the kitchen floor clutching his chest so I called the ambulance. They have taken him to Leicester Royal. I am going there with Farzana Auntie now. We will stay with him until you arrive."

"Thank you, *Uncleji*, I appreciate that. I will be on my way in an hour or so. It will take me two-hours' drive to get to the hospital."

"Don't worry, *betta*, drive safely. We will wait with him and pray for his *shiffaat* [recovery]."

"Okay, *Uncleji, khudda hafeez.*"

Abdel got some things together packed in a Gucci holdall first, and then he called Amna to let her know he was going back to Leicester tonight, updating her about the situation, and then called Jacob. He asked Jacob to call Amna in case he needed anything from the house as she had a set of keys in case, he needed access to the house for anything. The two-hour drive to Leicester seemed a lonely drive. He felt bad for Papaji. It was sad he had to turn to friends in his hour of need as everyone, except him, in the family seemed to have abandoned him. As much as he felt sorry for him, he wondered if Papaji was to blame for his own tragic predicament. Abdel could not help but wonder. Had Papaji behaved differently towards his children, just maybe his family would have surrounded him right now in his time of need, but the situation was his own creation, he thought to himself. He tried to listen to the radio. It was no good. His concentration was completely focussed on the situation at hand. How was he going to deal with it? If something happened to Papaji, it would put him firmly in charge. He was a male child and would be the head of the family. That would be tricky for him, if the situation did develop into one as he thought; his relationship was not exactly a close one with his sisters.

Thinking about things killed the journey time to the hospital. He arrived at the hospital car park, on Havelock Street around 9:30 p.m. The sun was beginning to make its descent to set in the distant horizon. As the light started to

169

slowly fade, the sun ebbing away ordered the sky colour to change from blue to bright red. The sunset was one beautiful sight.

David returned back to the village at around 9:00 p.m. He parked up on Hall Orchard Lane from where he had a good surveillance view of the house. Around 9:45 p.m., Tom left the house. He walked past the post office and carried on walking on Main Street. David disembarked from his car and keeping his distance, followed him on foot. Tom entered The Bell Inn public house. David did not wish to spook him, so he returned to his car.

Papaji was still in the A&E department as the day fell into early evening darkness. Abdel, upon his arrival, was met by Malik and Farzana in a busy hospital waiting area of A&E.

"Abdel, *betta, salaam alaiykum*. It is good to see you. Sorry we are meeting under difficult circumstances, *betta*."

"*Wa'alaiykum salaam, Uncleji*, nice to see you, you too *Auntiji*. How is he?"

"The doctor treating him has not been out to see us yet. We are waiting for him to come."

"All right, best thing we can do is wait, I guess."

"Allah is Almighty, *betta*. He is merciful too. He grants to those who are patient. Your Papaji has gone through a lot of bad times. I feel sure he will be fine."

Abdel paced up and down in the waiting area for five minutes, and then sat down on a chair for five minutes before standing up again. Malik could see the boy was anxious, troubled even.

"*Uncleji* and *Auntyji*, where are my manners? Please let me get something for you to drink and eat. What would you like?"

"I will have a cup of coffee, white with no sugar for me; and a cheese sandwich if they have any, if not, some biscuits will be fine," Malik said.

"I will have a cup of tea and any vegetarian sandwich, *puttar*, may Allah Bless you. Malik gives the boy some money," Farzana said.

"No, no, no, I will get it, don't worry."

Five minutes later, he came back holding in his hands, tea, coffee, Fanta bottle and some cheese and tomato sandwiches. The three of them went outside to eat. It was a warm evening. The sky had turned dark as the moon began to make its presence known in the sky.

As they returned back to the waiting area, a young Asian female doctor came out asking if there was anyone from the Rehman family there. Abdel stood up and walked over to the doctor.

"I am Abdel Rehman, Doctor, Faizali Rehman is my father."

"Hello, I am Dr Maisuria. Can we talk over there?" She pointed to an area in the waiting area. "It is a bit more private there. Your father has suffered an MI. In medical terms, it is called a myocardial infarction."

"In plain English, please."

"He has suffered a minor heart attack. I have given him some morphine, and he is comfortable right now. We will need to keep him in the hospital for a few days make sure he is fine. An orderly will soon take him over to one of the wards. It will be a few minutes as we are trying to find a bed for him."

"Can he be moved to a private ward? I can foot the bill for the private room if need be."

"I think that can be arranged. I shall go speak to the hospital administrator."

"Thank you, Doctor, can we go see him?"

"Yes, of course; he is in cubicle number 7."

Abdel walked to the cubicle with Malik and Farzana. Papaji seemed sedated. He looked old, very haggard, sad too as though he was about to give up on life. Malik and his wife, Farzana, stood on one side of the bed, Abdel on the other. Abdel held his father's hand; it was cold. He rubbed it gently with both his hands. Malik did the same to the other hand. Unsure what to do, the trio stood quietly in the room for a few minutes. Papaji opened his eyes. Seeing the three of them by his bedside, he smiled. His eyes began to fill up with tears. Soon the tears ran down his face all the way to his neck and his *kameez* top. Malik took a tissue from a side table and handed it to Abdel to wipe off the tears.

"Aray kew roh rahay ho dhost? Hum hey naa tumare key saath. [Why are you crying, friend? We are here with you.]"

"Abdel did you call *Amii*?" Papaji asked taking his time to take those few words out of his mouth.

"No, I have not had time to, Papaji, as I rushed over when *Uncleji* phoned me. I will call her when I get back to the house."

"What did the doctor say?" Papaji asked.

"You had a minor heart attack, friend, but it will be all right. You will stay here in hospital for a few days for observation, then they will discharge you," Malik said.

"Farzana, I have not thanked you for coming to the hospital with Malik to be with me. Please accept my sincere thanks."

"Aray bhaijaan kia bol rahey ho? Meri furz hey aney ki or mey Begum ko kia jawab du gee? Koi baat nahi. Jo chaiey to zurur bolna. [What are you saying brother? It is my duty to come otherwise what answer will I give to Begum up there. If you need anything, please tell me.]"

"Bohat shukhr aapka. [Thank you so much.]"

"Papaji, they will move you to a private ward soon. You will be comfortable there. I will go home and get some things you will need and stay with you until about 11:00 p.m., and then I will be back during visiting times tomorrow lunchtime and evening. I can bring some food with me tomorrow."

"You don't worry, I will make some food for you. Abdel will collect on his way to hospital," Farzana insisted.

"Please *koi taklif nay leynaa* [don't go to any trouble], I will be fine," Papaji pleaded with Farzana.

"Aray, no trouble at all," she responded.

An orderly, a young black fellow, came through the cubicle. He was in his late twenties, African descent wearing a green hospital top and matching bottom.

"Right then, Sir, I am here to move you to a private room, okay? Let's go," the orderly said as he unhooked the cables he was attached to the machines. He took off the brakes, got behind the bed as he began to wheel Papaji along the hospital corridors, taking the lift to the second floor then to a private room near the main ward.

"Thank you, Sir, hope all goes well for you. Goodbye now," he said as he left the room.

Abdel left the hospital at around 11:00 p.m. It took him ten minutes to get to the house. He opened the front door, and as he entered the house, it felt strangely quiet. There was no one there. The complete silence felt eerie. He remembered the times when there was laughter there, times also of sadness, women wailing in the house, especially when Saleena's body was brought home before her funeral, times when *Amii's* loud voice would echo in the house. There were people there. The house felt like a proper home. Now it was devoid of people. There were no sounds in the house. Papaji had driven everyone away, even *Amii*! Speaking of which he remembered he had to call her. He rummaged around the house for her number in Pakistan. Eventually, he managed to retrieve the note he had found on the dining table on Friday after returning from Manchester. It was in a waste basket in the sitting room. The number was written on it luckily. He picked up the telephone and dialled her number, not realising immediately it was around 3:30 a.m. in Karachi.

"Hello, *con bol rah hey eesi walkt ko?* [Who is calling at this time]?"

"*Amii*, sorry to disturb you. I am not sure what time it is over there, but it is Abdel here."

"3:30 a.m. *betta*. What is the matter?"

"Papaji is in hospital, *Amii*. He suffered a heart attack, said to telephone you and let you know. Are you able to, like, fly back soon?"

"Abdel, *puttar*, I am so sorry, I have decided to stay in Pakistan. I will not be coming back."

"Oh…err…what shall I say to Papaji then?" Abdel stuttered with his words, not expecting that response from her.

"Say just what I said to you. *Khudda hafeez, betta. Khyaal rakhna apna.* Thank you for everything you have done for me," she said putting the receiver down before Abdel had chance to say goodbye to her.

David spotted Tom at around 11:20 pm. He was unsteady on his feet. He swayed from side to side as he struggled to walk straight. The man was clearly very drunk. David took the opportunity to drive up to him.

"My friend, you could do with some help getting home?"

"F…uck…f…uck off you dic…dickhead motherfucker," Tom muttered.

"C'mon, I can help you, man, get home."

David hurriedly opened the door, got out and looked around to see if there was anyone there. No one seemed to be about. He opened the rear passenger door quickly, pushed Tom onto the backseat, lifted his feet pushing them inside on the backseat, and clicked the child-lock in the on position before shutting the door. Tom was out of it. He did not care. David hurriedly got in the car and began driving. Tom began snoring away in the back seat!

"That seemed easy," he muttered loudly with a grin on his face.

Abdel was still trying to process the information in his head about *Amii's* decision which seemed unexpected and sudden. His main worry was what he would say to Papaji. Without any doubt, he was sure Papaji would complain about *Amii* too abandoning him in his hour of need. But it is what it is, he thought in his head, something not within his control. Anxious to get to bed, he checked to ensure everywhere downstairs was secure, switched the lights off and went upstairs. He went into his old room. It seemed like being in a matchbox. The room was small compared to his bedroom at the estate. The bed creaked as he turned from one side to another.

Malik brought some food round at lunchtime which his wife had packed for Abdel to take to the Hospital. Malik accompanied him.

"Did you call *Amii*, Abdel, to let her know Papaji was in hospital?" Malik asked.

An awkward question, Abdel thought. Unsure how to exactly respond, he thought about the question for a few seconds. Malik was waiting for an answer.

"Err…*Uncleji*, I don't know how to say this, but I called *Amii* last night and let her know Papaji was in hospital so she should fly back home as soon as she could. But…"

"But?"

"Well, *Uncleji*, she said she was not coming back. She was staying in Pakistan."

"Farzana did say something about this to me the other day. I paid no notice as I thought it was just woman talk, gossiping, you know, like they do. I see. What will you tell your father, Abdel?"

"What is your advice?"

"It is sad that apart from you, all his family have abandoned him. He will be broken completely at the news. I say you don't tell him the truth until he is out of the hospital, maybe when he is bit stronger than the delicate situation he is now."

"I think that is good advice, *Uncleji*. It is good to have you with me today."

It was around 23 degrees Celsius, a pleasant summer's day. Papaji seemed a little better. He was sitting up in bed when Malik and Abdel walked into his room. He was still wired up to the monitor next to him which was making a beeping sound. The blood pressure reading displayed on it read '156/105'

"*Salaam alaiykum*, you look much better today. How are you feeling?" Malik asked.

"*Wa'alaiykum salaam*, I feel better today. As you can see, I am sitting up, no pain and my blood pressure has come down a lot. I feel hungry though. The food here is not our kind of food. It does not fill you up, fish fingers with mash potatoes. What did you bring?" Papaji asked.

"Farzana has made some dry aubergine curry, no oil, as you need to watch them oily foods from now on, *rotis* and rice. You will enjoy that," Malik responded.

"Oh yes, that sounds good. Abdel could you plate it for me, please? There is a microwave in the kitchen."

Abdel left the room to heat up the food for him.

"I don't know why Fauzia had to go to Pakistan right at this time. She knew I was on my own at home, the stupid trial as well; it's just not done," Faizali complained.

Abdel returned into the room at that point. Sure, enough as night follows day, the question came up.

"Abdel, did you speak to *Amii* last night?"

"Papaji, I did, she said she has some urgent matters to attend to first in Pakistan; plus, she said a family member was unwell or something. As soon as she was done there, she will see if she can catch a flight back home."

"What could more urgent than her husband being in hospital, possibly dying? Women these days do not know their place or the value of respect of one's husband or loyalty for that matter," he complained raising his voice slightly with a definite tone of disapproval.

"Faizali, my dear friend, she is in Pakistan. Let her sort her matters out now that she is there. We are here for you and can take care of you," Malik reassured his friend.

The news was unwelcome news for him. Seemingly rather annoyed at the news, his mood suddenly changed. He quietly ate his food. He made some inaudible muttering sounds as he ate. Malik attempted to make conversation, some small talk about the weather being lovely at this time of the year, how the grandchildren were growing fast, and so on, but Papaji seemed to have lost interest. He refused to be drawn into any sort of conversation. That was his classic trait, annoyance displayed by silence.

It was about 2:00 p.m. on Sunday afternoon. Tom woke up with a terrible hangover. His head was thumping. His hands were tied tightly behind him with plastic cable ties so much so they began hurting as he tried to struggle to wriggle free. He did not recognise where he was as he lay on a dirty mattress which stank of urine. His jeans were wet. The room was dark. The only light in the room was faint sunlight filtering into the room from the sides of what looked like a dark cloth covering one of the windows.

"Where the fuck am I? Is anyone here? I need to go to the toilet. Hello," he shouted. "If this is some fucking joke then you've had your laugh. C'mon mate, let me free."

There was no response; it seemed a deserted place. The quietness of it was hauntingly eerie. Tom continued to shout. An hour later, he heard what sounded like a door opening as it creaked somewhere in the place followed by sounds of steps approaching as the wooden floor boards creaked. Someone was climbing the stairs. The door to the room opened, David was carrying a torch in his hand. It silhouetted his figure onto the ceiling as he stepped into the room, closing the door behind him.

"Hey, mate, stop mucking about. You've had your little fun, now free my hands. I need the toilet."

"I can smell the stench on you."

"Yeh well, I need to go for a number 2, mate. Who the fucks are you anyway? What do you want from me? You look like the black geezer who came to my house yesterday."

David approached him and cut the plastic cable tie with a knife, holding the knife to Tom's neck.

"There is a toilet next door, but it does not work, I am afraid. Do not try any funny business or else you will not leave here alive, understood?" David warned his captive.

"Yeh, yeh, understood," Tom said as he dashed to the toilet in the dark.

David stood by the room door holding the torch in one hand and a seven-inch sharp bladed knife in the other. With the knife, David signalled him to return to the room where he was before when he was done.

"I am hungry, man, have you got any food?"

"No, I am not a restaurant. Sit back on the bed. Put those shorts on as you stink like hell." David instructed Tom as he tied his hands as soon as he changed into a pair of shorts with fresh cable ties.

"What do you want from me?"

"You will soon find out."

During the evening, Farzana joined her husband, Malik, to see Faizali at the hospital during visiting hours of between 5:30 and 7:00 p.m. They arrived at the hospital shortly after 5:30 p.m. Faizali looked perked up, seemed to be in a better mood. After exchanging the pleasantries for the day, Papaji ate the roasted chicken rolled into naan bread Farzana had made for him. He seemed to enjoy that as it perked him up even more.

"The food is so nice. Thank you Farzana." He paused for a minute or two finishing masticating the food in his mouth. "It is fine, I guess, if she wants to finish her matters in Pakistan," Papaji said randomly. "Tell her I am fine with that, Abdel, when you speak to her again tonight. But tell her she needs to get back home, perhaps, if not in a hurry, then with some speed."

"I will, Papaji. You have been thinking about it then?" Abdel said with a lump in his throat which made him cough slightly.

"Are you all right, boy? Have some water," Papaji said.

"*Bhaijaan* you look much better today, *Allah ka shukher*," Farzana interrupted. "You seem to be on the road to recovery, I feel. I am happy to see you looking and feeling so much better."

"Thank you so much for looking after me. I do appreciate it."

"Allah *rahem karey bhaijaan*. He is merciful, you know," Farzana said.

"Of course, He is. We are all His children; he looks after us all. You will see. I feel you will be home in no time at all. When we get to our age, it's best to put the brakes on, sit back sometime, and take it easy. Maybe pondering on life is a good thing also, as it is a gift from Him, to live life as it comes. Surely, we are from Him and one day we all must return to Him," Malik said.

"That is so, my friend. I think you are very right. It is perhaps better that Fauzia has gone to Pakistan. I can at least have a rest from her too."

It was funny and all four laughed. The visiting time was nearly over. Abdel advised he would not see him tomorrow lunchtime as he would need to travel to Manchester to get Mr Peggs-Green to make an application for the trial to be adjourned. He had already got a letter from Dr Maisuria stating Papaji was an inpatient at Leicester Royal Hospital. Malik said he would visit his friend at lunchtime and bring him some of his dear wife's homemade food.

It was Monday morning, would have been the sixth day of the trial. The sky was overcast. Grey clouds were looming in the sky threatening rain. It looked like it was going to pour down. Abdel reached the Crown Court just a few minutes before the Judge, Sir Christopher Norrington QC came into the courtroom. Mr Peggs-Green was looking around from side to side wondering where his client was. Abdel waived at him to attract his attention. At that very moment, the usher made his request for all to stand as the Judge walked into court.

"Good morning all. Mr Peggs-Green, where is your client? I see he is not in the dock. If there is not a good reason, I am minded to sign a bench warrant for his arrest."

"Good morning, My Lord, I…I err…I seek the courts indulgence. I have to say whilst I am not sure why he is not here, perhaps His Lordship can rise for say ten minutes in order to allow me time to make some enquires."

"Very well, Mr Peggs-Green."

"I am obliged, My Lord," Mr Peggs-Green said, as he made his way over to Abdel.

Ten minutes later, the Judge returned into the courtroom.

"Well, Mr Peggs-Green what is the position?"

"My Lord, I am grateful for the time. Sadly, my client was hospitalised at the weekend. Apparently on Saturday evening, he suffered a heart attack and was taken to Leicester Royal Hospital. He has not been discharged by the hospital. I have a letter signed by Dr Maisuria confirming what I have said."

"How long is he likely to be in hospital, and what is his condition? I suppose your application is for the trial to be adjourned, hmm?" the Judge asked.

"The doctor has not stated how long he will be in hospital, My Lord. He suffered a minor heart attack and I speculate that an adjournment for at least four weeks may not be unreasonable in the circumstances."

"Very well, having seen supporting evidence from the hospital, I am satisfied that there is a reasonable excuse for the defendant Faizali Rehman failing to answer to court bail today. I am extending his bail for four weeks from today.

Mr Peggs-Green, I would like you to update me of his progress. As soon as he is fit to return back to court, I would like to resume the trial."

"Indeed, My Lord, I most certainly shall do exactly that."

"We are adjourned then," the Judge said.

"All rise," the usher said.

Chapter 17

Tom, after a week in captivity locked up in the same room had become aggressive and agitated. Each time David made a visit to deliver some food and water bottles, Tom displayed aggression towards him threatening to kill him. David laughed at the feeble warnings reminding him who was in captivity and who was free. David, one afternoon, fired a warning shot across the bow, warning Tom if he did not calm down and cooperate with him, he would leave him there to die. Three days went by; there were no visits or supplies brought to him. He knew now he was somewhere in a remote place no one could hear or find him. His sanity began to wane. Concerned for his own safety, the threat of dying there became a stark reality for him. The living conditions had become totally unbearable too. The stench of urine, his body odour, state of being unclean and the awful smell emanating from an unflushed toilet focussed his mind on survival, even perhaps cooperation with his captor.

It was a Thursday that week. Abdel was in Papaji's room. The door was ajar when Dr Maisuria came in to see her patient.

"Good afternoon, Mr Rehman, how are you feeling today?" she asked.

"I feel fine, Doctor, thank you."

"Well, your recovery has been good, blood pressure is near as normal as can be expected. The heart trace has recorded a murmur in a couple of places, other than that the signs are good. The good news is, for now, I am happy to discharge you, so you can go home today. I would like you to see the senior cardiac consultant as an outpatient in two weeks' time. I have an appointment booked for you. The nurse will hand the appointment card to you when you are leaving. So that's it for now. Be good. Make sure you eat the right things, less salt and cut out all greasy foods."

"Thank you so much, Doctor. I will bring him for his outpatient appointment," Abdel said.

"Goodbye for now."

"Papaji, that sounds good. You can go home today. How would you like to come stay with me at my house? I have a housekeeper; her name is Amna. She is a lovely lady. She will look after you, I am sure."

"I will think about it. Let me get home first. *Amii* might be back anytime soon anyway."

"All right. In the meantime, I will hire a housekeeper to come look after you. Don't say no to that as I insist, Papaji."

"Very well, son, if you feel that is best."

Abdel knew he would decline the invitation as his house was purchased with lottery money. He would not agree to stay there for that reason. Farzana made some enquiries locally see if anyone would be interested in earning some cash looking after Papaji. There was no shortage of potential applicants. A middle-aged woman who lived two streets away had recently lost her husband from a heart attack so was desperate to earn some cash was hired to cook for him and keep the house clean for £100 for a week. Abdel was happy with that as it equated to just under £15 each day for a week. She appeared reliable as well as trustworthy too. Abdel picked a convenient moment to tell his father what *Amii* had said on the phone. Strangely, he did not seem as surprised as Abdel thought he might be. He seemed a little irked at hearing Fauzia was not returning back home though it did not bother him too much. All he muttered was women do as they please now and how times had changed for the worse.

It was Saturday morning. There was no sign of David still. Tom began to worry for the situation had turned dire, even desperate. He was terribly hungry. It was about 3:00 p.m. in the afternoon David came to the property.

"Hey, please, I am desperate, man. I need to eat, clean up, please." He pleaded with David as soon as he stepped into the room.

"Ah, I see you have changed your tune, have you? Let's see now if we can agree a few things first."

"Please anything. I will give anything you want from me," Tom pleaded with his captor.

"First, I want your absolute word that you will keep away from Sara. You will not go back to the property in Frisby other than to collect your things."

"Yes, I agree to that."

"Before the second condition can be agreed, tell me about the time when you met Nawaz Khan at the prison in Manchester and what you agreed to do for him."

"Do you mean the Pakistani guy?"

"Yes, I do."

"Well, he said he would pay me £3,000 to do a job in Leeds."

"All right, now the second condition. What I want you to do is…"

Mr Peggs-Green had sent Judge Norrington QC an email updating him on Faizali Rehman's medical condition. The Judge responded to him to say he had requested his clerk to list the matter for the resumption of the trial on any available days in July. Andrew Stanton called Abdel on the telephone informing him of the judge's decision. Sure enough, it was not long before a letter was sent to Faizali and Nawaz informing them that the adjourned trial would recommence on Tuesday 13 July at 10:00 a.m. and that they should answer to court bail.

Day 6 was a hot summer's day on 13 July. The courtroom was packed. The overhead ceiling fans were whirring at full speed. Mr Peggs-Green called Faizali Rehman to the stand. Faizali slowly stepped out of the dock holding the blue-coloured *tasbee* in his hand. Then slowly he walked at the pace of a tortoise making his way to the witness box, stopping at one point to catch his breath, head drooped low. He made sure the jury made particular note of this, as well as his age too. Slowly but surely, he made his way to the witness box eventually, demonstrably showing the jury that he was an old man. The usher approached him and asked if he would like to take the oath or affirm. He stated in a low voice that he would take the oath on the Koran as he was truly a Muslim. He picked up the Koran, raised it up with both hands, brought it towards his face, leaned forward towards the holy book, touched his lips on the book and kissed it first, then he raised it above his head before repeated the words on the card.

"I swear by Allah and on the Holy Koran to tell the truth and nothing but the truth."

"Mr Rehman, how many daughters do you have?" Mr Peggs-Green asked.

"I have five daughters," Faizali responded.

"Apart from your daughter Saleena, are all your daughters alive and well?"

"Yes. they are all sat in court over there," Faizali said pointing to the public gallery.

"If I can take you back to December 1997, please. I am sorry if this might be upsetting or painful for you, but could you tell the court how you felt when you first learnt of your daughter's death."

"Saleena was my fourth daughter. She was very pretty, intelligent and dear to me. I had loved her like I did all my five daughters. I was devastated at the news. I could not understand it."

"I will ask you straightaway, Mr Rehman, did you have anything to do with the tragic death of your daughter Saleena and her friend Mr Calvin Lenton?"

"No, I truly did not. I am a Muslim. I have practised my faith all my life and I have taken an oath on the Holy Koran. I had nothing to do with my daughter's death," Faizali said head bowed with tears in his eyes.

"Very well, could you explain why the Crown witness, Mrs Raazia Khan, told the police about the conversation she heard that night when she says she was in the kitchen on the day you had a first anniversary remembrance event for Saleena at your house?"

"I truly don't know. My son-in-law Nawaz had disappointed me very much. I thought he was a businessman when he first came to my house to see Saleena, but he constantly kept asking for money. My son Abdel gave him I think about £125,000 but he spent it all in no time at all. He was a big spender."

"Mr Rehman, could you tell the court why he gave him that sort of money and where did your son get that kind of money?"

"My son had won the lottery jackpot when he was seventeen. He gave some to every family member including Nawaz. I did not take any. As to why Nawaz was always asking for money? I don't know the reason. He may have been short of money, I guess."

"So being short of money, naturally, you being his father-in-law, he asked you for money. What was the amount can you recall, Mr Rehman?"

"Not exactly, but it could have been £5,000."

"So, when you were speaking about this matter, who were you speaking with and where were you in the house?"

"I was with my wife Fauzia, and we were in the living room."

"It was just the two of you in the living room, correct?"

"Yes."

"Where was your son Abdel?"

"He was upstairs in one of the bedrooms."

"What about your daughter Raazia, where was she?"

"She was in the kitchen cleaning up after the *barsi majalis*, oh sorry, the remembrance service for Saleena. Everyone had gone. It would have been about 9:00 p.m. I had put the television on to listen to the news. I always put the news on in the evening; it was my habit."

"So would you think your daughter Raazia might have been mistaken about the conversation relating to the money, especially if she was in another part of the house coupled with the fact the television was on making it difficult to hear the exactness of the conversation."

"Yes, most definitely. I do believe so."

"Did you give your son-in-law Nawaz Khan any money, Mr Rehman?"

"No, I did not."

"Let us now turn to the telephone calls that Nawaz made to your house. What can you tell us about them?"

"He called frequently asking for money. Some days he asked if I knew where Saleena was as he wanted to be reconciled with his wife."

"You are quite sure about that?"

"Yes, one hundred percent."

"The Crown says that you conspired with your son-in-law to have Saleena killed?"

"*Wal'Lahi*."

"What does that mean? Please translate for the jury."

"I swear by Allah I am telling the truth."

"I want to ask you about the honour system. The Crown alleges that Saleena was on a course unacceptable to your culture or tradition. She was killed because of that. What do you say to that?"

"What can I say, Mr Peggs-Green? It was her choice. Why would that concern me?"

"Thank you, Mr Rehman, stay there please. There will be some questions from my two colleagues here."

"Mr Rehman, did you and Nawaz Khan have a conversation about honour killing at any stage at all?" asked Mr Griffidam.

"No Sir."

"Thank you, Mr Rehman. No further questions."

"So, you had five daughters, Mr Rehman. Are they all married?" asked Mr Ravenstone.

"All but one."

"Which daughter is not married?"

181

"Sara."

"She is daughter number five, correct?"

"Yes."

"Why is that? Isn't it usual in your culture for you to arrange marriages for your daughters at a very young age?"

"Yes, it is. Sara did not wish to get married."

"Why was that?"

"I must confess I do not know."

"Really, Mr Rehman? Isn't it true that you arranged marriages for all your daughters as soon as they were turning sixteen, including Sara? They were still children at sixteen, Sir, and Sara refused to be compliant with what you wanted?"

"Yes, it is our tradition to arrange marriages for our children. I see nothing wrong with the tradition."

"We will come back to Sara in a second. Were your daughters happy to get married at that age?"

"Yes, they were."

"You compelled them to get married, did you not?"

"No, that is not true; they consented to marry."

"Let me take you back to your daughter Raazia's testimony. She testified, you will recall, that she was most certainly and unequivocally not happy to get married at the age of sixteen. In fact, she wanted to continue with her education but you did not allow that. Instead, you arranged her marriage without even consulting her, that is correct, isn't it?"

"As a father, I was merely discharging my duty to get my daughter married."

"When was the first time you had bought Raazia, or any daughters for that matter, any presents, birthday or Christmas, Mr Rehman, hmm?"

"On her sixteenth birthday, I bought her gifts."

"Really? That was a birthday gift, was it?"

"Yes, in a way it was. You see marriage and the union of two people is the greatest gift from Allah. The clothes were to mark the event. It was a happy time as it coincided with her birthday."

"Some might disagree with that very philosophical view, Mr Rehman!" A quick burst of laughter was heard in the whole courtroom. "Your daughter happens to clearly disagree with you. The reality was there were no celebrations for girls in your household, no birthdays or Christmas celebrations, no presents bought for girls ever, no spirit of joy and fun at Christmas time for them, was there? You might be like the Dickens' character Ebenezer Scrooge perhaps. This is what your own daughter said in her testimony, and I quote: 'There were no birthday celebrations for girls either. For a boy it was different. He had big celebrations planned for Abdel. We wanted to be children, Mr Ravenstone, but we were not allowed to be children. We used to sit there in the sitting room all huddled together under a blanket trying to keep warm, a small paraffin heater burning on low heat. We would fight to circle with a pen the movies or programmes we wanted to watch over Christmas. Schools were closed, and we were happy as we were just school kids, but Papaji would not let us watch anything. My sister Allia would beg and sometimes argue with him about how stupidly strict he was, but he did not let us have fun as kids, no birthday celebrations either ever I recall. The first time that I thought he had arranged a birthday party for me was on my sixteenth birthday'

"Raazia paints a very different picture of her childhood and that of her sisters. Something, I venture to think rather not unlike a tale from Victorian days or a Dickensian book. Do you still maintain you were a loving father to your daughters?" Mr Ravenstone asked with a raised voice.

Faizali sat quietly twirling the beads between his fingers. There was no response from him.

"I direct you to answer Mr Ravenstone's question," the Judge ordered him.

"I loved my daughters. That is all I have to say on the matter," Faizali responded.

"Very well, so you agree you arranged your daughter's marriages? I say you compelled them against their will."

"No."

"What do you say to this? 'Saleena had this dream that she would marry someone she chose as her partner, and unlike all her sisters, she would not be forced into an arranged marriage. She used to say to me 'I will run away and no one will find me if they do this to me.' She was wrong. Papaji and *Amii* chose Nawaz for her. She was not happy and wanted to run away, but she could not.'"

"I did not know she was unhappy. She did not tell me."

"Was not the reality in your house such that your children were petrified of you? They dared not speak out for fear of repercussions from a man who was domineering?"

"No."

"Let's return to your daughter, Sara. Did you not arrange a marriage for her in Pakistan when she was not yet even sixteen? You were to fly out to Pakistan as you had arranged for her to marry someone there from your wife's relative's side of the family?"

"No, that was a holiday."

"Was it now? Then explain why it was that she had threatened to report you to the police. She was not yet sixteen when you made those arrangements, was she? Subsequently, the poor girl packed some bare belongings and fled the house in the dead of night leaving home. Was that to prevent being forced into marriage she did not agree to, Mr Rehman?"

"No, I don't know."

"Mr Rehman, your daughter is in court over there in the public gallery. I can call her to give rebuttal evidence, hmm?"

"Yes. She left because she did not wish to be married."

"Precisely. I suspect for her to do that, Mr Rehman, it can't have been easy. It must have taken great courage to do that at her age. Was she in fear of her safety if she did not comply with your instructions?"

"I do not agree, but I do not know what you mean by fear for her safety. She was at home with her family."

"Mr Ravenstone, I hate to interrupt you whilst you are in full flow with your cross-examination. However, it is approaching 1:00 p.m. We did not break earlier for a short comfort break, and I feel it time for us to all have a break."

"My Lord."

"We will break for lunch now for an hour and fifteen minutes. The witness is reminded that you are under oath. You are not at liberty to discuss your evidence or the case with anyone, understood?"

Faizali nodded as the Judge rose from his seat. The usual cry of "all stand" by the usher followed. As usual, all the reporters made a dash for the exit door of the courtroom.

Maleeka noted David Mutembe was not in court today. She asked Raazia about him. She did not know why he was not there. As Raazia and her family walked round the corridor of the court busy talking about where to go for lunch, Nadine spotted David speaking with Mr Ravenstone in an inconspicuous corner of the corridor away from the crowds.

"Wonder what David is up to now?" Maleeka asked.

"He seems to be one mysterious character!" Nadine responded.

"You can say that again, Nadine."

Over lunch, Maleeka mentioned to Raazia and Akeel that David was spotted speaking to Mr Ravenstone. Maleeka started with her theories of some sort of international espionage going on. "You will see I will be proved right," she maintained, but everyone just laughed at her wild theory.

Returning to court for the afternoon session after lunch, Mr Ravenstone resumed his cross-examination. Papaji looked worse than he did in the morning. He looked tired, in a state of dire nervous disposition, almost trembling as he slowly got himself seated in the witness box. Mr Ravenstone wondered if the old man was performing certain theatrics playing or performing to his audience, the jury? The cross-examination was mentally draining for him, admittedly, and it was not easy when public eyes of the world were focussed on him facing harsh criticism.

"Mr Rehman, I was asking you about your daughter Sara before lunch, you will recall, I am sure. So, if she were safely at home with her family, why would someone of such tender years leave that safety in the middle of the night and take flight from a safe place, Mr Rehman?"

"I do not know. Children these days have different mindsets."

"I see, so that is your explanation. Very well, let me ask you this, did your daughter Sara ever return back home?"

"No."

"NO was your answer, was it not? Why, one wonders. Let me ask you about your relationship with Sara and your second daughter Allia. Do you have good relations with them?"

"No, they have chosen not to speak to me."

"Why is that? Is it because you have succeeded in alienating them by your traditions which they despise?"

"I do not know. Like I said, children have their own minds nowadays."

"Well, Mr Rehman, they are here in court, and they can be called to give rebuttal evidence should it become necessary. So, one child takes flight from home, another becomes estranged from you, Mr Rehman, yet you maintain to be a loving father, hmm?"

Papaji looked away from Mr Ravenstone turning his head towards the public gallery. He looked at his family one by one with one raised eyebrow, starting with Raazia who had tears in her eyes, then Akeel, then Allia who returned the favour with the same look of throwing daggers as he had done looking at her. You could almost see that pent-up hatred for him on Allia's face as it changed colour. Then he looked at Sara and finally, Sameena. It was an embarrassing position to be in. Mr Ravenstone had launched a full-frontal attack on his parenthood in public. It reminded him of Nawaz doing the same on the telephone after Saleena had left him. The consolation there was it was done in private. Faizali began to fidget in his seat passing the beads between his fingers at a faster pace than he normally would. A silent courtroom waited for an answer.

"I did my best as a parent. I woke up at 6:00 a.m. to remember Allah first thing after waking up. I worked hard in a factory all day. I did my duty and provided for my family, eight mouths to feed, you know. It was not easy, you know," he replied head bowed.

It was a pathetic effort, Raazia thought, at redeeming himself. She knew it was all an act for the jury responding with his head bowed, speaking in a low tone, as if it might make the jury feel sorry for him. To Raazia, the words felt hollow.

"Mr Rehman, parents who generally spend most of their time working at the expense of spending quality time with children at least compensate it by spending money buying gifts for them. It is odd that you did not do that, yet you say you loved your children?

"It does not really matter to me what you think. I know I did the best for my family," Faizali said with a slight force in his tone.

"I see. Let's move on to yet another member of your family this time, who again at your behest was estranged from you, your son Abdel. Well, how long were you estranged from your son Abdel?"

"Really, My Lord, objection to this line of questioning as it is simply not relevant," Mr Peggs-Green stated forcefully rising to his feet, as Ravenstone sat down. "I feel Mr Ravenstone is labouring the point unnecessarily, My Lord."

"Mr Ravenstone?"

"My Lord, this witness claims to be a loving father. Therefore, I am entitled to establish the credibility of what this witness claims. My line of questioning is merely to establish whether he was or was not."

"Objection overruled; I will allow it, but do move on Mr Ravenstone." The Judge decided.

"My Lord, thank you. Well, Mr Rehman?"

"I have made up with my son."

"That is not what I asked you."

"He had gambled whilst I was away abroad. When I returned back to UK, I found out from the papers he had won the lottery jackpot at the age of seventeen."

There were some, "Oooh, nice one," comments heard from the gallery.

"My religion says it is *haram* to gamble. I just wanted to show him, justifiably, my dissatisfaction at what he had done was wrong."

"*Haram* is an Arabic word. It means 'prohibited' does it not?"

Faizali nodded.

"So, you did not speak to him for some ten years then? He is your only son!"

"I have forgiven him, and he is the one who brings me to court every day. My relationship with him is good."

"Let us move on to the evidence of your daughter, Mrs Raazia Khan. She says in her evidence that she clearly heard what you said that night. Why would she tell the police what she heard if she was unsure? She was so distraught after hearing what she heard that she left the house via the back door without saying goodbye. Is that not the truth?"

"I do not know. She is mistaken."

"On the contrary, Sir, I put it to you, that there was no television on in the room. She overheard your conversation absolutely correctly about Nawaz Khan asking for £5,000 which you had agreed to pay him for taking care of his wife who was about to dishonour you, Mr Rehman, and it was blood money, was it not?"

"No, no, no, no, it was not, I tell you. Why do you torment me so?"

"This is not torment. It is the reality, Mr Rehman. Your honour was at stake, Sir, and you took whatever step was necessary to prevent Saleena divorcing Nawaz Khan and marrying a man not from your community. What you did was despicable in the name of honour. I therefore put it to you, that you with your son-in-law Nawaz Khan conspired together, did you not, to kill your daughter and her boyfriend to protect your so-called high honour?"

"No, it is not true."

"The telephone calls Nawaz Khan made to your telephone line were, I put to you, undoubtedly conversations relating to the conspiracy you two had hatched."

"No, they were not. It is not true."

"I have no further questions," Mr Ravenstone said as he resumed his seat.

"Mr Peggs-Green, any re-examination of your witness?" the Judge asked.

"Indeed, My Lord, just one question. Mr Rehman, how sure are you that your television was on that night?"

"I am one hundred and ten percent sure."

"Thank you, no further questions. My Lord, that is the evidence in defence for the defendant Faizali Rehman."

"My Lord…err. I am very conscious of the time," Mr Griffidam said rising to his feet, "and feel sure His Lordship will be thinking about adjourning for the day. However, I—"

"Yes, Mr Griffidam. Do you have an application to make?"

"No, My Lord, there is no application from me. I wish to indicate to His Lordship that I shall not be calling Nawaz Khan to give evidence as my client exercises his legal right not to give evidence. Furthermore, there are no other witnesses I shall be calling on his behalf."

Some faint gasps were heard from the gallery much to Mr Griffidam's dislike as he did not want any negative impact on his client.

"Well, thank you for that indication, Mr Griffidam. I must say that has surprised me, however be that as it may, we will indeed adjourn now. 10 a.m. start for closing speeches tomorrow."

"All stand." The usher's voice boomed across the court as people rose from their seats. The reporters, as usual, rushed to make their way to the exit door first.

Sherlock and Kiki were standing in the corridor just outside the courtroom discussing Nawaz Khan choosing not to give evidence when Mutembe approached them. He introduced himself first.

"Good afternoon, my name is David Mutembe. Could I speak with you in private somewhere, please?" he asked directly as he shook hands with both of them.

"We have seen you sitting in the court gallery since the start of the case, unsure of what your interest is exactly in the case. You do not seem to be an ordinary visitor, if I may say so, Sir," Sherlock said.

"Please come with me. We can speak privately in one of the rooms there," David said pointing to some rooms in the opposite side of the corridor.

The trio proceeded to one of the vacant rooms. David looked through the slim glass panel on the door making sure it was unoccupied. The signage on the door read 'Consulting Rooms – Reserved for Barristers/Clients – Private Only'. The lettering was in big font painted in black on a silver plaque. David asked them to take a seat as he closed the door behind him, then pulled out a chair from under the wooden table before sitting down. Both the officers looked rather puzzled.

"Who are you?" asked Kiki.

"My name is David Mutembe, I am a security aide to President Augustus Otambu who has, well, how shall I put it, shall we say, a personal interest in the case, Madam."

"What sort of personal interest?" asked Sherlock.

"Calvin Lenton was his nephew."

"Ah, the penny drops! So, the instruction to reopen the case was from high-up no doubt. It makes perfect sense now. No wonder we were not given a reason by the Chief instructing us to reopen the case," Sherlock said.

"What do you want from us?" Kiki asked directly.

"I am here only as an observer, those were my instructions," – he paused – "but what I am about to tell you must not leave this room. You may discuss this with Mr Ravenstone QC, but if I may suggest you exercise discretion in how you put the information to him," David said almost whispering.

"Go on, Mr Mutembe, you have our undivided attention, and we are all ears!" Sherlock stated.

"Being a security man, I have to say, I could not help myself when, quite by chance, I came by some useful information very recently to do with this case. It was in the very last three or four days." He handed the officers a folded piece of paper. "You will find scribbled on it a name and address of where you will find this man – Tom Ford. He had met Nawaz Khan in prison. He was the hired killer. Pick him up and question him. I am sure he will cooperate. And before you say it, I have not laid a finger on him. I have used some unorthodox methods, admittedly, which I do not wish to go into, shall we say, to persuade him."

"He has been coerced, you mean?" Kiki asked.

"No, well, maybe in a way, Madam. If you wish to punish those who are guilty, who have engaged in this horrendous crime, sometimes it becomes necessary to get some cooperation. What you don't know does not matter."

"We can't use the evidence if it has been given under duress!" Sherlock added.

"What duress, Sa? You have to obtain a statement, that is all. He can have a lawyer present if he desires. It will be an entirely voluntary statement given by Tom Ford. All I am saying is, you will have no trouble from him on that front, I assure you. He will cooperate, but you need to hurry. You do not have very much time. I suggest it would be best to send some police officers to his house in Frisby in Leicestershire, pick him up before he disappears. Don't worry, I shall be here again tomorrow if you need me."

Papaji was in a bad mood that evening. As soon as he entered his hotel room, he slammed the door, closed behind him throwing the key on the floor. Abdel tried to speak to him. It was no good, all he kept muttering was, "How dare that white man criticise my parenting in public like that. It was embarrassing." It preyed on his mind over and over. No matter how hard he tried to get Papaji's mind off the case, it was no good. Frustrated, he did not know what to do as all his father wanted that evening was to be left alone in his room. Before leaving his room, Abdel ordered room service for Papaji just in case he felt hungry.

Abdel opened the door to his room, closed it behind him, let out a huge sigh and dropped the room key on the bedside table. He felt dreadful at the same time completely helpless. Abdel flicked the TV on with the remote control. Physically as well as mentally, he was exhausted. He fell asleep to be woken up at around 10 p.m. by hunger pangs. His tummy was rumbling like a volcano. Feeling lethargic to venture out for a takeaway, he picked up the hotel restaurant menu. As he looked through, the news came on. Abdel turned the volume up slightly.

"This is Sean Denton reporting for BBC News from Manchester Crown Court. This case was adjourned on 21 June when the defendant Faizali Rehman failed to turn up at his trial. He was reported to have suffered a heart attack on 19 June and was admitted to hospital. This is a case where he and his son-in-law face charges of conspiracy to murder Saleena Khan and Calvin Lenton. The victims were found dead at a flat in Woodstock on 19 December 1997. The prosecution allege they were victims of honour killings. At the resumed trial, after slowly making his way to the witness box, Mr Rehman took the oath on the Koran. His barrister Mr Jeremy Peggs-Green QC asked him directly, 'Did you

have anything to do with the tragic death of your daughter Saleena and her friend Mr Calvin Lenton?'

" 'No, I truly did not. I am a Muslim. I have practised my faith all my life and I have taken an oath on the Holy Koran. I had nothing to do with my daughter's death,' he replied with his head bowed and tears in his eyes. He was asked how he felt when he first learnt of his daughter's death. He replied, 'Saleena was my fourth daughter. She was very pretty, intelligent and dear to me. I had loved her like I did all my five daughters. I was devastated at the news. I could not understand it.'

"Having established his defence, Mr Rehman, faced a barrage of questions when he was put under rigorous cross-examination from Mr Ravenstone QC for the Crown. Mr Rehman had stated in his evidence that he was a loving father to all his children, yet under cross-examination, it became evident that he was anything but a loving father. Apart from his son Abdel, there were no celebrations in his household for the children for birthdays or Christmases, no presents and certainly no festivities. For the children, it seemed like a drab Victorian life.

"Mr Ravenstone further tried to draw out information that he had forced his four daughters into arranged marriages at the age of sixteen. Saleena wanted to choose her own husband and had said to her sister Raazia when a child she would run away if she was forced to marry someone she did not like. Sadly, the reality for her was she was forced into marriage with the defendant Nawaz Khan who also faces the same charge of conspiracy to murder.

"Through cross-examination, it was established he had not spoken to his son Abdel for ten years. You may remember Abdel Rehman. He was the seventeen-year-old who scooped the jackpot of £6.6 million in 1990. Mr Rehman senior said it was not permitted in his religion for someone to gamble and he had stopped speaking to him to show him that it was wrong what he did. He went on to say he has a good relationship with his son now.

"Next it was put to him that his daughter had correctly heard his conversation with his wife about Nawaz Khan asking for £5,000 for sorting out the business with Saleena. He put it to Mr Rehman that it was blood money. 'No, no, no, no, it was not, I tell you. Why do you torment me so?' was his reply.

"Mr Ravenstone retorted, 'This is not torment. It is the reality, Mr Rehman. Your honour was at stake, Sir, and you took whatever step that was necessary to prevent Saleena divorcing Nawaz Khan and marrying a man not from your community. What you did was despicable in the name of honour. I therefore put it to you, that you with your son-in-law, Nawaz Khan conspired together, did you not, to kill your daughter and her boyfriend to protect your so-called high honour?'

" 'No, it is not true.'

" 'The telephone calls Nawaz Khan made to your telephone line were, I put to you, conversations relating to the conspiracy.'

" 'No, they were not.'

"It would have been Mr Griffidam's turn to call the defendant Nawaz Khan to give evidence next, but there were gasps in the court when he stated to the trial judge, Mr Norrington QC, that he would not be calling Mr Khan to give evidence as Mr Khan would be exercising his legal right not to give evidence. The case was adjourned for Counsel's closing speeches tomorrow. This is Sean Denton for BBC News at Manchester Crown Court."

A meeting was arranged in the morning of Day 7 of the hearing at the Crown Court between the Crown Prosecutor Carlie Singer, Mr Ravenstone QC, DCI McLean and DI Slater.

Mr Ravenstone sat down to hear some of the information and he stayed calm until DCI McLean finished speaking. Mr Ravenstone's face changed colour. Suddenly, he seemed uptight.

"Where is this so-called witness now?"

"In the cells, Sir," Sherlock replied.

"Bloody hell, you people. This case is a total mess, I tell you. The Crown has rested its case. I will be most surprised if the Judge allows the application to hear new evidence once the case is closed. He will also want to know if this witness has been in any way coerced to give evidence. This case has become more complicated than I thought it would be. I can't say I am happy about this at all," Mr Ravenstone stated angrily.

"There are two options here: one is to leave matters as they are and Counsel proceed to closing speeches, and the second option would be for you, Mr Ravenstone, to put together an application before the Judge and see what he says. My view would be there would no harm in doing so. What is the worst that can happen? He says no and we move on with the case as if we did not have this part of the evidence. Should he grant the application, Mr Ravenstone, you may have that added edge towards getting a result that we want, right? Do you wish me to look up the case law? I would be happy to," Carlie Singer asked.

"Thank you, but I know the cases. Hmm…very well, let's proceed then," Mr Ravenstone stated reluctantly.

"My Lord, I wish to make an application to His Lordship and would be grateful if the members of the jury were requested to leave the room," Mr Ravenstone asked.

"What for, Mr Ravenstone? The Crown has rested its case against the two defendants and so have the defence. Naturally, I was therefore expecting closing speeches from Counsel today so I may try and get my direction to jury completed, hopefully, today as well, but I find Counsel is seeking a *voire dire*! This had better be good, Mr Ravenstone."

"I seek His Lordship's indulgence. Yes, the application is for a *voire dire*, My Lord."

The Judge instructed the jury members to leave the courtroom. There was some chatter in the courtroom as the jury members made their way out of the courtroom.

"Thank you, I am indeed very grateful for His Lordship allowing my application at this late stage in the case. However, it is imperative that I discharge my duty to the Crown in the prosecution of this case with diligence, properly and above all having the interests of justice in my mind as a consideration of paramount importance. Since the Crown closed its case last week, new evidence, which was not available to the Crown until yesterday, has come to light. I therefore make this application for the Crown to reopen its case to enable me to adduce this evidence. DCI McLean and DI Slater spoke to me yesterday, My Lord, on the telephone in the afternoon after I left here. They advised they had received some new intelligence information which led to an urgent investigation resulting in the arrest of one Tom Ford. When the detectives spoke to him last night, he admitted to being hired by Nawaz Khan to kill his wife. I stress this is completely new evidence which was not available to the Crown before closing its case. My Lord, I respectfully submit to allow it in the interest of justice; not to do so would create injustice.

"His Lordship will be aware of the case law authorities, I am sure. They are cases of R v. Rice (1963) 1 QB 857 and R v. Kane 65 Cr Appeal R 270. Archbold page 506. The authorities cited state, in English law the general rule is that matters probative of the defendant's guilt should ordinarily be adduced as part of the prosecution's case. That rule applies (a) to matters put in cross-examination to a defendant and (b) to the calling of evidence. In this case, it was said that there is a general principle of practice, though not rule of law, which requires all evidentiary matters the prosecution intend to rely upon as probative of the defendant's guilt should be adduced before the close of the prosecution case, if, it is available then. Whether evidence subsequently available to the prosecution should be introduced at a later stage is a matter for the trial judge's discretion, which must be exercised within the limits imposed by the authorities and in such a way and subject to such safeguards as seen to him best suited to achieve justice between the Crown and the defendants, My Lord. This general principal was again considered by the court of appeal in the case of R v. Kane. The court in Kane stated where evidence could have been led as part of the case for the Crown became available for the first time to the Crown after the close of the Crown's case, the subsequent introduction of that evidence or its exclusion were matters to be decided by the trial Judge. Both authorities confirm the matter is for His Lordship to decide upon as the trial Judge."

"My Lord, on behalf of the defence, I oppose the application my learned friend for the prosecution has put before you. The police have had nearly two years following the tragic deaths to discover this evidence. It seems somewhat odd that it has now suddenly out of the blue become available after the Crown has closed the case. My concern is the defence will not have had any opportunity to consider that evidence beforehand as there is no statement from this witness. No doubt any evidence would be given on the hoof, unless His Lordship grants a long adjournment, should His Lordship be considering allowing the application. One has to also question the probative value of this evidence. I venture to think if there has been some deal done or offered to this Tom Ford.

Why otherwise would he agree to be a witness for the Crown at this late stage? The legal system would be dreadfully faulty if there were no safeguards in the justice system for the defendants, My Lord," Mr Peggs-Green asserted.

"I too oppose the Crown's application, My Lord. I concur entirely with my learned friend Mr Peggs-Green's argument. In addition, I would respectfully suggest that there must be, not just safeguards, but stringent safeguards which must go further in such circumstances ensuring there is no injustice suffered, especially where, My Lord in a situation, where a defendant has already made a decision to exercise his legal right not to give evidence but then allowing the application then creates such an adverse effect on the proceedings so as to bring about a conviction unjustly. It is for the Crown to establish sufficiency of evidence such that it creates a realistic prospect of a conviction and to place all that evidence before the jury and court in a timely manner. It seems to me that the Crown must feel that there is the lack of such evidence, which both my learned friend Mr Peggs-Green and I have argued all along to be the case here and that, therefore, it has become necessary to ask you to rule on admitting this new evidence," Mr Griffidam asserted for Nawaz Khan.

"Very well, gentlemen, I shall need to rise to consider the application. Before I make my decision, I need to speak to the two police officers, DCI McLean and DI Slater with all three Counsels in my chambers."

All three barristers looked at one another. Mr Ravenstone made a strange facial expression, flicking his head on one side at the same time raising one eyebrow as to suggest that the Judge must have something serious on his mind that he could not perhaps discuss in open court. Mr Peggs-Green responded with a facial expression by raising both his eyebrows at the same time. Mr Griffidam simply shrugged his shoulders. Counsel took off their wigs and placed them on the bench where they were seated.

The Judge's room was cool compared to the courtroom. The windows in his chamber were wide open letting some fresh air mingled with a slight breeze into the pleasantly cool room. The Judge had taken off his wig and gown, which were hung on a coat stand, preferring to have respite in the hot weather from the formal courtroom attire. The Judge was in his late fifties, wore a pinstriped suit, white tabs, perfectly starched wing collars, hair dyed dark blonde, the tell-tale signs where you could see the sideburns were still grey. His half-moon gold-rimmed spectacles were perched just in the right position below the bridge of his nose. As you would expect, the chamber had legal books all around. There was a wooden oak table with a pile of paperwork neatly piled up in one corner. There was a glass paperweight and a telephone next to the pile. In the middle, in front of the Judge, there was a freshly made cup of tea in a china cup with a matching saucer. The steam was rising from the hot teacup. Next to it was a white china plate with digestive biscuits arranged on it. The Judge took a sip of tea as the detectives with the three barristers walked into his chamber.

"Thank you all for coming into my chamber. You must all be wondering why I have asked you in here. There are no formalities in here; we can all speak freely and informally. Well, I will come straight to the points which I wish to clarify out there," the Judge said as he pointed to the courtroom holding his spectacle in the same hand. "Detectives, I get the feeling you have become aware now, have you not, why the case was reopened all of a sudden just like that. Well?"

"We truthfully said we did not know in court, Judge. We did not perjure ourselves. We genuinely did not at the time of giving evidence. However, Judge, some intel information came our way only in the last few days, Sir, which, shall we say, threw light on the matter. That, however, is not intrinsically important to the case Judge, is it?" DCI McLean said.

"No, but this is my courtroom, Detective, and I wouldn't want a foreign power influencing the Justice system. Can you assure me both of you have diligently been involved in investigating the whole case before bringing it to court and that you genuinely were not aware why the case was reopened?"

"We have Judge. Both Kiki Slater and I can assure you of that," McLean stated.

"Very well, what about this new evidence then? Why was it not available before and during the investigation? Where has it come from all of a sudden? Detectives, can you tell me or Mr Ravenstone? I remind you as officers of the law and you, Mr Ravenstone, being an officer of the court, there is an overriding duty not to mislead the court."

"Judge, I would never mislead the court. There was some intelligence gathered. I am not at liberty to reveal the source, Judge, for fear of compromising an informant's position which would not be right. Suffice it to say, however, that it was very recent. Last week, in fact, it was discovered quite by chance from Mr Rehman's younger daughter Sara who as you know from the evidence was estranged from the family. She had been living with this man Tom Ford who had assaulted her which forced her to leave her home. She quite by chance happened to mention that in a conversation to this individual source and it transpires that not only was he in Leeds on 18th and 19th of December 1997, but had incinerated the clothes he was wearing at the time in question upon his return home. Sara Rehman who works for the prison service as a probation officer apparently met Tom Ford whilst he was a serving prisoner. They subsequently had a relationship. He had kept the information to himself. It was by coincidence she mentioned that Tom Ford knew Nawaz Khan. They had met in prison when Nawaz served a short prison sentence following the assault on his wife Saleena. The police could not have possibly known this information earlier. Once the identity of this man was known, only yesterday the police picked him up and interviewed him. He stated that Nawaz Khan had asked him to take care of his wife, he would pay him £3,000, also stating the old man would be on board with this."

"And what sort of deal have you struck with him, Mr Ravenstone?"

"If he testifies for the Crown, pleads guilty to manslaughter, he may get eight to fifteen."

"If I were to disallow the evidence you wish to call, then what?"

"Depending on what the jury find, two guilty men may well be walking away scot-free from the court. There will be no justice for the victims nor will the Rehman family have closure, Judge," Mr Ravenstone said.

"Jeremy, Josiah anything you wish to say to me before I make my mind up?"

"Well, Judge, we both made our representations to you out there. It really is a decision for you. I must confess I do not envy you having to make the decision; it is a tough one," Jeremy said.

"I am of exactly the same view as Jeremy, Judge," Josiah said.

"Very well, go have some refreshments; you have fifteen minutes. It gives me a chance to consider my decision whilst I enjoy the digestive biscuits with my tea."

It was a hot summer's day. The court was packed with people, many wearing summer outfits to keep cool. Most of the men in the public gallery had taken their jackets off preferring to wear a shirt to feel slightly comfortable in the stuffy courtroom. The fans had been turned on at full speed, but they were not effective. The sheer number of people packed in the courtroom was making the room more humid from body heat.

"Well, gentlemen, having considered the two case authorities Mr Ravenstone relies upon in support of his application, as both cases confirm it to be a principle of practice and not rule of law, as the trial Judge in the case, it is my decision on the matter. I believe on balance, weighing up the factors and having considered the representations from all Counsel. I find it to be in the interest of justice to allow the application for the Crown to adduce this further evidence. However, I did take on board the valid points put forward by both defence Counsel and in safeguarding the defendant's right to a fair trial, I shall allow the defence wide latitude in their cross-examination of this witness. Usher, would you call the members of the jury back into the courtroom, please?"

As the member of the jury filed back into court, some of them began to feel the intensity of the heat in the courtroom. One or two removed their jackets and put them on their laps as they resumed their seats. As soon as they were all seated, Mr Ravenstone rose to his feet to address the court.

"My Lord, thank you for allowing my application, Usher, I call Tom Ford to the stand."

After affirming to tell the truth and nothing but the truth, he sat down on the seat in the witness box. He was wearing a white T-shirt. He had this hideous tattoo of a snake on the left side. Part of it seemed covered by his white T-shirt. The tattoo then extended from his neck upwards stopping just behind his earlobe. It characterised his display of macho-toughness. He wore a white T-shirt, denims and Nike trainers. The forearms had tattoos, names of women. He surveyed the courtroom from his position to see if he could spot his captor. As soon as he spotted him, Tom turned his head immediately away from him. Mutembe was dressed in military uniform. He could not be missed as he stood out in the public gallery crowd like a sore thumb.

Here was a man who seemed to display a tough exterior, but behind the ruggedness lay a tale of a sad life having been abandoned at the age of six by his mother and growing up in foster homes under local authority care.

"Your name is Tom Ford, and you currently live in Frisby in Leicestershire, is that correct?" Mr Ravenstone asked.

"Yes, it is."

"You were arrested yesterday and were taken to Leicester Police Station for questioning where you made a confession to the police about the killings in Leeds in December 1997, is that right?"

"Yes."

"Can you tell the court what you said in your interview, avoiding where you met the defendant Nawaz Khan?"

"Yeh, would have been back in 1990, Nawaz Khan approached me, offered me three grand for a job."

"And what was that job?"

"To find his missus and do her in."

"Anything else you can remember about the conversation with Nawaz Khan?"

"Yeh, he said summut about his old man would be on board."

"Were you in Leeds on 18th and 19th of December 1997?"

"Yes, I was."

"Thank you, no further questions. Please remain there in the witness box."

"Mr Ford, you made a confession just like that did you, or were you coerced by the police or anyone else for that matter?" asked Mr Peggs-Green.

"No, my partner, Sara, she is the daughter of that other guy over there in the dock, you know, the old one. She dobbed me in, so I wanted to get it off my chest, you know."

"Have the police offered you a deal in return for giving this evidence?"

"Erm…yes, they have."

"Is that why you have agreed to give evidence for the prosecution."

"Yes."

"What have they offered you?"

"If I gave the evidence today, pleaded guilty to the charges of manslaughter that the Judge will take this into consideration a significant discount on the sentence. The reason it is manslaughter is I went in the flat in Woodhouse just to scare her. I did not now she would have a fella there. Besides, I was heavily dependent on drugs at the time."

"I see, Mr Ford. So, you are here simply because the prosecution has offered you a deal?"

"Yes."

"Do you have a history of getting into trouble with the police?"

"If you mean do I have a criminal record, yes I do."

"Thank you, I have no further questions," Mr Peggs-Green said.

"Mr Ford, your criminal record you have referred to has quite a number of dishonest offences on there. Usher, here, would you please hand Mr Ford a copy of his record. Theft, dishonesty offences, driving under the influence of alcohol and a number of others, some you have served prison sentences for. You are, one could fairly say, a prolific criminal then?" Mr Griffidam asked as he commenced his cross-examination.

"Yes, the record proves it!"

There was a huge roar of laughter in response to the comment from the public gallery, reporters and the jury. Even the judge could not hide his smile.

"Indeed, Mr Ford, so you are a habitual criminal and an inveterate liar?"

"Yeh, that's a good expression, habitual criminal, but I ain't lying about what Nawaz asked me to do. He ain't even paid me for the job!"

"Yes, I put it to you that there was no such agreement. You are here simply to save your own skin and for no other reason, are you not?"

"No, I am telling you the truth."

"A man of your impeccable criminal record, you would not know what the truth was even if it hit you in the eye, Mr Ford. You like snakes, do you?"

"Yeh, I do, why?"

"Just curious, Mr Ford; they are cold-blooded creatures. I see you have a tattoo of one on your neck. No further questions for this witness, My Lord," Mr Griffidam said resuming his seat immediately after finishing speaking.

"My Lord, I have no questions in cross-examination. May the witness be released in the custody of the police officers there?"

"Yes, you may go," said the Judge. "It is a convenient moment for us to break for lunch at this time."

Closing summations from Counsel after lunch began with Mr Peggs-Green going first.

"Members of the jury, my client Faizali Rehman is sixty-six years old. He is a devout Muslim who regards his religion, traditions and culture important as all of them play a huge part in his day-to-day life. I will tell you that I do not intend to be on my feet a very long time but I need to put his defence to you. Now, as you know, the charge is one of conspiracy to murder Saleena Khan and her boyfriend Calvin Lenton. No one can deny reading the statement of the coroner that this was a terrible attack which resulted in the death of the two victims of the crime. You heard evidence form Tom Ford that he committed the murder. I shall return to his evidence later in my speech. My client has been charged with conspiracy to murder. The law of the land is that it is for the Crown to prove beyond a shadow of a doubt that he is guilty of the charge alleged against him. The Crown must bring evidence before you that proves the charge on the standard required. This burden is a heavy one not by any means a light one.

"Let us look at the evidence the Crown has presented to you in reliance to prove this charge. First, there is the evidence of Raazia Khan. She says she overheard a conversation from another room about her father stating that Nawaz had asked for £5000 for sorting out the Saleena business. Mr Rehman's explanation was he was talking about Nawaz asking for money as he had in the past asked for money as he was always short of money. He maintains that the television was on at the material time as he was listening to the news. He says she is mistaken in what she heard. Remember, members of the jury, Raazia was forced to marry at the age of sixteen by her father who had simply arranged for her to marry without any form of consultation with her or her consent. It sounds very much like, I speculate, someone who could have an axe to grind against him. What a perfect opportunity for her to get back at her father! Second, the Crown produced printouts of the telephone calls made from Nawaz Khan's home phone to Mr Rehman's number. They are simply records of telephone calls made from one number to another and nothing more. They prove nothing. You cannot therefore give weight to them as evidence.

"Thirdly, I suggest the Crown in desperation then brought and relied on the evidence of one Tom Ford. This was presented to you after the Crown had closed its case, you will no doubt recall. The witness Tom Ford says Nawaz had hired him to do his wife in and the old man was on board. Which old man he did not say surprisingly; simply an assumption is made that it was Mr Rehman. Tom Ford's evidence is neither credible nor reliable. The man has a criminal record with many dishonesty offences on his record. He has apparently, as he said, made a deal with the prosecution authorities that if he testified in this trial for the Crown his cooperation will be recognised by the judge sentencing him. He was open and candid about it speaking with a touch of bravado about it. I suggest you place a zero value on this piece of evidence for it is neither credible nor reliable.

"As for the motive, the Crown says that the motive was honour killing. This was introduced by the investigating police officers. That is pure conjecture on their part, and the two detectives' evidence does not add any weight to the evidence required to prove the charge. The Crown maintains that Saleena had embarked on a course of conduct which, to the defendants, was unacceptable. She had to be stopped by any means. They therefore entered into this enterprise to conspire to kill her. This is somewhat far-fetched, pie in the sky stuff I submit in my respectful submission. You have seen my client. He is an elderly gentleman, devout in his practice of his religion and a loving father of six children. He sat throughout the trial, you must have noticed, with his rosary in his hand. Is it possible that this religious man really be capable of a crime of conspiracy? I say not. "Members of the jury, there you have it. That's the lot. I would ask you to bring a verdict of not guilty as the strands of evidence required to prove the charge of conspiracy is neither compelling nor meets the standard required to be adduced by the Crown. The burden of proof has simply has simply not been discharged in this case. Remember members of the jury, if you have any doubts at all, you cannot convict. Thank you." Mr Peggs-Green stated.

Next to rise from his seat was Mr Griffidam:

"Members of the jury, the English criminal legal system requires the Crown to prove their case against each defendant. The burden of proof is entirely upon them, not the defendants. The standard required to prove the charge in law is beyond all reasonable doubt. You have to be satisfied that the Crown has discharged this burden in order to convict. If you are not satisfied, then you must not convict. My learned friend Mr Peggs-Green for the co-defendant has already gone through the evidence of the Crown, and so I don't really need to cover this ground again with you. It is for you to decide if the required standard of proof and burden has indeed been discharged. I say it has not been so discharged. My learned friend has already stated that the evidence is neither compelling to prove the charge nor does it reach the standard required in criminal law.

"Let me deal with the issues of motive and my client choosing not to give evidence. The motive for the conspiracy to murder, the Crown say was honour killing. Saleena Khan had left my client in 1990. She had been away for some seven years, and she was no longer in his life. What possible reason would he have to have her killed? The proposition of honour killing is quite frankly fanciful and preposterous to say the least. My client did not give evidence. It is his legal right not to do so if he decides he does not wish to give evidence at all as it is for the prosecution to prove the charge beyond all reasonable doubt, not him. All he has to do is enter a plea of not guilty and do nothing more than that. The law is not that he has to disprove the charge against him. On the contrary, the burden rests on the Crown to prove with cogent evidence the charge. For this reason, it would not be proper for you, members of the jury, to draw any adverse inferences from my client choosing not to give evidence. It seems clear from the evidence that Raazia Khan gave that she hates my client. She is a woman who is after vengeance. She merely suspects that he had a hand in her sister's killing. That is not proof of conspiracy, members of the jury.

"The evidence of Tom Ford, a man with a criminal record as long as his arm, with a tattoo of a snake on his neck, seemed unbelievable. The witness was simply trying to save his own neck. He had several offences of dishonesty on his record. Would you honestly believe his evidence as reliable? His evidence was not only dangerous but if you placed any weight on his evidence, the convictions would be unsafe. There are so many holes in the prosecution's case, members of jury, that it would not be safe to convict. The strands of evidence are not compelling for you to convict. Finally, I ask you all to hang on to the phrase 'beyond all reasonable doubt'. That is an important phrase. Thank you."

Next was the turn of Mr Ravenstone. He rose to his feet, stood silently as he closed his eyes for thirty seconds or so in a hot and hushed courtroom as everyone waited for him to speak. Mr Ravenstone then stated opening his eyes:

"Ladies and gentlemen of the jury, it is a hot day and I was thinking about how long should I be on my feet addressing you and at the same time I spared a thought for the two victims. It is important to get to the right result and for this reason, I would ask your indulgence and your concentration on what I have to say for a few moments. You will, I am sure, remember I said this in my opening of the case in June: 'Ladies and gentlemen of the jury, I state at the very outset that whilst the charge of conspiracy to murder is not in any way unusual, I confess the case I shall be presenting in this court will be. It is a case that is not one which we hear about every day, but it is a case which has all the hallmarks of an honour killing. Yes, members of the jury, you heard me right, it is a case of honour killing.'

"This case by no means is an easy case or an ordinary case. You have heard all the evidence to prove the charge of conspiracy to murder Saleena Khan and

Calvin Lenton. In order to prove the charge, the Crown presented two very important pieces of evidence, the evidence of the daughter Raazia Khan and the telephone printouts. Yes, the evidence is indeed circumstantial, but that does not mean it is not enough to prove a charge on the standard required. The credibility of the Crown witnesses evidence you have heard makes the evidence compelling members of the jury. Raazia Khan in her testimony on oath told you in clear terms what she heard. She is the accused's daughter. Do you think she would have come to court and tell you what she heard if she was mistaken? I don't. Her evidence was credible and believable. There are the phone call records which are there. Ask yourself, members of the jury, why would a man make those calls at or around the time the victims were killed? It sounds like too much of a co-incidence when his wife had been gone for some seven years. Saleena had left the marriage and was separated from him. She was planning to marry a man she loved and the couple were most likely going to live in Uganda. The father-in-law was no longer a father-in-law in the true sense and it made no sense for him to call his father-in-law just for a chit chat or talk about the weather. Note particularly the timing of those calls. You will see from the printout records; they were curiously around December of 1997.

"Then, of course, there is the evidence of Tom Ford. Whatever you think of the witness himself, I say that is not relevant. What he said in his evidence was important. He, in my judgement, corroborated the evidence you already had in front of you. There you have it. There is the motive of honour killing. All the hallmarks of it are there, members of the jury. You have a domineering patriarch of the family in control. As the control was ebbing away, it was time to regain that control by whatever measure necessary. I say there is plenty of compelling evidence for you to bring back guilty verdicts. Thank you."

It was getting late in the afternoon; the Judge made a decision to finish for the day and for the court to resume at 10:00 the next day.

Papaji seemed to be in a much happier mood that evening. He was pleased with Mr Peggs-Green's closing speech. Abdel enjoyed spending the evening with his father. After a short nap in the late afternoon, Papaji showered, prayed *maghrib namaaz*, changed his clothes and waited for Abdel to call for him. It was around 9:30 p.m. when he called for Papaji. The city was vibrant getting busier with it being a pleasant summer's evening. People were out enjoying the night. The temperature was twenty-one degrees with a moderate cool breeze blowing. Young men were mostly wearing T-shirts and shorts, the women, cool summer dresses. Lots of bars were open, people mingling outside holding drinks in their hands.

Abdel drove out to Stockport Road to Nawab Indian restaurant. It was busy there too. What mattered was Papaji was in good spirits. The trial did not seem to bother him that night. He hardly mentioned it, if at all, much to Abdel's surprise. The conversation spanned from talking about the weather to *Amii* and what Abdel's future plans were. Papaji asked him if he had found someone to settle down with as he was twenty-seven. It would be nice to have a *bahu*, [daughter-in-law] he expressed to his son. The subject was a delicate one which Abdel tried hard to avoid speaking about.

Sean Denton's report came on the late news as Abdel sat on his bed in his room with an ice cold can of Pepsi in his hand taking slow sips from it.

"This is Sean Denton on BBC News 24 reporting from Manchester Crown Court. It was day 7 at the court at the trial of the two defendants accused of conspiracy to murder. We can report certain parts of the trial today as Judge Norrington QC had placed reporting restrictions on some parts of the hearing. The day began with a dramatic situation where Mr Ravenstone QC for the Crown surprised everyone by making a legal application to the Judge to be permitted to reopen the Crown's case so he could call a prosecution witness who apparently had been discovered only in the last few days. Both the defence barristers objected to the application. However, rather surprisingly, the Judge granted the prosecution's application to call Tom Ford to the stand. This witness gave evidence that he had met Nawaz Khan who had hired him to 'do his wife in'. Under cross-examination, both defence Counsel severely attacked the credibility of his evidence which was challenged as he had a criminal record with several dishonesty offences on it. Mr Griffidam called him a snake and said he was only there to save his own neck which Tom Ford denied.

"All three barristers delivered the closing speeches to the jury. Counsel for the defence reminded the jurors that the burden to prove the conspiracy charge entirely lay on the shoulders of the prosecution. It was the Crown, they said to the jury, who had to prove the case against the defendants beyond reasonable doubt, not the other way round. The day was concluded with Judge Norrington QC stating he would resume tomorrow with his direction to the jury. The case therefore continues. This is Sean Denton reporting from Manchester Crown Court."

Sir Christopher Norrington QC's direction to the jury on day 8:

"Members of the jury, I thank you for your patience you have shown in this trial. My direction is not unduly long. You will be relieved to know we are nearly at an end of this trial now. It has been a long trial and you have heard plenty of evidence during the course of the trial. I am fully aware that the hot spell of weather has not helped at all, and it must have been difficult for you all to absorb so much evidence that has been presented in this trial. There was also a gap of three weeks which could not have helped though Counsel in their closing speeches covered the evidence presented in the first week of the trial. As the trial Judge, it is my job to direct you on the evidence and matters of law. Your function is to make a finding of facts only and to then deliver a verdict having heard the evidence and my direction on the applicable law.

"Every criminal act in law requires the Crown to show two elements in a crime. An *actus reus* and *mens rea*. Simply put, the *actus reus* is the carrying out of the act and the *mens rea* is the mental state of mind of having an intention to commit a criminal act.

"You have two victims here, Saleena Khan and Calvin Lenton, who were bludgeoned to death on the night of 19 December 1997 whilst asleep in their flat in Woodstock. Mr Ravenstone presented evidence on behalf of the Crown to you in relation to the charge of conspiracy to murder which each of the two defendants face in this court. The crime of conspiracy, members of the jury, requires an agreement between two or more persons to commit an unlawful act by unlawful means with the intention of carrying it out. It is the intention to carry out the crime that constitutes the necessary *mens rea* for the offence. You must be satisfied that they had the intention to be a party to an agreement to do an unlawful act. However, beyond the mere fact of agreement, the necessary *mens rea* of the crime is established if, and only if, it is shown that the accused, when they entered into the agreement, intended to play some part in the agreed course of conduct in furtherance of the criminal purpose which the agreed course of conduct was intended to achieve. Nothing less will suffice and nothing more is required. It is then not necessary for the Crown to show any action to be performed in pursuance of it. When the parties to the agreement entered into an agreement, the offence of conspiracy is complete. Mere acquiescence, in other words simply agreeing to what someone wants and remaining passive, may not be enough in law to establish a joint enterprise.

"You have the circumstantial evidence before you, namely the evidence of Raazia Khan, who seemed a very credible witness and her evidence may be compelling, then the telephone calls and, finally, the evidence of Tom Ford. Tom Ford's evidence must be treated with utmost caution. 'Why?' you may ask. Well, for one, the witness has a criminal record. Secondly, he gave evidence following a deal done with the prosecuting authorities. Such a witness's evidence in those circumstances must always be treated with a great deal of caution. How must you treat his evidence? Well, you either accept what he says or you do not. If you do, then it corroborates the evidence of Raazia Khan. Should you decide not to accept that witness's evidence as reliable, then you will be left with the evidence of the witness Raazia Khan only with the circumstantial evidence of the telephone calls from which you must decide if there was the required agreement of the defendant. There is the issue of honour the Crown presented to you as the motive. It is a matter for you to decide the credibility of it.

"As for the two defendants, they have pleaded not guilty to the charge of conspiracy to murder. Faizali Khan gave evidence and denied that there was such an agreement between the two of them. Was this defendant's denial and evidence credible? That is a question for you to decide. The defendant Nawaz Khan chose not to give evidence in his defence. That is his legal right not to do so. The question whether one can draw adverse inferences from it is a question for you to decide. You must not draw adverse inferences unless you have good reasons. Certainly, by not giving evidence, the Crown could not test whether his defence would have been credible or not. As I say, the question of drawing adverse inferences is not an easy one. What I would say is not to embark on that course unless you are sure of the reasons why you have done so and the reasons must be good reasons.

"You must remember it is not for the defendant to disprove the charge. It is for the Crown to prove the charge of conspiracy, not the other way round. The burden is on the Crown and it must discharge it on this standard of beyond reasonable doubt. You have been reminded time and time again by Counsel that you must be satisfied beyond reasonable doubt from the evidence presented. You must weigh up all the evidence. If all of you decide there was an agreement between the two and the evidence supports it on the standard required, you must bring a guilty verdict. If you have any doubt about their guilt, you must acquit them. I shall require a unanimous decision from you. Please choose a foreman amongst you who will speak on your behalf. Now you may retire to consider the verdict."

The reporters all dashed out of the courtroom whilst the jury filed to leave the courtroom guided by the usher to their room for deliberation. The jury deliberated for five hours but could not reach a unanimous verdict. As the jury failed to agree a unanimous verdict during the day, they were put up at a nearby hotel enabling them to continue their deliberations there.

The next morning, the foreman reported that they still had not reached a unanimous verdict. He indicated to the judge it was highly unlikely that a unanimous verdict could be reached. The judge advised that should they fail to reach a verdict after twelve hours of deliberation, he would accept a majority verdict whereby at least ten members must be agreed.

"In respect of the charge of conspiracy to murder, how do you find the accused Faizali Rehman?"

"Guilty," the foreman said.

"In respect of the charge of conspiracy to murder how do you find the accused Nawaz Khan?"

"Guilty," the foreman said.

The judge turned to the two defendants.

"Stand up Rehman and Khan. This was a wicked, inhuman and a most despicable thing you did. Any crime is unacceptable by a citizen, and I cannot fathom how a father could engage in an enterprise which involved the killing of one's offspring. I cannot but imagine the pain that the near and dear ones of those two victims must have suffered. I feel the sentence I impose upon you two must send out a clear message to those who choose to engage in such criminal acts, that society and the rule of law will not tolerate such deeds and for which they will be severely punished. The law must now take its course, and you should face the maximum sanction permitted by law and the sentence that must be imposed for this wicked crime. I therefore sentence you both to life imprisonment with a tariff that you must serve a minimum of twenty years. I express my deep sympathy to the victims' families, and I thank the members of the jury for your service in this case."

A barrage of reporters with cameramen had gathered outside the courtroom waiting for Raazia and her family and friends to come out of the court building. Raazia emerged from the court feeling elated with the verdict. She tightly held on to her husband's hand as she did the others. Allia, Sameena, Sara, Maleeka and Nadine walked out of the courtroom, with all their hands held stretched high up in the air. Raazia clenched her fist and punched the air with it in front of the camera.

"How do you feel about the verdicts, Mrs Khan?" Sean Denton asked her.

"Today is a day for justice for my sister Saleena and her dear friend Calvin. I am elated at the verdicts. The people who had a hand in my sister's death and her friend Calvin's have been found guilty, and they both deserve the punishment the court has given them. The punishment for them is not just here but in the hereafter. It should have been life for a life for Nawaz as he is a brutal and evil man. We all truly miss Saleena."

Sherlock and Kiki stood not far away from the group listening to her emotional statement. Raazia turned round to both of them and mimed 'thank you' with her lips. Sherlock nodded his head as he smiled back at her. Kiki came over and embraced Raazia as she whispered, "DCI McLean said to say, 'You are welcome,'" in her ear.

"This is a live report from Manchester Crown Court. This is Sean Benton reporting for BBC News. Behind me as you just saw Raazia Khan emerging from the court happy with the verdict. The jury finally, after some fifteen hours of deliberations, having spent overnight at the nearby hotel today delivered their verdict in the honour killing trial. The Judge sentenced the two men Faizali Rehman and Nawaz Khan to life sentences having been found guilty of conspiracy to murder Saleena Khan and Calvin Lenton.

"Judge Norrington QC said: 'This was a wicked, inhuman and a most despicable thing you did. Any crime is unacceptable by a citizen, and I cannot fathom how a father could engage in an enterprise which involved the killing of one's offspring. I cannot but imagine the pain that the near and dear ones of those two victims must have suffered. I feel the sentence I impose upon you two must send out a clear message to those who choose to engage in such criminal acts, that society and the rule of law will not tolerate such deeds and for which they will be severely punished. The law must now take its course, and you should face the maximum sanction permitted by law and the sentence that must be imposed for this wicked crime. I therefore sentence you both to life imprisonment with a tariff that you must serve a minimum of twenty years. I express my deep sympathy to the victims' families and I thank the members of the jury for your service in this case.'

"There were scenes of jubilation outside the courtroom. Faizali Rehman's daughter Raazia said this a few moments ago: 'Today is a day for justice for my sister Saleena and her dear friend Calvin. I am elated at the verdicts. The people who had a hand in my sister's death and her friend Calvin's have been found guilty and they both deserve the punishment the court has given them. The punishment for them is not just here but in the hereafter. It should have been life for a life for Nawaz as he is a brutal and evil man. We all truly miss Saleena.'

This is Sean Denton reporting for BBC News at Manchester Crown Court."

Abdel went to see Papaji in the cells of the court located in the basement area accompanied by Mr Peggs-Green and Andrew Stanton. Abdel went and hugged his father before they all sat down.

"I am so sorry, Papaji. I am dumbfounded at the verdict," Abdel said.

"Mr Rehman, I was convinced the jury would find you not guilty as the evidence was simply not to the required standard. The problem with the legal system is that your peers have found you guilty. To my mind, that is the flaw. Had it been the judge alone deciding the case, he would have thrown the case out of the window. I am not convinced at all the verdict is safe in law here and therefore I am going to prepare the appeal papers straightaway and send it to Andrew Stanton, your solicitor, to file them with the court without any delay. This is simply a case of miscarriage of justice, in my opinion. I shall also write to the Court with a letter urging given your age and health conditions to expedite the matter as soon as possible. I am so very sorry."

"Thank you, Mr Peggs-Green. I am sure you did your best for me. This must be Allah's punishment for being a bad parent."

The lawyers shook hands with him and left the cell. Abdel was in a terrible state. His mind said to him to do something.

"Papaji, I have a terrible confession to make to you."

"Whatever it is, son, it does not matter. I have no one but my creator now," he said looking sullen.

"Papaji, you had cast me out as some stranger from your love and the house I grew up in. I came to see you but you ignored me; you shut me out completely. I was only seventeen years old. I admit buying the lottery was a very foolish thing to do. It was just a whim. I never thought I would ever win. It was a hot summer's day; I just wanted to dream about it, that's all. I never thought I stood a chance of winning. I spent hours, days after I had won deciding if I should throw the ticket away. I saw a dream. My friends came to me dressed like angels informing me I was one of the chosen few. So, I decided in the end to claim the prize. It felt so good. What followed afterwards was a nightmare. I kept thinking I would wake up and it would be all over; things would get back to how they were. I craved for you and tried to make up with you, Papaji, but you were so tough," Abdel said with emotion, tears rolling down his cheeks.

"What has all that got to do with why I am here, son?"

Papaji sat there quietly listening to his son pouring his heart out to him. He too had tears in his eyes. The emotions for both ran to a high point.

"Don't you see? I was desperate for you to make things good between us. When Saleena came back, I thought I saw an opportunity to get back in your good books. I got this Pakistani old drunk, paid him £500 to phone Nawaz and pretend it was you. I told him what to say to him, that a payment of £5000 would be paid for the job. I knew that your honour was at stake and if Saleena had married that boyfriend of hers, it would have created untold harm to your reputation. If I took care of the matter for you, I felt sure I would earn the recognition of your love again. I craved day and night for you to hold me, hug

204

me, call me by my name, Abdel, and kiss me on the forehead as you used to do before. It was wrong, I can see now. We are in this terrible mess because of it."

Papaji stood up from his chair, as did Abdel. Papaji came to him and hugged him. Tears were rolling down his cheeks as he kissed Abdel's forehead. He put his hand on Abdel's head, brushed his hair back and rested his hand at the back of his neck.

"Son, you did this for me? I cannot believe you felt that way. I forgive you."

"Papaji, I am going to put this right. I am going to go to the police with my lawyer and make a statement. That will at least secure an immediate release for you."

"Son, no, no, no, don't do that. Listen to me carefully. I am an old man. Look at me and tell me how many years have I left on this earth. You are a young man with a future ahead of you, a whole life to live whereas I have lived mine. Though a sad one, nevertheless, I have lived my life. I have no one left at home, not even Fauzia who has deserted me too. The house is like a graveyard. What would I do at home on my own for you would be in prison? Think logically, *betta*, it would not do anyone any good if you went to the police, you hear me, Abdel?"

"Yes, I do, but how can I live with myself knowing you were in prison?"

"Son, it is fine. This is perhaps what I do deserve. I must admit I have not been a good parent. If I were able to put the clock back, I would do it in a jiffy and change the way I was. The hurt I caused to all my children is something I cannot forgive myself for. I now know growing up in this country is different for you children. Our old cultural ways don't work anymore. Look at our family; torn apart simply because I wanted to be a father who forced my kids to do what I wanted. I never once considered the feelings of my children. *Nateejah kiya nikla?* [What was the outcome?] The consequences were disastrous to say the least. I take full responsibility for it, *puttar*. I deserve this; it is my penance. It is a sacrifice that I must make for all my sins. You must not go the police; you hear me? It will not do anyone any good. Now look at me. I love you with all my heart. I want you to be happy, that is all I want. I know Raazia will not come but ask her to come and see me at the prison. I will write letters to Allia, Sameena and Sara. Now don't do anything stupid at all. Go back to your home and get on with your life. Come and see your Papaji from time to time which I will look forward to very much. Do this much for me, *puttar*, please, I beg of you."

After the emotional parting with his father, Abdel drove back to his estate, intermittently sobbing as he drove back home. He planned not to follow Papaji's advice as he called Andrew Stanton and spoke to him about accompanying him at the police station the next day without sharing any of the details. It brought some comfort to his heavily burdened mind as Abdel began to plan it all out.

Chapter 18

The security van driver transporting eight prisoners had driven the van via A6 Broad Street, taking the exit following signs for Pendlebury. His ultimate destination was HMP Forest Bank prison near Agecroft. He turned right on to A6044 Agecroft Road, when suddenly there was jolt from the rear of the van. The driver manoeuvred the van towards his right, taking measures avoiding colliding with a cyclist on his left at the same time applying the brakes, but the manoeuvre resulted in a collision with an oncoming articulated truck which jack-knifed as the van rebounded off it sliding all the way across into Pendlecroft Avenue before coming to a rest. It looked like chaos. The driver of the van crawled out from the passenger window, holding his head. His forehead was bleeding.

A passing ambulance that happened fortuitously to be passing by stopped seeing the accident. The crew first attended to the driver making sure he was fine. The road crash collision looked horrific. It was mayhem out there. Pedestrians soon gathered at the scene; traffic came to a complete halt as the road was blocked by the jack-knifed lorry. The ambulance crew pried open the door to get to the prisoners. Soon the place was crawling with police, fire brigade crew, ambulances and reporters with cameramen. No fatalities were reported; all but two prisoners were accounted for. It was assumed they had done a runner, as police scoured the area searching for them.

Papaji had been detained at a nearby hospital where in the night he managed to put the bed sheets together. He tied one end to the window and the other to his neck. He jumped out of the window. By the time the nurses discovered him, it was too late. Papaji had taken his own life.

Chapter 19

It was the morning on the day Abdel had arranged for Papaji's funeral. He telephoned all his sisters one by one to let them know what the arrangements for the funeral were. During his telephone conversations with all his sisters, he stated merely that Papaji had nothing to do with Saleena's death; he did not have the time to explain as he had a million things to do that morning but assured them, he would tell them in time. He pleaded with them to attend his funeral. Abdel made sure the pattern of the funeral was similar to Begum's funeral in 1972. The casket carrying his body was brought to the house and laid in the front room for an hour. Shaikh Ahmed was there as was his friend Malik. Shaikh Ahmed stood by the casket all the time reciting verses from the Koran. Much to Abdel's surprise, Raazia, Akeel and the twins had come with Sameena and Faraz briefly paying their final respects. Abdel welcomed them, shaking Akeel and Faraz's hands as they exchanged condolences. Raazia prayed *surah fateha*, the first verse from the Koran and left the house after with the twins. Akeel, Sameena and Faraz stayed on for the rest of the funeral rites.

It was a gorgeous sunny day in July. There were nearly a thousand people from the local community attending Papaji's funeral. His friend Malik took a moment after the funeral to reflect upon his friend's life then looked at his own life thinking how fortunate he and his wife Farzana were having abandoned their old archaic ways embracing changes for their children's happiness which brought comfort to him.

Fauzia arrived at the house later in the evening as people were ready to leave the house. She had come with two youngish men. They both looked to be in their mid-thirties. She did not introduce them to anyone. Abdel wondered if they were his stepbrothers. She came and hugged Abdel but did not speak to anyone else.

"*Amii*, the funeral was this afternoon. You should have telephoned me that you were coming I would have met you at the airport."

"The flight was delayed. I thought the funeral was tomorrow?"

"No *Amii*, it was Papaji's wish to be buried as soon as possible. Well, you did come which is the main thing."

Abdel got the distinct feeling of coldness about her. She seemed more casual about Papaji's death, not least bit upset at her husband's passing. When Abdel said he would stay the night at the house, she intimated that he could go back to his own home which seemed to be the first sign of *Amii* distancing herself from the family. She asked before Abdel left the house if Papaji had left a will. *A strange thing to ask,* Abdel thought to himself, a little surprised too she had asked so soon about it. He stated he did not know whether he had or not as it was not something he had ever discussed with his father. Before leaving, he picked up the small cardboard box which contained his father's personal effects, some letters, his watch, a ring, his *tasbee* and the clothes he was wearing at the time of death including his worn-out *topi*. She hugged him before saying goodbye to him. She said it in a strange way, he could not describe, but definitively there seemed to be some sort of finality about it, a final goodbye.

It was late when Abdel finally reached home. During the journey back home, he had wondered why *Amii* had changed so much. He had been closing to her, never said anything to offend her. For the first time, she made him feel like a stranger. It was an awful feeling, but his was not to reason why she was like that; she was not his biological mother. He remembered Allia calling her a bitch one time many years ago, something in common with Allia, he began to share.

Later, he sat in his bedroom at the estate in Oxshott with the cardboard box on his bed as he went through Papaji's items one by one. He looked at the *tasbee* first which had probably been with him most of his life. The beads had passed his fingers countless times and so was a precious item to him he would cherish forever. After looking at it for a few minutes he gently put it back in the box. He tried his *topi* on. It looked funny on his head as he stood up to look in the mirror, yet Papaji had worn it for so many years it had almost become part of him. It certainly did not look funny on his head though. He smiled as he put it back in the box. His Omega watch was very old. The glass face had scratches on it, the strap well worn. There were some letters in sealed envelopes addressed to him, and all his sisters. Abdel looked at the sealed envelopes putting back all but the one addressed to him. He slit the spine of the envelope with a knife, taking out the note Papaji had written to him. It had on it the final words written with his hand. He opened it, closed his eyes and ran his fingers on the pages trying to feel the writing on the two A5 pages, at the same time conjuring, in his mind, the picture of Papaji sitting in his favourite chair in the sitting room of the house watching the news. He began to read the letter:

"My Dear Abdel, my sweet child,
The moment I laid my eyes on you when Begum handed you over to me in the hospital in 1972, I had nothing but pure parent's love for you, my child. You were the greatest nehmat Allah had bestowed upon me. I was proud of you, son. I am so sorry I did not speak with you for 10 years. It must have caused you a great deal of pain, and I am sorry for that, I truly am. I wish I could have taken away the hurt you must have felt, but you were not a stranger to me all that time, but my son. In my heart, I loved you all the time, every minute, in fact, I lived in this world. I loved your sisters too. I shall have to face Saleena and ask her for forgiveness on the day of judgement when Allah calls me to account for the bad deeds I did in this world. I can only now ask Allah for his forgiveness for He is Almighty and merciful. Neither I nor you can change what passed by. You must live your life. I ask that you set up orphanages in Pakistan and India where you can house, protect and provide food, shelter and warm surroundings for as many orphans as you can. Build the orphanages in my name. Call them 'Faizali

Rehman orphanages. Bring love to those orphans who have missed out on their parents' love. This will bring you Allah's praise and inshallah wipe away our sins. For your penance, I ask that you spend three months every year of your life personally looking after and caring for the needs of those orphans. That will be enough for me for what you did. I forgive you.
Love you always and may Allah bless you and protect you.
Papaji.
P.S. Don't tell Raazia or anyone about you and Saleena."

Abdel sobbed uncontrollably for many minutes as he finished reading the letter. He put the letter on his chest, both his hands on top of it pressing it against him as though he was hugging the letter. He was worn out as it had been a very long day. He said a little prayer for his father then fell asleep. It was nearly 2:00 p.m. the next day Abdel had still not woken up. Amna wondered what she should do. She knew Papaji had passed away in bad circumstances but Abdel had only once or twice, she could recall, slept in so late. After some tortuous pacing up and down in the hallway, she mustered up the courage to go up. She knocked on his door gently.

"Sir are you all, right?" she said in a low tone.

"I am, I am. What time is it?" Abdel asked.

"2:00 p.m. in the afternoon. Would you like me to bring some breakfast for you?"

"No, Amna, I shall be down in 10–15 minutes."

Abdel came downstairs some minutes later in his nightgown. He sat in the dining room and began to cry. Amna came and sat next to him.

"I am so sorry for your loss, Sir. I don't really know what the right words would be to say to one's boss. All I can say to you is to exercise *sabbar* [patience], time does heal the pain, I know from when my husband died. If there is anything I can do to help, Sir, I am always here," Amna said with tears in her eyes which she wiped away with her fingers.

"Amna, thank you for being here; it means a lot to me. I thank you for your kind words too. I do."

"Please stay there, Sir, I will fix something for you to eat."

Chapter 20

David reported back to President Otambu in fine detail all about the case and his involvement with the final outcome much to the President's delight. He asked David about the cargo. David informed his President that the cargo was on its way.

"I am going to enjoy this one, David, I must say!" They both laughed.

David had developed a close friendship with Sara. They emailed each other every single day. David invited her to come and visit Uganda. He would take her to Soroti and show her the Orphanage where Saleena worked. Sara was chuffed at the idea. Feeling delighted, she handed in her resignation to the probation service declaring to her friends at work she was going out to Uganda to carry on where her dear sister Saleena had left her work unfinished.

Akeel and Raazia had firmed up the plans to visit Calvin's mother in the last two weeks of August. Allia and her family would be accompanying them.

Sara declared her news one afternoon at Raazia's house. It was a family gathering to honour the lives of Saleena and Calvin. Raazia and her two sisters were delighted at hearing Sara's news. It was timed perfectly.

"Raaz, did you know that bitch has put our old house up for sale? How dare she? It was not her house," Allia stated, recoiling with horror.

"Yes, Akeel did tell me," Raazia said.

"Can she do that? Surely the house would be ours, wouldn't it?" Allia asked.

"No, it's Papaji's wife's property so yes, she can put it up for sale, my dear *saali, Alliabenji*. Your Papaji left no will, so his wife will inherit the lot," Akeel stated.

"*Ay* my dear *Behnoi,* less of this 'Alliabenji', okay? And how do you know?" Allia enquired.

"It happened to Aziz Uncle, Jamshēd's and Chengez's family. Their father, Aziz *Uncleji* was remarried; he left no will, and his Mrs got the whole estate he had left behind!" Akeel responded.

"That can't be fair, can it?" Allia asked.

"Well, that is the law in this country, *Alliabenji*," Akeel responded.

"So Raazia, what we gonna do with Papaji's letters? I haven't opened mine. I don't know if I want to, if I am honest. I say we just burn them. Have any of you opened yours?" Allia asked.

Raazia, Sameena and Sara all shook their heads.

A huge cargo-bearing barge called the 'Finlandia' after sixteen days at sea docked at the Port of Cape Town. David was there to ensure his cargo container had arrived safely. A large crane lifted the container off 'Finlandia' and placed it on a nearby trailer which was bound for Uganda by road. Fifty miles into the long journey, David opened the doors to the container. As the daylight flooded inside the container, Nawaz and Tom covered their eyes immediately with their hands as the bright daylight was blinding. The stench of urine and human waste emanating from it was unbearable.

"Welcome to Africa, my gentlemen. You will be my guests now. I must say I am surprised you have not killed each other during your journey. Well, I hope you have enjoyed the company of each other as my President eagerly awaits your arrival," David Mutembe said with a gruesome laugh.

End.